A hammering sound drifted in and out of Anne's dream.

A man's voice called…and the pounding started again. "Nat, it's Tom. Unbolt this door!"

Anne's eyes flew open, her face nestled against Nat's hard chest, and the black curly mat of hair tickled her nose. His bare leg sprawled across her body, and his arm held her close. She peered up in time to see his eyes open.

He gave her a lazy grin. "Good morning, wife," he said.

Shocked, Anne pushed away from him, pulled her night shift up and straightened her bodice. He let her go, an amused expression on his face.

"A minute, Tom," Nat yelled, raking his fingers through his dark hair.

Anne started, unable to grasp how he could be so relaxed at a time like this. She watched, horrified, as he covered himself with a blanket and rose to retrieve his breeches hung over a chair. God's bones, he had lain naked as a babe next to her all night!

Dear Reader,

When we ran our first March Madness promotion in 1992, we had no idea that we would be introducing such a successful venture. Our springtime showcase of brand-new authors has been such a hit, that it has become a priority at Harlequin Historicals to seek out talented new writers and introduce them to the field of historical romance.

This month's titles include *All that Matters,* a haunting medieval tale about an imprisoned woman and her unwitting rescuer, by Elizabeth Mayne; *Embrace the Dawn* by Jackie Summers, the story of a woman kidnapped by a highwayman and forced to play his bride; a Western from Linda Castle that features a blinded hero and the woman who helps him recover, *Fearless Hearts;* and *Love's Wild Wager* by Taylor Ryan, a Regency-era story about a penniless heiress and the rogue who wins her heart.

We hope you will enjoy all four of this month's books and keep an eye out for all our titles, wherever Harlequin Historicals are sold.

Sincerely,

Tracy Farrell
Senior Editor

Please address questions and book requests to:
Harlequin Reader Service
U.S.: 3010 Walden Ave., P.O. Box 1325, Buffalo, NY 14269
Canadian: P.O. Box 609, Fort Erie, Ont. L2A 5X3

JACKIE SUMMERS

EMBRACE THE DAWN

Harlequin Books

TORONTO • NEW YORK • LONDON
AMSTERDAM • PARIS • SYDNEY • HAMBURG
STOCKHOLM • ATHENS • TOKYO • MILAN
MADRID • WARSAW • BUDAPEST • AUCKLAND

ISBN 0-373-28860-3

EMBRACE THE DAWN

JACKIE SUMMERS

believes in love at first sight. She and her husband, Tom, were married six weeks to the day after they first met and he proposed, many happy years ago. Home is a one-hundred-and-fifty-year-old colonial in Maine where they live with their Shih Tzu and Australian Terrier. When Jackie isn't writing romances, she's tending her garden of seventeenth-century roses.

This book is dedicated to my husband, Tom, who
never doubted. I love you, Bear.

My special thanks to a great writer, Linda Warren,
for her friendship and unflagging enthusiasm.
Thanks to Donna Martin, Trudy Zothner and
Kelly McClymer for the compliments when I
needed them. And to our daughter, Ellyn,
for always being there.

Chapter One

England
September 1651

*S*he felt someone staring at her.

Anne Lowell peeked through the leafy branches of the alders and studied the silent bank of the river. Too silent. The mallards had taken flight and a hush had fallen over the forest. From a nearby stand of oak, her mare whinnied. She drew back, clasping her arms in front of her. *Someone was there!*

Perhaps her own presence had quieted the woods, Anne reasoned, forcing the jittery feeling away. Aye, it was only her fear of being discovered that plagued her mind with devils.

At that moment, church bells pealed to signal the beginning of noon prayers. Dear God, she had no more time to behave like a poltroon. She must find her mother's locket—God rest her soul—and sneak back to her chamber before her uncle discovered she had gone.

With trembling hands, she scuffed off her slippers and woolen hose and tossed them aside. Next, she untied the blue ribbon lacings of her bodice. She yanked the loose-fitting day dress over her head, dropping it in a billow of white muslin on top of the slippers and hose. An unexpected breeze whipped the thin remaining undergarments about her young body. She shivered, feeling naked.

The rough grass felt harsh to her tender feet as she stepped to the bank, gathered her shift close to her body and inched her way into the cold river.

The slimy bottom oozed between her toes and she shuddered. By the time she had waded to the spot where Lyle, the scullery boy, had tossed the locket, the water reached above her knees. Damn that pesky little whelp! She'd nail Lyle's ear to the buttery door when she saw him.

Anne waded deeper into the rushing river. Taking a gulp of air, she dove beneath the river surface, stifling a gasp as the icy water engulfed her.

She forced her eyes open. Frightful images of water monsters bubbled up in her mind like witch's brew as her hands searched the swaying reeds and fanlike plants that danced along the river bottom. With shaking fingers, she scratched at the loose silt and pebbles, her mind willing the murky demons away.

Despite the illumination of the sun, nothing glittered on the river bottom. When her lungs demanded it, she stood up and inhaled deeply of the crisp September air. Blinking, she shook the streaming rivulets from her face and wiped her long red hair back from her eyes. Her teeth chattered, but she ignored her trembling. As she prepared to dip beneath the water, a branch cracked and a horse's whinny stopped her.

She whirled in the direction of the noise, her heart thumping wildly. A branch of oak leaves separated. A Roundhead soldier stared down at her from astride the largest stallion she had ever seen. The horse's white forelegs and blaze on its head flashed against the black sheen of its coat. Her heart doubled its rhythm when the soldier rode out of the shadows and stopped in a patch of sunlight near the shore.

Anne froze for only a moment. She plunged into the river and crouched low, only her head above water.

"What have we here, Shadow?" the soldier asked his horse while dismounting. Sunlight glinted from his round metal helmet and when he lifted his visor, she saw that his eyes were bold and dark. "I think she's a mermaid, and a pretty one, she is."

Her uncle's warning to keep away from the soldiers camped at Wycliffe Manor played back in her mind, although Anne didn't need to be reminded what black-hearted devils all Roundheads were.

The dark eyes flashed and brazenly assessed her with a gleam of satanic curiosity. "Who are you, mermaid, and what are you doing in the river?" His rich baritone voice with its blatant masculinity frightened her more than his question.

She wanted to run, but what if there were more soldiers with him? Her mare could never outrun his steed. Ignoring the shiver that passed through her, she answered with a defiant lift of her chin, glared back and clamped her mouth shut. She saw his angular jaw tighten in response as he released the stallion's reins, freeing the horse to drink.

All her instincts warned her that he was dangerous. She stepped back, the water rushing below her ears. "Be off with you." Her voice trembled as she hunched lower, water lapping at her chin. "You have no right to be here."

"No right to be here?" His deep voice feigned surprise, but his bold eyes glinted mockingly. "An officer of the Commonwealth not welcome at Wycliffe Manor? That'll make hearty laughter tonight when I sup with George Lowell and his guests."

God's bones! He would be at her uncle's dinner party! "You can't!" Anne's hand shot to her mouth. She saw genuine surprise light his eyes. "I—I mean...of course, you can, but..." She could see him thinking, measuring her. "But you're not welcome here...with me, that is."

He gave her a disbelieving glance, then concluded his assessment with a crooked grin. "I mean you no harm, lass. But these woods aren't safe. You might meet a straggling Royalist, limping home like a whipped dog from last week's battle."

Anne sprang to attention. How she wanted to shout back at this black-hearted enemy that she'd welcome the chance to meet one of the king's soldiers. Praise God, the poor soul might have news of her father. Instead, her mouth formed a tight line in answer; she dared not trust herself to speak out. He met her silence with interest.

"Could it be that the lovely maid hasn't heard of our victory over Charlie Stuart?"

Haven't heard, indeed! Her uncle had boasted of nothing else since word came that King Charles had barely escaped from Cromwell's armies and was fleeing for his life. If only she dared ask him if he had news of her father. Possibly, an officer in Cromwell's army might know if one of the most wanted Royalists, next to the young king, of course, had been captured.

But she dared not risk any action that might give away her identity. If this officer were to report seeing a red-haired maid in the river, even her uncle's feeble imagination would tell him she was the only soul who would dare do such a thing.

Silently, the soldier studied her like a fox waiting to spring at the henhouse door. "Tell me who you are, lass."

The sheep bells tinkled beyond the meadow and, with them, an idea sprang to mind. "I'm a shepherdess at Wycliffe Manor." Hopefully, the fib might keep her identity safe.

He gave her a skeptical look while he carelessly raked back the lock of hair that fell across his forehead. When he moved, she noticed the gold cords dangling from the wide shoulders of his jacket, signifying an officer's rank. "The other servants don't mind tending your sheep while you idle away the day?"

"What the servants do is none of your business, *Private*," she added, hoping the snub would wipe away his confidence.

The corners of his mouth quirked up. "Lieutenant," he corrected, "but why don't you call me Nat," he said softly

The bold familiarity of his intimate suggestion left her a little breathless. "If you must know," she managed, "a servant threw a trinket of mine in the river. I—I refuse to leave here until I find it." She hoped he hadn't heard her teeth chatter.

"Why would he do such a vile thing to a sweet maid as yourself?" His dark eyes seemed to ignite as he gazed at her.

"B-because I wouldn't k-kiss him, that's why." Despite the chilly water, Anne felt her cheeks flame with anger as she recalled what Lyle had done.

His mouth lifted slightly in a crooked smile. "And you didn't kiss him because your heart belongs to another?"

"Of c-course n-not." She rubbed her arms to warm herself, the water splashing bubbles to the surface. "I didn't kiss Lyle because he's an oaf and I—I hate him."

His smile broadened and her gaze lingered on his full, chiseled mouth and the white, even teeth that contrasted with his suntanned face. He looked no more than a few years past twenty when he smiled like that.

He strode to the edge of the grassy bank and stopped, booted legs spread apart, large square hands on hips. God's bones, he was going to wade in after her. Instead, he removed his helmet, revealing a face much younger than most of the officers who visited with her uncle. Younger and surprisingly handsome, for a Roundhead. Dark brown hair brushed his collar, a sharp contrast to the short, bowl-cut style of the officers who supped with her uncle. His straight nose and well-shaped mouth meant he could be gentle, Anne knew. She had overheard Daisy, the kitchen maid, talking about men. His thick dark brows and square chin meant he could be stubborn, if he had a mind. Aye, Daisy and the other maids would be all aflutter when they saw this turkey cock!

He peered out at the river, as though surveying the flow. "There's a dangerous look to the current," he said, his face serious. "There's a mean look about those dark swirls over there." He pointed toward the middle of the river. "An undertow if I'd have my guess."

"Nonsense," Anne tossed back, angry at herself for her girlish reaction to him. "I—I've no more time t-to talk to you," she added. "If I lose the sunlight, I'll n-never be able to find my trinket. I—I've known this r-river all my life and th-there's no undertow." She could tell by the way the soldier studied the current that he wouldn't be leaving soon. "I wish you'd go on about your business, and leave me to mine." With that, Anne peered down through the water where the sun glinted and flickered.

The officer remained on the bank, arms crossed, watching her. "You'd best come out of there, at once."

Ignoring him, she took a deep breath and plunged into the water. This time, she moved farther from shore. Trying to judge her bearings, she looked about the murky bottom. She remembered Lyle had been standing on the granite outcrop when he tossed the locket into the river, the same place where the lieutenant now stood. Her fingers carefully threaded through the soft ooze with steady motions. A flash of a shiny object beneath the silt caused Anne's heart to hammer. It was her locket! It had to be!

She reached out to grab it when a sudden rush of movement nearly toppled her over. A giant swell of bubbles pulled at her. She felt a tight constriction across her chest as if caught up by the relentless arm of a sea monster. The river demons had snatched her, just as her uncle had warned! God's bones, she was being yanked into the bowels of the river, down, down, down, toward the serpents of Neptune!

No, she wasn't! She broke the bubbly surface and gasped as she discovered it wasn't the serpents of Neptune, but the lieutenant. The powerful arms that fixed tightly beneath her armpits held her fast. He leaned low from his saddle and swept her out of the water. She sputtered and coughed as his sturdy hands clamped her sides and dragged her across his lap, then propped her against his chest, facing him.

Anne gulped a deep breath of air and coughed again. "Wh-what are—?" she choked. She struggled against his commanding grip. "Wh-what are you doing?"

"Saving your sweet neck, chit." His arms bulged with muscle as his grip tightened about her. With a jingle of spurs, he urged the stallion toward shore. High bursts of water splashed at their sides, spraying them as they lunged forward.

The horse leapt over the bank, its mane streaming like black silk ribbons in the breeze. Anne fell back against Nat's hard chest. Her heart skipped madly as she pulled the streaming curtain of hair from her face.

"Y-you've n-no right!" She drew a shaky breath. "There was no undertow. If you hadn't..." Her words trailed off when her gaze met his dazzling brown eyes sheltered beneath thick dark brows. Luxuriant black lashes fringed eyes the color of the dark, secret places of the forest. The wind snatched a lock of unruly chestnut hair, swirling it against his sun-browned forehead. The high cheekbones and strong jaw brought power and authority to his face; the full mouth brought sensuality. His closeness sent an unbidden thrill shooting through her. She felt as skittish as a newborn lamb.

His gaze lowered boldly to her breasts and her cheeks burned with indignation. Her hands flew to her bosom in a desperate attempt to cover herself.

He flashed a rakish grin before reaching behind the saddle and throwing a horse blanket over her. When he shifted, she felt his hard thigh muscles beneath her. Her flush deepened, and she was aware that her face must appear more scarlet than the crimson scarf tied about his waist.

Gratefully Anne covered herself with the scratchy blanket. She tried to speak, but no words came. Shivering, feeling deathly cold, she wanted to jump out of his arms, like a fish, and slide back into the river.

His arms tightened about her. "Stop fighting me, mermaid. I mean no harm, although I can't speak for all of the soldiers posted here."

She stole another glance at him, but his visor had slipped down about his face. She stopped struggling. She knew her efforts were futile.

His buff leather coat was unlaced at the throat. He didn't wear the gorget, or metal armor that officers wore around their neck while on duty. In its place she noticed crisp whorls of dark hair pushed up from his open collar. For an instant, she forgot her own embarrassment and flushed deeper at the strange sensations she felt at his nearness.

When they reached the small clearing on shore, he slid to the ground with her. She saw the mare toss her head, then whinny, as if in a relieved greeting.

"Is that what you went after?" he asked roughly.

"Wh-what?" Her eyes never left his.

"This?" The lieutenant squeezed her hand and she looked down into her own small fist to see her gold locket and chain.

"My locket." Clutching it to her breasts, Anne gave a little cry. "I *did* grab it when you came crashing in after me." She held on to the blanket with one hand while she slipped the locket around her neck and embraced it.

"Now that you've got your trinket, you'd best get dressed and return to your flock." Nat gazed into her wide blue-green eyes. Aye, those eyes, fringed by wet, long, spiky lashes—she looked like a water nymph sprung to life.

He watched as she wrapped the blanket about herself. "Turn around while I get my clothing," she ordered.

Nat raised an eyebrow. "Your sudden modesty is a bit late, wouldn't you say, wench?" He saw the blush stain her cheeks—more from anger than shame, he'd wager. Nonetheless, he turned his back as she scrambled toward the outcrop where her crumpled garments lay.

Frowning, Nat crossed to a rock and sat down, ignoring the sloshing at each step he took. His boots were soaked, his wool breeches drenched, and water splotches stained his leather coat.

She marched back toward him, her hastily gathered clothing over her arm. "It's your own fault you're wet," she said, her eyes sparkling with self-satisfaction. "There was no undertow, I tell you."

"If I hadn't come along when I did, you'd be food for the minnows, by now."

"Nonsense!" She strode past him on her way toward a copse of willows away from shore.

He pulled off his left boot and emptied the water from it, stealing a glance at her over his shoulder. She lifted her shoulder in an arrogant gesture despite her shredded dignity, before disappearing behind a small willow to change her clothing.

Nat chuckled and crossed his legs in front of him while he considered the tempting wench who had gotten him wet.

Tempting liar was more like it. Damn, but she was as much a shepherd maid as he was a lieutenant in the bloody Roundhead army!

He absently rubbed the dark stubble about his face as he remembered reading Babson's smuggled report that mentioned George Lowell's young ward, Anne. But nothing had prepared him for the beguiling vision of the lass in the river. The sight of those soft feminine curves had nearly undone him. And that mouth! How tempting her heart-shaped lips had looked—as sweet as a sun-warmed peach. And those eyes! Their blue-green color captivated him, changeable and turbulent like the first time he had seen the Mediterranean Sea during a tempest.

Nat pulled off his other boot and removed a sock, wringing it as dry as he could. He took a deep breath and frowned. How long had it been since he had been with a woman? If he'd had anything on his mind besides his own secret mission to meet up with the king, those bright eyes and generous mouth might be just too tempting to resist.

But when the dangers of these next few days were over, he'd have plenty of time to slake his desires with one of the lusty tavern wenches at the Pied Bull Inn. Until then, although she was a tempting lass, he'd best keep his mind on business.

Nat's jaw tightened when he remembered the gold locket. Had that bauble she had risked her pretty neck to find been a gift from Colonel Twining? he wondered. If so, Anne would be expected to wear it this evening, no doubt, when her betrothal to the colonel would be announced. No wonder she had been in such a bother to find it.

Babson. How lucky he was to have a loyal informant in such a crucial position as valet to Colonel Twining. Although Nat would ordinarily relish any information, however trivial, about the powerful Roundhead, the fact that Anne would soon become Twining's bride caused an unsettling feeling through him. How he'd like to taunt Twining with the fact that he'd held his betrothed's near-naked body close against him. And a very tempting body it was, too.

His mouth twitched. Too good for the likes of Twining.

Another of the items in Babson's report came to mind. Anne was the daughter of the Royalist, Jonathan Lowell. No doubt the wench followed her uncle's politics, Nat decided, since she was about to marry one of Cromwell's puppet officers. No wonder she had been so fearful of being recognized and the retelling of her actions getting back to her betrothed, Colonel Twining.

The bushes rustled again and Nat turned to see her snatch up the blanket, toss it over her shoulder and storm toward him. Her long red hair was knotted on top of her head. She wore a rumpled muslin gown that was at least two sizes too big, and by the damp marks already appearing across her bodice, it was evident she hadn't removed her wet undergarments.

She whipped her eyes back to his. "Are you still here?"

Nat shaded his eyes from the sun as he watched her approach him. "I'm waiting to hear you say thank you to me for saving your life, mermaid." He chuckled as he saw her shoulders stiffen and her hands ball into tiny fists in response.

He stretched his bare feet lazily in front of him and leaned back against the rock. "I'll see you to your flock, if you wait while I put my boots back on," he teased, knowing the last thing she wanted was for him to follow her.

When she neared, he saw the thought struggle in her blue-green eyes, just as he hoped. When she came to within a foot of him, she dropped the horse blanket over his head without breaking stride and marched toward the mare cropping grass nearby.

"I don't need an escort to find my way."

"You're not very friendly, considering you owe me your life," he shouted back, tossing the blanket to the side. "I've enough misery without ruining my uniform and boots trying to save the likes of an ungrateful chit." He tried unsuccessfully not to grin as he wrung out the other sock. "Remember, if you sprint about as a water nymph again, the next man you meet may not be a gentleman." He saw her cheeks redden and her eyes flash.

"You're not a gentleman," she replied. "A gentleman would have left the minute he noticed a maid in the water." She glared with undercurrents more dangerous than those of the river. Grabbing the reins of her mare, she trudged back toward him.

Nat squinted up at her. "You're a bale of trouble, wench."

Anne reached out and grabbed one of the boots he had discarded, then quickly mounted her horse. Narrowing his eyes from the sun, Nat stretched out for it, but a second too late. He heard her smug laugh as he scrambled to his feet and hopped after her, but the sharp stones and rough ground slowed his pace.

Without so much as a look back she goaded the mare into a gallop toward the river.

"Bloody hell!" Nat shouted. "Don't you dare...!"

She flung his boot into the water with all of her might. With a throaty chuckle, she whipped her horse around and faced him with a triumphant grin. "Watch out for the undertow, Lieutenant!" She wheeled her mare around and gave him a parting salute as she set off at a gallop along the hedgerow in the direction of Wycliffe Manor, her silver laughter ringing out after her.

Chickens squawked and flew in the air as Anne ran across the fowl yard toward the buttery, her black skirts flying behind her. At the garden post, she paused, her fingers toying nervously with her locket as she peered around the shrubbery before making a beeline for the servants' stairs at the rear of the kitchen.

It had taken her less than a half hour to sneak along the hedgerow to the milking barn and change into the proper dress which she had previously stashed in the hidden space behind the boards of her mare's stall.

Before scurrying toward the manor house, Anne stopped and looked back across the rolling autumn fields beyond. Her heart beat a little faster as she thought of the handsome lieutenant.

"Call me Nat," he had said.

Clutching her locket, she bit her lip. But of course the lieutenant hadn't followed her. He had believed her story and, by now, would think she had returned to her sheep. A warm blush swept over her as she remembered how his eyes darkened when he stared at her while he held her on his lap.

She had never been so near to a Roundhead, nor had she ever wanted to be. Of course, Uncle George was a Roundhead, but that wasn't the same. The lieutenant was a . . . soldier. Soldiers killed other Englishmen in the name of duty—Englishmen like her father, who had a bounty of gold sovereigns on his head.

Her dear father. Had it already been a year since he had risked his life to sneak into Wycliffe Manor late one night to see her? How handsome he had looked, dressed in his royal blue velvet cloak, the cavalier-lace sprinkling like crystals from his throat and wrists. He had risked capture even then, when he crept through the priest's hole—the hidden passageway—that led from the milk barn to the second-floor landing of the manor. She would never forget the moment when her father had promised to send for her, once Charles Stuart, God keep him, was restored and the despicable Oliver Cromwell driven into the sea.

"How much you resemble your mother," her father had said. "You have her beauty, Anne, but you must strive for her patience and understanding."

She had nodded, knowing her father wanted her compliance, but God's bones, she would never learn how to be patient. Besides, she really never wanted to understand the madness of politics that branded a man like her father a traitor. Still, instead of speaking her mind, she had stoically watched him go.

A cold shudder crept down her spine despite the fact the afternoon was unseasonably warm. What was the matter with her? She had been whisper close to her father's enemy, yet she had felt something so extraordinary it had taken her breath away.

Outside the buttery door the kitchen maid, Daisy, sat peeling apples and batting her eyelashes at several admiring soldiers. Anne gave a short huff. Apparently Uncle

George or anyone of importance must not be around, or those soldiers would never dare loll away in such a manner.

She straightened her prim white collar, brushed the chaff and weed seeds from her skirts and gingerly strolled across the cobbled path toward the darkened buttery. Humming softly, she made her way, as though she hadn't a care in the world. Without glancing at Daisy, she knew the servant would be much too involved with her own pastimes to pay her any mind.

Anne pushed open the buttery hatch. Smells of fermenting ciders and acrid pickles in brine rushed at her. She ducked around the table filled with covered crocks, cringing as she always did at the huge flies humming at the windows.

In the hall, boot steps clanked along the floorboards. Her pulse quickened as she waited, ear to the door, until the footsteps faded down the hall. Quiet. She drew a deep breath, hiked up her skirts and dashed toward the stairs. Grinning with success, she bolted up the steps, two at a time.

"Mistress Anne?" Uncle George called from the doorway of his study, down the hall. His ruddy face appeared more crimson than usual. Anne's spirits sank like a rock. She stopped dead still, her eyes wide.

"Mistress Anne. You're late. Come here this instant!"

Her mouth felt dry as she answered, "Yes, Uncle George." She patted the damp tendrils of hair that threatened to spill from under her cap, straightened her creased apron and turned to meet her fate.

Chapter Two

Fear and apprehension mixed in the pit of Anne's stomach as she strode toward her uncle, who scowled from the doorway.

Her mind scrambled for an excuse while she prepared herself for the violent tirade she knew was coming. "I'm sorry I'm late, Uncle George," she said as she came before him.

"I'll be interested to hear your explanation later, but I've something much more pressing to discuss with you." Although his tone was amiable, the hard lines of disapproval in his face betrayed his intent.

Anne eyed him suspiciously as she swept past. No sooner had she crossed the oak-timbered threshold of the study than she understood why her uncle had put off meting out her punishment. There, in front of the crackling hearth, sat Mrs. Jane Herrick, her uncle's goddaughter. Of course he'd never discuss his niece's errant behavior in front of company, she thought wryly.

Her relief for the slight reprieve mingled with curiosity. Usually, when George had important guests, Anne was excused from attending. She knew he believed that her presence would remind her uncle's friends that his older brother was an enemy of Cromwell's Commonwealth.

"Mistress Jane, you remember my niece, Anne Lowell?"

Jane dimpled beguilingly, the black silk fan in her hand fluttering in response. "Of course, Master Lowell. How could anyone forget your charming niece?"

Charming? Anne exchanged glances with her uncle. Although his eyes were unreadable, she guessed he thought Mrs. Herrick too refined to regard the gossip that blazed across Parliamentarian hearths about his rebellious niece, abandoned by her father like an unwanted kitten, for him to raise.

Anne bobbed a curtsy and took a seat as far away from her uncle as she could. Out of the corner of her eye, she watched George gaze with adoration as Jane charmed him with small talk that Anne usually found wearisome.

Anne pushed back a defiant red gold curl from under her cap as she studied the young woman. According to George, Jane exemplified everything a young Puritan woman should be. A few years older than herself, Jane had married a physician several months ago. A pristine cap covered Jane's silvery blond head. Her white skin with a pink rise to her cheeks contrasted becomingly with the Puritan black gown she wore. Her pale gray eyes and narrow chin spoke of an obedient nature, George had remarked more than once. For once, Anne had to agree with him. The woman was as perfect as an April crocus.

She felt like a toad by comparison. Anne nibbled her lip as she considered her attributes. Her mouth was too full to be considered comely, she knew. Her skin might be worthy except for the spill of freckles, Satan's tiptoes, George had called them, that peppered the curve of her cheeks and upturned nose. Who could blame her uncle for being ashamed of her?

"I was commenting to your uncle," Jane cooed, "how splendid the autumn foliage appeared this morning when we rode through the woods. The beech woods have turned a bright gold and the oaks—"

George pounded his fist on his knee. "I fail to understand how your husband thought it safe for you to ride without escort," he blustered, ignoring Jane's shocked surprise.

"Master Lowell!" Jane sat up with a start and touched her cheek with the tip of her fan. "I was perfectly safe. Besides my husband, our two menservants accompanied me."

"Humph! You are to be commended for your faith, dear lady, but your husband should have had the good sense to accept my offer of a military escort. The roads are teeming with ruffians, not to mention that . . . that . . . highwayman, the Black Fox."

"The Black Fox!" Anne's voice held a reverence that caused her uncle to shoot her a quelling glance. She had overheard Daisy, the scullery maid, say the outlaw robbed Roundheads of their gold and gave it to the Royalists for their fight to restore King Charles to the throne.

George snorted. "Enough of your dreamy thoughts, mistress. He's the highwayman who had the audacity to lighten the purse of Colonel Twining and his valet, Babson, only last week."

Anne stifled a laugh behind her hand. How she wished she could have seen that. The thought of a common rogue getting the better of that arrogant Twining was exhilarating. She despised the colonel, contrary to most females, if Daisy could be believed. Anne felt her cheeks flame with outrage as she remembered how Twining had leered at her whenever he had thought her uncle wasn't looking. But what truly irked her was that Uncle George had refused to take her complaints seriously.

Jane smiled reassuringly at Anne. "There's no need to worry, my dear. You can be sure the Black Fox is far from Wycliffe Manor since Colonel Twining and his soldiers have arrived."

Anne's gaze shot to her uncle. "Colonel Twining? You didn't tell me he's been invited to dinner."

A strange look passed between her uncle and Jane Herrick. Finally George cleared his throat while his gaze dropped to his lap. "Mistress Anne, I've something to tell you. Mrs. Herrick has kindly answered my request to coach you in the proper deportment for your appearance this evening."

A flash of foreboding skittered up her spine. "If you've paired Colonel Twining as my dinner partner again, then I'd prefer to remain in my chamber and go without food for a week."

George's ruddy face darkened. "Don't tempt me." He craned his neck and rubbed his finger along the inside band of his shirt, then glanced with pleading at Jane.

Jane dimpled back at him, then turned the dazzling smile on Anne. "Your uncle only wishes that you make your finest impression on his guests this evening. I thought we'd practice some polite phrases you may wish to use during dinner, and perhaps we might subdue your hair—"

"Aye, do something with her hair." George scowled back at Anne. "God's teeth! She looks like the devil's own spawn with that wild mane." His black brows knotted together. "Look how it threatens to unfurl from her cap like Lucifer's red banner fluttering on a windy Sabbath morn."

Jane smiled. "When I'm finished managing your niece, she'll be the paragon of acceptability. I assure you, sir."

Anne curled her fingers into the tufted ends of the chair. "Uncle George, I demand to know what's going on."

"You'll demand nothing!" George answered. "You'll do what Mrs. Herrick says. For once, you'll behave without embarrassing me when . . . when I announce your betrothal at dinner."

Nothing could have prepared Anne for the shock that coursed through her. She shook her head numbly. "Betrothal? To whom?"

"Colonel Twining has offered for your hand," her uncle continued, "and I've accepted for you."

Anne gasped, unable to get her breath. She could only stare at him while she tried to take in what he was saying. Her uncle continued speaking, but her mind blocked out his words. Betrothal? She was to *wed* Colonel Twining?

Shock and panic mixed with betrayal. Anne sprang to her feet, her knees shaky. "Uncle George, certainly y-you can't m-mean to wed me to that . . . that . . ."

"It's well time you're wed."

Anne rushed to him and knelt at his knees, her gray skirts billowing out behind her. "Please, don't do this. I promise I'll never disobey you again." She swiped at another rebellious curl. I'll do anything—''

George stood and jerked her to her feet. "Anne, calm yourself. Your behavior is unseemly."

Jane leaned forward in the chair, the black fan in her hand flitting like a wounded bird. "There are worse fates than to marry a handsome, wealthy man such as the colonel, my dear."

Anne jerked free and turned to face her, aware suddenly that not only Mrs. Herrick, but everybody must have known of the betrothal except herself. She felt like a fool, as well.

"Twining is a lecher and I'll never marry him!"

George glowered down at her. "Oh, yes, you will!" Then he turned and forced a smile at Jane. "Forgive me, my dear, but would you allow us a few minutes alone?"

"Of course, sir." Her gray eyes slanted toward Anne, her expression sympathetic. Then she folded gracefully into a curtsy before closing the door behind her.

George's blue eyes snapped with anger. "Your wedding will take place six weeks from tomorrow, and that's final. Now follow Mrs. Herrick and do everything she says. For once, you'll behave as your position dictates."

Anne squeezed her fingers on the edge of the chair. "What would my father say if he knew you've betrothed me to a—"

"Hold your tongue!" George's voice rose as his attempt at constraint dissolved before her. "I hold no loyalty to your father and you're old enough to have loyalties of your own. You'd best appreciate a man like Colonel Twining, not a dandy like your father, a fop who's disgraced himself and his family, flying his plumes against the Commonwealth."

Anne returned her uncle's fiery gaze with one of her own.

"How can you say that about your own blood?"

"A sorry fact I'd like to forget. He would rather chase romantic rainbows than be a father to you. He never wanted you or your mother. He's never coming for you, and the sooner you understand that, the better you'll be."

"How dare you speak of him so!" Anne squared her shoulders and faced him down. "He's been fighting side by side with the king at Worcester. For all you know, my father may be dead—"

"I pray to God every day that he is!"

A wash of renewed anger coursed through her. For the first time, she realized how vast was the well of rage and resentment that festered beneath her uncle's reproach. Her eyes stung with frustrated tears, but she blinked them back. "Nothing I do will make you accept me, because I'm your brother's daughter. You can dress me as a Puritan, threaten to bend me to your will, but I'll always be a Royalist's daughter. Unlike you, I'm proud to know my father is a man who had the courage and vision to stand with King Charles against the tyranny of Parliament."

Anne picked up her skirts and whirled toward the door to find Colonel Twining, resplendent in a crimson wool uniform, blocking her way. His granite gray eyes bored into her and she knew immediately that he had heard everything.

She felt like a chick with a hawk circling overhead.

Well, so be it! Maybe if he knew of her repulsion for him, he'd break the marriage contract. The idea gave her hope.

Anne pushed past him, but Twining grabbed her arm and half dragged her back into the room.

"My dear, what has upset you?" His stare glittered with feigned expectation.

"You know very well!" Anne's chin rose defiantly. "I'll never marry you!" She tried to wrench from his hold, but his grip tightened on her wrist like a vise.

"I wouldn't be so hasty, if I were you," he replied silkily.

"Let go of me, you... you... weasel-faced lecher."

Twining's thin lips lifted in amusement. "I'll overlook your passionate expression, my dear, as long as we understand each other." He pulled her closer, his voice as final as a death knell. "By Christmas, you'll be my bride." She grappled against his grip. His mouth twisted in what appeared to be enjoyment. "You may take your leave, my dear, but return to the study within the hour, when I'll escort you into the great hall for dinner."

Anne stopped struggling. His hawklike sweep of the nose and the square jaw quivered as if he were in pursuit.

"And if I refuse?" His smoky eyes sparked as though fired by her challenge. She almost thought he hoped she'd defy him.

"You'll obey," he said finally. "Because I'm planning a very special wedding present for you, my dear." His hard gaze raked over her. He was so close she could smell the tobacco and what she thought might be brandy. She was afraid if she didn't hurry and leave she might be sick.

"I don't want anything from you," she managed to reply.

His black eyebrows flicked up. "Very well, if that is your wish." His gray eyes glittered. "But I've already submitted a petition to Lieutenant General Cromwell to pardon your father from the charges brought forth by the Commonwealth." She heard a stifled gasp from her uncle sitting nearby.

Twining's face lit with amusement. "That's right, my dear Anne. When we're married, your father will receive a full pardon. That is, if you comply with your uncle's wishes."

Words failed her as she took in what he had said. The very generosity of his offer demonstrated his power. Would he truly grant his political enemy a pardon? His expression reminded her of a weasel crouched in the bushes waiting for the stray duckling. Certainly her father was too proud to take favors from the enemy—especially if he knew the cost.

His thin smile grew wider as she considered him. "And if I refuse?" she said finally.

The smile faded. "Then I'll see you immediately shipped off to the Bay Colony where you'll live with the Reverend and Mrs. Skylar." He leaned his face to within an inch of hers. "And I promise you," he whispered, his hot breath brushing her face, "you'll never see your father again!"

She gasped, fear tightening her words. Her heartbeat thrummed in her ears as her mind fought back the one thought she could never bear. For how would she endure if she were to lose the hope of seeing her father?

Anne caught the look of satisfaction on Twining's face and realized he knew he had won. He released his grip.

She squared her shoulders before she glared back defiantly, then clutched her skirts and ran from the room.

George came beside Colonel Twining, who stared after Anne. "I'll send for Mrs. Herrick. She'll know what to say to her—"

"It won't be necessary, old man." Twining faced him, his thin brows arched with triumph. "You see, Mistress Anne is like a beautiful, high-spirited filly. Reckless, perhaps, but she has a fine head on her shoulders." Twining flicked at an invisible fleck on his crimson sleeve.

Even the small gesture, George noted, the colonel did with a self-styled assurance. The coarse black hair styled in the bowl cut of the Roundheads gave him a striking demeanor, and did nothing to dispel the man's aristocratic bearing. Maybe it was that haughtiness some women found attractive. For a man of forty-five, his virility was well-known. Rumor had it several married women had risked their reputations with him, and it was fact that the colonel kept several mistresses in London.

"Your niece realizes what's at stake," Twining said with conviction. "That proud filly will come back of her own volition." He crooked an eyebrow. "Care to wager, old man?"

The thought of the dire consequences of denying this man anything brought a well of dyspepsia to George's throat. "I'm not a betting man, Colonel," he managed, his damp fingers pressing against his white collar. "But I'm certain my niece will do exactly as you foresee."

Twining responded with a smug lift of his shoulder, then turned and strode out the door.

After he had gone, George sank back in his chair and let the relief flow through him. God's teeth, Twining still wanted to marry his niece and he was pardoning Jonathan to boot!

For as long as he could remember, his older brother had been a bane upon his life. In one fracas after another, Jonathan's reputation would have been ruined if their father's

influence hadn't squelched the gossip. There had been some
gossip involving Twining, now that George thought about
it, but he never knew the details. God's teeth, but what did
it matter now?

And another question struck him, just as it had when the
colonel first offered for Anne. Why would such a powerful
man as Twining desire a hellion for a wife?

Nat crept around the corner of the manor house and
paused in the shadows of the dense ivy that clung to the
outer stone wall of the buttery. The last of the afternoon sun
slanted across the diamond-shaped panes along the gabled
front, mirroring the courtyard in its golden likeness. He
glanced at his reflection in the windows, then he pulled the
helmet down across his forehead, straightened the crimson
sash across his chest. Finally satisfied, he stepped out upon
the worn path toward the kitchen.

Ahead, the sound of spurs jingling alerted him to the two
Roundhead privates before they approached from around
the corner. Nat returned their hasty salutes as he marched
past them.

The tantalizing aroma from a dozen meat pies cooling on
the open windowsill filled the air. Nat's mouth watered, but
he brushed aside the thought that he hadn't eaten since
daybreak.

Parting the thick vines, he peeked inside the window. At
least ten servants bustled about the vast room. A side of
mutton sizzled noisily as it turned on the jack above the fire.
Several black iron cauldrons bubbled softly.

Nat crept to the next window. In the small storage room,
he saw Twining's valet, Babson, hunched over a table, unpacking candles. Nat tapped on the leaded glass.

Babson's snowy head shot up and his eyes widened with
recognition. "Quickly," he whispered, waving him inside.
"Soldiers everywhere."

"Don't worry." Nat gave the old man a crooked smile
while he climbed through the window. "In this lieutenant's
uniform, I'll fit right in."

Babson's worried frown melted into a wry grin, as though appreciative of Nat's boldness.

"Do you have the maps?" Nat grabbed a shiny red apple from a wooden crate beside the table and crunched a bite.

"Aye," Babson whispered, "an' news, too." He glanced over his shoulder before continuing. "The maps an' notes are 'ere." He pulled the folded parchments from his green tunic.

Nat took them and rolled the papers inside his jacket.

Babson lowered his voice. "Last night, while I served brandy to Twining an' 'is aides, I 'eard 'im say that Cromwell believed the king would probably be 'eadin' back to France through Scotland." Babson's face beamed with satisfaction.

"Good they think it." Nat took another bite out of the juicy fruit. "Anything else?"

"Aye. Twining said Cromwell 'ad agreed to the requisition for extra troops. 'E plans to stretch a trap to catch the Black Fox." Babson's eyes twinkled. "Later, I snuck back an' copied the marked locations of the roadblocks from 'is charts." A smile crossed his thin lips. "'E thinks I can't read or write."

"Good work, my friend." Nat patted him on the shoulder. "It would seem the colonel hasn't forgotten the night I lightened his purse in the name of Charlie Stuart," he added.

Babson chuckled. "That pompous ass speaks o' nothin' else."

"The added note I found in your purse, Babson, was well received. The list of the locations of their ammunition depots were clearly marked." Nat's expression became serious. "It's a brave thing you're doing, as well as a dangerous one."

Babson beamed with pride. "I'm honored to serve our king any way I can, Nat."

Nat nodded, feeling the familiar tug of kinship for the people who risked their lives for their king. "It's almost time for me to leave. If you need to get in touch with me, you know how."

"Aye, Nat, an' God be with you."

Nat had no sooner crept around the rear of the manor on his way to the stables than he heard footsteps pounding along the path. He darted back into the shadows and flattened himself against the shrubbery. The footsteps grew louder. Suddenly a young woman hurried past toward the rose bower nearby.

Anne Lowell! Nat frowned as he watched her dash across the leaf-strewn lawn, her gray skirts billowing behind her like a bell. Reason told him to ignore her. He had a job to do, and he didn't believe in allowing personal feelings to get in the way of duty. Yet something he couldn't quite explain drove him, instead, to want to follow her. It was more than the liking for clouds of coppery hair and blue-green eyes. She had gotten the best of him, and he couldn't help admiring her for that. He glanced across the courtyard at the stables nearby. Aye, he had a few minutes before it was time to leave. Enough time, surely, to satisfy his longing to see her for one last time.

A sweet fragrance drifted from the last of the summer roses and invaded Nat's senses as he approached the heavily entwined bower. The sound of muffled sobs came from the hidden bench; his heart went out to her, but he fought back the unreasonable response. She hadn't heard him approach, and for a brief moment, he watched her weeping, before he spoke.

"Rather far from your flock, aren't you, lass? Your sheep must be scattered all over the hillocks by now."

Anne lifted her white-capped head. "You?" she gasped, straightening. Her cheeks pinked at the realization he knew by her proper dress she was obviously not a shepherd maid.

Her eyes darkened and he noticed how the dappled foliage heightened the emerald shards of light in her eyes.

Nat reached for her hand. "The lady weeps as though her heart were broken." He brought her dainty fingers to his lips. "Agh!" He made a face. "How I hate the salty taste of tears."

Anne jerked her hand back. "What an ungentlemanly thing to say," she snapped, obviously forgetting her discomfiture. But when she saw his grin, she knew that he had made the joke only to take her mind off her troubles, and she rewarded him with her lovely smile.

"I'm glad that you've retrieved your...boot," she said finally, the memory lightening her eyes.

"Are you?" He felt pleased to see a spark of her former spirit.

"Aye," she answered, her fingers dabbing at her eyes. "And I'd be grateful if you said nothing to anyone of what happened this afternoon."

He leaned over her. "Would *anyone* perhaps be your uncle? Your uncle," he repeated with mock exaggeration, "Master George Lowell?"

He watched her pink blush deepen as she realized he'd known her identity all along. "Rest assured, Mistress Anne, you have my promise not to reveal our...adventure. However, to seal our bargain, little mermaid, there's a price."

She squinted her eyes knowingly. "You're a gull if you think I'd allow you to take any liberties with me. I've heard the kitchen maids whisper of what you soldiers do to a maid who forgets to keep up her guard."

Nat reached out and caught her by the waist with his left hand while he cupped her chin with the other. "I'm not some randy soldier..." His dark brown eyes flashed. "I've *never* had to beg a lady's favor, and I'm not about to begin with you."

Ignoring his boast, she jerked her chin free, then her gaze dropped to his hand at her waist. "Perhaps, but please let me go, should you decide to change your technique."

He chuckled as he released his hand and watched her spread out her skirt becomingly on the garden bench. "You're a tempting morsel, little mermaid," he drawled. Brushing aside her skirts, he sat down beside her. "All I had in mind was to ask you what happened to make you cry."

Anne gazed up at him with those incredible eyes. For a disorienting moment, he felt bewitched by their promise— huge liquid jewels fringed by dark sooty lashes. It must be the heavy scent of the roses that was weaving a spell over him, he decided.

Her delicate brows furrowed, her lips pursed as he watched her. She looked so vulnerable that, for a brief instance, a surge of wanting to protect her shot through him.

"It's a private matter," she said. Then, as though reconsidering, she added, "It's... that sometimes...I—I miss my father."

Nat remembered that Anne's betrothal would be announced later tonight. No doubt she was torn by her desire to marry Twining and being disloyal to her father. He felt a flash of regret at her judgment, but he cast it aside. It was no business of his, he reminded himself. "Your father is Jonathan Lowell?"

"You've heard of him?"

He caught the flicker of wary surprise on her lovely face. "Every Roundhead knows of the fearless Colonel Jonathan Lowell," he said in truth. "His name strikes fear into his enemies' bones whenever the king's men yell his name like a battle cry. With a price on his head, your father must be far away from England." No need to worry her if she was unaware of the many Royalists who had fallen by their swords at last week's battle at Worcester.

She shook her head. "Nay, he'll never stop fighting until Charles Stuart returns to the throne." Fresh tears glistened in her eyes.

"I see," Nat said gently. "It's natural for you to miss him." A pang of regret washed over him again as he thought of all the separation and suffering of innocent lives since the civil war. Yet he couldn't help thinking that if Lowell had died at Worcester, it might have been more merciful than to discover his daughter was betrothed to as cruel an enemy as Twining.

She brushed an errant copper tendril from her cheek. "When I was little, my father would listen to my childish troubles and offer his wise advice," she said wistfully.

He remained silent, watching her. After a while, he took her small hand in his large callused palm. "Now, you're a young woman. If your father were here, I'm certain he'd encourage you to make your own decisions."

Anne met his eyes. Her lovely face appeared so profound it nearly took his breath away. "Aye, I think he would," she said finally.

He considered encouraging her to go on, in fact, he would have enjoyed listening to her dulcet voice all evening, but it was time for him to leave. He knew he should offer her a simple solution: Forget her father and remember the solid future with one of the most powerful men in the Commonwealth. Besides, it would prove dangerous, if not impossible for Twining's wife to hold overt loyalty to the king.

"When I have a weighty matter to decide and I'm not certain what to do, I find that if I..." He watched her expectation grow, and for some strange reason, he couldn't encourage her to forget her father. Instead, he offered her what was in his own soul. "I find that if I listen to my heart the answer will always be there for me."

"But what does that mean?"

"It means the answer is within you, along with the courage to carry it through."

"But how?"

"You'll know." He stood and pulled her to her feet. Her hand felt warm and soft in his and she made no move to release it. "It's time I must leave."

"You've given me much to think about," she whispered. "Much to think about."

Nat smiled. "I'd escort you back to the manor, but my orders are to... to stay with my troops. They're expecting me."

"Of course." Anne stood for a moment, her heart fluttering beneath her breast like a captured bird. *What a strange man!* This handsome lieutenant was her enemy, her father's enemy, yet he had spoken of her father with respect, without judgment. She might never see this lieutenant again, but she'd always be grateful to him for that.

Impulsively she stood on tiptoe, only thinking to brush her lips to his. But the moment their lips touched, a jolt slammed through her and his mouth seized hers with an urgency that caused her heart to thunder. She went still with shock as a strange sensation poured through her.

His mouth felt firm and warm. Her heartbeat quickened when his lips moved over hers, deepening their kiss.

She drank in the smell of him. It reminded her of a cedar forest filled with sunshine. Her arms rose timidly around his neck, her fingers lacing the dark hair at his nape.

She felt her cap loosen and her hair cascade down her back. His hands roved up and down her spine, his fingers tightening the rebellious curls. She felt her breasts yield against his hard chest and her body trembled with delightful sensations she had never experienced before. She should beg him to let her go, but she didn't want to move. She wanted to remain like this, forever.

Her hands timidly explored his face. She heard him moan softly when her fingers lingered on the scar along his cheek. His breath shuddered as he lifted his mouth to kiss a line across her cheek, down toward her neck.

"I've wanted to taste those lips ever since I saw you at the river, little mermaid."

Her head buzzed with a light-headed feeling. Then suddenly, he released her. "And now, I'll always know your taste of honey, warmed with sunshine." His dark eyes glinted with something she didn't understand. "But if I don't leave immediately..."

Anne's swirling senses returned and she felt a blush rise to her cheeks. She lowered her lashes at his warm stare. Her fingers shook as she brushed her collar, straightened her skirts and snatched her cap from the bench.

A song thrush flew to an overhead vine. The throaty warble was answered by its mate nearby.

Nat reached up and plucked a rose from the bower and placed it in her cupped palm. "Farewell, little mermaid."

She clutched the rose and, with bittersweet longing, watched him disappear into the shadows and out of her life.

She sat back on the bench, not trusting her shaky legs to support her if she were to stand. Besides, for a few more minutes, she needed to gather her wits.

Never had she imagined a kiss could be so thrilling. She smiled, drinking in the fragrance of the roses as she trailed the blossom along the path of his kisses, across her cheek, down to the soft hollow of her throat, and her heart skipped a beat.

But never had she been so bewildered by her conflicting emotions. He was a soldier of Cromwell's New Model army. What would her father say if he knew? God's bones, it would kill him, as readily as if she fired the shot herself.

But she must be honest with herself. She had wanted to touch his sun-bronzed face, feel the shine of his tousled hair, the sinewy, corded muscles of his arms. She had wanted the enemy officer to kiss her.

Even though he was the enemy, Nat had helped her work through a difficult decision, without even knowing it. Without his gentle coaxing, she might have made a fatal mistake.

The acknowledgment gave her the jolt back she needed. Aye, she *had* made the decision. The answer had been in her heart all along, just as the lieutenant had said. How could she have forgotten that her proud father would never want her to bargain for his life? "Twining be damned!" he would have shouted.

For the next few minutes, she clutched the rose while she planned her escape from Wycliffe Manor, the first step in her journey to find her father.

And her only regret was she'd not be there to see Twining's pompous expression fade to surprise when he discovered she would refuse him, after all.

Chapter Three

By the time Anne returned to her chamber, she had decided how to put her plan into motion.

She smiled as she carefully pressed the pink rose in between the pages of her favorite romance novel. Her fingers lingered over the faded book cover for a moment before tucking it inside her bulging traveling valise.

"If you listen to your heart, the answer will follow," Nat had said. It was true. Her father would want her to follow her heart and search for him. To remain at Wycliffe Manor and cave in to Twining's threat was the coward's way out.

Her fingers shook with excitement as she tied the straps on the valise and lifted it from the bed. She would hide upstairs in one of the vacant bedchambers until dinner, then she'd sneak through the back stairs to the barn where her mare waited.

But first, she had to slip the note she had written to Mrs. Herrick under her door. Once Jane read that Anne had developed a megrim and had taken to her bed, even the callous Colonel Twining would realize his odious threats had made her ill. At dawn, when the maids would discover her missing, she'd be far away, searching for the king's scattered army and news of her father.

Surely someone would have heard of Jonathan Lowell. Then once she found him, they would sail for France with the other exiled Royalists until Cromwell's armies were driven into the sea and they could return to England. Hope surged through her.

A few minutes later, Anne arrived at the back stairs landing. She peeked down the passageway. No one was in sight. She tiptoed along the creaking floorboards toward Mrs. Herrick's room, the third doorway on the left. As she knelt to slip the note beneath the portal, she heard a hushed voice coming from inside the chamber.

"...searching the roads for her," Jane whispered. "Hurry, we must leave."

"Curse the luck," a male voice growled. "What if we're found before your husband gathers the horses?"

Anne stared, dumbfounded. *What was Jane Herrick doing with a man in her chamber who was not her husband?*

Anne pressed her ear closer to the door.

"...might prove too dangerous to warn him," the man continued in a low whisper. "Maybe Wilkens and I should..."

Unable to hear every word, Anne shifted against the wood. The board beneath her foot creaked loudly. She froze.

In a flash, the door flew open. A bald, barrel-chested man in a green uniform frowned back at her, then he grabbed her arm and pulled her inside the room.

Jane Herrick leapt from a corner chair and stared in astonishment, her face pale.

A young manservant, not much older than Anne, sat cross-legged upon the bed. "Who's this pretty thing?" His hooded black eyes twinkled as his gaze raked her up and down.

"She's Anne Lowell, the young woman I told you about." Jane folded her arms across herself and scowled at Anne. "How long have you been eavesdropping outside my door?"

"I—I wasn't eavesdropping."

"Sweeting, tell the truth and no one will harm you," offered the impertinent manservant, his black eyes glinting.

Anne felt herself redden at his insolent manner. A servant speaking to her like he was...an equal! She shot him a haughty look and directed her attention to Jane Herrick. "I came to your chamber to slip a note under the door."

The bald-headed man picked up the folded parchment from the floor and waved it in front of her. "This note?"

"Yes."

Anne reached for it but he handed it to Jane, who began to read it. After a moment, she glanced up.

"I can explain, Mrs. Herrick. I had only wished that you inform my uncle that I have a megrim and—"

"We can't take the chance that she might 'ave 'eard somethin'," interrupted the bald man.

She gave Anne a long deliberate stare. "If we let her go, she might try to haggle a bargain from Twining to let her out of the betrothal in exchange for what she's overheard," Jane said finally, pursing her lips together. She crumpled the parchment into a ball and tossed it into the roaring fireplace.

The black-eyed servant folded his arms. "She offers us no choice. The lass will come with us."

Anne's small fists flew to her hips as she regarded Jane Herrick and the two men. "Will you please stop speaking as though I'm not in the room? Go where?"

Jane crossed to the bed and sat down. "Very well, Anne, but first, there's something I must ask you." She motioned for Anne to sit beside her.

Without a choice, Anne obeyed.

Jane put her hand to Anne's shoulder. "Is it true that you're devoted to your father's cause?"

A charge of excitement coursed through her. "Have you heard something of my father?"

"Shh! Lower your voice." Jane's gray eyes narrowed. "Your father has risked his life for his beliefs, as many of us have."

Anne swallowed and tried to speak, but the words caught in her throat. Could it be that a Puritan like Jane Herrick could hold sympathy for the Royalist cause? Her father had often told her of the secret followers of the king: farmers, weavers, hoopers, you never knew who might be among them. Hope welled inside her. "Mrs. Herrick, do you support our exiled king?"

Jane's only answer was her smile. "For now, you'll have to trust me. Can you do that, Anne?"

Anne nodded eagerly.

"And do you believe in your father's crusade to restore a Stuart to the throne? Or do you merely flaunt his quest to rankle your uncle?"

"I'm devoted to my father's cause."

"Would you fight for those beliefs?"

"With all my heart," Anne answered. "I'd give my life for the young king. My heart breaks when I think of how he's forced to live in exile while that hateful Cromwell grips England by the throat."

Jane smiled. "You'll have your chance to prove it, my dear. You're going to help us save our king."

"The—the king?"

Jane swung her around to face the scraggly looking servant who sat in the middle of the bed, grinning at her. "Anne, it is my pleasure to present His Royal Highness, Charles Stuart."

Anne's mouth dropped as she stared at the servant. Her glance swept over the tattered leathern doublet, the coarsely woven shirt, the cloth breeches above the travel-stained stockings. "Charles Stuart?" she cried with disbelief when her gaze lifted to his swarthy face.

His black eyes twinkled with obvious amusement at her disbelief. "My fair and lovely subject." He reached for her hand and kissed it.

Anne snapped back and wiped her hand on her skirt. "Anne!" Jane gasped, horrified. "By divine Providence, this is our king! The sovereign every true subject serves."

Anne stared in shock while Jane pushed her into a curtsy.

"It's quite understandable, Mrs. Herrick." The king stood and touched Anne's chin with his fingers. "It's best she behaves as though I'm a servant. In fact, our very lives might depend on it." The hooded eyes glinted. "But what is to become of her once we reach Bristol?" The gleam in his eye reminded Anne of a ferret.

"I'm more concerned that we reach Bristol," Jane said.

The king's black gaze lingered reflectively on Anne. "She might make a lovely addition to the French court," he said. "What would you think of that, sweeting?"

Anne tried to comprehend that this unkempt servant was the one man she had always fancied would restore everything right in her world once he regained the throne.

"My cousin, King Louis, and his court would certainly be enlivened by your sparkle...and so would I," the king added.

"Your grace," interrupted Jane. "May I remind you that each moment we dally endangers your safety."

"Right you are, my dear. But please, remember to call me Will Jackson." His swarthy face became serious. "It might save our lives if another curious ear be pressed to the door."

Jane's face flushed. "Of course...Mr. Jackson."

"But you don't understand. I—I can't go to Bristol," Anne said. "I'm running away to find my father."

Jane turned slowly and drew a deep breath before she spoke. "Either way, you must leave Wycliffe Manor. The woods will be teeming with soldiers once they discover you're gone. With us, you'll have a greater chance to succeed than by yourself."

"How will you explain your disappearance, Mrs. Herrick?" Anne asked. "Won't my uncle wonder why you're not at dinner, too?"

Jane smiled. "We've already thought of that, my dear. My husband will deliver an urgent message to your uncle very soon, calling me to my mother's sickbed." Her smile broadened. "Don't look so puzzled, Anne. My mother, who's in very fine health, wrote the note long before we left for Wycliffe Manor."

The bald servant named Wilkens glared at her. "Besides, you 'ave no choice. You're leavin' with us, tied and gagged like a goose, if need be."

Anne bit back any further argument. She had no choice but to obey, and as sure as the sun rises, she'd be better off with them than to remain.

Wilkens gave her a sharp look before he hoisted the saddlebags and carried them to the door.

"If I'm a servant, then that's my chore, Wilkens," said the king. He swung the bag over his shoulder.

Jane lit two tapers from the burning candle on the table. "Take the back stairs and go behind the barn where my husband waits with the horses. Remember the story we've agreed upon if you're stopped. Anne and I will follow in a few minutes."

Both men nodded. Jane pressed her ear to the door before opening it, then peeked quickly into the passageway. "Godspeed," she said, giving each man a candle as he slipped out the door.

After the men left, Jane reached under the bed and pulled out a small bundle of clothing. Within minutes, she had selected a pile of assorted garments and tossed them to Anne. "Slip these on, and hurry," she instructed.

"But I've already packed a valise of my things. It's in my room. I'll get it," Anne offered.

Jane shook her head. "There's no time. Besides, it's safer if you're dressed as a man." She helped Anne pull an enormous muslin shirt over her gown.

Anne's fingers shook with excitement as she removed her unyielding underskirts before stepping into a pair of men's linen breeches that hung to above her ankles. The breeches were so baggy she could only hope the sash tied about her waist would hold them up. Next came the stiff leather jerkin. Finally, the disguise was completed with a red cap pulled down over her ears.

Jane frowned. "I'm afraid it will have to do."

After Jane tossed a black woolen traveling coat around her shoulders, she glanced about the chamber. "Put this on," she said, tossing the woolen blanket from the bed to Anne.

Anne wrapped the scratchy blanket about herself and followed Jane to the door. The latch creaked open, and she felt a rush of air as Jane nudged her into the hall. Her heart was in her throat while Jane led her toward the back stairs, their heels clacking along the creaking wooden planks.

In what seemed like the longest ten minutes of Anne's life, she and Jane arrived without incident at the outside entrance of the manor. The evening air hung heavy with the familiar animal odors drifting from the milking barn nearby.

A few minutes later, after they had crept around the back of the barn, Jane paused, her eyes searching the fields beyond the pasture. "There!" she whispered, pointing to a grove of willows beside the hedgerow path. Jane took Anne's elbow and hurried her along. Only when they reached the hedges did Anne see the three riders hidden in the shadows—the king, Wilkens and another man whom Anne assumed was Jane's husband, Dr. Herrick.

Clasping the blanket with her right hand, Anne yanked up the baggy pants with the other and ran the final few yards toward the waiting horsemen, her heart thumping wildly.

The full moon cast silvered light about the countryside as Anne and the riders charged along the high road that led from Wycliffe Manor toward the town of Bristol. Anne sensed that Jane had chosen the longer route rather than the shorter middle road because of the soldiers' camps fortified along the more widely used route. The horses' hooves splashed through mud puddles from yesterday's rain, tossing up mud clods along the way.

Dr. Herrick rode as scout and had a five minutes lead of the group. Anne rode double, behind the bald-headed servant, Wilkens. For what she thought might be an hour, she jolted back and forth, bouncing against the pillion that fastened behind the saddle. Wilkens lashed the reins in a futile attempt to keep up with the powerful bay stallion racing ahead, carrying Jane Herrick and the king.

As Wilkens spurred the horse faster, Anne held on with a ferocity that matched his and fought back the thought she might catapult off her seat and be left in the road. Good riddance, Wilkens would think and not even glance back.

Anne peered above his shoulder at the dark uncertainty of the road ahead and she felt torn between fear and exhilaration. She'd always known that someday she would leave Wycliffe Manor. It was one of her favorite daydreams to imagine her father's magnificent high-lacquered coach clattering up the driveway. Six white horses would prance impatiently while the footman helped her into the coach where her father waited. Together, they would bound away toward their new life, far from the strictures of Wycliffe Manor.

Instead, she was holding on for dear life, plunging head-long into the unknown. What if soldiers stopped them and forced her to return to her uncle? Colonel Twining would make certain she was punished and she knew she'd lose her father.

But if Jane Herrick was to be believed, each pounding hoofbeat brought her one step closer to her heartfelt dream. How she wanted to believe it, but her thoughts twisted in misgivings. Mrs. Jane Herrick, the fine Puritan woman Uncle George idolized, was nothing like he had imagined. Although the fact pleased her, it also provided a very dubious structure on which to build her hopes, Anne mused.

Suddenly a golden halo of light appeared up the road. Wilkens reined back on his horse and trotted alongside Jane and the king. Uneasily they waited for the lone rider to arrive.

"It's Dr. Herrick," cried Wilkens. Anne drew a sigh of relief as she peered out into the soft glow of the lantern the doctor held above his face.

"Roundheads," he warned, drawing rein. "A full squad riding off the middle road and they're coming straight on us!"

"We can't hide the horses," Jane said, twisting around in the saddle. "The trees aren't thick enough along this stretch."

"Aye," the king agreed. "It's too late for that." He pulled his wide-brimmed hat low over his face. "We'll talk our way out of this." Anne thought she heard him chuckle. "If our tongues fail us, we'll give them a taste of our metal."

Anne spied a small group of bushes a few rods from the road. "No, wait!" Anne cried. Four surprised faces turned her way. "If soldiers are riding from the middle road, they've been sent by my uncle. They're searching for me."

"She's right." Wilkens interrupted, shifting uneasily in the saddle. "The middle road cuts north through Wycliffe Manor."

"I'll hide in that copse over there." She started to slide down from the pillion.

"Oh, no you don't!" Wilkens reached out and caught her wrist. "We're on to yer tricks. You'll run out when the soldiers git 'ere and tell 'em 'bout the king."

"Release her, Wilkens," Jane ordered. "I'm sure Anne realizes if the soldiers take her back to her uncle, she'll never see her father again."

Wilkens grumbled but withdrew his hold.

Jane rode her horse beside Anne. "My dear, I give you my word, if you remain hidden and do nothing to give yourself away, I'll help you find your father. I have powerful friends who know the whereabouts of wounded and captured Royalists." Beneath Jane's black hood, Anne saw her wide eyes glitter with trust and assurance.

Anne desperately wanted to believe. "You can trust me, Mrs. Herrick."

Jane smiled. "I know I can, my dear. Remember, whatever happens, stay hidden in the bushes." She paused and her expression grew serious. "Don't be frightened, just think of your father."

Anne forced a brave smile, then hiked up the loose trousers and scooted across the deep rutted road. She tripped, but righted herself before splashing into a muddy puddle. When she finally reached the tall bramble of wild plums, she crawled inside the cover of low branches. A limb poked her head, pushing her woolen knit cap off. She grabbed the hat and stuffed her thick, unbound curls beneath the coarse band.

The sound of cantering hooves grew louder and six Roundhead soldiers, riding single file, came into view. Their armor clanked noisily as they approached.

A cool breeze lifted the loose tendrils of Anne's hair, and she shivered. Parting the branches, she held her breath and peered through the quivering leaves.

The first soldier trotted his horse beside Dr. Herrick's mount and raised the lantern. Before he had a chance to speak, Jane's dulcet voice carried on the night air.

"My prayers have been answered." She fluttered her hands and smiled becomingly at the soldier. "When we heard horses, we feared you were that highwayman my godfather, Master Lowell, warned us about."

Anne watched the soldier as he sat a little straighter on his mount. "I'm Sergeant Stone, at yer service, milady." He touched his helmet in the customary salute. "'Ave no fear of the Black Fox and 'is kind. 'E won't dare come near these shires, milady." He chuckled to his men. "Not with Colonel Twining's troopers garrisoned nearby at Wycliffe Manor. Aye, men?"

The soldiers cheered in unison. They were as pompous as their leader, Anne thought.

"George Lowell's niece is missin'. My orders are to bring all riders in the area back to the manor for questionin'." The stocky soldier held the lantern higher. "May I see yer travelin' passes?"

Anne's heart raced as she watched in trepidation while Dr. Herrick rode forward and handed the soldier the folded parchments. The trooper eyed him a moment, then examined the passes before returning them. "What brings ye to travel these roads so late, Doctor?"

"My wife's mother has been taken ill. We're on our way to be with her at her estate, Rosemoor."

Jane's face brightened in the sputtering light. "We've just come from Wycliffe Manor. I was visiting with my godfather." She pulled out several folded documents from her saddlebag and handed them to the sergeant. "These passes are for our servants."

The soldier inspected the parchments carefully before returning them.

"We're free to move on?" Doc asked hopefully.

"Aye. Yer free to go as soon as ye return with me to Wycliffe Manor for Colonel Twining's interrogation," he answered firmly. He waved his troops forward into escort position.

"But, Sergeant!" Jane fluttered a handkerchief in a demure gesture. "I—I'd never ask a soldier of Oliver Cromwell's to betray his duty..." Her voice trailed off while she batted her eyelids. "B-but my late father, a member of Parliament, was a close friend of Oliver Cromwell. Why, Uncle Oliver, as he insisted I call him, bounced me on his knee when I was a child." She laughed lightly, pausing, as though waiting for the effect of her words to settle.

In the lantern light, Anne saw the soldier's brow furrow in thought. Anne watched in amazement. How can Jane be so serene and collected when her own heart thundered?

Jane brushed a gloved hand along the soldier's forearm. "I'm sure Colonel Twining would understand if you could see beyond the usual enforcement of your office and oblige my sick mother this one small request." Her voice faltered and she lowered her gaze. "You see, if my husband and I don't hasten to her sickbed, she may..." Her voice faded as she bowed her head dramatically.

The sergeant scratched his neck, then turned toward the other troopers, as though hoping for an answer to his dilemma.

Anne watched, her apprehension growing by the minute. Unconsciously her fingers tightened into knots.

Finally, the sergeant's gaze fixed back to Jane. "Mrs. 'errick, under the circumstances, I'm certain Lieutenant General Cromwell, 'isself, would insist ye speed to yer mum's bedside without delay."

Anne saw Jane's shoulders relax and heard Jane's audible sigh. "You're a credit to your country, Sergeant Stone. When next I see *Uncle Oliver,* I'll remember your kindness to him."

"Thank ye, Mrs. 'errick," he said, touching his helmet. "It'll be me pleasure to escort ye to Rosemoor, meself."

"But—" Jane's eyes widened in the lantern's brightness. "That's—that's not necessary. We don't—"

"Aye, I'm sure Lieutenant General Cromwell would insist." Sergeant Stone turned to his men. "Attention!" he shouted. His spurs jingled as his horse bolted forward. "Flank position!"

Anne froze in terror. They were leaving without her! She'd be left out here for days before anyone would find her! She stood on tiptoe and folded the blanket about the leather jerkin. Shivering, her heart sank while she watched Jane and the others turn to leave.

Suddenly Anne heard a pounding of hooves and a loud rush as another group of horsemen thundered across the fields from out of nowhere.

The soldiers fell silent, listening.

Through the trembling leaves, Anne counted at least a dozen horsemen charging from the darkness toward the astonished huddle on the road. Moonlight glinted off their poised swords as the hooves sliced the turf all around them.

"The Black Fox," announced the soldiers, and Anne heard the fear in their cries. Sergeant Stone and his troopers drew their blades and waited.

From out of the night rode the most fearsome horseman Anne had ever seen. Her hands flew to her face and she gasped. Surrounded by masked men in Cavalier dress, he loomed larger than life.

A thrill coursed through her. *It was the Black Fox, and he had come to rescue them!*

He was dressed in black, from the wide-brimmed Cavalier hat with full black plumes cocked at a rakish angle, to the gleaming leather boots. Although his face was fully concealed by a silken mask, she knew he was the most handsome highwayman of all. A long cape billowed from his broad shoulders as he sat atop the majestic black horse draped in black skirts. The brace of pistols he held glinted in the moonlight. The steed reared back as the man's rich laughter rent the night.

"What have we here?" he yelled back to his men. "A party of wealthy Pilgrims escorted by ol' Noll's men?" He spurred the charger to circle the group. "You must be carrying valuables, my good woman," he addressed Jane.

Sergeant Stone's back flexed, his sword drawn. "A pistol against a sword isn't honorable, rogue."

"How very perceptive of you, Sergeant," mocked the Black Fox. "My compliments to your mum for raising a

bright lad!" A titter of laughter rang around the group and
Sergeant Stone swore under his breath.

"Be a good fellow and drop your weapon, if you value
your life," the Black Fox warned. "Besides, you'll need
both hands to dig into your pockets and hand over your coin
for the king's cause."

The sergeant swore again, then tossed his sword to the
ground, his men following his lead.

"Now, dismount and stand over there," the Black Fox
ordered, motioning with the barrel of his pistol. Grum-
bling, the Roundheads formed a line, hands raised, while the
highwaymen dismounted and emptied the pockets of the
soldiers.

Anne's eyes widened when the Black Fox slid from his
mount and strode beside Jane, Dr. Herrick, the king and
Wilkens.

"We have no money," cried Jane. "Please, let us be."
Her hand flew instinctively to the brooch at her throat.

Anne watched Dr. Herrick, who appeared as cold as a
steel trap. His hand went to his hilt, but the Black Fox saw
the motion, took his weapon and ordered his Cavaliers to
search the Pilgrims.

Shocked, Anne watched as a burly highwayman removed a small dagger from the king's vest pocket and
tucked it inside his own belt. Anne was outraged. This was
nothing like she had imagined. Didn't the Black Fox realize
that Jane and Dr. Herrick were loyal to the Royalists' cause?
How dare he take their valuables and arms?

"Your gold and jewels, fair lady," ordered the Black Fox.
"Be quick or I may take more." His demonic laugh gave
weight to his threat. Laughter from the other men made
Anne wonder what sort of loyalty these men really served.

"Please, this brooch was my grandmother's," Jane
pleaded, unfastening the glittering pin from her collar. "It's
of little value except to me."

The Black Fox caught it in his hand and examined it before he passed it to his men. "But, dear lady, one of my
women might take a fancy to it." He swept her an exaggerated bow and thanked her before turning to Dr. Herrick.

"Your purse or your life," he demanded.

The doctor scowled defiantly while he threw several coins to the ground. "I'm only a poor servant of the Lord, but take this, too, you despicable lout." Doc spit on the ground.

Anne froze in fear. This was the first sign of anyone disobeying the Black Fox.

With his hand on his sword, the Black Fox threw back his shoulders and strode purposely toward the doctor. "You've got starch, Pilgrim." He glanced back to his men while they shouted encouragements. After a moment, he faced Doc Herrick. "We're all poor servants, my good man. Only you and I serve different masters." The Black Fox reached inside the doctor's vest pocket and yanked off the gold watch and chain. "This will aid my cause quite nicely." Several of the masked men cheered when he tossed it to them.

"You black-hearted devil!" Dr. Herrick balled his fists at his side.

"That I am." The Fox swung around and from under his mask came a low chuckle. "As black hearted as you'll ever meet."

Anne stood horrified. This wasn't how she'd imagined the Black Fox. She was startled to see her hand shaking as she spread the leaves to afford a better view. *Could her uncle have been right? Could the Black Fox be a cutthroat who robbed in the name of the king, yet held no loyalty to anyone but himself?*

The Black Fox strode beside Wilkens and the king. They turned their pockets inside out in proof that they had nothing of value while Jane explained that they were only servants who didn't hold coin.

"Even the poor must give to Charlie Stuart's cause." He stroked his chin in feigned thought. "Take off your boots, lads. Your wealthy mistress will buy you another pair."

The king appeared dumbfounded, but quickly followed Wilkens' lead and removed his boots, tossing them to the amused men.

One of the highwaymen held up a fat bag of gold coins. "'Ere's what we gathered from the soldiers."

The Black Fox grabbed the bulging purse and peered inside. "It's not enough, I'm afraid." He tightened the cord on the bag and tucked it into his saddlebags. "Not nearly enough."

The highwayman shouted to several of his men. "Take the Roundheads down the road a modest piece from the eyes of the lady." He tossed his head in Jane's direction. "Then bring me back their britches." The robbers jeered as all but two of them flanked the Roundheads and prodded them down the road.

Although appalled by his antics, Anne watched the rogue with fascination. When the soldiers were out of sight, the Black Fox grabbed the reins of Sergeant Stone's sprig-tailed bay and brought it alongside the king. "Mount and follow me," she heard him say.

The king climbed atop the horse but cast a nervous glance toward Anne in the thicket.

The Black Fox called to the burly masked man beside him. "Tom, see them safely on their way," he ordered, motioning to Jane, Doc and Wilkens. "Hurry and be off with you."

Jane and her husband glanced nervously in Anne's direction then back at each other.

Anne's throat constricted in fear. She was going to be left! If the soldiers returned, they would find her and take her back to her uncle, or if the Black Fox found her... A shudder curled down her spine. Nay, she wouldn't think of that.

Doc Herrick assisted his wife in the saddle, then mounted his seat quickly. Jane wheeled her horse around. "There's another in our party... over there." She pointed in Anne's direction.

The Black Fox whirled around, his cape billowing in the wind. His hand flew to his hilt. Anne heard him ask, "Is he armed?" Before Jane could reply, the Black Fox drew his sword and swaggered over to where Anne hid in the bushes. She hunched deeper into the thicket. Her heart stopped as he drew near.

The highwayman circled the copse. Trapped, Anne crouched lower. Suddenly the branches above her head sliced apart and the masked face of the devil loomed over her.

Chapter Four

"Bloody hell. It's a tad."

A scream caught in Anne's throat. "I—I have no coin," she managed in a tiny voice.

His deep baritone laughter broke the tension. "What have we here?" He lifted her by the waist and pulled her from the brambles like a hare caught in a lair. She gripped both hands on her breeches, her blanket left behind, snagged on a limb. "Men, see what I've found in the briar patch."

The men's bellowed laughter infuriated her almost as much as this big peacock who enjoyed making sport of his victims. When he put her down on the road, she stumbled back, painfully aware of the comical sight she presented. She yanked up her breeches, then her stockings pooled down around her ankles.

The Black Fox held up a gloved hand to silence the laughter. "You must give something to the cause, lad."

"I told you I have no coin," she spat.

He tossed back the flap of his cape over his shoulder and studied her. "Then, I'll have to take something." He strutted about in obvious enjoyment while his men shouted encouragements. "I think I'll take this handsome hat of yours—"

"No!" Anne's hands flew from her breeches to her cap a second too late. He yanked off the hat and she heard a low gasp escape from under his silken mask when her long red gold hair tumbled around her. She shoved her hair from her face and glared up at him. "You son of Satan!" Anne yelled. Careful not to trip on the baggy stockings at her feet, she marched toward him, her fists gripping her breeches for dear life. "You want something else from me, eh?" Anne trudged to within a foot of him. "Take this!" She kicked the Black Fox squarely in the leg with the heel of her boot, just above where his wide cuff pulled down, to aim a square shot on his exposed shin.

"You vixen!" The Black Fox yelled in pain. His men hooted in merriment. He glared over his shoulder at his men, then down at her. She couldn't read his expression under the full black mask, but she heard his heavy breathing, like a charged bull, while his gloved fists knotted at his hips.

She faced him squarely, her chin clenched, her fists balled in perfect replica at her side. But she found it impossible to hide the triumphant smile that started to spread across her lips.

"Tom, tell the men to give the Roundhead soldiers back their britches so they can escort this hellcat back to where she lives. It must be past her bedtime."

"No, wait!" Jane called out. She urged her horse beside him, then leaned to whisper in his ear. No doubt Jane was informing him that Anne knew the real identity of Will Jackson, and she couldn't be trusted to be returned to her uncle. When Jane finished, the Black Fox jerked his head back to study her. When she heard his deep sigh, she knew she had guessed correctly.

Dr. Herrick and the king formed a small circle around them. "Well, what shall we do with you?" the rogue asked, the glittering eyes behind the mask fixed on her.

"I'm going with the Herricks," Anne whispered, careful to keep her voice within the small group. "Mrs. Herrick promised to help me find my father."

"You can't. If more soldiers stop them, how will you explain why you're traveling with the Herricks? Besides, I doubt if you have a traveling pass."

"I have an idea," the king offered. "She'll come with the Black Fox and me."

Anne's gaze flicked toward him in surprise. *So the Black Fox had known the unlikely servant was Charles Stuart, after all.*

"Nay. She'll slow us down," the Black Fox said. "Besides, by dawn, every Roundhead will be searching for her."

"Then there's no choice." Jane's face was serious. "She'll ride with Doc and me. We can't have the king endangered."

"If the soldiers find her, she'll endanger us all," Wilkens warned, scowling. "We can't trust her to keep our secret."

"We can't argue here on the road all night," the Black Fox said. "For tonight, the king will ride with Jane and Doc." He waved to a stockily built masked man. "Tom, guide them to the inn. Keep a close eye on them until morning, then I'll catch up with you and escort the king to the next safe house."

"What about me?" Anne stammered, her mouth dry as powder.

"*You're* coming with me." His voice held such a chill Anne was glad she couldn't see his evil face.

"Then it's settled," the king replied. He leaned toward Anne, his voice silky. "It's been my pleasure, sweeting." He blew her a kiss. "If you ever decide to come to France . . ." In the moonlight, his eyes were as black as stolen coal.

Anne pulled back a wisp of hair from her face and stared at the man who claimed to be Charles Stuart. Out of a confused sense of loyalty, she bobbed him a quick curtsy, just in case, she told herself. He responded with a crooked grin.

"Make haste," the Black Fox ordered the others. "I'll send word along the usual route," he added.

Jane waved to her, then gave that same dazzling smile she had bestowed upon Sergeant Stone. A sinking feeling washed over Anne as Jane, Dr. Herrick, the king and Wilkens galloped away with the masked outlaw named Tom in the direction of Bristol.

The Black Fox clamped his arm about her waist and carried her to his horse.

"I can walk." She squirmed beneath his grip. "Put me down!"

He mounted the huge animal with one easy stride and pulled Anne up onto his lap. She writhed beneath his grip, but the more she wriggled the tighter she felt his arm constrict around her. She tried to kick and beat her fists against his chest, but he caught her wrists in such a way as to leave her helpless.

"Throw me a blindfold," he ordered the last man. "I'll not risk a poor Royalist's loyalty for this she-cat's loose tongue." Aware that there was nothing she could do, Anne quit fighting.

The tall robber reached up and handed the Black Fox a silk scarf. The Black Fox grabbed it. "Cover your eyes with this," he ordered. Anne pursed out her lips and took the blindfold. With an indignant huff, she did as she was told.

"That's more like it." She felt his warm hands pull her closer. "Be still, or I'll stuff a gag in your mouth."

"I'll meet up the others tomorrow," he said to the robber. His commanding voice pierced the darkness. "Scatter the Roundheads' horses, then hide the soldiers' breeches in the woods." Blindfolded, Anne could hear the amusement in his voice.

The other man muttered a reply, then she heard the clink of spurs, and felt the horse's thrust throw her against the outlaw's chest as the animal beneath them broke into a gallop.

Behind her ear, she heard his heart pound, filling her with a strange sensation. The wind whipped her hair as the thundering hooves beneath them beat to an even rhythm. Wind tore at her face and she shivered. He must have felt her tremble, because he pulled his cape around her. When he did, she felt the heat from inside his cloak envelope her. Her heartbeat quickened. The smell of the soft wool reminded her of apples, and it triggered a familiar memory—one she couldn't quite put her mind to.

The wind whirled in Anne's hair while they flew through the rough fields. It was nothing like the jostling ride behind Wilkens when they rode blindly away from Wycliffe Manor. She could feel the power and strength of the man who held her, and the mighty animal beneath them.

She swallowed hard, fighting to keep her wits amid her fear. What if this outlaw murdered her, leaving her body in the deep forest, never to be found? Her insides twisted at the thought. Well, she'd fight him to her death, using the courage she knew she had. Hadn't the lieutenant named Nat meant that very thing when he spoke of the courage to follow her heart?

Well, she had the courage, and somehow she'd find her father. But first, she'd have to escape the fiend who held her.

For the next hour, Nat rode like the wind over the moonlit fallow land he knew from childhood, goading the stallion to the limit. Only a little farther through the overgrown woods ahead and the shape of the old, abandoned cottage would rise into view. Frustration raged in Nat's blood. He should be riding alongside the king, not minding this winsome bag of tricks who had fallen asleep in his arms. Bloody hell! Who was he trying to fool? It was his own fault! Why had he gone soft at the sight of that fresh-faced beauty acting so bravely in the face of the dreaded Black Fox? Why had he allowed her feisty charm to tug at him, just as it had earlier in the rose arbor? What was there about her that made him want to enfold her and comfort her? But he couldn't ignore the baser need—his growing desire to taste the sweetness of her innocence. It'd been a long time since he'd known lust burning in his loins for such a woman. Was she as full of fire in bed as out, he wondered?

Anne stirred in his arms, and he glanced down at the sleeping temptress against his chest. Only her head and one hand peeked out from his heavy cape. The blindfold had slipped from her face and rested softly below her chin. How he longed to touch her cheek, feel the softness of the silken hollows of her throat. He smiled to himself. How angelic she appeared in sleep. So peaceful, so serene, so—

Without warning, Anne reached up and yanked at his mask.

"You little—" Nat reined up and grabbed her wrist, snapping it back with his free hand. "Try that again, vixen, and I'll leave you here with the wolves!" When he straightened his mask, he noticed that two of the three ribbon fasteners had come loose. "Bloody hell!"

"What are you going to do with me?" she demanded.

Nat heard the brave note in her voice. She must be frightened to death, he thought, admiring her pluck. "You'll be taken care of. That is, if you don't try to rip off my mask again," he warned.

She huddled back against his chest, the black cape tightly wrapped beneath her chin. "Are you going to kill me?"

He grinned beneath his mask. "Although you tempt me, wench, I told you, no harm will come to you." He glanced down at her, but the high canopy of oak branches shaded the moonlight from her face.

He spurred Shadow onward. "We're almost to the farm cottage where we'll stay. Tomorrow, I'll sort out what to do with you."

He felt Anne stiffen in his arms, and although she said nothing, he knew that mind of hers wouldn't stop until she thought of a way to escape him and locate her father.

Nat urged the horse along the bank of a stream almost hidden by overgrown ferns. He chose the circuitous route purposely rather than ride through the overgrown weeds. Surely Anne would try to search out their trail the following morning. She'd find no tracks to follow along the riverbank, he mused.

Within minutes, the dark outline of the familiar thatched cottage of his childhood rose from the shadows. He swung down from his horse, pulling Anne with him to the ground.

Anne blinked and rubbed her eyes. The tiny cottage stood silhouetted against the moonlit sky, its thatched roof hung so low it almost touched the top of the latticed windows. "It looks ready to fall down," Anne muttered warily.

The Black Fox ignored the comment as he led the horse past her to the hitch. "Don't think about running away, wench," he warned while tying the reins to the post. "We're in the middle of a deep forest. If you run away, there will be nothing left after the wolves finish with you." His mouth quirked behind his mask at the gasp she couldn't quite hide.

He swung his cape over his shoulder and lifted the saddlebags with one hand. "Follow me." He strode toward the cottage door. "You start the fire," he ordered, "while I get water and tend to the horse."

"I won't spend the night with you, alone in that—" she turned a timorous glance toward the cottage "—that hovel. I'd sooner sleep under a tree than—"

"Suit yourself." His boot steps crunched along the stone path toward the cottage. He stepped over the stoop in one long stride, slamming the door behind him.

Anne bit her lip and strained her eyes against the dark canopy of trees that surrounded the cottage. The wind wailed low through their branches. Servants' tales sprang to her mind of horned, grinning beasties who dwelt in the forest, watching, waiting. The horse neighed and she inched closer to the animal.

Something hooted nearby and she jumped. The horse whinnied and pawed the ground. Something was out there! Horses sensed such things. She shuddered, pulling the jerkin about her.

Damn the Black Fox! He was as evil as her uncle had said. He held no loyalty to Royalists or he wouldn't be mistreating the daughter of one of the king's finest. More than likely, once the king was safely out of England, she'd be ransomed back to her uncle. *Providing there was enough left of her for him to find!*

What was she to do? She saw a candle flicker in the cottage window. Shivering, she watched his shadow dart in front of the warm light. Her stomach growled, reminding her she hadn't eaten since morning. Her body ached from weariness. How she longed to lie down, but the thick grass hung heavy with dew. The rogue had taken the horse blanket, leaving her no covering.

A faint smell of wood smoke drifted on the wind. He had lit the fire, no doubt. She pursed her bottom lip and stared at the warm, comforting glow in the window. On second thought, she'd rather be inside, but she'd die first than let him know it.

The stallion tossed its massive head and she noticed the animal was still saddled. If he thought she might be foolish enough to escape, he'd be forced to bring her inside. With a furtive glance at the cottage, Anne crept up to the animal and raised her right foot to almost reach the stirrup. When her fingers grabbed for the pommel, the stallion whinnied a bloodcurdling warning and reared up, throwing her back to the ground with a jolt.

Before she caught her breath, the Black Fox bolted out of the cottage and stood looming over her, his cape billowing in the wind. "Never give up, do you, wench?"

She bit her tongue to keep from replying that if he thought she was such a goose to try to escape, he shouldn't have left his horse saddled. But what did she care what he thought? Her plan had worked, and he'd have to bring her inside. "Your beast is as savage as you," she spat instead. "He nearly killed me."

"Don't give me any ideas, you little hellcat." He grabbed her by the wrist and yanked her to her feet.

Before Anne could fire a retort, he picked her up by the waist and tossed her over his shoulder like a sack of oats. Anne twisted in his iron grip. "You can't just carry me off—"

He gave her backside a hard whack. "The hell I can't."

"Y-you low-life . . . bastard!"

He kicked the door open, stormed into the cottage and flung her down upon a feather bed in the corner of the room.

"I'll do anything I want with you, understand?"

"I'll tell the king! I'll tell my father! I'll see you hanged!" She rubbed her backside, still feeling the sting of his hand on her bottom.

The Black Fox threw back his head and laughed. The rich, deep baritone reminded her of someone, but who?

"Don't laugh at me!" She floundered a moment before regaining her balance in the billowy feather bed.

He lit another candle and placed it in a holder. The soft glow illuminated his glittering dark eyes from behind the slits of his mask. He seemed oblivious to the loose ribbons dangling down behind his head mask. So, she *had* pulled the bottom ribbons loose. Her hands positively itched to snatch the black silk from his face, not only to see the devil beneath it, but to strip him of his arrogant manner.

"I'm leaving to bed down the horse," he said. He walked to where he had dropped the saddlebags next to a large trunk. "When I come back, we'll eat and have a glass of the finest French brandy." He reached in and pulled out a dark shiny bottle. "Compliments of your uncle's impressive wine cellar," he said as he placed it on the table. He strode to the door in two long strides. Framed by the doorway, he glanced back at her. "Mind yourself while I'm gone or I'll chain you to the hitch for the night." His dark eyes glittered with such intensity, she knew he meant it.

After he had left, Anne glanced about the tiny room. Modest, clean and tidy, it contrasted sharply with her first thought that the cottage had been abandoned. The plaster walls sparkled with whitewash. Fresh rushes had been strewn across the wide plank floor. The wood in the hearth had been laid in anticipation for their arrival, she noted, and now a fire crackled cheerfully in the stone hearth.

This was the Black Fox's hideout. But there was a decidedly feminine touch that piqued her curiosity: the delicate hand stitching of the muslin bed coverlet, the crisp lace that flounced above the window, the high beeswax polish on the plain wooden furniture, the dried bundles of herbs that hung from the rafters.

Her glance fell to a vase of pink gillyflowers on the corner table. She remembered what the Black Fox had said to Jane Herrick when he robbed her of her brooch: *Maybe one of my women might take a fancy to it.*

She sat bolt upright in bed, unsettled by the thought. What if he now considered *her* one of them!

Her gaze fell to the dusty saddlebags leaning against a large trunk. Anne knelt down beside the bags and lifted the flap. Inside, the plump sack of gold coins lay on top of loose papers and maps. Her heart hammered with excitement. Tucked alongside the pouch glittered Dr. Herrick's gold watch and Jane Herrick's brooch. Filled with elation, she glanced nervously toward the door. She'd return their keepsakes to the doctor and his wife when she found her way to Rosemoor. She'd return the gold to the Herricks, as well. They'd see that the coin would go to the king's cause. Besides, stealing it from that insolent rogue would help settle her account with him, she thought smugly.

With a surge of satisfaction, Anne removed her leather jerkin and spread it on the floor. Carefully she emptied the coins from the pouch onto it, then folded the garment into a packet and hid it underneath the feather mattress. Before she pulled the blanket over the saddlebags, she thought to fill the slack pouch with something. Her eyes scanned the small room. Nothing. Then she remembered the pebbled walk outside the stoop.

She opened the door a crack and peeked into the darkness. He must be on the other side of the cabin. With shaky hands, she gathered the damp stones in her apron, elation and fear fusing within her. Within minutes, she had filled the pouch with the stones, then sat back to wait for his return.

A short time later, she heard his boot steps scrape at the door. Her heart raced as she lay back upon the pillows, feigning sleep. The door creaked open and she felt a deeper tug of excitement.

She shifted her head and watched him through her thick lashes. He carried an armful of firewood and dropped it beside the hearth. After he stacked it, he moved to the shelf above the table. His back was to her, so she couldn't see what he was doing. Within minutes, he turned and she saw him place a trencher piled with biscuits on the oaken table.

He threw his leg over the seat of a chair, sat down and splashed a small portion of brandy in each of the empty tankards from the bottle. His mask hung loosely about his face by one ribbon, allowing him enough freedom to eat, yet concealing his identity. He took a sip from one of the mugs. "Fit for the gods." Then with a small knife, he whacked off a triangle of cheese from the large wedge and plopped it into his mouth. Anne's mouth watered and her stomach growled so loudly she was afraid he heard it.

"Mmm. What flavor!" He ate with slow, tantalizing relish. "I know you're not sleeping, wench," he said finally. "If you're hungry, come to the table."

Reluctantly she got to her feet and slid into the seat across from him. She bit into a biscuit, the flaky morsel almost melting in her mouth. Had the woman who baked his food provided the feminine touch about the cottage, as well?

Anne ate daintily, refusing to show how starved she was. Besides, his large masculine presence made her so nervous, she could hardly swallow. His man scent reminded her of her favorite glen at Wycliffe Manor, when the late afternoon sunshine permeated the air with the aroma of cedar.

He had removed his hat and his dark hair fell loosely about his mask. The sputtering candlelight shot deep auburn glints through the thick chestnut mane. He didn't need blades or pistols—just the sight of the fearsome rogue would strike terror into the hearts of those he robbed, she thought.

"Drink the brandy." The black silk fluttered about his chin when he spoke. "It will help you sleep. Tomorrow, I'll snare a rabbit. You'll be hungry by then."

She took a sip from the tankard. The liquid burned a line straight down to her gullet. She blinked back tears, but forced another swallow. He watched her silently, the only sounds coming from the crackling logs in the hearth. She couldn't help wonder what he was thinking and she would have given anything to see the expression behind that mask.

"More?" he urged, lifting the bottle, but she shook her head. He turned and the mask moved slightly about his mouth. She caught a brief glimpse of his chin. He wore no beard, she noted. Through the slits, his eyes glittered with something that strangely thrilled her, but terrified her, as well.

If only he'd say something to vex her again! His irritating words had taken her mind off her fear, her uncertainty, and the peculiar way he made her insides feel.

After they had finished, she watched him place the knife with the remaining cheese and return it to the shelf. She scraped her chair back and warily sat on the edge of the bed. He strode past her to the wooden trunk in the corner of the room. Anne dangled her legs over the bed and swung her long hair over her shoulder, watching him with interest.

He dragged the trunk into the middle of the room and creaked open the lid. Curious, Anne straightened for a better view.

After rummaging through the contents, he pulled out a gold-handled hairbrush, several folded undergarments, a blue silk gown and one more article before he sat back on his haunches and slammed the lid. "Buttercup is a bonny color for you," he said, tossing a bright yellow night rail at her.

Anne gasped, staring at the delicate lacy confection as though it were a coiled snake. "I'm not...wearing this, and you can't make me. It's not proper."

He chuckled under his breath, and she didn't need to see his evil face to imagine his don't-dare-me expression. "Proper?" He slammed the chest back against the wall with a booted foot. "It's a bit late to worry about propriety, wench."

Anne's face flushed with self-consciousness as she examined the exquisite gown. Delicate embroidered yellow rosebuds decorated the soft gathers about the neckline. She wondered how he came by such finery. "Whose clothes are—?"

"A rich merchant's wife, if I remember." He laughed softly beneath the mask. "I came by the lady's wardrobe quite innocently. She was so thrilled to meet the Black Fox that she kissed me boldly. I was so taken by her charms that I neglected to notice her husband's growing jealousy until he tossed his wife's trunks from the coach. I would have returned them, but I avoid possessive husbands whenever I can."

"I bet you do!" Anne hated his arrogance. Suddenly a fearful thought crossed her mind. "You're not sleeping with me!"

"You have nothing to fear." His devilish chuckle deepened. "I prefer my women...clean."

"Clean?" she repeated, aghast.

"Aye. You're mud from head to foot. Take off that silly man's disguise, at least. Tomorrow, I'll heat some water for a bath. And if you balk, I'll give it to you, myself."

Anne pushed back the veiled threat that he would sleep with her *then!* Her hand rose to her throat. "I hope they catch you and you swing from a gibbet." Anne tumbled forward and leaned toward him. "I'll dance a jig at your hanging and help them tug on the rope."

"My, my. Sounds like you're going to be busy. I suggest you get some sleep to keep up your energy." He unfastened his flowing cape and tossed it over the wood fireplace settle. "I'll sleep here," he said, pushing the bench nearer the hearth. "Don't try anything foolish. I'm a very light sleeper."

Anne tossed her head in stony response. She crept back to bed and peered at him warily. What could she do if he chose to ravish her? She was completely at his mercy. She watched him undo the ribbons at his wrist and neck. *God's bones! He was undressing in front of her!*

She turned her head into the pillow and squeezed her eyes shut, dismissing the disturbing image from her mind. She heard him chuckle in that insidious way, and she vowed to get even with him, somehow. Damn the rogue. She'd think of something!

Birds chirped in the distance and Anne stirred, pushing a wave of hair from her face. When her eyes fluttered open, it took her only a moment to orient herself and remember where she was. Already, pale morning light spilled in through the lace curtain above her head.

She knew without turning in his direction that the Black Fox was in the room. She could feel his presence. She threw back the blanket and sat up.

Low embers sputtered in the grate. Sprawled out like a loose doll upon the bench was the Black Fox, snoring softly before the fire. Even dozing, he appeared menacing. He had fallen asleep, fully clothed, without so much as removing his fancy wide cuffed black leather boots. His head lay on his shoulder, slumped against the hard wooden slats of the bench, the plumed wide brimmed hat on his lap.

The remaining ties of his mask were knotted behind his head. If she could only see his face, maybe he wouldn't appear so frightening. He wasn't some black spirit who haunted the highways at night, was he?

Suddenly she remembered the small sharp knife he had used to cut the cheese. Her glance darted to the shelf across the room. Sharp enough, she thought, to cut ribbons!

In her stocking feet, she tiptoed past the sleeping highwayman. She moved stealthily toward the shelf, unwrapped the linen and grabbed the small dagger in her palm. She pursed her lips together in concentration as she inched silently behind him.

Moving into position, she took aim. With one straight motion, she cut the ribbon and yanked off his mask.

"Wh-wh—" Startled, he jumped up. Seeing Anne standing over him, the knife in her hand, he lunged for her. He caught her by the right wrist and threw her down on the floor.

"Did you really think you could stab me, you hellcat?" He nearly took the air from her lungs while he shook the knife from her hand. Pining her to the floor, his hands squeezed her wrists so tightly she thought her bones would break.

From the flickering embers in the grate, she stared up into his dark, angry face. It was the lieutenant, *her* lieutenant from Wycliffe Manor! She gasped. "It's you!" Her voice rose with astonishment. How could the compassionate friend be the same blackguard known as the Black Fox? The question caught in her throat.

"Answer me! He raked back the chestnut lock that hung over his forehead. Did you really think you could kill me?"

"K-kill you?" *What was he talking about?* She had only wanted to remove his mask! But of course. He had awakened to see her poised with a knife in her hand and mistakenly thought—

"Don't think I wouldn't have tried if I had thought of it," Anne said, outrage adding to her shock. His face loomed inches from her lips. "But I only..."

"Go on!"

His grip tightened and she cried out in pain, but she refused to ask for pity. "I—I only wanted to see your face."

"My—" His hand let go of her wrist and flew to his cheek. "Bloody hell!"

She took advantage of her freed hand and rolled out from his grip, but he caught her again, pulling her to him. "Don't you know what you've done, you little fool?"

"Don't call me a—!" His chest crushed on top of hers, his arms gripped hers again.

"It means I can't send you back to your uncle, because now you can identify me as the Black Fox."

"I—I told you, I don't want to go back to my uncle." Anne stopped squirming, aware of her helplessness beneath his muscular power. She felt strange sensations at his clamped grip about her wrists. "Please, take me to Jane Herrick—"

"It's too dangerous. That fancy colonel of yours will search under every thatched roof until you're found."

"Twining might as well not bother. I'll never marry that weasel." Her breath came fast and hard. "Never!"

"He'll never give up the chase." His heavy-lidded gaze dropped to her lips. "I know if you were promised to me, I'd never stop searching for you."

Anne's stomach gave a tiny flutter. His dark brown eyes smoldered with something she'd never seen before. It both excited and frightened her. She stared back, unable to hide her fascination. Dawn's pale light filtered in from the window above, caressing the dark shadow of beard along his jaw, the powerful mouth, the sheer might of his body. She let out a small, involuntary gasp of vague understanding, and at the sound his hands tightened on her wrists.

Their eyes held and for a brief moment she wondered if he felt the same sensations as she did. The velvet heat of his eyes raked her with an intensity that left her weak. When her gaze fell to his full mouth, her lips parted expectantly as a prickly warmth spread throughout her body at the memory of their kiss in the rose arbor.

He lowered his head until his lips were barely a hair's breadth from hers. She trembled against him, aware of her own desire to touch him, to feel him against her fingertips...

Anne closed her eyes, her thoughts drawing back into the darkness. "Na—!" His lips caught hers before she finished saying his name. A shudder of passion ripped through her as his claim on her mouth intensified, pulling her deeper and deeper into the whirlpool of sensation she could never have imagined before. Now, enraptured by her own spinning desires, her breathing became as ragged as his own.

She felt his rough palm at the nape of her neck, his fingers tangled in her thick hair, all the while his mouth pulled at hers, drawing the heat from her very soul. She felt his strong hand slip inside the large waistband of her breeches. She gasped at the shocking realization that his other hand had parted her shirt as he caressed the sensitive skin along her rib cage.

She felt as though she were drowning in the onslaught of overwhelming intensity. Before she could cry out with longing, his tongue captured hers, his voice a guttural growl.

She thought to resist, but as their kiss grew more intense, these never-before feelings exploded with renewed passion, dissolving her struggle like a puff of smoke in a tempest.

Anne gasped when his hand cupped her breast. She began to tremble with an urgency she didn't understand as his rough thumb and finger stroked her, the bud growing taut beneath his touch.

"Tell me you want me as much as I want you," he whispered hoarsely in her hair. Then his mouth trailed a searing line of kisses along the smooth column of her throat, the sensitive hollow at her neck, down to the soft swells to seek the rosy nipples with his tongue.

As his hands possessively explored her, she felt his hardened desire press against her. A jolt of reality slammed through her mind. This man wasn't the sensitive, handsome lieutenant who had gently kissed her in the rose ar-

bor. Her eyelids fluttered open. A rush of despair invaded
her. Nay, he was the Black Fox, the hunted outlaw who took
women's virtue as easily as he took their gold. Hadn't he
admitted as much? The lieutenant who had befriended her
was an illusion, a lie. In fact, all of his words had been false.

"Let go of me!" She struggled from his grip. He jerked
back, his dark eyes smoldering down at her with what she
recognized as wild, insatiable desire; for those eyes mirrored what she had felt in her heart, as well.

Nat glared at her. His gaze, like burning embers, raked
over her naked breasts and she felt herself flush crimson as
she hastily covered herself with the crumpled clothing.

"You burn away my every thought of duty, my lovely
nymph." Without another word he got to his feet, picked up
his hat and stormed out of the cottage, leaving the door ajar.

Breathless, Anne stared after him, her heart beating
wildly. Remorse charged through her as she straightened her
rumpled garments. She shivered as a breeze, damp with
early dawn, brushed her flaming cheeks, still warm with his
kisses. She wrapped her arms tightly about her knees and
stared at the open door.

Never had she felt so abandoned in all of her life.

Chapter Five

He should have tied her up last night, as he had planned, Nat scolded himself, as he scraped the dark stubble from his chin with a knife blade. His mouth curved in a humorless smile. A little late to think of that, he thought wryly, feeling his body tighten at the idea of that tempting morsel who had turned his life topsy-turvy. Bloody hell, it had been half an hour since he had charged from the cottage and he wasn't able to control himself any more now than he had then.

He nicked his chin. "Damn!" From an overhead limb, a wren twittered an angry retort and flew away. Nat scowled after the bird, then swiped at the spot of blood on his chin. Swearing again, he dipped his knife into the river, this time determined to concentrate on his shaving.

When he had finished, he splashed water on his face, shook his wet hair and finished dressing, noting that since she had unmasked him, his lust hadn't abated one bloody inch.

Last night, when he covered her with the blanket, she had stirred, and in sleep turned her face to him. His heart melted. She appeared so helpless, despite her brave show. The firelight bathed her face, the long coppery hair fanning against the pillows, her thick lashes shadowing her high cheekbones. How he had wanted to cradle her in his arms and protect her... more than protect her, if he was honest.

Aye, she was too innocent to know the weapon she held. Those feminine charms would get her anything she had a wish for, when she learned how to use them. A rush of longing gripped him.

He should have taken her then, but it would be exactly what Twining would expect of the Black Fox. Nat kicked a stone with his boot, sending the rock into the air. He swore again while he filled both buckets from the river and lugged them back to the cottage, vowing with each step not to touch her again.

Nat kicked the door open. She knelt by the fire, quietly brushing her hair. He gave her a fleeting glance before he strode into the room. From the corner of his eye, he noticed she had changed into one of the frocks from the trunk—a high-necked, pink-striped long-sleeved gown that emphasized her full breasts and tiny waist.

A bowl of apples had been placed on the table. He shot her a suspicious glance as he set the water buckets beside it.

"I found an apple tree behind the cottage and I—I picked some fruit for breakfast." Her eyes met his briefly.

Searching for a way to escape was more like it. "While you were outside, I hope you noticed there are no paths to follow, if you're planning an escape." He tried not to smile at her feigned look of indignation. "I'm sure you found the river. Aye, boats and skiffs go by regularly, but if you're thinking of catching a ride with some kindly soul who'll promise to help you find your father, be forewarned." His eyes flashed with wariness. "Twining will have your description hammered to every oak in the shire. Show yourself at the river and that *kindly soul* will trade you for a few shiny coins without thinking twice."

Nat pulled the chair around and straddled the seat. "Listen carefully, Anne, because I'll only tell you once. I must leave you while I escort the king to the next safe house." He ignored the flash of worry that darkened the blue-green shards in her eyes. "I could tie you up, but you're a smart lass. You know, if Twining's men find you, they'll send you back to your uncle."

"What will you do with me?" she demanded. Her anger forced a bravery he knew she didn't feel.

"I've decided to keep you here until the king is safely out of the country. I'll send someone from the inn every few days to bring you supplies. You'll only be delayed a few weeks."

"Why should I believe you?

Nat flinched inwardly at her accusation, but he knew he could never explain why he felt deceit could be justified if for political gain. But how could Anne understand? That lesson occurred from witnessing war, or in his case, who his father was: Nigel Adams, the man who zealously carried out Cromwell's carnage against Ireland in order to satisfy his own vengeance against the bastard son he disowned. And until Nat could make up for what his father had done, he would lie or do anything else necessary to accomplish the task.

"Think what you will," he said offhandedly. "I promise I won't abandon you." He could only pray he could keep his word.

"Ha!"

"Whether you trust me or not, you know the chances of finding your father are greater with me than by yourself." He saw her lips part slightly and he knew his words hit their mark. Relieved, he added, "Help yourself to anything in the cottage you may need. During the day, don't burn a fire. If a search party smells smoke, they'll come to inquire. If I don't return tonight, I'll send a woman to stay with you."

"A woman? One of your harlots, I suppose?"

He tried not to smile. "You'll like Emma."

Anne arched her eyebrows and gave a disdainful sniff. "You're just saying that so I'll cooperate with you!"

"Cooperate?" He tried to keep a straight face. "Is that what you think you've been doing?"

Anne felt her temper ignite. "How else would you expect me to act? You insult me, threaten me, and..." A flush of heat rose to her cheeks when she remembered his intimate kisses. She shot him a sidelong look and, by the hint of a smile playing about his mouth, she knew he guessed what she was thinking. "Oh, you!" Her feelings burst forth like a bonfire. "You're a heartless, unscrupulous, mul-ish...bastard!"

"Unscrupulous, mulish, and certainly a bastard," he said, indulgently, "but not heartless, surely." He laughed in the same teasing way he had when he found her hiding in the bushes. "If I was heartless, I certainly wouldn't be sitting here, indulging you in—"

"Indulging me!" Anne's fingers squeezed into her palms. "You're the most impossible man!" She drew in a deep breath. "Well, if you're going to leave, leave!"

Nat strode to the saddlebags and hoisted them over his shoulder, then he glanced back at her as he opened the door. She refused to look at him. "What if something happens to you and you don't come back?" she asked, staring at her fingers.

Nat smiled. "You'd best pray that it doesn't."

That night, Anne slept fitfully, her dreams fraught with vague and frightening visions. She awoke startled, blood pounding in her veins. Moon glow from the window near the bed flooded across the blankets and into the room. By the low embers in the fireplace, she had slept longer than she first thought.

Had a noise awakened her? She drew the blanket around herself and tiptoed to the door, listening. If someone had snuck up the stone path, she would have heard the crunch of footsteps. Maybe it was nothing but her tightly strung nerves that fired her mind with devils, she reasoned.

But what if Twining and his search parties had caught Nat and tortured him into revealing her whereabouts? Anne dashed for the iron skillet and squeezed the handle for re-assurance. If someone was there, they'd not take her with-out a fight.

The door creaked open and before she could react, Nat stepped across the threshold, saddlebags slung over his shoulder. In the fireplace's glow, she saw surprise, then ap-preciation in the glittering dark eyes as his gaze lazily swept over her. Suddenly aware of how she must look brandish-ing the black skillet above her head—dressed in the thin night rail, her thick braid hanging over her shoulder—she dropped the weapon and snatched the long-forgotten blanket from the floor to cover herself. She felt herself blush with his bold perusal.

He glanced at the skillet, then back at her. "Expecting company?" His mouth tilted in a crooked smile.

A prickle of irritation washed over her. Did he expect to see her grovel with relief because he had decided to return? She had pride, after all.

She hung the skillet at the hearth and tossed another log upon the ash-covered embers. Behind her, she heard his boot steps across the floor, then the saddlebags slump in the corner.

"I didn't expect you back so soon." She poked at the embers until they burst noisily into hungry flames around the dry, peeling bark. The room brightened in a rosy glow.

She heard a loud creak of the bed ropes. She turned and in the brightening fire glow, she noticed the dark circles of fatigue beneath his eyes, shadowing his face. Her gaze followed him as he swung his long legs over the side of the bed and removed his boots.

"The king is missing," he said finally, the words sounding like a death knell.

Anne's knees felt weak and she slumped to a chair. "What happened?" was all she could think to ask.

"From what my cousin Tom said, a squad of Roundheads charged the inn just before dawn, looking for you." He cast her a sharp look as he dropped the first boot to the floor. "After they left, Tom returned to the king's room. His bed hadn't been slept in and he'd vanished."

And you believe it's my fault, Anne thought, but remained silent. "What are you going to do?" she asked instead.

"I'll strike out tomorrow, and God willing, I'll find him. He might have seen the soldiers and hid in the woods until they left. In the dark, he may have gotten lost." He dropped the last boot with a resounding thud.

Surely he didn't expect her to remain alone in this remote cottage while he traipsed all over the shire? "Before you

leave, please take me to Jane Herrick. You can't expect me
to wait until you find the king—''

"I expect you to shut up. I'm tired and I'm going to sleep.
We'll talk in the morning." He gave her a black look that
quelled any further argument before he fell back across the
bed.

"You can't sleep in my bed."

He lifted his head and squinted one eye. "Whose bed?
Damn it, wench, I was born in this bed."

Anne stepped back. "Very well, I'll curl up on—" she
glanced about the tiny room "—the settle."

"I'll warn you, it's damned uncomfortable." She heard
him chuckle as his dark head settled back against the pillow.

The next sound she heard was a soft snore.

During the remaining few hours before dawn's break,
Anne sat before the fire, listening to the soft, even breathing of the darkly charismatic man who held her captive. She
yanked the blanket closer about her shoulders, more to fend
off the shiver of dangerous fascination she felt than to ward
off the chill.

Leaning forward, she wrapped her arms around her bent
legs and rested her head on her knees. How she wished she
knew more about him. What kind of a man would become
an outlaw and take to the highways, risking danger at every
bend?

A devil, she answered to herself, a feral devil who was
destined to swing at the end of a gibbet. But when he looked
at her with hunger in his eyes, he was very much a man. A
dark, dangerous and alarmingly captivating man.

Anne awoke with a start. She sprang up in bed and stared
about the sunlit cottage. *She was alone.* For an instant, she
thought she had dreamed his return, but then she saw the
black caldron bubbling noisily from its hook over the roaring fire. Several skinned and dressed hares were piled on the
table beside a bucket of fresh water. No, he had not been a
dream.

An embroidered coverlet had been neatly tucked around her. She pressed her hand to her throat as she realized he must have awakened to find her asleep by the fire. No doubt he had carried her to bed. She felt herself blush crimson as her fingers brushed across her thin, wrinkled night shift.

Warily she crept to the door and peeked outside. He was nowhere to be seen. She dressed quickly. As she finished tying a green ribbon to her hair, she heard his steps along the path.

Her breath caught in her throat when she saw he was dressed in the buff-colored jacket and breeches of the Roundhead uniform he had worn when they had first met.

"What have you done with the gold, chit?" Nat asked as he strode into the room. Over his shoulder, he carried several cloth sacks. He dropped the smaller bag onto the table; several carrots and a potato rolled across the roughly hewn wood.

Anne blinked at the sight of him. "Gold?"

"Don't play the innocent with me." Nat raised an eyebrow. "I know you're the one who replaced the gold pieces with pebbles. Where did you hide it?"

She had completely forgotten the coin and jewelry she had taken from his saddlebags the night they had arrived at the cottage. She stumbled back upon the feather bed, staring at him.

"I—I only wanted—"

"I know what you wanted well enough. Where's the coin?"

"It's under the mattress." Anne scooted out of his way as he moved toward her. He lifted the bedding, untied the pouch from the bed ropes, then pulled out the bulging pouch.

"You have a natural flair for larceny, I'd say, pet."

Indignantly she straightened her skirts. "I only wished to give the gold to the Herricks and to return their keepsakes—"

"How noble of you." His mouth turned up with a slow grin. "Or perhaps, you'd thought Jane would be so beholden, she'd drop everything and hunt down your father for you?"

Her hands flew to her hips. "Only a despicable rogue would think such a thing!" How could she have forgotten he was as obstinate and unfeeling as the devil, himself? "Robbing a robber is just punishment, I'd say!"

"I'd say I've been punished enough having to put up with you. You've done nothing but nettle me since I met you, my pet."

"I'm not *your* pet," she shouted. "I'm not *your* little anything, and don't forget it."

"Aye, you're not," he said thoughtfully. Without looking at her, he stashed the gold pouch inside the saddlebags, picked up the sack, then strode toward the door.

A sudden fear that he might leave struck her. Anne jumped to her feet. "Wait! You said we'd talk about what you're going to do with me before you leave."

"I'm not leaving yet. I'm only going to feed my horse."

Anne's gaze lowered to the bag of oats he dropped to the ground. She felt foolish for her display of timidity. It was one thing to feel frightened, but another to show it.

His dark brown eyes held a warm look of compassion. "Aye, you're right, lass. Sit down, it's time we talked."

She took a seat beside him, her breath uneven.

"I'm leaving to make arrangements for you to stay at the Pied Bull Inn. You'll remain with my cousin Tom and his mother while I'm gone. He's a brusque but fair man. You'll work for your keep and give no one trouble. You'll be safe until I return from seeing the king safely embarked for France. If you obey Tom, when I return I'll try to find your father."

"But that might take . . . months. What if—"

"My word's final."

"But—"

"Not another word." He glanced at the hares piled on the table. "I trust you can cook. Busy yourself and make a rabbit stew. I'll be back in a while."

What was the use in arguing? When he clamped his jaw in that steely way she had come to recognize, words were futile. She eyed him warily. "Very well, I agree to your terms. But remember one thing. If you're hoping to quiet my fears with more lies . . ."

The warm glow in his dark eyes faded. "While you're feeling sorry for yourself wondering how trustworthy *I* am," he said, pointing to himself, "what about the king?"

"The king?"

"Aye, the king" he repeated with mock exaggeration. "Do you think he's wondering if he'll be found, while he stumbles about the forest lost, hungry, thirsty, dodging squads of Roundheads who are out searching for you?"

Although he hadn't said it, he *did* blame her for the king being lost. If she hadn't left Wycliffe Manor, the king would be with Nat, en route to the coast and safe passage for France.

"Although I didn't plan what happened, I understand why you blame me." She glanced back up at him through her thick lashes. "I'm sorry for my show of temper."

His only answer was an amused, indulgent smile, the kind reserved for naughty children.

How she would love to wipe that expression from his face! Instead, she sniffed disdainfully as she lifted the sack of vegetables. "I hope you like your stew as I do. Extremely salty," she added, trying to keep her face straight.

Nat chuckled softly. "Prepare it any way you wish, lass. I'll be leaving before supper."

Anne dipped a ladle into the bubbling caldron and wrinkled her nose. God's bones, what had Nat put in this pot? It smells like moss! For the past hour while she prepared the stew, the earthy aroma of the mysterious contents nearly drove her out of the small cottage.

She would ask Nat to carry it out when he returned. Wondering where he was, she had peeked outside long enough to watch him brushing down his horse. Good! He could stay there all day, as far as she had a mind.

No sooner had she added the vegetables to the stew than Nat returned to the cottage. He gave her a cursory glance as he leaned over the boiling kettle and dipped the ladle into the dark, acrid-smelling brew.

Although curious, Anne preferred to wait for his explanation. "Aye, it's dark enough," he said finally.

"Dark enough?" she wondered aloud.

"Dark enough to change your lovely red hair to a deep walnut brown." He smiled at her growing confusion.

Anne stared at the vile concoction in the bubbling vat, then back at him. Had he really planned to stain her hair?

"Before each ride as the Black Fox, I dye Shadow's white front forelocks and the blaze on his head." Nat's eyes crinkled with amusement. "It's never failed to protect the horse. Let's hope it'll do the same for you."

Later that afternoon, Anne knelt beneath the shade of the apple tree, her head bent over the black kettle as she dipped her long hair into the murky, acrid smelling liquid. Her stomach knotted with dread. What had she gotten herself into this time?

Although Nat had told her to steep her hair in the liquid for only a few minutes, already Anne's back ached from the hunched position. She wrapped her head with a linen cloth and carefully avoided the messy drips, while she strained the remainder of the dark liquid into an earthenware jug, as he had instructed.

When she had finished, she strolled to the apple orchard behind the cottage. The September sky was cloudless, and the sun heightened the smell of autumn in the forest. The tall grass whipped her skirts as the soles of her boots crunched unseen apples. Seating herself in the notch of the tree, she removed the stained rag from her head and tilted her head back, letting the warm afternoon breeze catch the damp ringlets. In the limb above, a cock chaffinch warbled cheerfully, his reddish breast bright with the sun. His mate picked at the strewn windfalls scattered below.

Would Nat like the change in her? she thought while towel-drying her long tresses. As if what he thought mattered a fig!

Her hair dried quickly in the warm afternoon breeze. Half an hour later, she toyed with a lock. Deep, rich walnut. She could hardly wait to brush the long, glossy curtain of hair and catch her reflection in the river.

She lifted her face to the warm sunshine. Had Nat played soldier in this orchard and swung from these branches as a child? Aye, how could any child resist? She could imagine children's voices at play on the breeze. Maybe young Nat had brought his first maid here, and kissed her beneath these branches ablaze with white blossoms on a warm May afternoon.

She closed her eyes, imagining she were that maid. She could imagine Nat walking toward her. She could hear the ferns brushing the tops of his boots as he strode near. She sat waiting for him, perched gracefully upon a low branch of an apple tree. She would be dressed in a robin's-egg blue gown, the billowing skirts waving to him in the breeze. The delicate scent of blossoms carried on the wind as she watched Nat come near. She smiled, imagining his smoldering dark eyes, the thought making her heart pound.

Anne leaned forward, her lips parted, eager for his kiss. She felt as if she could float away with this sense of dreaming.

"Ahem."

Anne's eyes flew open and she grabbed the trunk of the tree to keep from falling off the limb. Her face flamed as Nat's dark eyes gazed down at her.

"I—I..." Anne swallowed. "I was...napping."

Nat gave her a slantwise glance. "I didn't mean to...wake you," he said with a grin, "but I couldn't wait to see your dark locks."

She had trouble breathing when he stood so close to her. He reached out to brush back a strand that tumbled into her face. The tender gesture caused her heart to flutter like a bird's wing. How could this man be so incredibly gentle one minute and so incredibly irritating the next?

She glanced down at the buff uniform he wore and she knew he had come to say goodbye. This time, she refused to behave like a frightened child, even though inside, she felt like the little girl whose father had come to say farewell.

Anne bit her trembling lip. "I pray you find the king quickly, and that you'll both be safe."

He rewarded her with his handsome smile. "I'll be back as soon as I can," he whispered, and brushed his lips to her cheek. Then he strode from the clearing, and in several long paces, slipped from sight through a blur of tears.

Her hand lingered on her cheek. The gesture, so sweet and gentle, filled her with yearning. What was the matter with her? The man was a rogue, a devil who had made her his captive.

And who had captured her heart.

Chapter Six

The next morning, Anne trampled onto a dense patch of weeds behind the cottage, and if she hadn't recognized the scent of lemon verbena drifting above the crushed leaves at her feet, she would have never found the overgrown garden. On her hands and knees, she discovered rue, woodruff, lavender, artemisia and several other plants she recognized from the servants' kitchen garden at Wycliffe Manor.

Time passed quickly while she dug up the choking weeds, gently dividing the woody old plants as the infusion of crushed fragrance delighted her senses.

Had it been Nat's mother who first planted this garden? she wondered, working lovingly in the rich, dark earth. How delighted Nat would be when he returned and found the surprise of a newly cared for garden. Perhaps she might edge the planting with stones before he returned.

When she had finished, she decided to wash her hands at the river before returning to the cottage. Stepping across the flat rocks where the stream flowed into the river, she heard the sound of wood banging along the shore. She hesitated, her heart racing. She crept back to the edge of junipers and peeked through the boughs. A small woman, wearing a wide brimmed straw bonnet had poled a boat to the bank and was tying the craft to a fallen log onshore.

Warily Anne studied the stranger. A shapeless black dress, white apron and homespun shawl—she certainly wasn't a highwayman's fancy lady.

The woman lifted several bulging sacks and stepped ashore. Anne watched as she made her way, with familiarity, through the maze of junipers. When the woman was almost to her, Anne stepped forward. "Let me help you with the bundles," she offered, feeling a mixture of relief and wariness.

The straw hat lifted, and Anne gazed into the flushed, round face of a woman old enough to be Nat's mother. Strands of black mixed with gray hair peeked out from the edges of her straw bonnet. She squinted a blue eye at her. "Yer legs are younger 'n mine," she cackled. "Lug them supplies up from the bank for me."

"Has the king been found?" Anne asked, ignoring the woman's terse manner. "When did Nat say he'll be coming for me?"

"First things first, missy." She jerked her head in the direction of the river, then without another word, she trudged up the hill, leaving Anne staring after her.

By the time Anne had brought in the supplies and helped the woman pull the boat in and cover it with fir branches, darkness had fallen. Inside the cottage, Anne lit the candle while the woman covered the window with a blanket. After an exchange of measured looks, the woman explained that she was Nat's Aunt Emma, who lived with her son, Tom, the innkeeper of the Pied Bull Inn.

"I'll sleep in the loft," the old woman said. "I like to roost abovestairs."

Like the old crow that you are, Anne mused. While the woman climbed the rope ladder to prepare a bed in the tiny alcove, Anne banked the fire for the night, her curiosity growing as to why the woman wouldn't answer any of her questions.

A few minutes later, Emma clambered down the rope ladder from the loft. "My sister and I slept up in the loft when we were tots," she said wistfully. A soft look brightened her eyes, but it disappeared as quickly as it came.

So this cottage had been Nat's grandparents, as well as his parent's, Anne decided. Hopefully, she might have a chance to ask this unfriendly woman about Nat's childhood.

"Has there been news?," Anne asked again, determined not to be put off. "Has Nat found the king?"

Emma's blue eyes glared at her. "Nay, the king's still lost, God bless 'im. Nat's out there somewhere, riskin' 'is life against Twining's Roundheads, who're beatin' the bushes for ye."

Anne averted her eyes. So that was it. Emma blamed the king's disappearance on her. "We must try to be hopeful," she managed, unpacking the earthenware jugs of milk, ale and wine from the cloth sack.

Emma's head shot up. "Humph! Easy for ye t' say, missy. Yer safely looked after, while our king is, God only knows—"

Anne's hands trembled with frustration. "It's not my fault, and I resent your implication that it is!" Anne blinked back the thought that Nat was enjoying a good laugh, knowing what sour company he had inflicted upon her.

"Not yer fault?" Emma narrowed her eyes. "Me son, Tom, says ye ran away 'cause you don't want t' marry the man yer betrothed to." She folded her arms. "Ye've endangered the king, Nat an' all 'is men with such foolishness. I know yer kind, missy. Yer a spoiled, ill-tempered chit who—"

"Spoiled and ill-tempered?" Anne drew in a breath. "I didn't ask to be kidnapped and brought here!"

Emma's disapproving expression didn't waver.

"I'm sorry the king is missing, but—"

Emma huffed.

"But my father is lost, too." Anne slumped in a chair, her hands bracing the worn edges of the table. "God knows I'm worried about the king, but my father is an officer in the king's army. Her throat tightened. "For all I know, he may be dead."

Emma listened, her blue eyes unblinking.

"I'm all my father has left, and if he's lying somewhere, wounded, I want to be with him." She bit back the sting of tears. "If that makes me spoiled and ill-tempered, so be it."

Emma remained silent.

"And don't call me 'missy'!"

For the rest of the evening, Emma said nothing until bedtime, when she shuffled to the rope ladder. "Best get some sleep," she said finally. "We've much to do tomorrow an' little time to do it." Without another word, she went to bed.

The next morning, Anne awoke to the sound of Emma's humming. Sunlight streamed across the embroidered coverlet over her bed, bathing the room in a cheery glow that didn't match her mood.

"I've made ye a bowl of gruel," Emma said, bending over the grate. "Eat it while it's warm. I've let the fire go out till dark. If the soldiers come back, we can't 'ave the smell of wood smoke leadin' 'em to us."

The image of Twining and his men filled Anne with real fear. Without comment, she dressed, then forced the tasteless porridge down her throat, wishing that Nat would return soon.

Emma gathered her sewing and stitched beside the fire. When Anne rose to clear the table, Emma lifted her white-capped head. "Try this gown on fer size," she said, snapping the thread with her teeth. "Watch the pins, I 'aven't basted the seams."

"But I have a trunk full of beautiful clothing," Anne said, moving toward the chest and lifting the lid. "I've already worn several and they fit perfectly." Anne placed a huge feathered hat upon her head while she held her favorite, the robin's-egg blue gown. "Aren't they lovely?"

Emma lifted a thin brow. "Those clothes belonged to a rich Roundhead's wife. What if that very lady stopped at the inn an' saw ye wearin' 'er finery?"

A wave of disappointment stilled her. Of course! The Black Fox's booty could be used as evidence by the authorities. Many innocent people, like Emma, might risk arrest if even a hint of suspicion aroused notice by the wrong people. "But it's a pity to waste such lovely things," she said wistfully, running a finger along the silken fabric.

"They'll not go to waste. I remake the gowns into plain garments for our girls at the inn."

Anne glanced at Emma. "Girls?" Were these the fancy women Nat had referred to?

"The servin' maids," Emma explained. "We're short two maids now. I'll be glad fer yer 'elp."

Anne straightened. "I'll be working as a serving maid?" She found the idea intriguing.

"No, lass. Ye'll be cleanin' the abovestairs chambers."

Disappointed, she decided there was no use arguing. More than likely, Nat thought she would be safer if out of sight. Anne sighed, slipping into the loose-necked muslin gown. It was the color of melted tallow and just as shapeless.

Emma studied the fit, her hand on her chin. "If I take it in 'ere," she said, her bony fingers catching several inches of the neckline, "an' 'ere..." She gathered a handful of muslin at the waist. A look of satisfaction spread across her features. "It'll do, an' the cream color goes well with yer 'air."

"This dress is the color of bread dough and it does nothing for me," Anne said before she remembered her dark-tinted hair.

Emma's mouth twitched. "Nat will like it."

"I care nothing what Nat thinks," Anne scoffed.

Emma pulled away a gray strand of hair from her face. "I'm not so old that I don't remember what it's like to be in love."

Anne snapped her head up. "Whatever do you mean, Emma?"

"I've seen that starry look in yer eyes, lass."

"With all respect for you, mistress, that look isn't love," Anne answered hotly. "It's the look of dismay at why you defend a blackguard like Nat, even if he is your nephew!"

"Every maid," Emma continued as though Anne hadn't spoken, "falls over 'erself for me 'andsome nephew." She sighed. "Aye, I wish me own son, Tom, 'ad a splinter o' 'is charm."

Anne gave an exasperated huff.

"Nat's a rogue, Anne. I'm not sayin' he ain't." Her round face grew serious. "'Ave ye ever seen a black fox, lass?"

Anne shook her head.

"When a black kit fox is whelped, the other kits in the litter sense 'e's different." Emma's voice lowered. "A black kit's life is fraught with dangers, besides bein' a priceless trophy to a gamesman."

A shiver curled up her spine, but Anne said nothing.

"Nat's always known 'e's different. When 'e first put on 'is mask an' rode as the 'ighwayman, I knew in me 'eart why 'e called 'imself, the Black Fox." Her gaze drifted to the window and the overgrown fields beyond. "Nat knows 'll never know a normal life with a wife, children, a cottage." Her blue gaze shifted back to Anne. "Yer father'll contract a rich man fer ye in France. Ye'll be mistress of a manor as grand as Wycliffe Manor, I've no doubt."

That had been Anne's dream for as long as she could remember, but now, somehow, that vision of the future held little of its magic. Instead, for these past few days, her dreams lingered on laughing, dark-eyed children skipping playfully along rose-covered bowers outside a tiny hidden cottage. Was she the romantic dreamer Emma suggested?

Nat came from a different world. He took his women as he found them. Women—like the tavern wenches at the Pied Bull Inn—who were more than willing, and asked nothing more from him than he was willing to offer.

Besides, she could never understand his need to embrace the political wrongs of the world. Wouldn't the world be a simpler place if everyone just took care of their own?

Emma's simple words had provided wise counsel. Nat was a charming rogue, but he had no place in her world, and she'd be a silly fool to believe otherwise.

Emma lifted the sewing from her lap. "I've finished the skirt of the blue gown, lass. Come try it on."

Before noon, Emma went to the orchard to pick windfall apples for a sauce. She had just left when Anne heard her shriek. Bolting from the cottage, her chores forgotten, Anne dashed behind the cottage and ran headlong into Emma, fists on her hips, an angry frown on her face.

"Whatever's the matter?" Anne asked.

Emma pointed to the garden behind her. "Did you do this?"

For a moment, Anne didn't understand. "If you mean did I weed the garden, then the answer is yes."

Emma tugged on her straw bonnet in a gesture of frustration. "An' what do you think a nosy Roundhead might wonder if 'e ambled behind the cottage and found a garden, all neat and tidy?"

For that brief moment, Anne felt like bursting into tears. Of course, Emma was right. Why hadn't she realized the garden had been purposely neglected to provide the look of abandonment so necessary to a highwayman's hideaway? She should have known, instead of wishing away the afternoon, dreaming of the romantic cottage by a bubbling brook. She bit back her regret. She had been a fool, but she would not make the same mistake, twice.

As though Emma could tell what went through her mind, she smiled wistfully. "I'm sorry to be so gruff, lass, but it caught me by surprise to see Sarah's garden..." Emma glanced back at her. "Of course, you couldn't 'ave known."

"Aye, I should have realized, Emma. I'll cover the plants up again with—"

"I'll lend ye a 'and gathering oak leaves, dear," Emma said gently as she led the way toward a grove of trees.

While they worked silently, Anne finally asked, "Sarah was your younger sister?"

Emma lifted her eyes, moist with memories. "Aye, Nat's mother. I always feel 'er presence 'ere, among the garden." She smiled brightly. "You should 'ave seen the garden then, lass."

Anne poured the final basket of leaves over the mound. "What were Nat's mother and father like?"

Emma's face became stonelike. "Me sister was a servant at a wealthy manor. When she fell in love with the younger son and found 'erself with child, the rogue denied 'e fathered the babe."

"What happened to her?"

"Sarah came 'ome to this cottage to live with me, me 'usband an' our son, Tom."

"Did she ever see Nat's father again?"

Emma shook her head sadly. "Nay, child. Although 'e never tried to see 'er, she never stopped lovin' 'im. She never became bitter over it, but sometimes, I wish she 'ad."

"Did Sarah die in childbirth?"

"Nay. She lived to see 'er beautiful baby boy. But the year of the smallpox, we lost our parents, me 'usband an' Sarah. Nat was only four years old."

"Has Nat ever met his father?" Anne asked.

"Nay. 'E joined the Roundhead army an' died durin' the Irish campaigns." When Emma had finished, Anne saw the moist gleam in her eyes. She swallowed the hard lump in her throat as she compared her own loneliness after her mother died with the dark-eyed little boy's whose father renounced him at birth. What must it have been like to grow up without a father's love? Her throat welled with sadness. At least, her father had wanted to be with her, even though he couldn't.

Midmorning of the next day, Anne sat on the three-legged stool by the hearth and cleared away the ashes from last night's fire. Scraping the last of the white ash into the hod, she had barely lifted the container and turned toward the door when she heard a horse whinny.

A bolt of fear surged through her. Could the Roundheads have found the overgrown trail through the woods? Her first thought was to warn Emma, who had been picking fruit in the orchard for the past hour. She opened the door a crack, and her heart leapt when she saw Nat tie Shadow's reins to the rail.

Nat! Anne's heart beat wildly with excitement. Her hands felt trembly and she almost dropped the unwieldy hod of ashes as she ducked back from the doorway into the cottage. Her hand flew to her long, unbound mane; her gaze swept the wrinkled, faded chemise and skirt she wore to scrub the hearth. She had dreamed he would return to find her wearing the robin's-egg blue gown, her dark tresses brushed until they shone like burnished walnut. God's bones, she looked like a street urchin!

Before she could think what to do, the door creaked open and he strode inside. Their eyes locked at the same moment. Her stomach flip-flopped when his dark gaze hungrily swept her loose, flowing hair, low neckline of her chemise and full sweeping skirt. She felt a blush deepen in her cheeks at his bold perusal.

She had missed him. She hadn't wanted to admit it before, but seeing him now, tall and fierce, she had truly missed him. Her mouth felt full of wool. For all the world, she wished she knew if he had missed her, as well.

He reached out and wiped a speck of ash from her nose. "Where's Emma?" he asked, grinning. Her spirits fell.

"Emma's in the orchard," she managed finally, chiding herself for her foolishness. Had she expected him to spout honey-coated words to her? She drew back a wayward lock from her face. "I'll go get her," she offered, but her feet didn't move.

"No matter. I'll see her in a few minutes." He slipped off his cape and hung it on a peg beside the hearth.

"Have you news of the king?" she asked, her wits finally returning.

"I've not found him, but I think, now, I know where he is. Hopefully, in a few days I'll locate him." His mouth twitched. "I've some other glad news you might be willing to hear." His voice held a ring of excitement she had come to recognize. She saw the dark eyes twinkle merrily and she knew.

"My father!" Anne stared, the words hanging in her mind. "You've found him! He's alive? He's well?" Suddenly she was afraid to learn the truth.

"Aye, he's alive." His smile faded slightly. "He was wounded at the battle of Worcester, and from my sources, I'm told he's well and recovering at a safe house. I'll arrange passage to France for you both. You can sail with the king, if that's what you want."

"If that's what I want?" Her heart overflowed with gratitude. Certainly this news hadn't come to him easily. Despite the weighty issues burdening him, Nat had found the time to seek out what she had longed to hear: *Her father was safe!*

For a disorienting moment, she was filled with such incredible happiness she wanted to wrap her arms about him. "Thank you, Nat," she said instead.

"Hurry and pack your things. We'll leave for the Pied Bull Inn at dawn." The familiar wicked grin curled his mouth.

She felt a flicker of warning. Suddenly, leaving the little haven of the cottage seemed fearful. Could she believe him? Was he telling the truth about her father, or was it a lie to force her into submission until the king was safely out of England?

He waited for her answer. Grinning the same charming way—identical to how he had looked at her that night in the rose arbor. Anne narrowed her eyes at him. She hadn't forgotten how easily he could beguile and tangle her feelings with his silky words. He was a rogue and a liar, and witless if he thought she would melt like hot tallow with his sugared ways.

She stepped back. "You told me Twining has posted a reward for me. How do I know you're not turning me in for the gold?"

"Because you could identify me as the Black Fox."

"Even with me to identify you, Twining would have to catch you first. What would prevent you from taking the ransom and sailing to France to rob there?"

He gave her a diabolical half smile. "You'll just have to trust me."

"I'd sooner trust ol' Beelzebub than you."

A devilish twinkle she had come to recognize flickered in his eyes. "You have very little choice, pet."

She drew in a resigned breath and gave him a side glance. "There's one bright spot. At least I won't have to put up with you once I'm at the inn."

He slipped his cape from the peg and strode to the door. "Well, lass... there's one small matter I don't think I've mentioned." He drew open the portal, then turned back at her. "Did I say we're registered as man and wife?"

Anne's eyes widened with disbelief. "We're what?"

He cleared his throat. "I've a few words to say to Emma," he mumbled, rushing out the door.

"You've a few words to say to me," she shouted with a lift of her chin. "If you think I'm going to act as your wife—"

Nat stepped back inside the cottage, his hand still on the portal. "I think you promised to do as I say." He took a deep breath. "We're posing as man and wife because it's the only proper arrangement that won't raise suspicions. If you'd think before you light up like a torch, you'd know an obedient farmer's bride will blend in with the other families, but a single—"

"B-but..." Her blue-green eyes pleaded. "I can't act like I'm...I'm your..."

Nat tried not to smile. "You have nothing to fear. We'll share the same chamber, but you'll sleep alone on your pallet." His mouth quirked in a grin. "That is, unless you'd rather—"

"You rogue!" Anne snapped her head back and glared at him. "I must be mad to believe the word of a...highwayman. You'll take advantage of me, and...try to kiss me again!"

Nat tossed his head back and laughed. "You kissed me, too, lass." His rich laughter deepened when he saw the blush brighten her cheeks and the fury blaze blue-green sparks from her eyes. "It's the only way I know to still that lovely mouth of yours!"

She stepped back, her tiny fists balled to her side. He forced the grin from his face and watched her with amusement.

"I'll give you fair warning," she snapped. "If you try to take advantage of me, I'll tell the first soldier I see that you're the Black Fox."

"I'll say you're my young bride, miffed at her new husband over some puffed-up marital trifle. Emma and Tom will back me up, and you know it." He cocked a brow. "Besides," he added, his tone suddenly serious, "if you try a stunt like that, you'll never see your father. Remember, pet, I know where he is, and if I'm arrested, that knowledge goes with me to the gallows.''

He knew his threat hit the mark from the wince that splintered, if only for a moment, her defiant challenge.

Satisfied, he added, ''Pack your things. We leave at dawn.''

He turned and strode over the threshold. As he closed the door after him, the dull thud of earthenware hit the door and bounced off the wood directly behind his head.

Chapter Seven

For the rest of the day, Anne tried to quiet the flurry of excitement that grew whenever she thought of leaving in the morning with Nat, but the more she tried, the greater her nervousness became. Occasionally a snatch of his deep baritone or the sound of his hearty laughter drifted back inside the cottage, causing her feelings to go all aflutter.

He had kept out of her way, as well, except when he brought the cock pheasant he had dressed for their meal. "I'll make yer favorite bastin', lad," Emma had said, her eyes smiling.

"Find me some rosemary in the garden," she said to Anne, in an attempt to draw her out. But before she had a chance to put down her needle, the door had shut, and Nat's boot steps faded down the path.

Emma caught her eye and winked sympathetically. "Nat's not 'imself, lass. 'Is thoughts are on the king.''

Certainly what Emma said was true, but Anne knew his cool detachment toward her was his attempt to keep her at arm's length. Her cheeks warmed at the realization that instead of relief, the thought filled her with disappointment. What was the matter with her? Her wits seemed to scatter like dandelion seed on the wind whenever he came near.

After dinner, the rich aroma of roast pheasant with rosemary and spiced apples lingered in the cottage while Anne scurried about the table, scraping the bones and carcass from the wooden trenchers. As she moved about the table, the candlelight wavered, casting shadows about the room.

She glanced up to see Nat watching her, but he quickly averted his eyes.

Emma reached for her straw bonnet. "I'll be in the orchard," she said to no one in particular. "There's daylight enough to pick some apples for yer journey tomorrow."

After Emma had left, Nat drained his tankard and plopped it down with a thud. "We'll leave at first light so pack your things tonight," he said without looking at her. "The militia have the roads blocked, so we're forced to take the wood path. It's a full day's ride to the inn." He glanced up and their eyes held. She couldn't help wondering what he was thinking.

He pushed the chair back and got to his feet. "I'll sleep in the barn. The wind has the scent of rain, so dress warmly tomorrow." He moved to the door and paused. "When we get to the inn, we best call you another name besides Anne. Do you have a preference?"

As she thought, a wren warbled to its mate from an unseen bough outside the window. "My mother was called Elizabeth Rose. I'd like to be called Rose."

"Aye." His mouth quirked. "Rosie it is."

"Help me, Anne! Help me!"

"Father? Where are you, Father?" Through the ghostly veils of fog, Anne tore the gossamer webs, searching the thin fingers of mist.

"I'm here, Anne. Help me!" His voice grew louder.

"I'm coming," she cried, running toward the voice, hope building with every step. A hand appeared from the swirling cocoon of darkness. "I knew I'd find you, Father."

She grabbed for him, relief replacing her panic as she tugged on his icy hand, to free him from the brink of darkness. But the hand dissolved through her fingers like thin wisps of fog, leaving her only to stare in horror.

Anne's eyes flew open and she bolted upright in bed. Her heart pounded in her breast. The fire crackled in the hearth, splashing the cottage walls with warm assurance, but not enough to touch the chill that shook her. Emma's snoring drifted down from the loft. It was only a dream.

She wiped the damp hair from her brow and pressed her face into the pillow. Her breath came unsteadily as her mind fought back the familiar terror of the dream. Dear God, why would her childhood nightmare haunt her now? Was it an omen?

Long afterward, Anne tried to sleep, but she couldn't shake the feeling of forewarning. "God, please protect Father," she whispered, her fingers clenching the locket at her breast. "Protect the Black Fox, as well!"

The early morning fog blanketed the cottage with ghostly tendrils, the gloom intensifying Anne's sense of foreboding. Her hands trembled as she dressed in the black Puritan traveling suit Nat had chosen for her. She patted her locket reassuringly at her bodice, then slipped on the heavy woolen cape. She turned in a circle for Emma's inspection.

Emma smiled approvingly. "One more thing," she said, reaching for her straw bonnet. "If the fog lifts, the sun'll freckle that white skin o' yers." She carefully placed the hat over Anne's dark curls. "Now ye look like a thresher's wife."

"It'll be a comfort to have your bonnet with me," Anne said, grateful for her sacrifice. She packed the cloth grain sack with her folded garments. "When will you return to the inn, Emma?" Anne hoped the question didn't betray her uneasiness.

"Soon, but I thought I'd linger awhile before rowing back." Her blue eyes gazed wistfully out the window to the gnarled trees hung heavy with fruit. "I love the smell of the fog 'long the river. So many memories." She shook her head, then glanced back at Anne. "Ye must think I'm a foolish ol' woman."

"Of course not," she answered, knowing firsthand the soothing balm of happy memories.

"Don't forget about yer jug of walnut stain," Emma warned.

"I've packed it with my things," she replied.

"Anne?" Nat's deep voice called from the rail outside the cottage.

Anne felt the knot in her stomach tighten. After a quick hug with Emma, she burst out the door.

Nat adjusted the horse's bridle as she tucked the grain sack inside the leather traveling pouch. Nat's gaze dropped to the glimpse of gold chain at her neck. "Leave your locket at the cottage, Anne. That bauble links you to Anne Lowell."

Her eyes glistened with a dread that touched his heart. Damn, he knew what that trinket meant to her, but if a poor man's wife was seen with a gold bauble, it would draw questions.

She stood without moving, her fingers toying with the glittering oval, a spark of defiance in her eyes.

"You trust Emma. Leave it with her." Nat felt his mouth go dry. "I'm sorry, lass. If there was any way..." He stopped, silently cursing his unbridled response to her. Too many lives had been risked for her, already. But damn him, when she gazed up at him like that, those eyes could melt a cannon. "Go back and leave your bauble with Emma."

He saw the wars raging within her, but finally she ran back to the cottage. Relieved that she was going to accept his decision without any fight, he sighed. She had lost so much, her mother, her home, her reputation. Now he was forcing her to lose the only thing she had left—her mother's locket.

When Anne returned without the locket around her neck, he knew by her determined step that she was angry. She gave him a frosty scowl as she stepped into his laced hands to be helped onto the pillion behind his saddle.

Good! Maybe she finally realized that she had no choice but to obey him. Thank God for that. Otherwise, he knew he'd suffer the agonies of the damned before he got her safely to her father.

The rain began at noon. Droplets splattered from the overhead canopy of autumn leaves as the horse splashed along the muddy trails known only to Nat. Occasionally an acrid trace of smoke from a peat fire threaded the rain—the only sign of a cottage tucked along the edge of the forest. In cadence with the rhythm of Shadow's hooves, Anne's heart hammered with trepidation at what the next few days might bring.

Night had dropped its mantle of shadow by the time they reached the Pied Bull Inn. Anne pulled the cape's hood back from the rim of her bonnet and stared through the rain at the welcoming candlelight blinking from the diamond windows of the inn. Larger than she had imagined, the two-storied, half-timbered thatched building looked like a sprawling haystack. The smoke from the chimney hung in the damp air and her stomach growled at the thoughts of a hot meal before a roaring fire.

Her sodden cape hung heavily from her shoulders and beneath it her clothing stuck to her skin. Earlier, Nat had positioned her sack of clothing beneath her pillion to shelter the garments from the rain. Hopefully, her night rail would be dry. Her bones ached from the exhausting ride. How she longed to change into dry clothes and jump into a feather bed.

Tension tightened her stomach like the strings of a viol whenever she thought of sharing a room with Nat. Emma's gentle urging that she must trust Nat and do whatever he said came back to haunt her. Aye, if she wanted to see her father again, Emma repeated, she'd obey Nat without quarrel. However, Emma didn't know about the way he had kissed her, or how it made her feel.

Several minutes later, Anne followed Nat into the smoke-clouded tavern. A chandelier hung from the low-beamed ceiling, the gutted candles sputtered deep shadows against the half-timbered plaster walls. Oak plank tables and benches filled the room. Logs from an open fireplace snapped cozily. When Anne saw four Roundhead soldiers sipping frothy ales at a table, her stomach lurched. She pulled her cape across her face while Nat led her past them toward the fireplace.

A soldier hammered the table with an empty tankard. "Moll! Another mug." He yanked on the skirt of the passing barmaid.

Moll slapped playfully at his hand. "You'll tear me skirts, luv." Her tone was teasing but firm. The soldier whispered a retort that caused the circle of men to howl uproariously.

Anne kept her head down, knowing that any minute the soldiers would recognize her as Anne Lowell.

"Dry yourself by the fire while I order some food sent up to our chamber," Nat whispered.

"Don't leave me." She grabbed his arm. Regretting it immediately, she added, "I—I mean, will you be gone long?"

"I'll be right back." His reassuring grin did little to quell her fear as she watched him move toward Moll, who was filling mugs at the tap behind the bar.

Anne shook her skirts at the hearth; droplets hissed on the hungry flames. She heard Nat's rich laughter join a high feminine titter. From the corner of her eye, she saw Moll place her hand possessively along Nat's arm, and Anne felt the sting of jealousy she was unable to stifle.

A few minutes later, Nat returned to her side. Hoisting the saddlebags to his shoulder, he led her by the elbow through the room to a hall that led to a narrow flight of steps. When they reached the first landing, Nat took a candlestick from the table before putting a key into the last door down the hall.

When he pushed open the portal, a cold, stuffy smell of dust and mildew rushed out at her. She shuddered as she glanced about the chilly room. Dim lamplight shimmered against the austere, white plastered walls. It had no fireplace. A window—no wider than a man's shoulders—centered the outside wall. An oak table, a stool and two rolled-up pallets lay on the rush-strewn floor.

Nat held a finger to his mouth to warn her that they might be overheard. "The walls are thin," he whispered. "Twining could be in the next room as far as we know."

Anne wondered if Nat had mentioned Twining's name to frighten her into silence, lest she complain about the room. In any event, the result was the same. Fear gripped her by the throat and she said nothing.

He hung their capes on a hook behind the door, then flicked back the thin curtain at the window. In the tiny chamber, his wide shoulders and tall frame made her feel dwarfed in comparison. She glanced timidly at the rolled-up pallets stuffed with straw. Her thoughts were interrupted by a soft rap at the portal.

Anne's heart hammered. Nat shot her a warning look, then called out, "Who's there?"

"It's Moll, luv," the feminine voice trilled. "Brought you an' yer bride a bite to eat."

Anne pulled the bonnet about her face, then Nat opened the latch. Moll pushed inside and placed a covered tray on the table. The dark-eyed girl, not much older than Anne, stared back at her. "So this is the bride, eh? Not more 'n a babe, are ye?" she said to Anne. "Tom said you'd be workin' here—"

"Thank you, Moll." Nat interrupted before Anne had a chance to speak. "We'll see you in the morning."

"Lovebirds want to be alone, eh?" Moll said as she winked at Nat before ducking back into the hall. "Oh, I almost forgot," she said from the hallway. "Tom told me to give ye a message when ye arrived." Anne could almost imagine Moll's beguiling smile as the maid blinked her eyelids at Nat. "He says the men will be haying at the Danbury farm at daybreak."

Anne rummaged through the rain-soaked cloth sack and wrung out a sodden gown to wear in the morning. With a shake, she hung it on a wooden peg, her spirits as wet and soggy as her clothing.

Nat shut the door, walked to the small table and uncovered the cloth-covered plate. "You must be hungry."

"Not really." She lifted her eyes and scanned the meat pie, cheese and two small tankards of ale.

"I'm going to leave for a while," he whispered.

"But...but we just arrived." The thought of him leaving her in this strange place full of soldiers filled her with dread. "Must you go?"

"Tom's message. It means he's left a note for me in a secret place." The lamplight wavered about the planes of his handsome face. "I'll be back as soon as I can."

"But... what if soldiers come searching—?"

"With the heavy rain, the searchers will get an early start tomorrow. The soldiers belowstairs are local lads. They're not on duty." His words didn't ease the dread of his leaving. "You'll be safe here." He gazed thoughtfully for a moment, then strode to a small wooden cabinet that hung along one wall. He opened the door and gave her the tiny mirror inside, then held up the candlestick for her to see her reflection.

Anne stared into the mirror and gasped. She looked nothing like the reflection she had seen of herself when she stared into the rippling river after she had darkened her hair.

The thick, lustrous dark curls contrasted becomingly with her creamy skin. Since leaving Wycliffe Manor, she had lost weight, because the hollows beneath her cheekbones were more pronounced. Faint violet shadows circled her eyes from lack of sleep. She appeared older, somehow. A faint blush crept into her cheeks. She looked like a woman.

"What do you think?" Nat asked indulgently.

"Aye," she said modestly. "I don't recognize myself."

Nat smiled. "You're Rosie Braydon, a poor thresher's bride." His mouth curled in a smile. "Remember that while I'm gone. If you do what I tell you, you'll have nothing to fear."

Anne gazed back into the mirror. Aye, she certainly looked different. She felt differently, as well. She pulled a few wisps of dark hair loose from around her face. She was pretty. Did Nat think she was as pretty as Moll?

"I'll be back as soon as I can. Push the bar across when I leave, and don't let anyone inside."

Anne nodded, her hand on the bolt. After he left, she slid the bolt across the door. Still holding on to the latch, she listened to his receding boot steps echo down the hall. A feeling of loneliness welled up inside her. Wistfully she rubbed the rough door with her finger. Why was she feeling like this? It must be that she missed Emma and the peaceful sounds of the birds and wildlife at the cottage.

Already, it was near midnight. The din from the tavern below seemed to have increased. Outside the window, several off-key voices rose in song.

Worriedly she wondered if the door would hold against strong, burly shoulders, if the drunken louts decided to break in. She glanced around the room. The metal candlestick would do a bit of injury, she decided.

It took her only a few minutes to undress and change. Luckily, her single night rail had remained dry from the rain. Shivering, she wrapped the thin wool blanket around her and pressed her ear to the wall of the adjoining room. Nothing. The lodgers were still downstairs, she thought, a feeling of alarm coursing through her as she remembered the Roundheads.

Anne glanced at the door. Why was it that Nat could throw her into the most unsettling turmoil by his presence? But now that he had left, all she could think of to comfort herself was his return.

The jingle of spurs along the hall brought Anne's head up with a start. The gutted candle sputtered low in the holder. *How could she have fallen asleep?*

The footfalls stopped outside her door, bringing her fully awake. She held her breath, afraid her heart would explode in fear. Wrapping the blanket around her, she blew out the taper and gripped the candlestick as a weapon.

A soft rap on the door. "It's me, wife," Nat whispered.

Anne's fingers shook as she struck the flint and lit a fresh candle from the table. Carrying it, she walked unsteadily toward the portal. She drew back the bolt and edged open the door.

In the flickering light, their eyes met, sending shivers dancing up her spine. She opened the door wider and stepped back as he strode inside. The earthy aroma of his rain-soaked wool cape reminded her of their ride together through the September rain, and she knew the fragrance would always remind her of him.

His dark eyes lingered on her bare shoulder. Heat rose to her cheeks as she tightened the thin woolen about her, hoping he hadn't seen her trembling hands.

Nat's gaze drifted to the iron candle holder in her hand.

Anne's chin rose. "It's a fine weapon, don't you think?"

"In your hands I've no doubt it would send an enemy to his maker," he said, grinning. He dropped the saddlebags in a corner and turned to give her an appraising look. "No one bothered you while I was gone?"

"If trouble had come courting, I'd have sent it packing." She returned the candle to the holder. He smiled and she caught the flash of admiration in his eyes. "Remember that," she added, "in case you think to act other than gentlemanly,"

"You'll have nothing to fear from me tonight, wife."

"Don't call me—"

"Wife," he repeated, coming beside her. His eyes flashed with warning. "Every minute we're together, we'll keep up the ruse," he whispered, cupping her chin. "Our very lives depend on it, so don't forget it."

His breath feathered her face and she caught a whiff of rum. She couldn't help but wonder if he had been with Moll. Although curious, she dared not ask him. It would be just like the arrogant rogue to get the ridiculous notion that she was jealous.

His fingers still gripped her chin and her stomach did a little flip. When his dark velvet gaze swept her face, coming to rest on her pout, she felt breathless. The touch of his fingers inflamed her, and when she wondered if he might feel the same, he released her.

Oh, why should she care if he had been with Moll? She moved to her pallet and sat cross-legged, watching his every move. He walked to the other pallet and, with a tug, unrolled the straw mattress and kicked it in place beneath the window.

"Did you find Tom's message?" She knew he wouldn't confide in her, but it was the only way she could think of to learn if he had been with Moll. When he nodded, she added, "No trouble, I hope."

He raised a dark brow. "If trouble had come courting, I'd have sent it packing." He failed to keep a straight face.

Although he mocked her, she kept her poise. Trying a different tack, she asked, "I hope you thanked Moll for bringing up our meal." She hoped to match his nonchalance.

His mouth hinted his amusement as he unlaced his vest. He removed it, exposing the rain-soaked shirt plastered against his wide shoulders and hard-muscled chest before giving her a knowing grin.

He knew she was curious about Moll, damn him!

She turned toward the wall, laying her head against her bent arm. As he moved about the tiny room, his shadow splayed across the wattle and daub plastered wall above her head.

What did she care how he wasted his evenings as long as he fulfilled his promise to take her to her father? Suddenly the thought faded from her mind when she saw his shadow untie the laces at his waist and slide out of his leather breeches.

"Don't remove your clothing in front of me!" Anne gasped as she pulled the blanket up above her head.

"Be still!" She heard him stumble about. "There. I've blown out the candle."

"Well, I would think so!" Anne peeked her head out from the covers and peered into the darkness. She heard the rustle of clothing and fasteners unclasp, then after his final boot fell, she heard what sounded like the chair being knocked over.

"Bloody hell!"

A warm blush rose to her cheeks and she wondered how much of his clothing he had removed when another question struck her. Had he just returned from lying in the dark with Moll? A flash of unbidden emotion stirred deep inside her. Had he left the candle burning while he kissed her?

An agony of torment washed over her as her mind whirled with forbidden thoughts. Just how many of his clothes had he removed then? Had he helped Moll disrobe? A memory flickered of how his deft fingers had worked the fasteners of her shirt and had it opened before she was aware of it.

She chewed her bottom lip. Despite her experience garnered from eavesdropping on the servants' gossip, she knew very little about what went on between a man and a woman.

Well, at least he wasn't bothering *her*, thank goodness!

From the time his straw pallet rustled with his weight to when his breathing drifted off to an even slumber, it seemed less than a minute. Somehow, knowing he was asleep made her feel terribly alone.

Even the rain played solitarily against the mullioned window. Somewhere in the distance, an animal howled. The plaintive cry reminded her of the tales Uncle George told her to instill righteous behavior.

Anne shuddered and fumbled for the gold locket she had hidden in the pocket of her skirt, safely tucked inside the grain sack. Feeling the familiar keepsake, she felt comforted momentarily, then she placed it back into its hiding place.

How long she lay there before a welcome drowsiness overtook her, she didn't know, but she remembered her last waking thought being how devilishly handsome Nat had looked when she opened the door to him in the flickering candlelight.

"Help me, Anne! Help me!"

"Father? I can't see you." Anne *frantically peered through the spreading mists, but his voice came from everywhere. Suddenly a hand appeared from the thick fog rolling toward her.*

"I see you, Father," she cried. *"I'm coming."* She *reached out, running faster, knowing if she didn't hurry . . .*

She stumbled and fell. Her legs felt like lead. Unable to move, she watched in horror as the curls of fog slid around her.

"No!" she screamed, tearing away the threads of mist as *his voice faded into the swirling abyss of fog. "No! No!"*

"Shh, lass. It's only a dream!"

Anne's lids fluttered up and she looked into Nat's eyes; candlelight flickered about his caring face. She gasped in ragged breaths. His rough hand wiped the damp hair from her face and his naked arm held her in a warm embrace.

"A bad dream," he soothed, rocking her slightly against his hard chest.

"M-my father. I couldn't—"

"I know, lass. It's all right."

The room was chilly and she noticed he had taken his blankets from his pallet and covered her with them.

"Before, in the dream, I've always sensed where my father was, but this time—" A sob overtook her.

He watched her blue green eyes fill with terror. "This time? You've had this dream before?"

"Since my mother died." He felt her body tremble. "But this was worse. I couldn't—" Another sob racked her, and he rubbed small circles along her tense shoulders to soothe her. He held her closer and kissed the soft curls at the top of her head.

She gazed up at him warily. "I—I'm all right, now. I'm sorry to have awakened you." He felt her stiffen beneath the thin night shift and a soft blush pinked her cheeks.

The fragrance of lavender drifted up to him. Although a warning played through his mind, he allowed himself the pleasure of feasting on her beauty. Her shiny nut brown hair swirled down her back, the silken strands brushing against his arm. His eyes lingered on the gentle rise and fall of her breasts pressed against him.

How he wanted to hold her for as long as it took to erase the doubt he saw in her eyes. The doubt that said she didn't quite believe he thought her need to find her father important enough. She was right to be wary, he reminded himself. His first duty was to the king, and to somehow make up for the savagery his father had caused. But somehow, he needed to be her hero, as well.

But how could the Black Fox, a common rogue, be a hero to a lovely maid who deserved a man without a price on his head?

But already his body was responding to her closeness, and he cursed himself for not being able to control it. He had released his embrace and started to return to his pallet when her small hand touched his bare arm, sending a bolt of lightning through him.

"Please, stay...until I fall asleep?" Her whisper reminded him of a mewing kitten. "I won't mind if...you move your pallet closer to keep warm."

"Aye, if you want," he answered hoarsely. His words hung in the silence that followed. Finally he added, "You've nothing to fear from me, lass," more for himself than to reassure her.

He slid the pallet alongside hers, then tucked the blankets around her.

"Try to think of the pleasant things you'll tell your father when you see him," Nat offered, "but I suggest you omit this particular venture."

He heard her soft chuckle, then she shifted her knees and turned over on her back. He felt a rush of admiration for her spunk and courage. Anne Lowell was made of strong mettle, unlike the pampered niece of an indulgent uncle he had first thought she was. And if her father was anything like his daughter, by now, he'd be mended and ready to take on the bloody Roundhead army single-handedly, Nat thought with a grin.

She sighed contentedly, nestling beside him. Her small hand sought his in sleep while he watched her narrow shoulders lift and drop with her breathing. He felt the familiar stirring again. Sweet and innocent, she had no way of knowing what her simple request was doing to him. Damn, he wouldn't have it on his conscience to take advantage of her now, after she finally trusted him enough to relax beside him.

Before his traitorous stirrings took over his common sense, he released her hand gently and pulled away. She fluttered her long lashes, and murmured something before settling back into the lavender-scented blankets.

The chill of the room brought back the harsh reality of where he was and why. Tomorrow, at dawn, he'd follow the route the Fairfax family's carriage had taken the night the king disappeared. From what Moll had told him tonight, she had been in the livery haystack with a tall, gangly servant of a young couple who had arrived late that night. From Moll's description, the man and woman were Doc and Jane Herrick. If Nat's instinct was correct, Moll's randy admirer was none other than the king.

Moll said when the squad of Roundheads called everyone together, she had left the man in the livery, discovering only later that he had not followed her inside. Although Moll didn't know what had happened to him, it was Nat's hunch that the king might have hidden inside the boot of the coach owned by the Fairfax family, who were sleeping at the inn. However, Nat had learned later from Tom that the family had left in a fright when the soldiers did—and if Nat's hunch was correct, with the king as stowaway.

Nat blew out the candle. He sighed, hearing Anne's soft stirrings beside him. He sighed again. It would be a devilishly long time before he drifted back to sleep, he knew.

Far off, a hammering sound drifted in and out of Anne's dream. A man's voice called...she couldn't quite make out the words.

The pounding started again. "Nat, it's Tom. Unbolt this door!"

Her eyes flew open. Watery sunlight flooded the tiny room. She blinked. Her face nestled against Nat's hard chest, and the black curly mat of hair tickled her nose. His bare leg sprawled across her body, and his arm held her close. She peered up in time to see one of his eyes open.

He gave her a lazy grin. "Good morning, wife," he said.

Shocked, she pushed away from Nat, pulled her night shift up onto her shoulder and straightened her bodice. He let her go, an amused expression in his eyes.

"A minute, Tom." Nat yelled, raking his fingers through his dark hair. He stopped to lift a long lock of Anne's hair that splayed across his chest.

Anne stared, unable to grasp how he could be so relaxed at a time like this. She watched, horrified, while he covered himself with a blanket and walked to where his breeches hung over the chair. God's bones, he had lain naked as a babe next to her all night!

Anne averted her eyes, her face flooded with embarrassment. After what seemed like an eternity, Nat whispered, "Ye can turn around now, wife." She peeked through her fingers to see him standing barefoot at the door, dressed only in his breeches.

"Tom, quit your pounding, we're awake," Nat called through the portal. Before pulling back the latch, he gave her an appraising glance. She had smoothed her hair, pulled the covers modestly to her neck and nodded consent to open the door.

Nat unbarred the door and Tom pushed inside. His frown swept Nat's half-dressed form, the two pallets pushed together, the overturned three-legged stool, the scattered clothing and boots and Anne's flaming cheeks.

Tom's ham fists flew to his side and he scowled back at Nat. "'Ope I ain't disturbin' the bride and groom."

"Not at all," Nat answered lightly. If Anne didn't know better, she would have sworn Nat found their embarrassing situation amusing. "And to what do we owe this visit?"

"As if it's not enough ye've slept the mornin' away, or that yer *wife* is late cleanin' the chambers for the new guests, it's urgent I talk with ye."

"Before I forget, *Mr. Thackery...*" Nat grinned at Tom's surprised reaction at the formal use of the surname. "Since my bride and I'll be staying during the harvest, we'd like a larger room with a fireplace for the remainder of our stay."

Tom stood with his mouth agape. "Well, I beg yer lordship's pardon. Maybe I could dainty up the room fer ye, as well!" He narrowed his eyes. "I'm a wee bit low on ribbons and love knots," he continued sarcastically, "but I might be able to turn up a streamer or two!"

Nat chuckled as he gathered his clothing, boots and saddlebags. He strode to the door and turned to Anne. "I'll see you at breakfast, wife. Hurry, I'll need your warm embrace before I leave for the fields." He winked at her.

Anne made a face at him.

"There'll be no meal for 'er til she readies the rooms for the guests waitin' downstairs." Tom folded his burly arms.

"We'll see about that." Nat shot a fortifying look at Anne. "Come, Mr. Thackery. I've a few words to say to you, as well."

After Nat stepped into the hall, Anne recognized Moll's feminine giggle. She padded across the room to bolt the door, in case the nosy servant dared enter. She couldn't help the swift, outraged thought that Moll was laughing at the young bride whose husband had been dallying with her last night!

A few minutes later, Nat and Tom stepped into the small antechamber off the inn's kitchen, which afforded them privacy. Nat finished tying the shirt laces across his chest, then he glanced at Tom. "I think I know what happened to Will Jackson." With the ever-present danger of a Round-head ear overhearing them, his words were cautious.

Tom folded his arms about his chest, his bluster cooled to mild annoyance. "An' I suppose a little mouse whispered where 'e is in yer ear, eh?"

Nat adjusted his sword belt, ignoring his cousin's sarcasm. Until the king was found, Tom had a right to be worried. Anne under his roof only added to the risk of discovery that the Black Fox had ties to the Pied Bull Inn. It could mean death to Tom, his mother, Emma, and all both men held dear.

"Take care of Rosie while I'm—" Nat's words faded when he saw Moll enter the kitchen, a small package in her hand.

Tom's scowl deepened. He followed Moll's lazy saunter while she moved beside Nat. Her dark eyes brightened as she shoved the linen-wrapped bundle of food under Nat's arm.

"You'll be starved workin' the fields without somethin' in yer belly." Her hand slid against Nat's chest, her fingers toying with the laces of his shirt. She leaned against him, seemingly unaware that the drawstring of her blouse loosened and her neckline slipped low over one shoulder.

Tom's face darkened. He scowled down at the lunch, then back at Moll. "'E 'as a wife to do that."

"But Rosie's still abed." She batted her lashes at Nat.

"Then 'e'll go 'ungry!" Tom grabbed the bundle and threw it on the table. "Get yerself back to the taproom, wench. See to feedin' the payin' customers for a change." Tom gave her a slap across the backside, but not before Moll tossed him a saucy look.

After Moll left, Nat studied his cousin and shook his head. "Why don't you tell Moll you're sweet on her instead of behaving like an ugly old bruin?" Nat picked up the lunch Tom had thrown down on the table and stuffed it inside his saddlebags.

"One lovesick pup around 'ere is quite enough," Tom replied. "Besides," he stated, his voice tempering, "the wenches never give me a glance when yer around. I learned that long ago," he added with resignation.

"Moll is trying to make you jealous. Anyway, she knows I'm a happily married man," Nat stated with a wicked grin. He watched the brief flicker of surprise mix with hope cross his cousin's face and it was all he needed to know that he had guessed correctly. Tom really cared for Moll.

Nat gave him a playful punch. "Give Moll a smile now and then, or at least try not to frighten her with your ugly scowl!" Nat grinned when Tom's face turned beet red.

"As I was saying before Moll interrupted—"

"Ye don't 'ave to ask it," Tom answered, picking up the bellows at the fireplace. "I'll watch out for yer wench, an' I'll think up a likely tale if ye don't come back in a few days."

Nat tossed his cape over his shoulders. "Thanks, Tom. She's a helpless victim of all this."

Tom gave a huff of laughter while he stoked the fire. "Aye, an' in more danger than she knows. An innocent maid with ye as 'er protector!" Tom rolled his eyes, his mouth curled into a grin. "But Rosie'll be safe with me. An' ye knew that or ye wouldn't 'ave left 'er 'ere."

"True enough." Nat fastened his outer cape and pulled his hat brim down over his face. The men shook hands quickly.

Tom watched as Nat left, his head down as he strode purposely across the courtyard toward the livery.

"May God 'old ye in 'is palm, my friend," Tom muttered, his gaze fixed on Nat until he slipped out of sight.

Chapter Eight

The following evening, Anne glanced up from the dusty corner of the tavern where she had been scrubbing, and sneezed.

"God bless ye," said Tom as he hoisted himself upon the bar stool and peered down at her. The clink of a tankard being removed from the hook along the ceiling beam and the swoosh of ale being drawn from the tap told her that he was helping himself to a brew. "Did ye empty all the chamber pots?" Tom asked her, before taking a gulp from his tankard.

Anne moved her mop bucket. "Aye. They're washed and back in the rooms. And I've swept and placed fresh rushes on the floors and changed the linens on the beds, as well," she said, putting on her best imitation of a broad Shropshire accent.

Tom glowered down at her. "An' 'ave ye shook an' fluffed the pallets?"

"Aye." Anne bristled with resentment at the way he had ordered her about all day, then sat back and appeared to enjoy her toil, but she held her tongue. She knew Tom considered her a hindrance and he blamed her for the king's disappearance. She wiped her brow with the hem of her apron. "And now that I've finished scrubbing behind the bar—"

"Yer through when I say ye are." Tom's glance swept across the wet floorboards where she had been scrubbing.

"It's still dirty. Do it again." He smirked at her unspoken fury.

How she wished she could scrub the sneer from his face. "It is *not* dirty!" Anne got to her feet and threw her scrub brush down on the floor. "That floor's cleaner than it's been since Jesus was a babe," she retorted, pleased that she sounded nothing like her uncle's ward.

"Enough, wench." Tom's thick dark brows furrowed a warning. "Get back in the corner and do it again, I say."

"Do it yourself!" Anne untied her apron, flung it in his face and stormed past him. He reached out to grab her, but instead, his arm knocked over the full tankard of ale he had drawn, sending it splashing across Anne's gown.

Anne shrieked.

"Now look at the mess ye've caused!" Tom yelled.

"Look what *you've* caused, you lout." Her accent had ceased to matter. She was screaming and glaring in a way that would give credit to a London fishwife. She shook her skirts. The large stain spread across the front of it, soaking her to the skin.

"Damn ye, wench," Tom hollered. He caught her wrist and pinned her to the bar. "I'm not some mooncalf, like Nat, ye can twist 'round yer apron strings. Ye'll do as yer told, or I'll tie ye out back like the wild filly ye are." His grip tightened.

"I've had enough of your rudeness. Where's Emma? Has she returned from the cottage yet?"

"Aye, but the miller's wife is birthin', and me mother went to stay with 'er fer a few days." He gave her a smug look. "Now that ye know she ain't here to bail ye out, change yer clothes and git back 'ere in a blink."

She knew Tom would never believe her friendship with his mother was genuine. "My clothes are soaked from last night's rain," she said instead.

Tom rolled his eyes. "Moll, lend her one of yers till she dries the one she's wearin'."

Anne craned her neck and peered under Tom's arm. Moll stared from the doorway, eyes round, surprise and expectation brightening her face. After an awkward moment, the dark-haired girl stepped forward. "Follow me, Rosie."

With her head high, Anne traipsed behind Moll, copying the swing of Moll's hips as she followed her from the room. When they were safely from earshot, Moll whispered, "Pay no attention to Tom. Under all that thunder, 'e's a sweet puddin'." What looked like admiration shone from Moll's black eyes.

Anne said nothing, but she decided then and there that Moll was a very bad judge of men.

A few moments later, Moll pushed open a door onto a small, stuffy chamber below the stairs. "Tom would ask me t' marry 'im in a blink if 'e wasn't so shy," Moll said. "I could 'ave any man I sets me bonnet for," she added with a snap of her fingers. Her barbed stare begged for a rebuttal, and Anne knew that Moll included Nat in her quarry.

So it hadn't been her imagination that Moll had appeared overly friendly to Nat. Surely, if he had gone to Moll last night, she would have welcomed him gladly.

Anne bit back the surge of jealousy raging in her veins. She had no call on Nat. He was free to do whatever he pleased.

Moll sniffed. "Ye'll be sorry ye got married. By summer, you'll 'ave a babe swingin' from ye an' yer man 'll be off flirtin' with another wench. That's what marriage'll git ye."

Anne swallowed back the angry words that tore from her mind. But if Nat had been with Moll, there was no need to make herself look more pitiful with a watery excuse. Instead, she forced herself to keep her composure.

"I must get back to my chores," Anne said. "Do you have a gown or not?" She amazed herself that she held her poise.

Moll strolled to a wooden cabinet in one corner, then swept Anne an appraising glance. "Hmm. Apples, I'd say."

"Apples?"

Moll burst out laughing. Finally she explained with open candor. "Ye know...melons," she said, cupping her breasts. "Some are plums, some are apples, and some of us are melons." Her laugh deepened. "An' the gents like the melons the best," she declared with an exaggerated lift of her shoulders.

A loud rap sounded at the door and Tom's voice boomed, "'Urry up in there."

"I'm tryin' to find Rosie somethin' that'll fit," Moll called back. She turned toward Anne. "Gimme your soiled gown. I'll tell Tom ye'll be along as soon as ye've changed."

Anne unfastened her dress, then stepped out of the crumpled heap at her feet while Moll rummaged through the cabinet.

After a few moments, Moll held up a plain gray frock. "'Ere, Rosie. This'll do," she said with an impish grin.

Anne grabbed the gown and gave her a dark look. Moll only chuckled as she picked up Anne's discarded clothing and tossed it over her arm. When she was about to leave, she stopped.

"What's this? Moll felt about the folds of the skirt. "There's something in the..." Reaching into the skirt pocket, she pulled out the shiny object and stared at the gold locket in her outstretched palm.

"My locket!" Anne reached for her precious keepsake.

Moll's eyes rounded with surprise. "Looks costly. Did ye steal it?"

"Of course not! How could you think such a thing?"

Where did ye get it, then?"

"A...a wedding present." Anne said the first thought that she hoped Moll would believe.

Moll lifted a brow in disbelief. "Fit for a queen, it is."

"Give it here!" Anne snatched for it, but Moll playfully dangled it from her reach.

"I—I promised my husband I'd never take it off." What would Nat do if he found out she had kept her locket? His words of warning came back to haunt her. Not only could she be identified by the locket, but she had jeopardized Nat as the Black Fox, as well.

When she heard Moll click the locket open, she felt a sickening feeling in the pit of her stomach.

Moll's face clouded with puzzlement. "Why'd yer man give ye a locket with another lady's picture?" She fixed Anne a steely look. "It *is* stolen!"

"I'm telling the truth!" Anne countered. "The locket's been in my husband's family for years. The miniature is his grandmother. She *was* a lady." Anne wrenched the locket from Moll's hand and slipped the chain around her neck, the gold oval falling safely between her breasts. "I kept it hidden because I feared I'd scratch it."

Moll's eyes slanted, but if she thought otherwise, she was silent as she left the room, slamming the door behind her.

Anne slipped the gown on, then surveyed herself in the mirror. The collar hung from the austere neckline, and the waist hung past her hips. Glancing in the mirror, Anne cupped her breasts. In this gown, no one would know whether they were plums, apples or melons! Suddenly a mischievous thought crossed her mind. She moved to the cabinet and searched for a few minutes before she found what she was looking for.

She dressed quickly, her thoughts on how Nat's eyes would light up when he saw her in what was obviously Moll's best gown. After she folded the shapeless gray dress and placed it back inside the cabinet, she glanced at her reflection one more time.

The gown, the color of the red roses in June, set off her dark hair and creamy skin to perfection. Her waist appeared so tiny she believed Nat could span it with his fingers. The thought thrilled her. She twirled around, the full skirts fanning gracefully below her hips.

The neckline dipped along her smooth white shoulders down to the swell of her bosom. The tight lacings pushed her breasts out in the most provocative manner! *Melons!* she thought smugly.

No doubt Moll would force her to return the borrowed finery, but to see Moll's face when she strutted into the tavern would be worth the trouble, she decided with a grin.

Anne's finger traced along the gold chain at her neck before she removed it and hid the locket deep inside her cleavage. She prayed nothing would come from her foolish act of defiance.

A sharp rap at the door startled her. "Let me in," Tom's voice boomed. "We've got trouble, lass."

Anne opened the door, and Tom rushed inside. "Saints!" His jaw fell when he saw her. "For a moment, I didn't know ye!" Tom shook his head as if trying to believe his eyes. "What a disguise! Twining won't even know ye."

"That's not funny, Tom." She moved toward the door, but Tom yanked her back.

"I wasn't being funny. Twining is expected any minute. Already, 'is Roundheads are 'ere, an' they've captured the king. They don't know who 'e is yet, but when Twining shows up, that dog'll recognize 'im."

Shock froze her to the spot. Her hand flew to her mouth. "Dear God, what are we going to do?"

Tom moved to the window and twitched back the curtain. "We've got to 'elp 'im escape before Twining gets 'ere."

She felt as though her legs might collapse from under her as she stumbled to the window to watch the drama unfold in the courtyard. At least a score of soldiers swarmed around the tall man in the prison cart while another held him at sword point. Fear hammered away as she watched the prisoner's familiar wiry shoulders brace back in a prideful manner. Her mouth went dry with fear. "How can we save him?"

For several minutes, Tom studied her, his brow furrowed. "I've an idea that might work. 'Urry, an' follow me." He grabbed her hand, but she shook him off.

"I—I can't go out there. What if Twining comes—"

"Ye'll be found if ye try to hide, lass. How will ye explain yerself, then? But if yer out in the open, tendin' bar in the tavern, he'll never notice ye."

Fear tore at her throat and she could barely speak.

"Besides, Twining won't be lowerin' 'isself with the likes of the public tavern," Tom said. "After 'e's settled in, 'e'll be sendin' 'is aide down for a bottle of me best canary, if I know 'is kind."

"But I can't—"

"Ye must, lass. If ye work the tap, then I'll be free to try and help the king." He grabbed her arm and pulled her from the room before she had a chance to say another word.

Moll glanced up when they entered the tavern, her face livid when she recognized the dress Anne was wearing. Tom glared back at Moll, his jaw set.

"Rosie is 'elpin' me at the tap. I told 'er she can borrow yer gown, so not a peep out of ye."

Moll's eyes narrowed to angry slits, but she said nothing as she served a full tray of mugs to a crowded table of soldiers.

Anne drew in a shaky breath and began to fill the empty mugs from the tap. "I'll be right back, lass," Tom whispered. She trembled as she watched his burly frame leave the room.

Perhaps Tom was right. Certainly this rowdy tavern filled with boisterous soldiers was hardly a place Colonel Twining would visit. Besides, she had no choice. She had to obey Tom in any way possible if they were to help the king.

Anne ignored Moll's black looks as she refilled the trays of empty tankards Moll slid along the bar. Finally Tom returned.

"The guard said the prisoner was found without papers," he whispered. "He was stranded when the carriage 'e was ridin' in broke a wheel. But when the soldiers couldn't find 'is master, they thought 'is story seemed suspicious an' they brought 'im 'ere for questionin'."

"Where is he now?"

"They've tied 'im to the mulberry tree behind the livery. Two guards are watchin' 'im. I wish Nat was 'ere. 'E'd know what to do."

Anne had been thinking the same thing. "Well, Nat isn't here, so it's up to us to save the king!" Anne hoped her words sounded more confident than she felt.

"There's somethin' else, lass." Tom's frown deepened. "Colonel Twining just arrived." He wiped his sweaty palms on his leather apron. "'E's abovestairs waitin' for 'is supper. I'm sure 'e's plannin' on seein' the prisoner afterward.''

Although she had prepared for the worst, Anne hadn't prepared for the wrench of fear that twisted in her gut. Although she was paralyzed with terror, she couldn't stand by and watch when Twining recognized Will Jackson as the king. He'd be strung up to the nearest tree, in a blink, as Tom would say.

A sudden burst of courage welled inside her. "I have an idea that might work, Tom." She bent low as she whispered her plan into his ear.

Tom had said the prisoner was tied to a tree behind the livery stable. With any stroke of luck, she might be able to convince the guards to move the prisoner into the storeroom for the night, then once the king was untied, she could flirt with the guard as she'd seen Moll do, while the king escaped through the woods.

But what if the guards asked to see the military orders for moving a prisoner inside? Aye, that would be too risky. She felt a flash of dismay. Perhaps she could say that the prisoner was her sweeting, and that she came to plead for a brief moment alone with her lover. A surge of hope raced through her. Of course, *that* would work.

The door to the outside passageway was unlocked, just as the soldiers had left it. She crept toward the outside entrance and stepped out into the moonlit courtyard. She paused in the shadows, her heartbeat thumping wildly. As she dashed toward the livery, a short, stocky soldier stepped from the bushes, his fingers hastily fastening his breeches. Anne blushed, guessing he had just relieved himself. He glanced up, surprised. She pressed on, taking advantage of his embarrassment.

The night air felt cool against her flushed skin as she ran across the cobbled yard, jumping over puddles until she reached the far corner of the livery. She stopped, listening for footsteps. So far, no one had followed her.

Men's mumbled conversations from inside the open window of the livery and the sound of horses nickering uneas-

ily carried on the night air as she crept around to the back
of the livery. She planned to distract the soldiers inside in
order to enable the king to steal a horse. How, she wasn't
sure, but there was no need to upset the king about that little fact. Compared to the danger of what would happen to
her if Colonel Twining found her, stealing a horse from the
livery once she managed to have the king untied from the
tree seemed like an easy task.

Blades of grass soaked her stockings while her slippered
feet felt their way across the supple, mossy ground until she
reached the far corner of the livery. Another few feet and
she would be near the mulberry tree where the king was tied.

A horse whinnied and she jumped. The hammering in her
heart beat inside her chest; she prayed her plan would work.

Her fingers caught the rough stone of the edge of the
building. She stopped. Tipping her head around the side,
she searched the back pasture. There, in the center of the
field between two hedgerows, stood the giant mulberry tree,
its sweeping branches reaching heavenward. Her gaze lowered to the dappled shadows below.

But no one was tied to the tree. In fact, there was no one
in the pasture that she could see.

Before she could think what to do, the sudden clank of
armor and chink of spurs drew Anne back against the livery building. Someone struck a lantern, the light spilling
only a few feet from her. Her heart thundered beneath her
breast. *Soldiers.* Once they turned the corner they would see
her!

She had to make a run for the hedgerows. With luck, she
could hide in the thicket until it was safe to escape. Hiking
her gown up to her knees, she bolted toward the cover of
trees.

"There she is! Grab 'er!"

Metal clanked behind her until a viselike grip wrapped
around her waist, forcing the air from her lungs. Arms and
legs flailing, Anne fought back, but the Roundhead's armor was impervious to her kicks and thrusts.

"Pl-please, I—I only wanted t-to speak to the prisoner,"
she begged. "Where is he?"

The soldier ignored her question. Her blood chilled as they laughed and carried her, head down, toward the inn. Her cap fell off and several of the ribbons holding her hair came undone. She fought to speak but could hardly breathe.

Anne jerked her face around and looked up at the Roundhead who carried her. "The prisoner...he's my...lover," she managed. "I only wanted to say goodnight."

She heard a soft chuckle from beneath his visor, but he continued his deliberate march toward the back entrance

"Please..." Anne's mind whirled as they approached the rear steps of the tavern. "I—I must tell him something—"

"Don't worry, wench," the second soldier called out from behind. "We'll pass 'm yer message."

The tavern door pushed open and the smell of smoke, ale, sweat and melted tallow assaulted her nose as her feet hit the floor. She grabbed the edge of the rough-hewn table and leaned against it to catch her breath and quiet her racing pulse.

A tumble of dark hair fell in her eyes; she left the rebellious locks in front of her face and studied the faces through her hair.

The Roundhead remained at her side, staring down at her. Modestly she straightened the neckline of her gown, her fingers probing the valley between her breasts for the locket. Thank God, she hadn't lost it.

"Where did that wench come from, Private?" Colonel Twining's question thundered from across the room.

A chill of black terror engulfed Anne. Through her curtain of hair, she saw Twining, flanked by two aides, charge straight toward her. Hair streaming in her eyes, she averted her face. She was caught!

The soldier beside her snapped to attention. Twining marched in front of them. Anne bowed her head, her heavy mantle of loose waves covering her face. Her hands clutched her chemise where her locket and chain lay hidden in the valley between her breasts. Even if Twining didn't recognize her, he'd remember the locket instantly as belonging to

Anne Lowell! Dear God, why hadn't she obeyed Nat? She prayed for a miracle.

A woman's scream and men's shouts rose from the far end of the room. From the corner of her eye, she saw a soldier dash from behind the bar. "Colonel, sire. The innkeeper's been knocked out, the men are 'elping themselves to the ale."

"Devil's work!" Twining cursed and turned on his heel. "Private Hobbs," he yelled over his shoulder to the man beside her. "Fall in and bring the tart with you. Boggs and Smith, return to the prisoner."

For the first time, Anne noticed Moll. She sat on the floor, her shoulders lifting in silent sobs, Tom's head cradled in her lap. "Is he dead?" Twining asked her.

She looked up, pale with shock. "I dunno." She sniffed and wiped at her eyes.

"See to him," Twining ordered one of the soldiers.

"'E's only 'ad the wind knocked out of 'im," the Roundhead said after examining him. "'E'll come 'round anytime."

Moll cradled Tom's head again and rained little kisses across his forehead, her brows knotted with worry. She buried her face in Tom's dark, curly hair. Just then, Anne saw his eye flutter open and wink at her. Tom was only pretending to be unconscious!

Through her long tangle of hair, Anne watched in amazement. Romance between a man and a woman was much more complicated than the stories from her French romance novels. Maybe the English did it differently, she thought.

Twining broke up the handful of soldiers drawing ale from the keg.

Suddenly a loud blast roared through the room. "What was that?" Twining yelled. The soldiers scattered about the room.

The stunned aide beside her said, "It was a flintlock, sire." Anne held her head down, her unbound mane wild about her face. She edged toward the door, waiting for a chance to escape.

Another loud blast rent the room. "It was a flintlock!" Twining shouted, hand on hilt. "Who fired it?"

"I did!"

Anne turned around and looked up to see the Black Fox! Nat's large presence filled the doorway like a black specter. He held a brace of pistols in the air. From beneath the black Cavalier hat, his mask covered half his face, hiding his expression. A black stubble appeared along his jaw. His mouth looked hard, but when she partially lifted her hair from her face and caught his look, his mouth curled into a lazy smile. Her heart filled with joy, yet she feared for his life, as well.

"You've overstepped yourself this time, Black Fox!" Twining drew his sword, candlelight glinting menacingly from its steel blade. "What have you done with Mistress Lowell?" He strode forward, soldiers leaping out of his way. "So help me, if you've harmed her, I'll rip you apart, myself!"

"Women who come under my, eh...protection, are never harmed, Colonel." A deadly tone of sarcasm edged his voice. "In fact, ladies whom I've sheltered have been most unwilling to leave my care. I daresay, Colonel, if you couldn't keep track of your fiancée before, heaven help you now."

"You insolent bastard! You'll pay for those words." Twining shouted to the two Roundheads who suddenly appeared in the doorway behind the Black Fox. "Arrest him! Then take him outside and wrap him in chains!"

Anne's fist flew to her mouth as despair shattered through her. Twining was right. How could Nat outfight such numbers?

The Black Fox threw back his head and laughed. The Roundheads, instead of obeying the colonel, charged Twining, swords drawn. Anne gasped in surprise. They were Nat's men dressed as Roundheads! Were they the same men who had escorted her from the livery only a short time ago?

A hush fell across the room. "Wh-what's the meaning of this?" Twining froze, looking as if someone had struck him. Then, the drunken soldiers who had moments ago appeared deep in their cups, suddenly burst into sobriety, their blades flashing threateningly at the few remaining Roundheads who looked about, dazed. Twining stared, mouth agape, while the realization of what was happening played on his sharp features. Twenty or so men, dressed in Roundhead uniforms, circled his handful of men and held them at their mercy.

Anne glanced up at the Black Fox. She thought she might burst with admiration. She had prayed Nat would come, but never had she dreamed he would be able to stage such a victory against Twining and his men.

Nat put his pistols away and pointed to a tall, well-built Roundhead. "Relieve the colonel of his coin purse, and you," he ordered, pointing to another of his men, "bind and gag our important guest and take him out to the livery." Nat tossed a rope to the shorter cavalier, who quickly obeyed.

"I'll see you'll hang for this," Twining called out as he was led away. "And I'll not rest till I hunt you down and Mistress Anne is found."

Anne felt her blood run cold.

"Perhaps," Nat replied, derisively. "But hollow promises will be of little comfort now, Colonel."

Twining snorted contemptuously as the soldiers led him out the door.

Thank God you've come, Anne thought to herself as she reached up to touch Nat. Instead of taking it as she expected, Nat cocked his head and chuckled. "A willing lass, she is." He threw his head back and the half circle of men joined him in laughter.

Anne shot him a desperate look. But of course, Nat was playing a role, and if she gave any sign she knew him, it would place them all in jeopardy.

"Yer not goin' anywhere!" A young private leered at Anne. "If anyone's goin' to 'ave ye, by God, it'll be me."

A slow smile spread across Nat's face. A dangerous smile—his teeth, even and white against his tanned face—betrayed the cold malice in his voice. "And I'm taking what you think is yours." Nat grabbed him by the shoulders and pushed him to the floor, then he circled his arm around Anne's waist. He picked her up like a feather and cradled her against his chest.

Nat looked at her. "This must be my lucky night, men. I only planned on making off with a few sacks of Roundhead gold." Through the slits in his mask, she could see his eyes glitter menacingly. "And I promise you, wench. This will be *your* lucky night, as well."

The men's cheers and laughter echoed around the room, but his mouth held no hint of a smile.

She felt herself flame with embarrassment. Beneath the silken mask, she saw his mouth lift with a wicked grin.

The private stumbled to his feet, rubbing his shoulder. "We'll see 'bout that! The wench stays with me or you're a dead man."

Nat shifted Anne protectively to one side. Her fingers felt the cords in his neck stiffen. "Save your pluck for the battlefield, lad. You're a bit outnumbered at the moment."

The soldier reached down to his boot and Anne saw a glint from a dagger. "Watch out!" she screamed.

Nat ducked back. The metal whooshed directly above the Black Fox's head, then fell harmlessly with a thud upon the floor.

"Keep your games to dicing instead of knife throwing," Nat said mockingly. "You'll live longer."

The men roared with laughter. Nat pulled Anne around to face him. In a voice loud enough to be heard across the room, he said, "You better be worth all the trouble you're causing, wench." Even with his face half-masked, Anne felt a tingle of feminine response. She should have been frightened, but in Nat's strong embrace, she felt safe and protected.

"Let's have a taste of those luscious lips." He pulled her head back and kissed her. She felt his lips work hungrily upon her mouth. The cheers and cries from the men rang in her ears. After an embarrassingly long time, he released her, then he gave her a wicked smile.

"Damn you!" Anne sputtered, hoping her act of outrage would convince the staring Roundheads that she hadn't

enjoyed his kiss. Her hand shot up to shove him away, but
he caught her wrist, as though expecting it. He took her
mouth again. This time, the men's cheers became louder,
but his lips were tender, caressing. Surprised, she hesitated,
her mouth opening slightly beneath his feathering touch.

He groaned low in his throat, their kiss deepened and
when his tongue demanded more, she heard her own moan
of pleasure, shocking herself that she wanted it as much as
he. She felt him hesitate for a moment, as if taken aback by
her response. When his mouth moved upon hers again, she
shivered. Oh, how she had missed him! Her senses swim-
ming, she was only vaguely aware of the cheering faces
around her.

When he finally released her, he wasn't grinning. This
time, he stared at her for a moment, his eyes molten behind
the silken slits of his mask. She drew a shaky breath. The
men watching appeared not to have noticed what passed
between them, their gibes as loud and coarse as ever.

Had she imagined it? She stared at him, wishing to see his
face, but his rakish smile returned. He lifted her in his powerful arms and carried her to the far corner of the room
where several of his men collected coin and valuables from
the assembled soldiers.

Nat glanced at the private, who glared back at him with
malice. "Men, take him with the others to the livery, then
tie them up." Swords clanked against armor as the few remaining Roundheads were led away by Nat's men.

"You're coming with me," Nat whispered in her hair. His
words caused her heartbeat to quicken. Hoisting her over his
shoulder, he strode to the door.

"Wait. Th-ere's some-thing I—I must t-t-tell you." She
had to tell him about the king, but her chest bounced off his
shoulder at each of his jostling strides, forcing the air from
her lungs.

"Tell me when we're on the road." He carried her outside like a sack of grain, until they reached the far edge of
the moonlit courtyard.

She blinked, her eyes becoming accustomed to the night. In the shadows, three riders waited upon horses alongside Nat's black stallion.

"I must tell you—" she whispered, glancing around at the other three riders, but Nat mounted the stallion in one fluid motion, then helped her into his lap. The first Cavalier, dressed in a brown cape and wide-brimmed feathered hat, lifted the corner of his mask. In the moonlight, she saw the smiling, freckled face of Doc Herrick. The man beside him was Wilkens, the Herricks' servant. The last rider urged his horse from the shadows. Tall and thin, the man swept off his large comical hat in a mock salute. "Welcome, sweeting." The king, dressed as the servant, Will Jackson, grinned.

Relief and joy filled her heart. Anne glanced up at Nat's face. "You knew Twining had arrested him?"

Nat removed his mask, his crooked smile confirming it. "One by one, we overtook Twining's soldiers, then my men dressed in their uniforms until we had the Roundheads whittled down to size." He flashed her a rakish grin as he threaded his fingers through his hair.

"I gave you my promise, my darling, and now I'm keeping it. I'm taking you to your father, and by this time tomorrow, God willing, you'll be with him."

"Oh, Nat," she cried joyfully, her arms circling his neck. Tears of relief and happiness welled in her eyes. How could she have doubted he would come for her? He could do anything, this man she loved. Her pulse quickened at the realization. *This man she loved.*

Aye, she loved him. A delightful shiver of wanting ran through her. He had stolen her heart, this black rogue, and she would love him until the day she died.

"This way," Nat called out as he wheeled Shadow and spurred the animal into a wild gallop down the road. The king, Doc Herrick and Wilkens brought up the rear.

Cold wind whipped Anne's face as they raced along, thrilling to the danger. With her cheek against his chest, he urged the horse faster. His strong arm tightened around her waist. Her heart raced with exhilaration as Nat's words pounded in rhythm with the thunderous hooves beneath her: *By this time tomorrow, God willing, you'll be with him.*

Nat's cape billowed out from his broad shoulders, slapping the night's shadows like a devil's challenge. She thought excitedly of how he had kissed her, moments ago, as if she were his love. She had wanted more—much more. The truth surprised as well as startled her. A flush rose to her face, flaming her skin against the night's cold rush.

How powerful and strong Nat had looked when he confronted Twining and how brave he had been when he swept her up and carried her away! She owed Nat her freedom, for if he hadn't arrived when he did, Twining would have recognized her . . .

But thanks to Nat, she needn't think of it again. She would think only of her future with Nat and her father.

They would be sailing to France together. *And the Black Fox, as well?*

The idea caused her to burst with happiness. Could Nat have come to realize he loved her? Her heart sang with hope. Of course! Nat must have planned this surprise all along! He planned to ask her father for her hand. They would be married in France, where they would live safely until the Royalists delivered Oliver Cromwell's head on the end of a pike!

Joy and excitement swelled within her as the clamoring hoofbeats roared, each strike of the hooves bringing her nearer to her dreams.

Chapter Nine

Far off, a rooster crowed as the rosy streaks of dawn stretched across the horizon and touched the far corners of the Pied Bull Inn. Twining sat by the window, his fists tight with rage as he watched his aide lead Tom Thackery and his wench across the courtyard toward the tavern.

The Black Fox could never have ridden in, captured his Roundheads, stolen their horses as easily as he did last night unless someone at the inn had helped him. And he was almost certain who that someone was! His fingers traced the heavily engraved gold miniature he always carried inside his vest. He snapped it open and gazed down into the lovely face of his Elizabeth. *Trust me, my love. I'll find your daughter and bring her back safely, so help me, God. And I promise you, my love, by all that's holy, Anne will stand by my side when I string up that bastard and make him pay for his crimes. So help me!*

The action invariably soothed him, but now, it fueled a vengeance for the truth if he had to whip it out of the peasants, himself.

"The two civilians are here, sire," The aide called from the doorway. Behind the young lieutenant, the wench clung to the innkeeper, her dark eyes wide with fear.

Twining studied her, and a thought came to him. "Bring the wench here, but have Thackery loaded into the prison cart and prepare to take him to London."

"Nay!" Moll screamed, throwing her arms around Tom's neck. Lieutenant White called two guards, who rushed Tom, pushing Moll aside, and they dragged his writhing form from the room.

Moll's face twisted in horror as the soldiers led the innkeeper away. She lashed back at Twining. "Tom's done nothin' wrong. An' 'e knows nothin' 'bout what 'appened 'cause one o' yer drunken soldiers knocked 'im out with 'is tankard." Her lips quivered. "Sire," she added, as though suddenly realizing she was speaking to a superior.

Twining watched the wench's obvious concern for the innkeeper. If there was a link between Thackery and the Black Fox, it would be only a matter of time before the wench told him. "Perhaps you might be able to help Thackery." He gestured to the wooden bench in front of him. "Have a seat, my dear."

She glanced warily, her hand clutched fearfully to her throat. Finally she seated herself across the table from him.

Twining leaned back and tented his fingers. "Tell me about the fracas between the soldiers when Thackery was hit on the head. Was this before the Black Fox and his men arrived?"

"Aye," Moll answered.

Just as he thought. No doubt it was one of the highwayman's rogues, dressed as a Roundhead, who feigned the blow to Thackery's head, supplying the innkeeper with an excuse.

"It was all me fault, Colonel." Tears brimmed in her large dark eyes. "I was angry at Tom. I tried t' make 'im jealous. Then the men got t' fightin' an' Tom tried to break it up—"

"I've read the men's reports, and I know all about your lewd behavior." He sniffed. "You and that doxy, Rosie."

Moll's eyes widened. "Rosie? She ain't no doxy. She stole me best dress an' was wearin' it, that's all."

Twining straightened. "I saw her for myself."

Moll shook her head. "Saints! Rosie's no tart. She's the wife of one of the men workin' the 'arvest. Rosie was carried off by the Black Fox!"

Obviously Moll was lying, but why? Twining's thoughts went back to the dark-haired wench. She had kissed the

Black Fox, and at the time he thought the wench had only pretended to thwart the bandit's advances. Something had been vaguely familiar about her, but what? Suddenly he had an idea that left him feeling as if he had been struck by a thunderbolt.

His hand shook as he fingered down the list of the inn's guests' names. "Her husband, Nat Braydon. Where is he now?"

Moll shrugged and shook her head. "I dunno."

Twining leaned closer. "See here, Miss Standish. The Black Fox didn't ride in here, overtake my men as easily as he did without Thackery's help. Whether he's taking payments or he's foolish enough to be one of them, I'm going to find out." He glowered at Moll, his voice menacing. "And I don't need to prove it to send Thackery to jail for questioning."

Moll gasped.

Twining grinned with satisfaction. "Now, where's Braydon?"

Moll burst into tears. "I—I dunno."

"Unless you have something to say, Miss Standish, you may leave." Twining dismissed her with a wave of his hand.

"Wait" Moll shot him a fearful glance. "I do remember somethin'."

Twining hid the glow of satisfaction. "I'm glad, my dear. What is it you remember?" He leaned forward, his fingers drumming the table.

"It was Rosie, sire." Moll's fingers knotted in her lap. "Somethin' unusual about 'er."

He grunted. "The woman the Black Fox carried off?"

"Aye, the same." Moll blinked. "Rosie 'ad a stolen locket.

"The woman stole a locket? From whom?"

"I dunno, sire." Moll peeked nervously back at him. "I thought she . . . I mean . . . she 'ad so little—"

"I've no time for fimble famble! You either know something or you don't."

"Aye, I do!" Her voice steadied. "Rosie 'ad this locket. Gold, it was." Her mouth pouted in thought. "An' inside was a picture of a lady. A beautiful lady. She said 'er man gave it to 'er as a wedding present." She rolled her eyes. "An 'eirloom from 'is family, but . . ." Moll's eyes narrowed. "I didn't believe 'er. The woman's picture didn't look a bit like 'im."

"Enough, wench! You're wasting my time."

"Rosie stole me gown! That proves she's a thief, an' she lied about the locket." Moll glowered back at him.

A muscle above Twining's jaw twitched when he suddenly remembered the delicate gold locket Anne always wore. "Tell me more about the miniature inside the locket."

Moll's eyes brightened with his encouragement. "She wore a yellow gown, she did. Looked like a queen." Her fingers toyed with the ribbons at her low neckline while she thought. "The locket was this big." She circled her thumb and forefinger to show its size. "An' Rosie stole it," she added.

A chilling thought formed in his mind: *If the locket was Anne's, he knew she'd never relinquish it willingly.* Rage coursed through him as he imagined the heartless devil ripping Anne's locket from her neck, or worse! Twining shifted and pulled out the miniature from his vest pocket. "Was the locket larger or smaller than this?" He clicked open the gold lid and stared at the portrait of his beloved Elizabeth, Anne's mother, before he showed it to the wide-eyed wench.

Moll's jaw fell. "It's . . . the same . . ."

"The same lady?"

"Aye, sire. The same lady!"

For a moment, the realization that it was Anne's locket filled him with heavenly jubilation. He could hardly contain his excitement. "Think carefully," he crooned. "You're positive?"

Moll's voice lowered, as if she sensed the importance of her discovery. "Aye, Colonel, 'tis the same lady."

Twining studied her, choosing his words for their most dramatic effect. "The locket you've described, my dear, is the very one that my betrothed, Mistress Anne, had with her when she was abducted by the Black Fox."

Moll's eyes rounded in shock. "Oh, sire!"

He felt encouraged. "I believe Nat Braydon, the man living at the inn with his woman, Rosie, is the Black Fox! You must tell me everything you remember about Nat Braydon and his woman, Rosie. If you give me any information to help me find them, I'll release Thackery and you'll be richly rewarded."

"Oh, sire, gladly," Moll exclaimed, "b-but, how? I've told ye all I know."

Twining looked at her reflectively. "You're a pretty lass, Moll. I noticed how Thackery looks at you." He paused. "I'm sure you've noticed, as well." Two red circles stained her cheeks and she batted her eyes self-consciously. He knew his plan couldn't fail. "With your feminine charms, my dear, I'm sure Thackery will tell you anything you ask him."

Moll's eyes glittered like shiny coals. "Tom knows nothin' 'bout the Black Fox and 'is men," she answered defiantly.

He could see the fear flash across her face at the realization that her lover might hang along with the nefarious outlaw. His mouth twitched in satisfaction. Aye, the wench would do anything to keep that from happening, he mused.

Moll studied him cautiously. "An' you promise if I find out somethin', you'll free Tom?" she asked, her voice hopeful.

"Of course. In fact, I'll release Thackery immediately so you'll be able to question him. In payment for your information about the locket."

Moll gave a small squeal of delight.

"But be warned! I'm leaving by tomorrow's light and I'll expect you to have a report by then."

Moll's brow knotted in a frown. "Th-that's not much time."

Twining stood and pushed the chair back, its legs scraping the oaken floor. "Thackery would be on his way to jail if it hadn't been for your cooperation." Shuffling the parchments in front of him in a pile, he stuffed them inside a leather pouch. "But fail me and I'll have Thackery hanged from the nearest elm."

Moll shrank back like a frightened kitten.

He felt encouraged at the fear he saw in her eyes. "Think of your reward—a fortune in gold sovereigns and your lover's freedom." He hesitated a moment, then added, "I'll even drop any charges found against Thackery when this is over."

"Ye . . . ye promise?" Uncertainty edged her words.

Twining straightened, fingering the baldric at his throat. "You have my word as an officer and a gentleman."

Ribbons of dawn's light broke through the heavens as the four riders galloped across the half-moon bridge. Hooves thundered over the ancient stone above the river, pounding the valley's stillness like the devil's heartbeat. When they reached the other side of the waterway, Nat reined back and gave the signal to halt. He flashed a rakish grin at Anne in his arms. "We'll stop for an hour to rest and change our clothes."

She smiled back at him, breathless with anticipation. Soon she would have the opportunity to speak her heart.

As the others rode up alongside and dismounted, Nat spoke to them. "Take the horses down by the stream out of sight from the road. You'll find a change of clothing and food in your saddlebags. Best try and eat. The next time we stop, we may be dodging Roundhead musket balls."

The king shot Nat a mischievous glance. "Then let us break out that special leather flask I gave you earlier. He doffed his hat and wiped his forehead on his sleeve. "I'd not fancy leaving good French brandy to the Roundheads. They'd never know it from green beer, anyway."

Anne joined the men's laughter. As the flask was passed around, she couldn't help but remember the way she had seen Charles Stuart shackled and held prisoner. How she admired the king's courage in the face of what he'd been through. Although he was only a few years older than herself, he showed the measure of a great sovereign. She put her hand to her throat. For the first time, she felt a deep understanding and appreciation for what her father had risked of their family's happiness in order to bring this man to the throne.

"Anne," Nat whispered. "I hope the clothing suits you. It's the best I could do on short notice." He snatched Shadow's reins and walked toward the hill, his cape swirling about him.

"N-Nat, wait." An urgent need to tell him how she felt before the others returned prompted her to follow after him.

When he turned back to her, the early morning light stroked his handsome face. "Change into dry clothes, first. I don't want you sick with the ague—"

"Please, before the others return."

"Very well." His voice gentled. "There's something I have to tell you, as well. Come with me." He reached down for her and lifted her up and set her atop the stallion. Nat's gaze fixed on her mouth and when his dark brown eyes finally met hers, she felt she would drown into those liquid dark pools. A sudden heat heightened the thrill she felt.

"From the top of the knoll, we can watch the entire countryside awake to the dawn." During the few minutes it took to reach the top, Anne's stomach fluttered with expectation of his news. Dawn had barely touched the horizon as pale streamers of rose and gold rested on the treetops of the sleeping landscape below.

Nat lifted her from the saddle and held her in his arms. "I never had the chance to tell you how enticing you look in that gown." His moist breath hinted faintly of brandy. "But with your beauty, adornments would pale in comparison."

His words thrilled her. She circled her arms around his neck as he carried her through the tall dew-kissed grass. How long had she waited to hear him say those words?

"Even so, you deserve to wear beautiful silks and laces," he said as he unfastened his cape and threw it across the high seat of a fallen log. "No doubt, *you'd* be happier wearing rich threads and precious perfumes, instead of dresses of homespun, and smelling of ale."

Anne frowned. This wasn't what she'd expected to hear, and it made her uneasy in a way she couldn't define. "But wouldn't anyone rather be rich than be poor?"

His mouth quirked in that certain smile she had come to love. "Of course, they would."

He turned and she watched him tether the animal, still feeling disturbed by his words. How silly of him to believe she needed finery to be content. Was he trying to prepare her for the hardships of living in exile? But of course! That must be what he had in mind, she decided, her mood lifting. She'd have plenty of time to convince him she could be happy anywhere, as long as they were together.

A sweet sensation of yearning filled her as he walked back toward her through the meadow grass. He bent over and picked something up, examining it in the half-light. Then he reached down and gathered more handfuls. He smiled as he handed her a bouquet of bright blue star-lavender. She gasped with delight and she buried her nose in the heady fragrance.

"Its sweet scent will always remind me of you," he whispered, sitting beside her on the cloak. "The blue spikes remind me of your eyes when you're happy. But when you're angry," he added, his eyes twinkling, "the green in your eyes sparkles like the Mediterranean on a stormy day."

She wasn't used to compliments, and she could feel the blush creep up her face. She didn't know what to say, so she said nothing. To hide her awkward feelings, she hid her face in the wildflowers, their intoxicating spicy bouquet engulfing her.

His eyes surveyed the valley below, which glowed with each passing minute of sunrise. She thought maybe he was choosing his words, or gathering his courage to ask for her hand....

"It's getting late," he said, instead, his gaze lingering along the harvested cornfields, golden squares of pasture set against amber rolling hills.

Impatiently she thought to ask him of his plans, but she didn't want to break the spell of this moment. She found it impossible to take her eyes from him: The dark, thick hair wind-tossed around his handsome face, thick black lashes spiked his large brown eyes beneath majestic brows. Overwhelmed by her feelings, she watched as the pale light brushed his profile, softening the fine scar across his left cheek. Even the black shadow of a day's growth of beard emphasized his maleness.

"Dawn is my favorite time," he said, a myriad of emotions playing in his eyes. His thoughts were not on the autumn beauty of the view below, she knew, but of serious things of the heart.

"Dawn is another beginning, another chance, don't you think?" His eyes rested on her again, his face enthusiastic.

"Another chance?" What was he talking about? Another chance for them to be together?

"Each dawn is God's gift for us to try to reach for whatever our heart dares to dream," he said.

Sharing the dawn with him made her think of her own dreams: she would be reunited with her father; she would become Nat's wife. She touched his hand, her heart swelling with gratitude. "If it hadn't been for you, I might never have had another chance at my dreams." Nat's hard, callused fingers clasped hers in his large, warm hand. She lowered her head and fell silent for a moment before adding, "Not only have you risked your life for the king and for me, but my father will be indebted to you, as well."

He smiled at her, then looked back over the valley. How noble he was. She thought her heart would burst with love.

A moment later, his eyes captured the questioning azure of hers. She felt a heady reaction to his unwavering stare. She wanted him to take her in his arms and love her. Her mouth went dry, a rush of desire flooded her. "Thank you for keeping your promise to me," she managed to say without wavering.

"Did you doubt my word, lass?" He cocked a brow and she knew by the teasing glint in his eyes and the grin tugging at his mouth that he was remembering the morning at the farm cottage when she had told him as much.

His fingers toyed with her tangled locks. Each time his fingers brushed her cheek her heart skipped a beat.

"Who would trust the word of a rogue?" she teased, imitating her words of that first morning at the cottage.

The devilish gleam in his eyes darkened and his gaze came to rest on her lips. "I gave you my word as a man, not as a rogue."

She wished she could have saucily tossed back that it was the same thing, wasn't it? But she knew her voice would betray her intense feelings. Besides, Nat knew how she felt.

What was this unspoken thing between them? It was as if they could see into each other's very soul whenever they looked into each other's eyes.

"Look at me." The low, husky tone of his voice sent tingles of excitement darting up her spine.

Obediently she met his dark velvet gaze. "Yes," she heard herself say. She reached out and touched the scar along his cheek. "I knew you'd never forsake me."

He stood up and pulled her to her feet. Behind him, the sun's rosy brilliance exploded ribbons of color across the heavens. "And I promise you, I never will, my heart." Curling his fingers around her hand, he brought it to his lips. "I'll never forsake you." He kissed her fingers, his eyes smoldering down at her. "Promise me, you'll always remember that, regardless of what might happen."

Alarm coursed through her at the uncertainty of his words. But, of course, he meant only that he couldn't promise her total happiness over things that were beyond his control. She relaxed. "I promise," she whispered.

"Have you any idea, my Anne, how precious you are to me?" His whispered words felt like a soft caress. He pulled her to him, his head lowered as he tipped her chin, his expressive eyes half-closed. Her pulse quickened in thrilling response, and her insides felt light and fluttery.

"Nat—" Before she could say another word, his mouth took hers with fierce tenderness. His hand curved around her nape, his fingers tightening in the thick tangle of her lustrous hair. He pulled her closer, his other hand circling her waist.

A soft moan of pleasure escaped her while her hands eased through the opening of his black silk shirt. If he hadn't been so gentle, she might have been frightened by these strange, overwhelming thoughts of hers. Her fingers slid up his bristly, muscled chest, only to linger at the pounding of his heart.

Oh, Nat. You have the same feelings for me, as I have for you! She thought she would burst with happiness. Timidly she opened her lips to his, allowing his tongue to slide inside, filling her with unbelievable desire as their kiss deepened. Her arms curved around his neck, fastening themselves as she innocently and unconsciously molded her body against his length.

At that moment, Nat could no longer fight his feelings. God knows, he had fought against the desire that exploded within him. But this innocent, bewitching enchantress was the most enticing woman he had ever known. Drowning in a sea of ecstasy while his tongue tasted and courted hers, his body thrilled to the hungry insistence of her desire.

She returned his kisses passionately, teasing him unknowingly, unaware of her power over him. Her fingers gently kneaded the corded muscles of his back. "Oh, Nat," she whispered.

He caressed the soft curve of her shoulder through the silk of her hair. Brushing aside the shining, dark cloud, he trailed kisses along her neck. His fingers shifted from her waist to her midriff, sliding upward until his large hand cupped her breast.

He heard her breath catch when his mouth slid beneath the soft fabric covering her breasts. His tongue, finding the sensitive tip, teased the rising bud until it hardened. She whimpered low in her throat; her heart beat like a captured bird, begging for release.

Passion exploded in him as he kissed the satin skin of her breasts, his hands caressing, exploring. Her soft moan of longing whispered in his ear. Intoxicated by her quivering response to him, his mouth traveled over her soft, heaving mounds. The spicy aroma of crushed wildflowers and the subtle scent of woman invaded his senses. "So soft, so incredibly sweet."

God, how he wanted her! He drew back and gazed down at her. Her beautiful oval face, flushed from passion, cried out to him. His mouth came down hard on hers. Her fingers raked his back with need as their kiss deepened. He caressed her breasts; when his hands lowered, his fingers caught something hard and metallic.

Nat pulled back and stared at the golden oval and chain that had been hidden deep within the soft folds of her bodice. He grabbed it, gaping at the glittering object dangling from the chain twisted around his fingers.

Anne reached for it, but he snatched it from her grasp. His eyes fixed on hers in shock and accusation, while her hands flew back to cover her breasts.

She stared at her locket swinging back and forth from the delicate chain tangled in his fingers, then looked away, regret tightening her face.

"I'd forbidden you to bring this!" His face was a glowering mask of fury. "I waited outside the cottage while you went to give your bauble to Emma for safekeeping."

She pulled back a tangle of curls from her face, then straightened her shawl over her shoulders with trembling hands. Her lips were swollen from his kisses, and her face still flushed with passion.

He cupped her chin. "Don't you know the danger you could have put us in if anyone had seen this?" He watched her avert her eyes, her face pale. "Anne, look at me."

She jerked her chin free from his grasp. Her dark lashes hid the truth she prayed he wouldn't see in those blue-green depths. Finally she met his sharp gaze, then he knew someone *had* seen the locket—he knew it as well as if she'd told him.

"The locket fell out of my pocket at the inn." Her soft voice was edged heavily with remorse. "I told Moll that—"

"Bloody hell! Moll saw this?"

"Aye. But you needn't worry." Her eyes brightened. "I took care of the matter."

His brow furrowed with doubt. "How?"

"I told Moll that my locket was a wedding gift from you. An heirloom from your family."

He thrust his fists on his hips. "And you think she believed it?"

"Of course," she responded innocently.

He raked his fingers through his hair. After an awkward silence, he stared back at her, his eyes pained. "If you had kept the locket, you should have told me."

"B-but I—I didn't know you then, as I know you now."

Nat glared down at her. "You know me not, wench. You only think you do." He whirled around and strode several feet from where she stood. He reached out and angrily swiped at a tree branch, snapping it off with a crack.

Curse it! He'd known all along that she had an effect on him. If only he had remained steadfast to his duty, none of this would have happened. That damned locket was as dangerous to the Royalists as a Roundhead's blade or flintlock. He should have taken her locket, just as he would have disarmed an enemy.

God in Heaven, how could he be so blind? It wasn't the locket that fueled his anger, but what the locket symbolized. The golden oval felt like fire in his hand as his fingers turned it, over and over. Aye, the woman he loved wasn't Rosie, a wench of his own invention, who could fall in love with a bastard and never yearn for more. She was Anne Lowell, daughter of a proud Royalist who would see that she marry into her rightful world. Her future in France would guarantee a marriage contract, wealth and security. *Damn his soul, if he loved her, he'd let her go!*

The realization hit him with the force of a cannon only to be followed by a torrent of self-rebuke. God, he'd have eternity for reproach. Now, his mind must be on the mission at hand, and best he give her an example to follow.

Reluctantly he strode toward where she stood, her head bowed, clutching the drooping spikes of lavender. Ignoring her surprise, he placed the locket in her cupped hand. Forcing all the emotion from his voice, he drew a steadying breath. "While I'm here to protect you, keep your trinket, but keep it hidden. It's little enough you have of your family." *It's little enough of what you deserve, my love.*

His heart wrenched as he saw her large sad eyes glittering with unshed tears.

"I have news from your father. My cousin Jane Herrick sent word that he's been brought to Rosemoor. He's been

notified you're coming to him." He watched her chin tremble slightly, but she clenched her jaw in steely resolution.
The slight fortifying gesture endeared her all the more to
him. "If the rains hold back and all goes according to plan,
we should arrive at Rosemoor tomorrow. After a few days'
rest, we'll leave for the coast where a ship waits to sail for
France."

"And will you . . . ?" Hope filled her as she laid her hand
upon his cheek, as though her touch might magically bring
the answer she desperately needed to hear. "Will you sail
with us?"

Beneath her fingers, she felt the muscle in his jaw harden
and he pulled away. "I can't leave England, Anne."

Shock jolted through her. "But, I—I thought . . ."

"I know, and I'm sorry."

Anne stared at him in stricken disbelief. *He didn't love her
enough?* Only her constricted throat kept her from verify-
ing it as her dreams shattered before her.

A detached tone edged his voice. "Once the king is safe,
my place will be here, raising money to restore the throne."

Anne buried her face in the bouquet of lavender.

"Anne, please." She felt his hands touch her shoulders,
but she flinched away and threw the flowers to the ground.

"You never planned to see me again once I sailed for
France, did you?" She forced herself to look at him. In his
dark brown depths, she saw the truth in her words. What a
silly little fool he must think her to be! She swiped at the
salty tears that ran down her cheeks. Whirling around, she
lifted her skirts and stumbled blindly down the hill. She had
to get away from him.

Nat opened his mouth to call her back. God, how he
wanted to comfort her, to tell her how much he loved her,
but what good would it do? All he could offer her was a future with an outlaw whose destiny would be to swing from
a gibbet.

He watched her run toward the shore, her red skirt billowing behind her as she scampered toward the willows

where the horses grazed. And where he knew, when alone, she could let the tears flow unchecked.

How he wanted to run after her, hold her and kiss away the tears. But pride was all he had left her.

Chapter Ten

The clank of harness and men's voices caused Anne to lift her head from the cradle of her arms. Through blurry tears, she watched the king and Doc, followed by Wilkens with the horses, trudge back through the tall weeds toward the knoll. "Hurry, Anne. Time to leave," Doc called to her.

She swiped at the tears that ran down her cheeks as she gathered her things and proceeded to follow the men. How she treasured the plain but lovely muslin yellow gown she had found inside the saddlebags that Nat had packed for her. Among the starched cap and apron, stockings and underskirt was a blue-green bodice—had Nat chosen the color because it reminded him of her eyes? Inside the cap, she found several buttercup yellow hair ribbons. Fresh tears stung her eyes. How Nat must have planned to find such feminine luxury for her. For a moment, she caressed the ribbons against her cheek.

After she closed the saddlebags, she slipped the locket yaround her neck, the cold metal shocking her skin. How her locket had always sustained her, but now, she couldn't help but compare the feel of cold metal at her breast with the heated passion she felt in Nat's arms only a short time ago. If only she could undo her foolish action! A sudden cold gust tore at the skirts beneath her cape. If only a chilling wind could blow away the heated yearnings from her mind as well as her body, she thought bitterly as she followed the crushed path through the grass toward where the others waited.

At the sound of footsteps, Nat glanced up from polishing the flintlocks and scowled when he saw Doc Herrick wade through the tall grass toward him.

"I saw Anne by the stream," Doc said as he sat cross-legged upon a rock. "By her tearful face, I'd say you told her you wouldn't be leaving with her."

"She'll get over it." Nat said, his eyes on his work.

"But will you?" Doc asked compassionately.

Nat threw the cleaning rag to the ground and glared back at his friend. "I'll thank you to mind your own business." He mounted his horse, then brought the stallion up sharply. "I'll go ahead and follow the river trail," Nat said brusquely. "You lead the others in about five minutes. If I see any militia, I'll head back and warn you. Otherwise, meet me at the Averys' farm. We'll stay there for the night."

"Will Anne be riding with you?"

"Nay. It's best I keep my distance." Without another word, he spurred Shadow into a gallop and disappeared through the lacy golden foliage.

The next two hours of slow, calculating travel felt more tedious than a full gallop along the highway, Nat thought glumly. But since Anne's confession that Moll Standish had seen her locket, there was no other choice. If Twining suspected that Anne and Rosie were the same woman, he'd probe the countryside looking for her with the determination of a forest fire.

Up ahead, a pheasant flew out of the dense thicket, its loud crowing *cuck-cuck* sound and the resonant beating of wings filled the stillness. Nat swung down from his horse, then removed the water bags that hung from the saddle. A few minutes later, a horse's whinny rang out behind him. Turning at the sound, he forgot everything at the disarming sight of Anne as she rode up alongside him on the gray mare. From the far distance, he heard the others approach, but for a greedy moment he gave in to his desire to drink of the sight of her while he could.

She pulled off her black riding hood and shook loose the heavy waves of hair from around her lovely face. Sunlight beamed through the leafy canopy of branches, lighting the fiery chestnut highlights that fought brilliantly against the walnut stain she had applied to her hair.

Anne averted her eyes from him, but the blossoms of color deepening her cheeks told him she was aware of his stare. God help him, but he couldn't resist. Her soft mouth parted slightly, her thick sooty lashes shaded her brilliant eyes.

So lovely, so fresh, so unspoiled. A lump formed in his throat as he tried to endure the feelings that warred within him. What he was thinking was insane, but he could no longer deny it. He had not even believed in the kind of emotion he felt for her, but this early morning beside her on the knoll, he knew he loved her. He loved her with all his heart. *And how, in God's name, would he gather the strength to send her away?*

Shadow shied nervously as Will Jackson rode into the clearing, his horse a few strides ahead of Doc and Wilkens riding double on the last horse.

Anne dismounted, then her gaze locked with his, but it was Nat who forced himself to break away.

The men dismounted while Anne walked stiffly out of sight of the others. Doc strode to the privacy of a thick copse to relieve himself while Wilkens led the horses to the shore.

The king pulled a flask of water from his saddlebags and, after a healthy swig, offered it to Nat. "Tell me about the safe house we'll be staying at this evening," the king asked.

"Sam Avery is a cooper. His wife rents rooms to help feed their ten children. The vicar said Avery fought with your father and Prince Rupert at Naseby, but he has no idea who we are."

The king's hooded gaze lingered on the fast-moving current. "Naseby. I'll never forget that defeat. So many casualties."

Naseby. Nat's stomach tightened on the word. The battle when the Royalists fought and lost against his father, Colonel Nigel Adams! A trembling rush of remorse and anger claimed him before he could shunt it aside. Although it had been six years since the battle, Nat knew time would never fade his anger at what his father had done.

His eyes shifted to Anne, who appeared from a shelter of trees. She brushed her dusty cape as she sauntered toward them.

The king studied Nat thoughtfully, his black eyes serious. "Did your father die at Naseby, Nat?"

His throat tightened. "Nay."

"I had no idea your father fought at Naseby," Anne said, hearing the last of the conversation. "My father fought there, as well. They might have known one another."

Nat bit back the bitter taste in his mouth. "*My* father rode with Cromwell, not with King Charles." Anne's aquamarine eyes widened with puzzlement, confusion, and then dawning disbelief. He had never felt the shame cut so deeply as it did now, watching her stare back at him, too shocked to speak.

A thrush flew to a nearby bush. Its soft warble amid the rustle of autumn leaves was all that could be heard.

"My father died of a fever in Ireland," Nat said finally. "But not before he had led Cromwell's dragoons against the Irish in one of the most savage bloodbaths in history."

Anne came forward, forgetting herself, and placed her hand gently to Nat's cheek. Her eyes glistened with unspoken words.

Nat turned away. "My father was one of the chief supporters against Charles. He even signed the king's death warrant."

"Nat!" The king clamped Nat's forearm. "You can't blame yourself for that." His voice lowered. "Learn to leave the fallen on the battlefield, my friend. It becomes quite a burden to carry the dead around with you."

Nat swallowed. "Of course," he answered, not wishing to disagree with the king. But how could Charles Stuart understand how it felt to know the blood charging through your veins was of a father who had betrayed his king?

Anne clambered toward the grassy slopes where Doc knelt, watching the river. Nat watched her, wanting to run after her, but instead, he turned back toward where the horses grazed, resigned to let the matter die. Shadow twitched his pointed ears and tossed his massive head in greeting. Grabbing the reins, Nat called out to Doc, "Wait fifteen minutes, then follow me."

Doc waved in acknowledgment, then turned back toward the river to his thoughts. If Anne heard Nat leave, she gave no sign of it as she leaned against the towering elm, its lacy branches tossing autumn shadows about her in the golden sunlight.

Nat had barely ridden out of sight when Anne came to within a few feet of where Doc crouched on one knee, skipping stones across the silvery ripples of the river. His freckled face remained impassive as he stared across the water.

"What did Nat's father do that was so terrible?" Anne asked Doc as she spread her cape upon the grass and knelt beside him.

Doc scowled back at her from under his hat's wide brim. "It's not my place to tell ye."

"I'm asking you because you're his friend." She ignored his loud sigh as he tossed another pebble into the water. "It's not just curiosity on my part." A heavy ache went through her as she thought of the pain in Nat's face when he spoke of his father. "I care about Nat," she confessed, a blush warming her cheeks.

Doc pulled back his hat, revealing the sandy shock of hair. "I know you do, Anne, but it's not my place to tell you. Besides, what's done is done." He shrugged helplessly.

She tugged on his sleeve. "Please, I know so little about Nat." She felt starved to learn all she could in so little time.

Doc squinted a hazel eye at her. "Might as well. You'll only pester a body till you find out, and best it comes from me." He tossed the remaining stones into the river with a loud plunk, then grabbed at a wand of timothy weed. His gaze dropped to his fingers as he stripped the outer blade, gathering his thoughts.

"Nat's ma wasn't much older than you when she went into service at Rosemoor," he began. He stuck the weed into his mouth. "My wife, Jane, was no more than a babe at the time," he said, the weed moving up and down while he spoke.

"Emma told me some of the story when I stayed with her at the cottage," Anne said wistfully. "What was Nat's father like?"

"A devil, that one!" Doc shook his head. "Nigel was nothing like his older brother, Alexander, my father-in-law. A finer man never lived. But when Nigel learned that Nat's mother was with child, he denied being with the maid. There was a terrible uproar. Bridget took the side of Nat's mother against Nigel, and Nigel never forgave her."

Anne leaned forward, her chin resting on the palms of her hands. "Many men don't acknowledge their bastards. What I saw in Nat's face was something a great deal worse than that."

"Aye." Doc shifted on his side and leaned his head on an elbow. "A few years later, when Nat's mother died, Bridget had lost her firstborn, a son. Bridget wanted to bring Nat to live at Rosemoor, but when Nigel heard of it, he was outraged. He vowed if Nat was brought into the family, he would leave it.

"Alex ignored his brother and young Nat came to live with them. Nigel's threat proved true. He left, joined Cromwell's legions and when the war ended, Nigel marched with Cromwell to revenge the Irish for befriending the Royalists. But Nigel had his own ax to grind." Doc's hazel eyes darkened. "He slaughtered Bridget's kin and put a torch to their home. Only Wilkens and several maids escaped to tell the bloody tale."

Understanding replaced Anne's immediate shock as she caught her breath. "What did Nat's uncle do?"

"Before Alex died, he vowed to make up to Bridget for what his brother did to her. With his Roundhead connections, he helped Bridget and Jane set up an underground web to smuggle valuable military information back to the Royalists. This web grew and will continue to do so until our king is back in power." Doc smiled. "Your father owes his life to them, as well."

A surge of gratitude tightened her throat. "You must be very proud of what your wife and her parents have accomplished."

"Aye, but it's Nat and his work as the Black Fox who has made their efforts successful."

She felt a tug of remorse at the jeopardy her selfish act had put him in.

Doc rose, brushed off the loose chaff from his clothes. "Time to leave. We don't want Nat to have to wait too long for us." He reached out and helped her to her feet.

"Thank you for telling me, Doc."

She snatched up her cape, shook it and, in a swirl of skirts, strode toward her horse. Somehow, Nat had to be made to understand that if he could aid the king safely from England, that was enough to pay back his debt for his father's crimes.

Somehow, she had to make him believe it. But how?

From behind the hatch door of the tavern's storage room, Tom Thackery peeped through the knothole and watched Colonel Twining in his resplendent red uniform march back into the inn after talking to his aide in the courtyard. "That speck of puny ass is exactly the sort of runt who can cause large trouble."

Moll knelt beside him. Tom reached out and rubbed his broad hand along Moll's smooth bare leg. Her heart hammered in fear as she thought of Twining and remembered his threat to have her Tom strung up from the nearest elm. She had so little time to find out from Tom all she needed to know about the Black Fox! If only she had more time...

"Don't go," she whispered, rubbing her body against his.

"B-but...what if 'e finds us together?" Tom's eyes belied his words, as he watched her, transfixed, while she slowly untied the ribbons at the front of her chemise.

"No one will find us." The thin fabric fell from her shoulders and brushed down her arms to fall in a soft gather around her waist. She reached out and cupped his curly head and hugged his face to her breasts.

"But..." His voice faded in a groan of desire.

Her lips met his mouth hungrily. Giggling with pleasure in her knowledge that his longing equaled hers, Moll hiked her skirts up and straddled him, pulling him down to the floor. She raked her fingers along his chest, dropping to the knot in the belt of his trousers.

Tom responded with the same wild passion that he had the first time. A thrill she had never felt with any of the others raced through her at the memory.

Tom's wide hands explored her body; she moaned with delight. She squirmed above him, her mind marveling how, in the two months since she had worked as his tavern maid, Tom had been too shy to have shown her any sign that he cared. Funny how men could be sometimes.

She had been as stubborn as he, probably. But how was she to know that beneath Tom's unpleasant brusqueness and serious frown beat the gentle heart of man who could love her for what she was—despite her lack of schooling and questionable morals?

How lucky she was to have finally found him, and if anything were to happen... "Easy, luv. Remember, like I showed you."

"I can't wait—" His breathing was ragged.

"But ye 'aven't told me what I asked ye," she coaxed, knowing from experience that if Tom didn't tell her before he was sated, he might never tell her what she needed to know.

Tom rolled her over, and she felt his need urgent and ready. "Not now," he rasped, his mouth probing, searching.

"I don't think ye trust me," she whispered, her hands kneading him gently. "Or else you wouldn't keep secrets."

"Moll, please..."

"Is Nat the Black Fox? Tell me, or I won't go no further."

"Moll..."

"He is, isn't he?"

Tom groaned.

"Isn't he?" *Please tell me, luv. It's your life I'll be savin'.* "Tell me, luv."

"Ahh!" Tom cried out.

Her hips arched with him in need.

Later, after they were sated, she smiled as she lay beneath his powerless embrace.

So, she would have to try again the next time!

Afternoon sunlight spilled through the shutters of the small room Rosie and Nat Braydon had shared. Moll sat down on the straw pallet, her spirits low. Despite her best efforts, Tom had refused to tell her what she needed to know about Nat and Rosie.

Besides, Twining would want proof. She'd tell him anything to save Tom, but if she could only find something to link Rosie with Anne Lowell, she'd have a better chance to save Tom's life.

She had hoped to find a Bible, a prayer book, anything to prove Rosie had stolen something else from the Puritan Mistress Lowell. Instead, she had found a faded night rail, several day dresses, underclothing, hose and a straw sunbonnet.

Exactly what a poor young farmer's wife would wear!

Moll sighed as her eyes fell back to the clothing tucked inside the muslin sack in the corner. Then her eyes rested on the earthenware jug Rosie had hidden inside her underskirts, the silly twit. At first, Moll had almost missed seeing it.

She examined the small crude jug. Had Rosie saved brandy or rum from their wedding party, perhaps? Moll pulled off the cork. The bottle was full of dark liquid. She sniffed. It wasn't liquor. In fact, the smell reminded her of... the forest!

Curious, Moll walked to the sunny window. She squinted inside the neck of the bottle. What was it? Didn't smell like sage juice—that foul stuff what wives drank to help them make babies. Didn't smell like rue, or marjoram, thyme, parsley or bracken—all to be drunk for them that *don't* want babies.

A love potion? Moll chuckled, remembering the handsome dark-eyed highwayman who terrorized men but who stole feminine hearts as easily as he took their coin.

Moll poured the thick liquid out into her palm, rubbing it between her fingers. Dark walnut brown, sticky and glossy.

Did Rosie mix it in Nat's ale? Moll stood at the window, staring at her fingers. Well, she wouldn't have a use for such a thing, not with her randy Tom, she thought, smiling.

It was when she put the cork back into the jug that she noticed her hands were stained dark brown. Wiping her fingers on her apron, she gasped in dismay. The color wouldn't come off!

Moll dashed to the end of the hall where a pitcher of water and a washing bowl stood upon a bench. After repeated scrubbings with strong yellow soap, the stain remained steadfast.

She sighed, finally giving up. As if on the edge of something, and not knowing what, Moll returned to the tiny room and studied each of Rosie's garments. If there was a clue hidden among them, she couldn't find it.

The straw wide-brimmed bonnet, its band faded to white. Nothing unusual about the coarse weave of the straw, like hundreds of other hats she had seen. Moll turned the hat over, her stained fingers running idly along the brim while she thought. Then her gaze dropped to the crown. The pale straw was stained at the crown and sides. It was as though Rosie's dark brown hair had left its color...

Moll felt a jolt of astonishment as she excitedly examined the bonnet. She didn't care if it was true. All she needed was a link to build a story, and she had found it. Colonel Twining would believe it, too, if she was any judge of men.

Moll gathered up her proof and hurried toward the stairs, her insides pounding with excitement. *Oh, Tom, if you knew what I'm about to do for us! We'll get married and buy our own cottage with the gold Colonel Twining will award us, and we'll make love, over and over and over, for the rest of our lives.*

Colonel Twining scowled as he looked up from the letter he was writing to Oliver Cromwell. "I'm busy, Miss Standish. See Lieutenant White if you want something."

"But Colonel..." Without asking permission, Moll took a seat in front of his table. "I know where Mistress Anne is."

Twining glared at her, dropped the quill and jumped to his feet. "Where is she?"

"She's with Nat Braydon. He's the Black Fox. Rosie and Mistress Lowell are the same person!" His eyes narrowed.

"Rosie Braydon has dark hair. Mistress Lowell has red gold hair."

"Aye, but that was 'fore I found this jug hidden with Rosie's things." Moll opened her stained fingers and waved the jug in front of him. "Look at me hands, Colonel." Moll saw the look of surprise on Twining's face. "The Black Fox forced Mistress Anne to stain her red hair. An' look. This is Rosie's... I mean, Mistress Anne's bonnet she wore when she came here with 'im." Moll showed him the stains inside the hat. "The Fox knew yer soldiers wouldn't be lookin' for a brown-haired maid." Moll's dark eyes widened as she waited for his pleased reaction.

Twining grabbed the jug, sniffed the contents and looked back at Moll's fingers. "Walnuts, with some coal dust mixed with it, possibly." He looked back at her warily. "Who told you Nat Braydon is the Black Fox?"

Her hand fluttered to her throat, her face drained of color.

"It doesn't matter," Twining said, knowing full well that Tom Thackery had probably bragged his secret to her. He was in league with the Fox, and no doubt had drugged the ale he served the Roundheads.

Twining sat down, stunned. The disheveled woman, dressed as a doxy, who averted her face to him not in shame, but in fear of recognition was his Mistress Anne! A sharp pain shot through his temples. How he had wanted to believe that Braydon had gone off to search for his bride, Rosie, but in his heart, he had known it wasn't true.

Nat Braydon had used the perfect foil against the militia's blockades: farm worker permits that allowed the bandit to roam from hamlet to hamlet, unlike common citizens.

And the answer to his other question came glaring back, as well! The Black Fox had chosen *this* inn—not to rob the few poor soldiers and guests of their measly coin, but to make a fool of him—Colonel Edward Twining—and to let him know that the Fox had stolen Mistress Anne and forced her to share his bed.

"Leave me!" he yelled, his fury barely under control.

"But Colonel—"

"Leave!" Twining glared back at the foolish wench, her face white with fear. "Get out of my sight!"

"But the reward? When do I get me gold you promised?"

Twining leapt from his chair, blind with rage. He tore from the room, stormed into the courtyard, fists balled at his sides. He'd find Nat Braydon and kill the bloody bastard with his own bare hands. But first, he'd have Tom Thackery loaded in a prison cart and hauled off to jail. Aye, he'd hang with the rest of the pack, but in the meantime, let Thackery mull over his fate. *And when the devils from Hades come to seize him, we'll see if he still swears fealty to the Black Fox!*

He never looked back to see Moll Standish, mouth agape, staring after him.

Chapter Eleven

The bleating of sheep and the mooing of cows were the only sounds that broke the late afternoon hush as Anne dismounted in front of the Avery cottage. Her legs almost buckled when her booted feet touched the ground. Every bone in her body throbbed from the long day's ride, but she only had to glance about at the weary faces of the others to know they felt as bone tired as she.

Traveling ahead, Nat had already made the arrangements with the farmer's wife for their stay and awaited their arrival at the half-timbered barn. While Nat spoke with the king, she stole a glance at the man who stirred her so to distraction. Nat's sun-bronzed face, preoccupied with strategy, looked devilishly handsome. Her gaze lingered on his rich chestnut hair. A careless lock fell across his forehead and he mindlessly raked it back in a familiar gesture that warmed her heart.

His dark eyes met hers unexpectedly and her heart jolted. She gave a little smile, hoping he wouldn't shut her out for the short time that remained for them.

She felt further rewarded when he returned a faint smile. Suddenly she was filled with hope. If only he would talk to her of his feelings about his father, surely she could help him understand how useless it was to carry his father's burden. But would he grant her the chance to speak to him?

Two baying hounds interrupted Anne's reverie. The animals lumbered down the cottage steps, followed by a thickly set woman with a crying babe in each arm, a youngster yanking at her apron and another toddler hanging from her skirts. After introducing herself, Mrs. Avery cheerfully showed them their quarters.

Wilkens led the horses to the barn where he would spend the night. Anne agreed to share a chamber with three of the Averys' young daughters. Doc and Will Jackson shared a tiny room behind the kitchen. Nat chose to lodge at the woodcutter's shed in the woods behind the wash hut. Anne knew Nat had picked the outbuilding to be as far away from her as possible.

When Anne offered to assist with the meal, Mrs. Avery gratefully accepted the help and the company. Inside the cottage a calico cat preened itself before the crackling fire. A Bible lay open upon a tall, polished oak stand, out of reach of little hands. The shiny plank floor, the faint odor of beeswax, and a spinning wheel surrounded by baskets of fluffy wool caused a faint stirring of envy as Anne realized, again, that if she were unable to convince Nat to leave England, she would never know the pleasure of providing a home and children for the man she loved.

After supper, Anne welcomed the woman's generous offer of a bath. By the time she had finished washing out her only change of clothing and spreading the garments across a rack in front of the roaring fireplace in the washing hut, Anne had decided what she would say to Nat to convince him to leave with her for France.

By the time she had finished her bath, towel-dried her freshly washed hair and changed into the blue woolen gown Mrs. Avery had let her borrow until her clothing dried, she had committed her speech to memory. With a fortifying breath, she pulled the hut's door open and went to find Nat.

Sunlight filtered through the lacy foliage overhead, dappling the forest trail with glints of gold. The bouquet of freshly split cherry pervaded the air. Her stomach tightened as she heard the crack of wood rending the September stillness. She knew she was near where Nat would be splitting firewood.

Her blood pounded when the granite shed came into view. The door was ajar. She steadied herself against the cool bark

of a linden tree and swallowed back the strangle of fear
when she realized what was at stake. No, she had no time to
think of failure. She must gather her wits and concentrate
on being the most persuasive she knew how to be.

The verdant moss felt springy beneath her slippered feet
as she crept closer to the shed. Stepping upon the worn
granite step, she hesitated a moment and peeked inside. She
could see Nat's shadow flash across the inside wall as each
sharp crack rent the air. She took a deep breath and tried to
swallow.

The sound stopped. Ignoring her skipping heartbeat, she
stepped inside the open door. Nat's naked back was to her.
A breath caught in her throat at the sight. His broad muscular shoulders glistened with sweat as the sunlight slanted
through the broken slats of the shuttered windows, bathing
him in light. He bent to lift an armful of wood and his
powerful arm muscles bulged from the weight as he carried
it to a tall pile in the opposite corner, stacking it neatly. He
stood up, then yanked a white rag that had been loosely
wrapped around his waist and wiped his face, neck and chest
with it.

Watching him, she remembered the first time she had seen
him without his shirt—the night they shared the same
room—at the Pied Bull Inn. But unlike that night, when she
had been too embarrassed with their closeness to study him,
now she gazed as if she could never get her fill of the sight
of him. He was truly a beautiful man. Dark thick hair curled
down along his neck as the dampness shone on his deeply
tanned body. He straightened and, without looking, tied the
linen back around his narrow waist, fastening it loosely at
the band of his breeches.

He casually lifted an arm and she saw a muscle flex when
he pulled a chestnut lock from his face, the dark hair along
his tanned arms glistening in the sunlight.

Longing swelled within her.

Nat swung the ax, arcing it over his head. With a powerful thrust, he drove it into the wood, splitting it in two with
a loud crack. A strange feeling came over her. She swallowed, chastising herself for her sensual thoughts and re-

minded herself of her purpose. Blushing, she forced her eyes away.

His shirt and leather vest lay in a careless heap across his saddlebags. A blanket, water pail and jug stood nearby.

"What are you doing here?" Nat's sharp voice startled her.

Their eyes met. Suddenly she felt dwarfed by his towering size. "I—I came to ask you, I mean, to tell you something." She brushed her damp palms against the soft folds of her gown.

Nat leaned the ax against a stack of wood. Pulling the linen from his waist, he dipped it in the water pail, wrung it out and wiped his face and neck with it. "You shouldn't be here. It's not proper."

"Not proper?" She threw her shoulders back indignantly.

"Don't act all innocence with me. You know what I mean." In one long stride, he moved to where his shirt lay and picked it up. "What would Mrs. Avery think if she knew you were with me?"

"Mrs. Avery does know! She told me where to find you."

"Then ask me what you must, then leave."

"Nat," she began, her mind spinning as she tried to remember her rehearsed speech. She took a deep breath. "Nat," she repeated, commanding the fluttery feeling in her stomach to quell. "I must tell you how sorry I—"

"I know." He picked up another log, balanced it, then stepped back. "There's no need to say anything." He swung the ax, cracking the chunk in two.

"You don't understand." Exasperation, frustration and confusion chased her composure. She planted her fists on her hips. "Nat, look at me!"

He narrowed his eyes in warning. "I know what you've come to say, and it's not necessary. Now leave." His voice whispered in desperate longing, betraying the stern face he tried to present. Her heart filled with despair.

She moved toward the door, then stopped. "I'll leave when I've finished what I've come to say."

She heard the imprecation under his breath, but she ignored it, staring at the door. "I only wish to say that I understand why you believe it's important to remain in England..." Her memorized words were returning, as long as she didn't look at him. "In order to succeed with your mission to..." She peeked at him over her shoulder, feeling hopeful.

He leaned against the stack of wood, his arms folded across his chest, a dark scowl on his face as he studied her.

She took in a shaky breath and glanced away. "To save our king. And I'm so sorry for my childish behavior this morning on the hill..." She felt the flush of warmth spread up her neck and face as she remembered their kiss and her unbridled response to him. She shot a glance at him, wondering if he remembered it, as well. Her blush flamed when she saw the spark of reluctant humor in his eyes.

She wiped her moist palms along the folds of her skirt, again. "I understand your duty, Nat," she concluded, "and I'm asking your forgiveness for my behavior."

"I accept your apology. Now, leave."

"And...and for all the problems that I've caused..." She couldn't leave now! Her mind whirled as she repeated her speech. "That I've caused, to you, to Tom and..." *Damn him. Nothing was going right!*

She whirled back to face him. "And to ask you something."

He put on his shirt, his eyes never leaving hers. With a lift of a dark brow, Nat gave her a look that said, finally we're getting down to the matter.

She moved to within a foot of him. His male scent, combined with the smell of freshly splintered wood and the autumn afternoon unsettled her, but she made herself meet his gaze. "When the king and my father and I are safely boarded for France..." Her gaze lingered on the familiar curve of his mouth, the well-known line between his brows when he frowned down at her like that, and her heart lurched. "Will you...?" She didn't recognize her own voice. "Will you...?" She wanted to reach out and touch the fine scar along his cheek. "Come with us? You can continue to raise money to restore the king in France as well as England."

Only a flicker of surprise crossed his face. It disappeared as quickly as it came. Waiting, she held her breath. How had she asked him? She couldn't even remember her words.

Finally his eyes shifted to the floor. Then he moved to the open window, his broad back to her as he braced himself against the window frame with his outstretched arm.

Recovering her composure somewhat, Anne followed him. How she wanted to touch him, to feel the sun upon his face. "Please, Nat, you must leave with us. If Twining discovers it was you who helped the king escape, he'll never rest until you're hanged."

Nat stared out the window, his face expressionless. She reached out and touched the dark stubble at his chin.

He flinched, as though her touch set off a charge. "It's impossible." He turned and strode to where his vest lay atop the saddlebags, giving it a hard shake before putting it on.

"Why is it impossible?"

"Because if I remain, I can help crumble Cromwell's grip on England. It will take soldiers and munitions, and that takes money." He gave her a sharp look. "Since our loss at Worcester, the Scots won't help us again."

"But you can raise money on the Continent. France's coffers are so much larger than England's, and Louis XIV is the king's cousin. Surely, you can convince Louis to help the cause."

His dark gaze softened. "Young Louis has his own money worries, my pet."

Nat was the most stubborn man! How could she convince him? "Uncle George has always said Spain is rich," she said in her most persuasive tone. "You could seek King Philip's help," she added.

"Besides the fact that Louis is at war with Spain, and that keeps Philip's coffers thin, it's the family link between Louis and Charles Stuart that keeps Spain from aiding the king's cause." He looked at her thoughtfully. "As the Black Fox, I can raise money for the king by depleting Cromwell's coffers. Two birds with one volley, you might say." His mouth twisted wryly. "But that won't happen if I leave England."

"It won't happen if you're dead!" Fear swept through her at the real fear she might lose him forever.

He said nothing. But those unfathomable brown eyes held her and she felt his pain. Finally he tossed the blanket across the saddlebags, then squatted cross-legged beside them. He glanced back at the golden forest outside the window.

Dear God, she didn't come here to quarrel. Anne knelt in front of him on the edge of the blanket. Her voice grew soft. "I—I can't bear it if something were to happen to you."

His eyes smoldered with the desire she had hoped to see, and for a moment she thought he might kiss her. She only knew she wanted him to.

Instead, he took her hand in his rough palm and lightly brushed her fingertips across his lips. "Try and understand, my Anne. I have a debt to repay. A debt of my father's making."

"I know." She saw surprise light his eyes. "I pleaded with Doc to tell me what drives you. I needed to understand. He explained what your father did to your aunt Bridget's family." She blinked back the tears that stung her eyes at the memory. "But God help me, I still don't understand you."

His thick eyelashes lowered, shielding the struggle she knew mirrored in his eyes. She swallowed the hard lump in her throat.

He refused to look at her, then slowly his brown eyes met hers. "Did Doc tell you what my father did was because of *me?*"

"What do you mean?" Anne leaned closer.

"My father felt that Bridget was responsible for proving that he had seduced my mother. When my grandfather discovered my father had lied to him—a much more serious affront than debauching a maidservant—my father was disinherited."

"Was Bridget responsible?"

He shrugged. "In seducing my mother, my father had written her love poems, not knowing she couldn't read." His mouth twisted in irony. "My mother, ashamed to admit it, asked Bridget to read them to her, without revealing the man who gave them to her.'' He shook his head in disgust. ''Bridget recognized my father's handwriting. He had merely copied the poems of the Cavalier poets. She showed the evidence to my grandfather.''

''What happened then?''

''My father swore vengeance against Bridget, then fled to join Cromwell's campaign against the Irish.'' His voice lowered. ''He'd been gone for almost a year before we learned the extent of his revenge.'' Nat's voice tightened with emotion. ''I was only eleven years old, Anne, but I'll remember that day as long as I live. A rider arrived with a letter. Later, Bridget and my uncle Alex called everyone into the great hall. Framed by their loyal staff from her ancestral home in Ireland, my aunt read the letter, her words as solemn as when she said her rosary.''

Anne saw the anguish twist his face. Remembering Doc's words when he told her of Nigel Adam's cold-blooded assault against Bridget's ancestral home, the slaughter of innocents, her voice caught and she was unable to speak.

She brushed his cheek with her fingertips. He clenched her hand in his, and kissed it briefly before he continued.

''Only Bridget remained dry-eyed. She rose from her chair, the letter drifting to the floor. I ran and picked it up, but she said, 'Throw it in the fire, Nat. What's done is done. We can't bring them back.' Then she gazed down at me. As young as I was, I knew that if I hadn't been born, Bridget's family in Ireland would still be alive.''

Anne shut her eyes to his pain. But she couldn't blot out the image of a small dark-haired boy with huge, sad brown eyes, who believed he was the cause of such carnage.

''Bridget must have seen my remorse, for she bent down and kissed my cheek. 'It'll be all right, wee laddie,' she whispered in her soft brogue.''

Anne's voice choked with empathy. ''What did your uncle do?''

''Alex vowed to do everything in his power to make it up to her. From that day, my uncle, from his seat in Parliament, covertly aided the king's cause in every way he could.

Bridget and their daughter, Jane, worked day and night aiding the Royalists against Cromwell. Bridget and Jane, as a loyal Parliamentarian's wife and daughter, had the perfect cover." He squeezed her hand gently. "When Parliament beheaded King Charles, Alex retired. He never fully recovered from that." Nat drew his gaze away. "He died soon after."

Anne wondered about Nat's father, but she hesitated to ask. Finally, as though sensing her question, he said, "My father spent the remainder of the war risking his life in the most daring way. A more heartless soldier never rode with Cromwell."

Maybe he had hoped he would be killed, Anne thought, but she said nothing.

"I enrolled in Oxford, but after a year, I left to travel abroad. While in France, I was held up by a highwayman outside a small inn near Marseilles. I had only a few sous. He felt sorry for me and gave me a twenty franc gold piece. It was that night I knew what I wanted to do with the rest of my life. With the money from the robber, I booked passage the next day for home.

"When I returned to England, I found out my father had died of a fever. Things were very bad in England. It was the second year of the drought and famine was everywhere. Roundheads fought with the poor, overtaxing them.

"With Tom, Doc Herrick, and a few men I could trust, I took to the highways, using the gain to feed the hungry and help the Royalists' cause."

And the Black Fox did what he could to make up for his father's crimes, Anne thought to herself. Her eyes blurred with tears. How she longed to comfort him, to soothe away his pain.

Nat turned and he tenderly brushed a tear from her cheek. "Now, do you understand?"

With a finger, she gently lifted the dark silk of his hair from his forehead and pressed her lips in a chaste kiss to his brow. Shifting back, she saw a strange expression in his eyes.

"I don't want your pity, Anne." She saw his mouth twitch, then his eyes darkened as his gaze fell to her mouth.

Her hand trembled as she touched his lips. "It's not pity I want to give you," she said, her voice quavering.

"Don't do this, Anne," his voice rasped.

But she couldn't leave without showing him how much she cared. *Maybe, if he knew, it might change his mind.* He was only inches from her. Bolder this time, she leaned forward and brushed her lips along his ear, then traced a trail of tiny kisses across each crevice.

His eyes remained closed. He barely breathed.

She leaned down and delicately traced her tongue along his mouth, teasing his lips open with tiny flicks of her tongue.

He pushed her away. "Bloody hell! Do you know what you're doing?" His dark hair hung tousled about his sun-bronzed face, and his dark velvet eyes smoldered with something she could sense but didn't understand.

"I only want to kiss you."

"Merciful God!" He drew an unsteady breath.

"A farewell kiss." She pouted and leaned closer. "What harm can that do?"

He squeezed his eyes shut and leaned back against the saddlebags. "Go back to the cottage," he whispered hoarsely.

Anne sat back on her knees. "Very well, I will!" But before she did, she would make him confess that he cared for her as much as she knew he did. When he finally admitted it, if only to himself, maybe he'd find another way to help ease what his father had done. Then he'd leave England, while he had the chance, and they could be together, forever.

Bracing her hands against the floor, she leaned over him. "Farewell, Nat." She lowered her mouth to his.

When she felt his shuddering breath and pounding heartbeat, she knew she had almost won. But when she felt his hands claim her waist, pulling her down against him, it was her own muffled cry that surprised her.

His lips moved on hers, demanding and possessing. He shifted, rolling her down on her back, his mouth never

leaving hers as their kiss deepened, stirring a greater need in
her than the last time he kissed her.

She moaned and brought her arms around his neck. She
trembled as his mouth became more seeking, more possessive. Unaware of the effect she had on him, she timidly slid
the tip of her tongue to meet his, her only thought to pleasure him back with the same tingling delight he gave her. She
never expected the tumult of passion she would release as his
tongue tangled in hers. A groan of pleasure escaped him as
he pulled his mouth from hers, moving his lips over her
cheek, along her ear.

"How can I let you go?" he growled, the words lifting her
beyond her wildest dreams. He raised his head, and she
suffered a pang of frustration when he pulled back from her.
She tightened her hands behind his neck, wanting more.

"I can't get enough of you," he moaned as his hands
moved restlessly across the front of her gown. She gasped
when his fingers fumbled with the ribbon fasteners along the
opening of her bodice. In the next moment, she felt his callused fingers against her bare breast. She trembled with
pleasure as his hand cupped and stroked her delicate rosy
nipple with exquisite tenderness.

Desire exploded in her as his fingertips lightly flicked back
and forth against the sensitive tip. "My Anne." His eyes
darkened with desire. He caught the hardened bud between
his fingers, rolling it between them, as she moaned with desire.

She gazed into his handsome face, his eyes drugged with
longing. She released her hands from behind the dark silk
at his nape, her fingers trailing along his broad shoulders,
to rest on his muscled arms. "You're the most beautiful man
I've ever seen," she said, smiling up at him.

His mouth twisted in pleasure. Watching him, she shivered in delight as he lowered his head. But she had no way
to anticipate the shock of quivering sensation that burst
through her when his lips caressed her sensitized breasts.

Her fingers curved into his muscled forearms, her senses
reeling. Just when she thought she would die of pleasure, his
lips closed around the sensitive tip, pulling gently, then eas-

ing, then drawing hard on it. The thrill caused Anne to arch and writhe beneath him.

He paused and regarded her, drinking in every detail.

Her hair tumbled back across the soft blanket he had carelessly thrown on the floor when she lifted her face to him. "Don't stop," she begged. "Please..." She pulled herself up against him. She felt him shudder.

"You've bewitched me," he whispered in her ear, his voice husky as he buried his face in the silken tangle of her walnut colored hair. "God help me, but I want you so."

Anne's eyes opened to meet his, and she saw the desire rage against something she didn't understand. "And I want you," she said, hoping the knowledge of her need would quench his torment.

"My darling Anne." The words tore with the beating of his heart. "Not like this—"

"Aye, like this," she finished, and put his hand on her heart. "Before I leave, I need to know what it feels like to be loved by you."

"You don't know what you're asking." The fires of conflict raged in his eyes. "This isn't right."

Her finger brushed back the dark lock of hair from his brow. "But it feels right," she whispered, "and...I love you."

The muscle in his cheek softened as he smiled at her. He stroked the line of her jaw. "You're so incredibly sweet and innocent." His loving glance swept her face. "Let me try to explain." His voice thickened with passion.

"You have a gift, my darling," he said unsteadily. "A gift to give for one time only...." His fingers trailed along her cheek. "And I'm cursed not to be the man who can have it."

"You'll always be that man, my love." Her gaze fell to his mouth and her lips parted. "I'll never love anyone but you."

Nat pulled her to him, muttering thickly against her ear, his words tangled in her hair. "And you'll always be the woman who'll own my heart."

A feeling of intense joy shimmered through her. She cupped his face with her hands. His brown eyes, torn with the battle within him, gazed hungrily back at her. Then his dark lashes lowered, casting spiky shadows on his cheek-bones.

Please don't be at war with this wondrous thing between us, she wanted to say. Instead, she whispered, "Take my gift, my love." Her voice sounded husky, uneven. "And never has a woman offered it more willingly."

He lost control. His mouth came down hard on hers, and she felt the indescribable urgency of his desire.

He kissed her endlessly, his tongue coaxing, exploring. She wanted to shower him with the same return of desire, but she didn't know how. Her tongue followed his teachings with the gentle plunging and retreating again and again, but when their mouths formed the forbidden rhythm it was *she* who felt the urgency of passion explode wildly within her.

His hands slid possessively along her spine, her breasts, moving across her back, pressing her to his hardened length. Anne felt herself plummet into a strange whirl of awakening sensuality. She clung to him, aware of the primal calling but unsure of how to answer its urging.

His hard, muscled arms surrounded her, cradling. Then he scooped her up and carried her to the other side of the room. A soft moan of surrender escaped her lips as he laid her gently down upon the narrow bed

Chapter Twelve

Anne felt cool air touch her shoulders and legs, and her eyelids fluttered open. Above the cot, sunlight slanted through the shuttered window, bathing the narrow bed in autumn gold. Birds chirped melodiously from the lacy branches outside.

Nat knelt over her. A tumble of sun-burnished hair fell down over his forehead as his fingers unfastened the waistband of his breeches. His shirt was opened to the waist, the laces loose and dangling down in front. He yanked off the linen shirt, revealing the powerful lines of his tanned shoulders and arms.

Her skirts fell in disarray beneath him. Modestly she tucked her feet up under her skirts, their eyes fixed upon each other all the while.

Anne felt mesmerized by his raw masculinity and primitive drive. She swallowed back a sigh of self-conscious admiration at how splendid he was. Splendid and unsettling at the same time.

Shyly she reached out to him, her fingers brushing the heat of his skin. His large hand clamped over hers, moving her fingers across the wiry dark thatch covering his muscular chest to finally rest at the hard beating of his heart.

Nat trembled beneath her feathery touch. Gazing down at her, he thought she had never looked more beautiful. Passion heightened her natural coloring, blossoming her cheeks into pink roses. He kissed her fingertips and released her hand while he filled his palms with her soft lustrous hair. Its fragrance reminded him of a meadow of violets. God, how he ached for her.

She raised her arms about his neck, her soft fingers twining gently into the hair at his nape. He thrilled to her delicate touch.

Damn his soul, but he needed to have her. God knows he had tried to resist her, but she awakened such need in him that no other woman could ever satisfy him. He was possessed by her, and all he knew was that when she was in his arms, nothing else mattered, nothing in the past or in the future.

He stroked her back from under the tangle of her hair, her silken skin warm and exciting. Gently his fingers played with the ribbons, finally releasing the soft folds of her gown, baring her breasts. He felt her shiver beneath his fingers. Slowly he lowered his lips to the rosy nipple, teasing it with his tongue. This time, she arched with need. He flamed at her unbridled response to him.

"It's all right, love. There's much, much more. I want you to enjoy what I do to you." His tongue trailed across her breasts, the nipples hardening at his touch. Her arms tightened around his neck, drawing him closer. His mouth took hers with a passionate urgency that plummeted them into the fleeting world possessed only by lovers.

"Nat." Her voice, shaky with passion, spoke his name as if it were a song.

"Not yet, love," he whispered hoarsely as his tongue played, nibbled, dallied, while his hands teased, fondled, stroked. From her breasts, down across her flat stomach to the waistband of her underskirts, his fingers worshiped her. Her skin's fragrance reminded him of a meadow after an April rain.

His hand slid downward to the junction between her thighs. "I've dreamed of this, Anne. So many, many times." His breath mingled with hers as their mouths hungered for each other. He could feel her heart thundering beneath her breast, her breath quickening to match his own.

She arched against him, instantly becoming conscious of a burning heat spreading languidly up through her body.

Delirious with need, she squirmed and writhed beneath him, wanting more but not knowing exactly what that might be. "Please, my dearest," she cried out, her fingers pressing into his shoulders.

"Are you certain, my darling?" His voice was ragged.

She nodded, her eyes wide with trust. She had only thought she knew what to expect. She felt on the brink of a wide chasm, but she wouldn't be afraid because he was there with her. Aye, she was ready to offer whatever he willed of her, for if this was to be their only time together, then she needed to give whatever could be given. She opened for him, lost in a sea of sensations.

"I don't want to hurt you..." His voice was unsteady. "But the first time will hurt a bit." His fingers found her moist and hot. When he touched her there, she cried out, her back arching. "Don't be frightened," he whispered against her mouth. "I'll be as gentle as I can." He kissed her deeply, then lifted his mouth from hers to gaze into her eyes. He could see, mirrored in their blue-green depths, all of the confusion, desperation and wild urgency he knew she felt.

He was between her legs. She felt him pressing against her, huge and hard.

"Don't be afraid, love." He stroked her gently, caressing her, arousing her to madness. She pushed up against his probing fingers, demanding more. She was drunk with his kisses, the warm male scent of his body, the sure hands that made her ache with desperation. She surged up again. She felt him move slightly and widen her for himself. Breathless, she felt him come into her and without realizing it, lifted her hips, offering herself more fully to him.

He groaned, closing his eyes for a moment, and arched his back. "I wish I could take the pain for you..." The words were raw. He plunged forward, the small maidenhead detaining him for but an instant before tearing.

Anne cried out, caught by surprise, and clung to him. He thrust again. Drawing a stabbing breath, he shuddered as she trembled beneath him. He held still, letting her body accept him, holding his own passion in check to wait for her.

When he finally started to move slowly, she shivered. Her aquamarine eyes blazed with passion, fanning the fires within his soul.

"Easy, my Anne, let me love you." A soft moan of pleasure escaped her. He knew her pain eased and he began the slow, deep strokes. Sliding upward and withdrawing, repeating deeper each time, he could barely contain the forces racing through him.

His thrusts flamed a hungry desperation that was nothing like Anne had ever imagined. She matched his rhythm, instinct and love guiding her. Filled with his pulsing heat, she felt the wild and primitive building that flamed as he thrust into her. Suddenly the exquisite pleasure exploded, rapture tearing his name from her lips.

Nat drove, pouring himself into her, overwhelmed at the full force of his passion. His body racked again and again, as he coupled her, her name a broken cry against her cheek. His heart thundered in ecstasy with hers until the last of his release burst into her.

Several minutes later, Anne, still dazed from reality, was only dimly aware when he slid from her. She caressed his face with fingers that felt weak and trembly.

Nat lifted his head from her tangled hair and closed his eyes. "I should have been stronger, but I wanted you so much."

"And I wanted you, as well." She smiled up at him, aware that his hand still cupped her breast. "Never could I have dreamed of such as what you gave me." She pulled herself up to kiss his lips, and his mouth took hers again. She felt him shudder and a thrill blossomed within her at the realization of her feminine power over him.

Anne's heart hammered with joy. Never had she believed she could ever be so deliriously content. She curled her fingers in the thick hair at the nape of his neck. "We'll be so happy in France, my love."

He stiffened and pulled back enough to see her face. "What do you mean?"

She smiled beautifully at him. "Don't tease me. You know what I mean." Her fingers twisted the hair at his nape.

Nat stared back at her. She saw not the ecstatic look of wonder that she had expected, but the dark, tortured look of remorse. He shut his eyes, as though tormented by the sight of her.

"I'd give anything to undo this."

"Undo what? What's the matter?"

Nat arched back and sat up on his knees, staring down at her while he pulled at the lacings at his breeches. "I thought you understood." He reached for his shirt, pulled it over his head and stuffed the ends inside his trousers, not bothering to fasten the ties. "You know I want to be with you," he whispered, "but I thought I made it clear that I can never leave England."

Confused, her mind raced with denial. She pulled herself up, straightening her skirts about her. Her fingers twisted at the ribbons of the gathers at her neckline. "But I thought..." A crushing emptiness quaked through her at how foolish she had been to think she might have changed his mind.

"I couldn't have you leaving me, thinking I wanted you to go." Pain and sadness etched his magnificent dark eyes.

"But Nat, don't you see?" She sat up, straightening the bodice of her gown, retying the crushed ribbons. "Cromwell won't be stopped. I overheard Wilkens tell Doc this morning that the people might offer him the crown."

"Nay." Nat stiffened, getting to his feet. "The people will never forget their sovereign. Nor will I."

"But Doc said Cromwell is grooming his son to succeed him, and it may be years before the monarchy is restored."

"Doc and Wilkens have the right to think their own opinions." He gave her an icy look as he rolled up his sleeves. "I won't stop working for the cause until the Roundheads are destroyed, regardless how long it takes."

"But Twining will run you down until..." Tears choked her words and at that moment, she hated him for being so noble. Angrily she dabbed at her tears with the hem of her gown. "What's so noble about hanging like a common rogue?" she cried.

His mouth twisted slightly. "I *am* a common rogue."

Tears spilled down her cheeks before she could stop them. "Nat, are you so blind that you can't see?" She swiped at her eyes. "You're not just destroying Cromwell's armies. You're trying to destroy your father, as well."

He glared at her as though she had slapped him. Then he grabbed the blanket and saddlebags and strode toward the door.

She immediately regretted her words. "Nat, I'm sorry." She went to him, pressing her head to his chest. "I didn't mean it." She felt his heart hammer beneath the heat of his shirt.

He lifted her chin and she saw love shining from his eyes. "My Anne, of course I know why you want me to leave England." He pulled her head against his chest, his fingers crushing the tangle of her hair. "And I'll always love you for that."

"Then d-don't send m-me away," she pleaded. "I—I'll never love another. I'll never get married. I'll—"

"My precious Anne." He stepped back and held her at arm's length. To see the glaze of pain in her eyes was like a dirk in his heart. If only she'd remain angry. Lash out at him. It would be so much easier. His throat constricted with emotion. "Always remember, I love you."

A sob wrenched her as she collapsed against his chest. He cradled her face with his hands and kissed her lips gently. "But if I left England with you, I'd always know that I ran away from my duty. You'd come to hate me for it."

"Never, my love. I could never hate you."

"You'd come to hate me because I'd hate myself." Nat placed his hands on her arms. She stood limply, tears streaming down her cheeks. "You're so beautiful. You've a life of happiness ahead of you."

Anne shook her head. "N-no, not without you."

"Aye, because of me." His eyes held such adoration it took her breath away. "Our love will give you strength." He tensed his grip on her arms. "Our love will help you to be brave."

She shook her head, overcome with despair. "No, I can't live without you."

"You must, Anne. Because that's what will sustain me in the days ahead. I'll have my memory of you and that, my heart, will keep me strong. You must do it for me."

Anne's fist tore to her mouth. "I'm not noble like you. I don't want to live if...if I thought I'd never see you again."

"You *are* noble. I've never known a woman as courageous, determined, or as strong. Remember your father, your duty to him. He's waiting for you." His words were as much a reminder to himself as to her. He gazed at the silver tears glistening her eyes. Her long, spiked eyelashes, the fiery highlights burnishing the walnut hair tumbling down along her shoulders.

"It's late. You should be getting back to your chamber. Tomorrow, we'll act as though this never happened. Try and forget—" His voice broke as he let go of her hands, then he turned and strode out the door.

A circle of leaves whirled outside the woodcutter's shed, spinning upward in the early morning light like golden doves winging to heaven. From the window above his bed, Nat watched their ascent—higher, higher—until a sudden gust, like an invisible finger, scolded them back to earth, as though reminding them of their place in the scheme of things.

Nat tossed aside the coarsely woven blanket and rose from the bed. He moved to the shed door and opened it. The smell of wood smoke hung heavily in the damp mist. He studied the gray sky. Last night's rain had dwindled to a mist, thank God. They'd reach Rosemoor by late day if only the rain held off.

His hand scratched the rough stubble along his cheek as he remembered last night when he had left Anne. After rubbing down the horses for the night, he had walked along the split stone fence toward the washhouse to shave and take a bath when he caught a glimpse of Anne in the garden. She sat beneath the rose bower, her head bowed over the Averys' baby. She wept softly as she rocked the sleeping infant in her arms.

A fresh stab of remorse washed over him as he remembered listening to her muffled cries. How he had wanted to take her in his arms, kiss the red-rimmed eyes that glittered with tears and somehow undo the pain he had caused her. Instead, he had turned and walked away. A gold leaf swirled down in front of him. He felt another tug at his soul as he was reminded of his place in the scheme of things.

Very little was spoken between Anne and the men while they saddled their horses and prepared for the last full day's ride before arriving at Rosemoor. Anne rode on the pillion behind Nat. Only the raw wind in her face and the thud of Shadow's hooves beneath her gave testimony of her numbed senses. She felt mercifully lifeless, and she hoped she would never feel again.

She read Nat's own sorrow in the tight-lipped silence, the rigid line of his back as she rode behind him.

At the first rest, several hours later, Nat reined in the horse, swung his leg over the pommel, then helped Anne dismount. Before she could gather her thoughts to speak them, he turned away from her to confer with the others.

Anne watched him walk away from her across the clearing, feeling unaccountably lonely at the small desertion. Tears threatened her and she wanted to run away, to hide, to give in to them, but she needed to be close to him, as well. She hungered for each precious minute they had together. On shaky legs, she willed back the tears. Her gaze remained fixed on him as he crossed his arms in front of his chest with that commanding presence he assumed so easily when he spoke to the men. The breeze ruffled his dark hair, and when he raked back the errant lock in that familiar way, she felt a fresh threat of tears.

As though he felt her watching him, Nat turned and his dark gaze caught hers. For a moment, she saw something that fueled a hope...then, he glanced away. It was only folly that kindled the fancy that he might change his mind. A rush of anguish jolted the breath from her. Aye, she could feel, after all.

Damn, would he never be rid of this anguish? After Nat had braced himself against his inevitable reaction to her, his fingers only had to touch her as he lifted her from the pillion and he was filled with an incredible urgency to sweep her into his arms, hold her and comfort her with his loving.

And he almost did....

My lovely, beguiling Anne, how I want you!

But she wasn't his. She never could be, and the sooner he put an end to the tormenting idea, the better. She would be leaving, and somehow, he must find the strength to let go. Let go of his feelings. Let go of his memories. Let go of his love.

He shuddered as the plea twisted his soul, coiling and pressing until he could barely breathe.

But it was useless to lecture himself. He would forever hear her laughter like the tinkling crystal chandelier in the great hall at Rosemoor. Or forever see her changeable blue-green eyes defiantly sparkle at him each time he gazed at the morning sunlight upon the dew-kissed grass.

But he never wanted to forget how her warm, sweet passion flamed beneath him, and he felt his steel will shatter and blow away as easily as a whirl of gold September leaves.

The soft shuffle of Doc's boot steps upon the damp, pungent earth forced Nat's attention back to the task at hand. He grabbed a handful of dried grass, twisted it into a loop and, with long motions, rubbed Shadow's black satiny coat with it.

"Want me to work down the other side?" Doc's wide-brimmed black hat hung heavily with mist and obscured his face, but Nat didn't have to see his friend's expression to know that the real reason he had come was to ask what was troubling him.

Nat shook his head, not missing a stroke along Shadow's shiny haunches. "Help yourself to the brandy from the saddlebags. It will take a bite off the dampness."

Doc nodded and, after removing the flask, took a swig. He made a face, then handed the container to Nat.

Nat threw the twist of grass down at his feet, took several healthy gulps and gave the flagon back to Doc.

"Trying to drown your sorrows?" Doc asked lightly, throwing a leg over a mossy stump and sitting down.

Nat wiped his mouth with the back of his hand. "Nay, teaching them to swim."

Doc chuckled softly, but the gentle hazel eyes appeared concerned. "I thought you might want to talk."

Nat grabbed another fistful of weeds, twisting them in his tanned fingers as he stared across the gently rolling valley. "Ah, Doc. You know me too well." He sighed. "At least I'll be comforted to know she'll be with her father. After a time, she'll forget all about me."

They sat listening to the squirrels high in the treetops rustle the coppery chestnut leaves. Finally Doc spoke. "Anne will never forget you, Nat." He shoved his hat back from his forehead, his eyes fixed steadily on Nat. "We never forget our first love, regardless of the happiness we find later with someone else." His voice was tight, caught in his throat, and Nat knew Doc was referring to the loss of his first wife.

"A bastard rogue with a price on his head could never give a woman like Anne the life she deserved," he said, his voice a hoarse whisper.

Doc's fingers traced the leather brandy flask in a helpless gesture. "You're only human, Nat," he said without glancing up.

"Nevertheless, I should have kept away from her...." Nat squeezed his eyes shut from the reality.

Doc sighed and glanced to where Anne rested, her dark head bowed. "I wish there was something I could do...." He shrugged and got to his feet. "But I'm afraid there's no easy way out, my friend." Doc's sympathetic gaze shifted back to Nat. "Would it help if Anne rode with me?"

"Nay." Nat jabbed at another hank of grass. "Thanks, but ... I'm not up to having her anywhere but by my side."

Doc nodded with understanding before he strode back down the hill to the others. In the short time it had taken Doc to offer a fortifying portion of brandy to the king and Wilkens and return the flask to the saddlebags, he noticed that Nat was approaching the leafy spot beneath the grove of chestnuts where Anne rested.

A slight smile lifted the corners of Doc's mouth and he hurriedly retraced his way along the path toward where the men waited. At least he could provide a few minutes of privacy for the young lovers, he mused. It might be the only happiness they find, he thought sadly.

Anne had finished braiding her long thick hair into a single plait when she recognized Nat's boot steps upon the damp carpet of leaves behind her. She would recognize his step in the black of night for as long as she lived. Although she braced herself, her breath caught when he came up beside her.

"May I have a word with you, Anne?" His expression was unreadable, but the naked anguish in his voice was unmistakable.

Anne's hand fumbled with the coarse braid at her breast. "Aye, of course," she whispered.

He turned the full force of his deep brown eyes on her. She was taken aback again by how handsome he was. The damp mist curled his dark hair in loose waves that brushed the collar of his cape. Despite the bone-weary ride, his deeply tanned face showed no sign of the fatigue she knew he must be feeling.

"I was thinking..." Nat dropped his gaze, and the thick black lashes obscured the tormented expression in his eyes.

He was a few inches from her and she could feel his heat and smell the arousing woodsy scent of him.

"Thinking what?" she urged, hopeful of what had brought him to seek her out after his previous detachment. When their eyes finally met again, the dark velvet depths clung to hers in such silent pleading, it nearly took her breath away.

Afraid to move, she stood silently. The only sound was the low rustling of the wind through the trees. She felt her blood stir and she trembled, hoping he hadn't noticed. In his torn gaze, she recognized his genuine suffering was as deep as her own. For a brief moment, she forgot her own torment and wanted somehow only to keep him beside her and comfort him. Unable to think what to say, she reached out in a helpless gesture and touched his cheek.

As if waiting for her signal, he crushed her into his arms, his mouth frantically seeking hers. She was too stunned, too incredulous to react. But it took only a fleeting moment for her to cling to him, to cherish him for whatever precious time they might have.

He swung her around and lifted her up into the cradle of his powerful embrace. Her arms curled around his neck instinctively as he carried her to the shelter of shimmering poplars and laid her down upon his heavy woolen cape spread across the crush of gold and copper leaves.

She held fast to her grip around his neck, afraid suddenly that he might disappear as he did from her daydreams. He knelt above her, his darkly tanned face dappled by shadow, and she watched him in adoration. Aye, she wasn't dreaming. An aching lump in her throat grew as she recognized the molten passion in the cinder-dark depths of his eyes. At that moment, all she knew was that he needed to comfort her as she needed to comfort him, he wanted her as she wanted him, and for now, nothing else mattered.

Nat's strong hands were gentle when he pulled her back and began to unbraid the thick nut brown hair. "I love to see your shining curls tumble loose and wild about you," he whispered hoarsely, his eyes sensual and heavy lidded. Slowly his fingers unworked the thick, shining tresses and she thought she would die from wanting. She could feel his manhood strain against his leather breeches. Her heart pounded when he finally threaded his fingers through her unbound hair. "My darling Anne," he murmured, over and over in her ear as he came down, slanting his mouth over hers.

She closed her eyes, welcoming him as her mind fought back any thought except that she hungered to remain with him for as long as she could. She closed her eyes, welcoming his loving as it hammered away the anguish from her heart.

Chapter Thirteen

Church bells echoed throughout the hamlet the call to prayer. Nat shielded his eyes from the afternoon sun and studied the valley below. A few leagues beyond where the river twisted like silver rope through the wheat fields, stood Rosemoor. He climbed over the meadow gate and called to the waiting riders, "Only a few more hours and we'll be there." The men cheered and Anne's smile revealed the relief that he knew was in her heart. His relief would come when the king, Anne and her father sailed to France. He wanted so much more, but for the few precious hours left to them, he would treasure her and keep her safe.

"Anne and I will enter through the main entrance," Nat said to them. "Wilkens, let Anne ride your horse. Doc, you lead Wilkens and Mr. Jackson. Follow the river path until you come to the cave near the stream. Once inside, follow the tunnel that leads to the granary. Then send Wilkens to find Bridget and she'll come for you when it's safe."

Anne watched the men's excited faces, and she felt her exhilaration quicken. She had come so far for what this day held. Within hours, she would finally see her father. Her father. The man who had made everything better when she was little. Now, perhaps her father might do so again.

She would ask her father to convince Nat to give up his impossible quest and sail with them for France. Surely Nat would listen to reason from such a noble patriot as her father. Weren't they both hunted men, fleeing their land to gain strength to return another day and restore Charles Stuart to the throne?

Hope rose within her as each moment brought her closer to her final chance to save the man she loved from himself.

Later that same day, Anne rode up beside Nat and caught her first sight of the honey-colored limestone manor house of Rosemoor. The diamond-shaped panes in the triple rows of windows mirrored gold from the setting sun. Against the verdant hillside the house sparkled like a glittering jewel encased in flowing green velvet. "Rosemoor is exactly how I knew it would be," she exclaimed. "It's magnificent."

"Aye, it's that." The note of irony in his voice caused Anne to look at him. Suddenly she realized all he must be feeling. Besides the happiness at seeing his loving aunt Bridget, Nat would again face the painful reminder of his father's evil deeds.

She wanted to reach out and smooth away his ache. "I can hardly wait for my father to meet you," she said instead, smiling. "He'll be so proud to meet the Black Fox." Without waiting for his reply, Anne prodded her heels into the mare's side. "I'll race you," she called over her shoulder, forgetting her bone-weary, aching muscles. Her high-spirited laughter rang in the crisp air as she bolted ahead, the green turf flying past her. Nat tore after her. The sound of horses' hooves thundered along the cobbled road toward the main house.

"You let me win," she teased, catching her breath in short gasps when her mare arrived first at the steps a few minutes later. A horse's length ahead of Nat, she pivoted in the saddle to catch the innocent gleam in his laughing dark eyes.

Several grooms appeared, as though from nowhere. After they dismounted and the servants led the horses toward the stables, Anne brushed at the dust on her clothing, painfully aware of her soiled appearance. Nat squeezed her hand. "You look beautiful," he whispered, love shining from his deep brown eyes. His look of adoration restored her confidence.

"Let's hurry." Hand in hand, they raced up the steps. Before they reached the top, the black-lacquered portals creaked open and a plump servant woman beamed down at them.

"Peggy, tell the mistress we've arrived." At the sound of his voice, the maid's hands flew to her round face. "Saints be praised!" Nat swooped up the chubby maid in an affectionate hug.

After he had put her down, she swiped at her moist eyes with her fingertips. "Praise God! Wait till the mistress sees you."

The maid escorted them into the hall, above which arched a domed ceiling of robin's-egg blue, with oval medallions of ivory plasterwork. The stairs, of ebony wood, climbed to the first landing and disappeared behind the second-floor wall.

"Mistress Bridget and Mistress Jane are at the Wellingtons'," Peggy said, taking their capes. "They'll be back later tonight."

Anne noticed Nat's face tense, but he quickly recovered. "This is Mistress Anne. Show her to a chamber in the south wing, then have my room readied."

"We've been expectin' yer arrival, sire. Besides, yer room is always kept ready, Sire," Peggy answered brightly. "I'll light the fire an' send 'enry up directly."

From the devoted gaze on her motherly face, Anne knew the old servant was thrilled to have the young master home again.

"Where is Colonel Jonathan Lowell's chamber? Mistress Anne is eager to see her father."

Peggy's smile faded and she glanced toward Anne. "Aye, the colonel is finally sleeping after a fitful night—"

"He's improving, isn't he?" Anne felt a thread of worry.

"Aye, mistress. Yer father grows stronger each day."

"Thank God." Anne swallowed, her enthusiasm dampened. "Let him sleep, Peggy. "His rest is more important."

Peggy bobbed a curtsy, then hobbled off, her footsteps hushed along the thick maroon ribbed carpet.

Anne glanced wistfully toward the staircase leading to the second-floor landing. She could sense her father's presence, so close, after all this time. Nat watched her as he leaned against the banister. How happy she would be when

these two men finally met. Her throat tightened with longing. Surely her father would convince Nat to leave with
them. She knew it in her heart.

"Oh, Nat. I'll never be able to repay your aunt and Jane
for saving my father's life."

Nat held her face between his hands. "In a short while
you can thank them, yourself."

Anne thought of the many times Jane Herrick had visited Wycliffe Manor and had charmed her uncle's guests.
How she had resented Jane then. Regret washed over her at
her naiveté. Jane had really been risking all she held dear for
any scrap of information that might help the Royalists'
cause—or help bring a wounded Cavalier, like her father,
through enemy lines.

She pulled away gently. "But you don't understand. If
only I could have been a help to the cause, like Jane, during my stay at Wycliffe Manor!"

He grinned. "Somehow I don't think your uncle thought
of you as a...*help* to his cause," he said, a glint in his eyes.

She nudged him playfully. "You know what I mean. If
only I could do something to repay how I've been helped."

Nat gave her a rakish grin, then kissed the tip of her nose.
"I think I might be able to think of something. . . ."

She felt herself blush crimson at the double meaning of
his words. "You're incorrigible," she replied, and before she
had a chance to tell him she loved him for it, his mouth took
hers in a deep, lingering kiss that drove everything from her
mind except thoughts of him.

"Ah-humph!"

Anne jumped back from his embrace to see Peggy, red
faced, hands on hips. "Yer room's ready, mistress."

"Thank you, Peggy," Nat said calmly. "Mistress Anne
will be with you shortly. And close the doors tightly when
you leave." Nat gave the servant a glance that warned if she
dared listen at the door she might be shot.

Peggy sniffed with disdain, bobbed the tiniest curtsy and
left the room, slamming the door after her.

Anne dissolved into laughter. "You behaved like an
ogre."

"I'd have to be far more an ogre than that to intimidate Peggy." He grinned back at her. "The servants have been with my aunt's family from birth. They're loyal as old dogs and Bridget spoils the pack of them."

The thought of Bridget's manservant, Wilkens, came to mind. Never would such an outspoken servant have been tolerated at Wycliffe Manor. Anne tilted her head back. "I'd best hurry. After I've changed, hopefully, my father will be awake."

"Aye, leave, wench, before I show you what you've started." She shivered as his rough palm caressed her cheek and lifted to burrow beneath the thick tangle of her unbound hair. His dark gaze followed his fingers as they traced the loose curls before he reluctantly released his hand and let her go.

Anne stared at herself in the reflecting glass, unable to believe the change that had taken place in the past hour.

Peggy had thought of everything! A bevy of maids had filled a copper tub by the fireside. Castile soap with lavender for her bath, rosewater rinse for her hair. After Anne had soaked in the warm, luxurious water, Peggy oversaw the final shampoo that removed the remainder of the walnut stain, leaving her hair fire red with spun-gold highlights.

When Anne saw the navy blue watered silk gown with flounced red skirts underneath, her mouth flew open in delight. Two maids helped her dress while Peggy brushed her thick tresses until they shone, catching the sides with pearl combs. The rest of her hair cascaded down her back in a tumble of shining waves.

She studied her face in the glass. Would her father recognize her? She had lost weight; her cheekbones held a more mature line. The dark blue of her gown picked up the blue-green shade from her eyes, giving her a more enigmatic appearance.

The gold locket felt cold in her fingers as she polished the only adornment she wore. She would return it to her father, as she had promised him. She clicked the locket open. Her mother's gentle face smiled back at her. It was rightfully her father's keepsake, and she felt solace knowing it was her mother's love that would sustain him now.

A soft tap at the portal and a black-haired maid bobbed in the door. "Mistress Bridget has returned, mistress," she said in a soft Irish brogue. "They're waitin' for ye below-stairs."

"Praise God, you're safe," Bridget cried out in a strong Irish lilt. She let herself be folded into Nat's embrace. The slight weight of the woman, trembling in his arms, made him suddenly aware of how frail his aunt had become in the three years since he had last seen her.

"Wilkens and Doc met me at the stables with *him*." Bridget's face beamed at the reference to the king. "All of England will be so grateful to you, Nat." Her pale blue eyes brightened. "How I wish your uncle Alex could have known the Black Fox."

"The danger isn't over, Bridget. But with God's grace, we'll be on our way tomorrow and no longer be a danger to you."

Bridget waved her thin hand. "Rosemoor is a fortress." Her lips tightened with resolve. "The servants patrol the grounds like troopers before a battle." She strode to the small writing desk and chair, her walk reminding Nat of a cocky general.

"Jane offered to help Mrs. Wellington with the children." Bridget lowered her voice. "Actually, one of the Royalists, Lord Wilmot, is still listed as missing from the Battle of Worcester. Jane had hoped to learn from the major the names of other Royalists who had been captured."

Nat knew that Mrs. Wellington tried to ingratiate herself with Bridget and Jane, hoping the friendship of a devoted widow and daughter of a great parliamentarian like his uncle Alex would weigh heavily in Roundhead society. "I hope you didn't tell Doc of Jane's intrigue. He tries not to let on, but I know he's been very worried about her."

She rolled her eyes. "Doc knew without my telling him." She seated herself and drew a parchment and quill. "I assured Doc that I'd send Wilkens with a note to fetch Jane immediately."

Nat watched his aunt's deft black strokes scratch the paper, her mouth set to one side in the familiar way that told him she enjoyed the intrigue, as well.

Bridget rang for Wilkens, and after he had left with the note, she moved beside Nat. "Let me take a look at you," she said after a moment. "I've missed ye, laddie." Her face brightened with unspoken words.

Without maudlin endearments, Nat knew she cared as much for him as if he were her own son. "I've missed you, too."

She began to speak, but footsteps at the landing stopped her. Nat's gaze drew to the procession of maids scurrying down the stairs, followed by Anne.

The sight of her nearly took his breath away. She descended the stairs in a rustle of silk. The austere lines of the gown only accentuated her feminine curves. Her red gold hair shone in waves down her back, bouncing with each step as she came near. He was reminded of a wild red rose, fresh with the morning dew. He strode to the staircase and extended his arm. "You look radiant, my love."

"You're quite handsome, yourself, sire," she whispered as she stepped down beside him.

Bridget dismissed the maids and went to meet them.

"Aunt Bridget, this is Anne." Nat grinned as Anne spontaneously embraced the smiling older woman.

Bridget drew back and gave her a long look. "Your father speaks of you so often, lass, I feel I know you." Her smile lit her pale eyes. "Seeing you will be the best medicine for him."

"Is he awake? May I see him now?" Anne could barely hide her impatience. She had waited so long for this moment.

"Aye, but may I have a few words with you first?" Bridget reached for her hand.

Anne glanced uneasily at Nat, but if he knew what Bridget had in mind, he said nothing.

Bridget turned her attention to Anne. "Your father's wounds were grave. After surgery, he developed a fever. It has left him very weak and frail—"

Anne's throat went suddenly dry. "Are you saying he—he'll...die?"

"Nay, the doctor feels he's making strides, however..." Her voice dropped. "Your father suffered the loss of his right arm."

The loss of his right arm! Shock surged through Anne as she tried to comprehend Bridget's words. Her vibrant father, galloping through the fields of Wycliffe Manor, fencing with an expert parry and thrust, embracing her with his love of life. Her stomach twisted with the agonizing truth. Dear God, all she cared about was that he was alive. He was her father, and she needed him.

But how had he taken it? The shock of the loss of his arm must have been devastating. Questions formed in her mind, but she would only learn the answers when she saw him.

"Please take me to him, immediately," Anne pleaded.

Anne hesitated beside the door. She trembled as she raised her hand to knock. For the moment, she had discarded every thought except her father. How things had changed. Now he needed her, yet her journey began because she had needed him.

"I'll wait here for you," Nat whispered, releasing her hand. She smiled at him, thankful that he would be waiting for her.

A blond-haired maid answered the door. "Follow me, miss."

Anne was escorted down a narrow corridor to a small bedchamber. She looked about the silver tapestry-lined walls to the windows covered outside with ivy. A white silk chaise longue, delicately curved, was placed before an unlit marble fireplace. A spinning wheel and box of wool stood to one side. But the room was empty! Where was her father?

The servant moved to the fireplace and reached inside the opening. Anne watched as the servant pulled at a hidden knob. With a click, the fireplace wall opened to reveal a secret door.

The servant grasped the latch. "Colonel Lowell is expecting you, but if you'll wait, mistress, I'll tell him you're here."

Anne drew a shaky breath while her cold fingers toyed with her locket. Her hands were damp as she straightened her skirts. The maid turned the latch and pushed open the door.

"Anne? Anne, is that you?" called a faint voice.

"Father!" Anne pushed past the servant and rushed into the shadowed bedchamber. She blinked at the unaccustomed darkness. The only light came from the fire in the hearth. Firelight danced off the white plaster ceiling, darting long shadows across the walls and the canopied bed.

Behind her, she heard rustling movements. She turned and her eyes settled on the figure of a man sitting in the corner.

She threw herself at him, her arms circling his neck. He hugged her with his left arm, and she couldn't help notice the wasted muscle in his shoulders. She shivered as she clung to him. After several minutes, she drew back to look at him.

His hazel green eyes looked sunken in his pale face, his hair, once so lustrous and black, now was shot with gray. "Darling daughter," he whispered. "I feared I'd never see you again."

She forced herself not to show the anguish on her face. "When I heard you'd been wounded, I had to come...." Emotion tightened her throat and she pressed her cheek on the smooth blue silk of his jacket. She floundered with the raw and primitive anger that raged within her—fury at the politics that had changed this once powerful man into the thin shell of his former self. But she bit back her wrath; she needed to reassure him that everything would be all right. He was alive. That was all that mattered. "I love you, Father." The words seemed to convey everything that was in her heart.

His eyes glistened with tears. "Aye, and I love you."

The servant bustled over. "Colonel Lowell, you shouldn't be out of bed." The tapestries shuffled as she pulled them back from the bed. "Come, I'll help you—"

"Leave us alone, Mattie. I'll be fine now that—" His voice dissolved into a cough.

The servant wavered, eyes round with alarm.

"I'll call you if I need you," Anne assured her. The maid relinquished her patient with a curtsy, then turned in a bustle of starched black skirts, closing the door after her.

Concerned, Anne knelt beside him. "Let me help you back to bed." Although worried about his fragile condition, she couldn't help but feel heartened by his familiar spark of defiance.

"Later." He leaned his head back against the red velvet chair. "First, let me look at you."

His gaze clouded, and she could tell from his expression that he was surprised at how grown-up she had become. She knew he would be somehow saddened by the fact, as well.

"You're the picture of . . . your mother."

"Nothing you could have said could please me more, Father." She rested her head on his knee as she used to when she was a child. Her fingers wrapped around the chain at the front of her dress. She lifted her head. "Father, I have something for you." She removed the gold locket and placed it in his palm.

His chin quivered, and his hazel green eyes filled with memories. "Do you remember when I gave it to you?" he asked.

"Of course."

"I'm so glad you brought it." His thin fingers clicked open the gold oval and he smiled down at the miniature of his wife.

"I almost didn't. I lost it several times . . . Once was the day I met Nat Braydon, the Black Fox. Maybe I shouldn't have brought it. Nat wanted me to get rid of it because he felt it was a danger, but . . . I couldn't bear to part with it."

His tired eyes lifted to her face. "It means a great deal to me to have it."

She smiled. "Whenever I felt alone, I would hold the locket and think about you and our future together."

His thin lips spread faintly. "Now I have it to keep and think about you and what a lovely woman you've grown up to be."

She knew he was also thinking of all they had missed together, as she was. He was overtaxing himself emotionally. "Please, let me help you to bed." She offered her arm and with the reluctance of a child, he accepted it. He rose stiffly to steady himself. The right arm of his jacket dangled loosely at his side and a sudden jab of grief overwhelmed her. He had lost so much. His wife, his ancestral home... She felt him shudder when he drew in a sharp breath.

"They told you what happened to me, didn't they?" he asked, as he settled into bed and let Anne draw up the coverlet.

"Aye," she whispered. For a moment, she was at a loss for words. "I'm so sorry," she said after a long moment.

"Left me for dead." His hazel eyes glittered with anger. "When I awoke, it was dark. I remember crawling from the battlefield until I lost consciousness. When I came to, I was here, at Rosemoor." He leaned back against the pillows.

Thank you, God, for allowing me to arrive in time. He would gain his strength, now. She and Nat would make him well.

"The king. Tell me, daughter, is he here with you?"

"Aye. But you must rest now. I'll be back later and we'll tell you all about the plans to go to France."

His thin lips twitched and his body jerked as though a pain shot through him. He quickly recovered. "Praise God."

Anne took the hand he offered. "I want you to meet the Black Fox. I owe him my life."

"Ask him to come so I can thank him for bringing you to me."

She lowered her eyes, her cheeks warmed at the thought. *When you meet him, Father, you'll see why I love him. Together, we'll convince him to give up this folly. The Round-*

heads have won. Who has learned that better than you, my father?

His hand felt cold. "He's eager to meet you, as well."

He closed his eyes. No doubt, her visit had weakened him. She leaned over and kissed his forehead. "Rest now, Father. I'll be back later."

He released her hand. "Aye, that might be best."

After she closed the door behind her, she rushed past the servant, who sat spinning and ran to where Nat waited.

Nat glanced up, his face serious. "How is he?"

"He's...in good spirits," she said, striving for Nat's calm. "He's determined, though frail..." But it was no use. She couldn't pretend with Nat. She fell into his arms. Her body shuddered as she clung to him.

"Don't worry, my love. He'll regain his strength now that you're here," he whispered into her hair.

She drew back, wiping her eyes. "He's so feeble. He can't possibly leave tomorrow with you and the king." She buried her face into his chest. For the moment, she tried only to think of the comfort of Nat's strong arms.

A few minutes later, Anne walked with Nat into the study. The low hum of conversation stopped as they entered the room. The king glanced up from the leather chair, his black eyes narrowed in concern. Bridget, seated on the sofa, her embroidery in hand, paused with needle in midair. Doc, who had been watching out the window for his wife's return, flicked back the heavy velvet drape and took a seat in one of the fireside chairs.

"I'm sorry to hear of your father's injuries, my dear," the king said as Anne sat opposite him.

She acknowledged him with a brave smile. "He feels fortunate to have fought alongside you at Worcester. But he's much too weak..." Her voice broke, and she gazed up at Nat.

"It will be weeks before Anne's father is able to travel," Nat finished, taking a seat beside Anne on the mahogany settle. He glanced at the intense faces staring back at him, then he directed his gaze to Anne. "I know you'll want to remain with your father until he's strong enough to travel."

Anne nodded, her blue-green eyes glistening.

Nat peered back at the king. "Tomorrow, you and I will leave for Shoreham as planned. After you're safely out of England, I'll return to Rosemoor. When Anne's father has recovered, I'll arrange passage for them at that time."

Bridget's face relaxed. "Aye, that's wise. Besides, Twining's troops are still searching for Anne. Without her, your chance of success will be greater."

Doc leaned closer, his expression grave. "I'll go with you, Nat. The villagers know me, and if we run into militia, I might be able to lend support to your alibi."

Nat knew his friend would rather remain with his wife at Rosemoor, but he also knew that Doc was a well-respected physician in the area, and his word would go far if Nat needed vindication. "Aye, I'd welcome your company."

The king slapped his hand on his knee. "It's settled then."

"Now that that's resolved, tell us of your plan," Bridget whispered, her needlework forgotten.

"Tomorrow, we'll leave for the coastal hamlet of Shoreham." Nat pulled out some crinkled parchments from his vest pocket and unfolded the official-looking documents. "I'll be disguised as a coal merchant in need of a ship bound for the Isle of Wight."

Anne leaned forward, absorbed with the details.

"Shoreham is a market town, as I remember," the king said. "You'll have no trouble finding a good sailing vessel."

"Aye. Once I hire a boat and the captain agrees to the price, Doc will go and ask the same captain for passage for Mr. Jackson, who needs to leave town because of a duel." Nat waited for their reaction.

"Any captain would be a fool not to want to earn an extra passage on top of payment for his ship," Doc said quickly.

Nat folded the papers and returned them to his pocket. "After the captain sets sail for the Isle of Wight, you'll convince him to set a course for the channel for France, once the ship is out of sight from Shoreham."

The king's eyes lit with understanding. "Excellent! By then, if Twining has sent a fleet of ships to search the coast, they'll be too far away to notice our new direction."

"But do you have enough gold to bribe the captain to change his route?" Bridget asked worriedly.

"That's the least of our problems, dear lady." The king gave Nat an expression of indebtedness. "Thanks to the Black Fox, we've more than enough, plus a generous bonus for the crew."

"This news deserves to be celebrated," Bridget said, but before she got to her feet, the study doors flew open. Jane Herrick rushed into the room, her maroon cape flowing after her as she ran to her husband's side. After a hurried embrace, she pulled off her hood and stared at the faces in the room.

"Major Wellington had just returned from Twining's headquarters as I was preparing to leave." She paused to catch her breath, then she turned her intent gaze on Anne. "He said Tom Thackery has been arrested for aiding Anne's kidnapping, and a tavern wench is being held who can identify Nat Braydon as the Black Fox!"

Chapter Fourteen

Anne gasped. Her heart pounded in her throat. Frightened, barely able to hear the excited voices around her, she prayed for it, somehow, to be a mistake.

But there was no mistake. She was to blame for this, as surely as if she had told Twining, herself. The tavern maid was Moll—it had to be. Somehow, Moll had told Twining about the locket, and he must have recognized it as Anne's.

By her foolish disobedience, she had jeopardized Nat, the king and everyone she held dear.

Bridget turned to Nat, her expression incredulous. "Surely, that's impossible. Tom would never give you away."

"Someone did," Jane answered, pacing in a tight circle. "The major knew too many details about Tom and the Pied Bull Inn." Jane peered back at Nat. "Have you any idea how the tavern wench could learn of your identity?"

Anne studied Nat's strong profile, the flames from the fireplace shadowing his clenched jaw. "That's not important, now," he said, sidestepping Jane's question. "The important thing is to get the king safely out of England, then we'll find a way to free Tom from jail." His brown eyes watched Bridget's ashen face. "It's best I leave alone for Shoreham, tomorrow," he said gently. "I'll rent a ship, and Doc and the king can follow in a few days."

A knot of fear tightened inside Anne. It was much too dangerous for Nat to go alone. She clutched her fingers inside her palms but remained silent. *She had already done enough.*

"Don't worry, Aunt Bridget." Nat's dark gaze settled lovingly upon his aunt. "Everyone believes your illegitimate nephew died in France. Even if Twining discovers that his name was Nat Braydon, he'll never prove that I'm still alive or that your nephew's demise became the birth of the Black Fox."

Just thinking of it shattered Anne. She trembled as fearful images built in her mind. "But what if, somehow, Twining proves the connection?" she asked.

"Impossible," Bridget answered. "Nat's right. There's no link to my nephew who died in France and the Black Fox. Besides, no one would dare doubt the Braydon family's loyalty to Cromwell. Jane and I have done everything to insure that image."

Jane knelt beside her mother. "That's true, Anne. Even if Twining believes Nat is alive, that alone can't implicate us." Jane's lift of the chin and resolute tone made Anne want to believe her, although she remained doubtful.

Nat took her small, cold hand in his. "Anne, let's step outside," he whispered. Grateful for a chance to speak to him alone, she took his arm and excused herself from the group.

Nat led her to the upstairs gallery. While he lit a taper, she moved to the fireplace where a low fire burned in the grate. Her gaze was drawn immediately to the magnificent painting above the white marble mantel. The portrait featured a country gentleman beside a majestic white steed. She studied the man's face: Thick chestnut hair, magnificent dark eyes, thick brows and a strong, determined jaw. For a moment, the likeness took her breath away.

"My uncle Alex." Nat smiled down at her. "Everyone comments about the likeness. Hopefully, the resemblance won't be recognized now that Twining is aware of my identity—"

"Nat, I'm so sorry I disobeyed you about the locket." She clung to him, fighting back tears of regret. "If only—"

"Shh. No harm will come of it, you'll see." He lifted her chin and gazed into her eyes. "After I see the king off, I'll return to you before Twining will be the wiser."

She felt his body heat infusing her in waves. His large dark brown eyes smoldered with passion, his gaze so full of love, she thought her heart might break if she lost him. She swallowed with difficulty, then found her voice. "It's true, Nat. I've endangered everyone."

His finger gently stroked her cheek, causing a tingling warmth to course through her. "The maid who selfishly refused to give up her locket no longer exists, my love." His low voice whispered like a soft caress. "In her place is the unselfish young woman who has stolen my heart."

She clung to him, her mind torn with unexpected bliss. He loved her, he forgave her. She buried her head against his hard chest, exhilarated by the rapid beating of his heart. She drank in the familiar masculine scent of him. "Hurry back to me," she murmured into the soft folds of his shirt. His strong arms tightened about her, and for the moment, her fears took flight.

Time seemed to stand still. She sighed deeply, trying to hold to memory the feel of his powerful embrace, the bewitching sensations his nearness caused in her. She needed to remember the hot searing passion of their joining, the sweet ecstasy that had rocked her soul. Memories. Loving memories. Memories would be all she would have to sustain her until he returned.

Finally he drew back, his gaze serious. "You and your father will be safe here. Rosemoor is an impregnable fortress dating back to Edward II. There are more secret rooms than you'll ever imagine. If Twining searches Rosemoor with a thousand troops, you'll still be safe."

His mouth tightened. "But you must promise me you'll remain here, regardless of what might happen."

A warning premonition swept over her, but she dismissed it. "Aye, I'll promise. I'll never disobey you again."

He turned her face upward and she saw the desire in his eyes. "Promise me you'll think only of when we'll be together again."

Anne smiled, and before she could speak, he silenced her with his lips. The gentle force of his tongue exploring her mouth caused such a hunger for the feel of his body next to hers that she thought she might die when he drew back.

"I want you so much, but first, I must speak to your father. Do you think you might find out if he's well enough to see me?"

Feelings of frustration were forgotten when the moment Anne had been waiting for finally arrived. "Of course," she answered, joy welling inside her. "I'll ring for Peggy." She dashed for the door, then tossed a smile back at him. "My father is going to be so happy when he hears about us. Just wait and see."

Nat studied the impressive face above the fireplace while he waited for Anne to return. How Alex would have appreciated the strong-willed, beautiful woman he had chosen for his wife. Aye, she was as much his wife in his heart as she would be when they finally exchanged vows.

"I thought you might be here," Bridget said as she came beside him. Her gaze lifted to the painting of her husband. "I come here when I'm troubled or in need to be alone," she said, her eyes never faltering. "Sometimes I talk to him, and somehow, I'm always strengthened."

"I was wishing he could have met Anne," Nat said softly.

Bridget's light blue eyes met his dark eyes, her approving smile subtracting years from her face. "I know you love her. Your feelings shine from your eyes, as they did when you were a lad," she added with sentiment. "Alex would have been pleased with your choice, as I am."

"Anne deserves more than I can offer. Life on the continent will be hardship at best."

"Then you're leaving England with them. Have you told her yet?"

"Nay. First, I thought I'd ask her father for her hand," he said, trying out the idea on her. "As soon as I see the king to safety, when I return, we'll be wed."

Bridget kissed his cheek. "Aye, lad, your news makes me so very happy." Her fingers touched the brooch at her throat. "You know, Nat. When they brought Anne's father here, I didn't think he'd survive the surgery. But later, when Jane told him that the Black Fox would bring his daughter to him, well..." Her thin brows arched. "I saw his will to live suddenly blossom. It was as if his life force hung in the balance with his daughter."

A host of the old doubts stormed Nat's thoughts. "You think he'll disapprove because I'm an outlaw?"

"Not if he were well, Nat." Her eyes narrowed in thought. "He's extremely weak—emotionally—and it might take him time to realize his little girl has grown up." She paused, as though deciding to keep further thoughts to herself. She gazed down at her hands, then back at him. "But when has it ever been easy for the Black Fox?" She smiled and the admiration he saw lightened his heart.

Bridget took his hand. "Anne asked me to tell you her father is anxious to meet you. She's in the library."

"Before I go, I want to ask you something. In case I don't return—"

"Nat!" She drew back, her face suddenly pale.

"Aunt Bridget, please. See that Anne and her father arrive in France. If they need anything, take care of them as though she were my wife." He felt his aunt's frail fingers grow cold in his palm and her chin trembled slightly.

"Aye, laddie," she said, her eyes bright with unshed tears.

Five minutes later, Nat and Anne stood outside her father's door. Anne rapped on the wood. "Father," she called softly. When he answered, she pushed the door open and Nat followed her to the shadowed profile of the man seated beside the desk.

Jonathan wore the blue satin suit of a Cavalier officer, white frothy lace at his collar and cuffs, and Nat noticed the black Cavalier boots had been buffed to a mirror finish.

Anne took her place by her father and introduced them. Jonathan rose and extended his left arm. Nat shook the frail hand gently. "I'm honored, sire." He couldn't help but notice the wince of pain that crossed the older man's face from the small effort.

"To finally meet the man..." Jonathan drew a breath. "The man who brought my beloved Anne to me, and who will aid our king to safety, the honor is mine, Braydon." Jonathan bowed slowly. His left hand gestured a flourish.

Nat returned the bow. "Thank you, sire."

"The king honored me with a visit only a few minutes ago." Jonathan paused for breath. "He told me of your brilliant plan for his escape. How I wish I could go with you and help carry it off, but..."

Anne's lovely face brightened as she gazed back at Nat. "Oh, Father, Nat saved my life, more than once." Her aquamarine eyes glistened with adoration. "Once, when we were fleeing from Wycliffe Manor..." As she recalled their escape, Jonathan's hazel green eyes hardened behind an unreadable mask.

"And again," Anne continued, "at the Pied Bull Inn when the soldiers came and—"

"That's what the Black Fox is paid to do," Jonathan interrupted unexpectedly, his voice sharp.

Anne tilted her head back to her father. "Paid? Certainly you don't believe Nat did it for the money, Father!"

"The Black Fox doesn't risk his neck for the folly of it, child. Isn't that so, Braydon?" His eyes glittered defiantly.

Instead of answering, Nat watched the drama unfold between father and daughter. He knew all along that Jonathan might never approve of a rogue for his daughter. He only prayed that her father would be gentle with her.

"Didn't you explain to my daughter," Jonathan took a breath, "that gold and valuables are raised among our supporters?"

"Of course Nat told me, but that money is for the cause. Nat protected me because—"

"My dear child." Jonathan patted Anne's hair as though she were a little girl. "You're too young to understand politics."

"Father, it's *you* who don't understand!" Anne drew her hand from her father's and stared at him as if for the first time. She pulled back and moved beside Nat. "I love this man, father, and I thought you'd be happy for us."

Jonathan's eyes widened with rage in the brief moment it took for the meaning of Anne's words to settle in. He glared at Nat. "Leave us alone, child."

"No, I'm not a child—"

"Hush! You *are* a child, and a foolish one at that."

"Anne, do as your father asks." Nat placed his hands gently on her shoulders. "Let's not upset him."

"Keep your hands off her." Jonathan's eyes rounded in challenge.

Anne glanced at Nat, then her father. She felt like a small, trapped bird, her feelings divided by the two men she loved.

Nat removed his grip. "Anne, wait for me in the hall," he whispered as he strode toward the door and opened it.

Anne's gaze settled on her father. "I'll be in to see you before bedtime, Father."

After she had gone, Nat waited for the older man to speak.

"The king spoke highly of you, Braydon. But when I..." Jonathan gasped for breath. "I saw the hopeless infatuation in my daughter's eyes, I knew you had taken advantage of a poor girl, frightened and alone." He drew a labored breath. "I'll never forgive you for that."

Nat studied the old Cavalier, the flat sleeve of the faded blue satin jacket folded across the gaunt chest and tucked inside the loose belt. A wave of compassion flowed through him. The man had lost so much, and Nat knew the old soldier feared losing his daughter, as well.

"I've had the same doubts as I see in your face, Colonel Lowell. I've told myself every day since I met Anne at Wycliffe Manor that I don't deserve her and I never will, but we love each other, and I promise you, I'll make her happy."

"How can the Black Fox promise such a thing?" The question echoed the room like a shot. "Can you deny that my daughter isn't at risk just being with you?"

There would be no progress in further discussion, Nat knew. Anne's father needed time to accept that his young daughter had grown up and fallen in love. "With due respect, Colonel." Nat bowed and strode toward the door. "I'll be leaving very early in the morning, so I'll say farewell."

"Mr. Braydon?"

Nat turned back to the tense, frail man glaring at him.

"I'll spend every waking moment trying to change my daughter's mind about you." He gasped and continued. "But if you love her, you'll end it now, before you leave. Her whole life is before her. Don't ruin her chance for happiness with her own kind." The emotional effort racked the older man as he dissolved into a fit of coughing.

Nat opened the door. The servant jumped to her feet and rushed to the older man. "Colonel Lowell, yer not to get upset."

Nat held his frustration in check as he strode from the room. When he marched to where Anne waited, he felt as if his heart had been ripped from him. She rose from a heap of dark blue silk and fell into his arms.

"Nat, why is he so blind?" He could feel her shoulders tremble with forced control. He sighed helplessly. "He believes he knows what's best for you," he said into her fragrant hair.

"I'll talk to him tomorrow. I know I can dissuade him." She lifted her head, her face streaked with tears. "He'll feel differently when he regains his strength." She blinked blue-green eyes spiked with wet lashes. "I know he will." She flung her arms around his neck and pressed her lips against his.

The rapture of her almost nearly overcame his reason. But he would always be helpless with her. Nothing could ever stir his soul with such desire as this incredibly passionate woman. Reluctantly he pulled her arms from his neck and gazed down at her. "I'll love you until I die."

Her fingers silenced his lips. "Don't speak of death," she whispered, her brows furrowing.

Nat took her fingers and kissed her fingertips. "Don't worry, my darling. Nothing will happen to me," he promised before their kiss deepened.

* * *

Somewhere in the distance, a cock crowed. Nat knew it was time to leave, but as he listened to Anne's steady breathing and felt the warmth of her soft, supple body against him, he resisted the mission calling him for one more selfish moment.

It would be the last time he would see her for almost three weeks, and it would take all of his discipline to tear himself away from her. Her silken hair, streaming like the red rays of morning sunlight, splayed across the pillow. Her ivory, heart-shaped face was etched against his deeply tanned shoulder. She stirred, then cuddled deeper into his embrace, a slight smile on her mouth. He wanted to reach out and kiss those tempting lips, but he knew it would wake her and he needed to watch her for one more glorious moment before it was time to leave her.

He had refused to think of her father's warnings until now, but just as surely as the daylight steals away the darkness, his thoughts kept turning into a deep melancholy.

"I'll spend every waking moment trying to change my daughter's mind about you!"

But Anne was a strong-willed woman whose thinking couldn't be changed by the overprotective rantings of her father. She loved him as he loved her. Certainly her father couldn't deny that.

Anne stirred deeper into the warmth of him, and he glanced down at the woman he treasured. So beautiful and loving. He remembered how she had come to him last night. One look at that wild temptress who gave everything to him with such abandon, and his reluctance had melted like warm honey; just thinking of her made him go hot and weak inside. But would their all-consuming, passionate lovemaking—so satisfying and complete—be enough for her against the trials of their separation?

Her eyelashes fluttered open and he smiled. "Feigning sleep, eh, temptress?" He kissed her enticing mouth. Her small hand touched him, igniting him into instant need.

"If you don't stop, I'll never be able to leave you." His voice was a husky growl.

"That's my plan," she teased, before his mouth took hers.

Several hours later, Anne pulled back the tapestry cover from her bed and leaned against the stiff, cold pillows, her slippered feet dangling over the side. She watched the dawn rain pelt the diamond panes of glass of the bedroom window as she heard the clip-clop of Nat's horse ride along the cobbles of the courtyard below.

I'll be back in three weeks, my love, he had said. He had only been gone a few minutes, and her heart twisted as though it were breaking. Nothing had prepared her for the anguish of his leaving. Dear God, how would she manage if...

She squeezed her eyes shut. No, she wouldn't think such a thing. Nat was larger than life, and he would return. She must hold on to that.

He had told her not to watch him leave. *Remember only the happy times,* he had said. Aye, but she needed to see him, even to catch the slightest glimpse of him. She ran to the window and watched the tall shadowy figure ride past the gates into the swirling mist. Then, through a veil of tears, he was gone.

Anne spent the next three days tending her father: Steeping medicinal herbs to cleanse and dress his wounds, reading *The Tempest* aloud to him, and listening to the stories of his war adventures against the Roundheads.

The king's prolonged visits with her father gave Anne a chance to hear the stories of the court of Charles I. How she had relished the tales as a child growing up at Wycliffe Manor! Now, the opulence seemed pretentious. She knew she could find happiness anywhere... with Nat.

She realized her father's incessant talk of life at court was only his way of keeping her mind from Nat. She admonished him silently, for he had only her best interests at heart. Despite her tiring duties, the nighttime hung heavy with desperate longing for Nat.

By Wednesday, the excitement grew as Wilkens, Doc and the king prepared for the journey to meet Nat. Jonathan was too weak to leave his room, so the men said their farewells in his chamber. The king graciously thanked everyone, flattered her father excessively, and the old Cavalier beamed with pride.

"God watch over you," Bridget said, then gave her son-in-law a hug. "Pray, be careful."

Doc reached over and kissed Jane on the cheek. She gave a gallant smile, although her swollen eyes betrayed her bravery.

Before the king left, he took Anne's hand. "I'll never forget how you risked that pretty neck to attempt to unchain the scruffy Will Jackson from the mulberry tree," he said, squeezing her palm. He winked at her outrageously.

"Your father has a glorious, courageous daughter," the king added. "A true Royalist's daughter."

The smile she gave him was genuine. She curtsied low. When she lifted her gaze back to his face, the king's mouth twitched wickedly. "Remember, sweeting, if you ever decide to leave that handsome rogue of yours..." His hooded black eyes glittered mischievously with the unfinished offer.

She blushed, not taking offense at his boldness. She couldn't help admire his lighthearted bravado against all he had been through. Impulsively Anne stood on tiptoe and kissed his cheek. "Godspeed, Mr. Jackson."

"Godspeed, sweeting."

Doc shook her hand. "Don't worry, Anne. Nat and I will be back in a little more than a fortnight."

She nodded, determined to put up a brave front like Bridget and Jane. She kissed Doc on the cheek. "For luck," she said, and was rewarded by his broad smile.

While the women waved farewell, Anne wondered who were the bravest, the men who saddled up to war or the women who waited stoutheartedly for their return?

When Anne returned to her father's room, he appeared to be sleeping. He had been too weak to attempt to see them off. She didn't light a candle. Instead, she quietly placed a fresh log on the fire. The orange flames licked greedily upon the fresh wood and illuminated the room.

"This will be a day to tell my grandchildren," he said.

Your grandchildren will be Nat's children, Anne thought.

"Someday, Charles Stuart will return, and all England and Scotland will rejoice," he continued.

If the Black Fox is successful, she mused. Her fingers twisted in the blankets as she listened absently to his familiar baritone. Thoughts of Nat and the dangers of the next few weeks tumbled forth in her mind. She couldn't help worrying about Twining's militia posted everywhere.

Nat and I will be back in a little more than a fortnight, Doc had said. She could pretend to be brave until then.

Chapter Fifteen

During the long weeks that followed, Anne could do nothing but wait. Thank God for her father's constant demands, or she would surely go mad. Despite reading Shakespeare to him, playing chess and retelling his stories of battles, the days dragged on.

But in her heart, Nat was always with her. She would spend hours in the gallery, taking comfort with her favorite portrait, the chestnut-haired, dark-eyed man who gazed down at her.

Jane spent as much time as possible at the Wellingtons'. Anne knew her purpose was to hear news of any Royalists' arrests or the militia's movements. Major Wellington enjoyed boasting of his importance, and Jane provided an obliging ear.

In the month since Anne had come to Rosemoor, she had become very close to Bridget. Sometimes the cold grip of fear would return, forcing its hold upon her. Bridget had noticed something was troubling her, but Anne had dismissed it. But what would the older woman think if she knew that because of Anne's thoughtless mistake, their very lives might be at stake? If Bridget knew, would she dismiss Anne's fears as readily? Would Bridget ever be able to forgive her?

"Yer father's awake, Mistress Anne," Peggy's soft brogue called out to her from behind the library door.

"Thank you, Peg. I'll be right there." Anne took the folio of Shakespeare's works from the shelf and swept past the

servant into the hidden room. The smell of lavender drifted
from the dried bouquets on the mantel. A roaring fire in the
hearth dispelled the damp gloom of the world outside as she
padded silently across the thick carpet to her father's bed.

His head rested upon several pillows. "Each time I see
you drift in, I'm certain I'm dreaming."

"You're not dreaming, Father." A thread of alarm rippled through her at his trembling voice. He had seemed to
grow weaker with each passing day. She forced away her fear
with a smile. "I'm here." She took a seat beside the bed.

"Aye, but your thoughts are sometimes elsewhere." She
studied the hazel eyes and wondered, for the first time since
Nat had left, if her father might speak of him. "Has there
been word from Nat?" he asked, pursuing the subject head-
on.

Surprised, she stilled her fingers. "Nay. He's two weeks
overdue, but I expect him anytime." She couldn't hide the
apprehension in her voice.

His face flushed and she noticed a tiny bead of sweat
upon his brow. "I've been thinking..."

Her hopes swelled, but she remained silent, waiting.

"You know I love you and want the very best for you."

Anne nodded. "If there's one thing I'm certain of, it's
your love and devotion, Father."

He smiled. "When you first spoke of being in love with a
highwayman, I was very much opposed."

A wave of hope burst within her. "Have you reconsid-
ered?" she blurted out, leaning across the bed.

"Nay, Anne. Don't interrupt me."

Anne held his cold hand. "I'm sorry, Father." Anne
blinked, aware of her heart hammering beneath her bosom.

"My lovely, impetuous daughter..." He shook his head
slowly. "You have your mother's beauty, and I'm afraid you
have my stubborn will." He smiled weakly, his dark head
sunk against the pillows. "I fear if we ever had a test of
wills, you'd be the winner, my girl."

She heard his soft chuckle and she smiled. "I'll consider
that a compliment, Father."

He squeezed her hand, then his gaze drifted toward the velvet curtains hanging from the canopy over the bed. His eyes took on a faraway look. "Your mother, Elizabeth, and I were very much in love, but her family insisted she marry into a wealthy, powerful family." He released her hand and pulled the gold locket from his vest pocket and snapped it open. "When your mother sat for this miniature, she was betrothed to another man."

Anne stared in astonishment. "I never knew..." She had never imagined her parents betrothed to anyone but each other. "Did you ever meet the man?" she asked with genuine curiosity.

"Aye, a black-hearted soul. Edward Twining."

"Tw—" The shock caused the name to wedge in her throat.

He glanced up at her. "Aye, Colonel Edward Twining of the New Model army." His hazel eyes darkened. "An unscrupulous bast—" He paused, then took a steadying breath. "Twining was obsessed with her. When Elizabeth refused to marry him, he made a scandalous scene and vowed to run me through." His eyes hardened at the memory while his gaze shifted back to the velvet curtains, his mind lost in his own thoughts.

Colonel Twining had almost married her mother! An uneasy feeling rippled through her as her mind tried to grasp the idea. All the years her father had been away fighting, he had mercifully been spared knowing how close his nemesis had become to his brother. Thank God she had decided not to tell her father about her betrothal to Twining; it would have upset him far more greatly than she would have imagined. Thankfully, now there was no need.

Her mind whirled while her father continued reminiscing. Remembering the lustful way Twining had looked at her at Wycliffe Manor, she now understood his drive to possess her.

"Twining had gone to the artist and commissioned a copy of your mother's portrait." He looked down at the miniature inside the locket. "I wonder if the scoundrel had it completed?"

One thought broke through her astonishment as a curl of fear raced up her spine. If Twining had a copy of her mother's miniature, he would have real evidence to prove the gold locket was truly hers. Because of her, Nat faced a real danger.

She felt her hands shake with an uncontrolled anxiety. Surely God would keep Nat safe.

Anne leaned back and gazed at her father. They had come to know and understand each other so much these past weeks. He was a proud man, but she might help him to admit he had been wrong about Nat. "If my mother disobeyed her family and married you," she said, a flicker of hope rising, "perhaps I have my mother's will, after all."

Jonathan's jaw tightened. "I might remind you, young woman, that I was a respectable landowner with excellent lineage. Our line goes back to Edward I—"

"There's no need to become upset, Father. Quit beating the bushes and tell me what's on your mind." She leaned back and waited for his game playing to end.

"Very well, my dear." He cleared his throat. "In case something happens to me—" he paused to take a deep breath "—I want you to know that I've given your future happiness a great deal of thought." His hazel green eyes glittered with challenge. "And I cannot abide you marrying beneath your station."

She gasped in astonishment. How could she have been so wrong? "I love Nat, and I'll marry him, without your blessing," she said, her voice low and controlled. "I feel I owe you my honesty."

"I know you do," he replied, "and that's why I want you to promise me you won't." His eyes brightened with an unfamiliar intensity that frightened her. "A deathbed promise. Now do it."

She was too stunned to cry out. Anne backed away toward the door, his glaring eyes fixed on hers. Her knees felt weak and a trembling threatened to overtake her as she fled from the room.

* * *

From her bedroom window, Anne watched the snow-
flakes whisper across the diamond-shaped panes of glass as
Bridget's coach clattered up the driveway. It had been five
weeks, four days and nine hours since Nat had left. A sense
of urgency beat beneath her breast as she watched Bridget
and Jane alight from the coach and enter the snow-covered
front walk.

Let them have heard good news, Anne prayed as she
dashed to meet them. "Is there any news?" she asked expectantly, but when she saw their grim faces, Anne knew
there had been no word.

Bridget pulled away the gray woolen scarf and shook her
dark head. "Mrs. Wellington droned on, but nothing of interest, my dear." She gave Anne a sympathetic look. "We
can only take it as a good omen," she added optimistically.

Knowing Bridget and Jane were as worried as she was,
Anne smiled with the same courage. "I have a feeling everything is going well," she lied, hoping to match their
mettle.

Bridget gave her a quick hug. "I thought I'd go to chapel.
Would you like to join me?" she offered softly.

"My father should be awake from his nap, mistress. But
I'll attend chapel with you this evening," Anne replied.

Bridget nodded and turned toward her daughter. Jane
removed her blue hood and cape, her pale face drawn.
"Listening to that dreadful Mrs. Wellington has given me a
headache, Mother. I think I'll lie down before dinner."
Turning to Anne, Jane added with a courageous smile, "I
feel certain they're safe."

Anne nodded politely. Since Doc had left, Jane hadn't
spoken of her husband, but she couldn't hide her worry.

After Jane left, Bridget glided up the stairs, a black cloud
of silk skirts swishing softly behind her. Anne listened to her
footsteps fade above her, then suddenly the light-headed
feeling that had been frequently overtaking her caused her
to cling to the banister and steady herself on the bottom
step. Maybe she should ask Peg to make her a posset, but the
thought of the creamy drink made her sick to her stomach.

Besides, she wouldn't have the servant running back to Bridget or Jane with tales that she was ill from worry.

At that moment, Peggy stepped into the hall. "Mistress? Are you all right?"

"Don't fuss, Peg." Anne pulled away. "I'm fine." She took the stairs, clasping the handrail for dear life. *Please, don't let me faint in front of Peggy,* Anne prayed as she dragged herself up the stairs, fighting the dizziness. *God's bones,* she'd be as stoic as Bridget and Jane. She'd be damned if she'd admit to feeling sickly.

Another wave of nausea threatened, and Anne bolted for the gallery, the nearest room with a necessity closet. Afterward, feeling weak and chilled, she slumped into the fireside chair, gathering strength to make it to her room abovestairs.

The fire earlier that afternoon still burned and she leaned forward to light a candle from the iron candle holder nearby. The small movement brought on another attack of sickness which brought Anne to her knees. She knelt before the flames, her gaze upon the huge portrait above the mantel.

"Oh, Nat," she cried, her head spinning. "Why haven't you come back to me like you promised?" The firelight cast unnatural light about the dark eyes and hard, chiseled mouth, making the face eerily come alive. "Nat, please let me know you're all right."

A few minutes later, she wiped her face with the hem of her apron, willing the dizziness to ease. When it did, she returned to her room, carrying the telltale chamber pot with her. Her head throbbed and her body felt sluggish as she crawled between the icy sheets, and an incredible sense of longing lurched through her. When she thought she would die of it, she threw back the quilts, went to the window and twitched back the velvet curtains.

"Oh Nat, wherever you are, my darling, I pray you're safe." She stroked her thick braid as she peered out into the swirling darkness. Her breath frosted the pane, clouding the night's shadows. With a trembling finger, she drew a tiny heart upon the glass, her words giving comfort to her worry but providing nothing for the yearning in her heart.

* * *

A horse whinnied. Anne sat bolt upright in bed, a cold finger of fear gripping her spine. Had she been dreaming? She stilled, listening in the darkness. By the low embers crackling low in the grate, it must be near dawn.

Another whinny. A jingle of harness. The sound of rushed boot steps upon the cobbles below caused her blood to pound with excitement. Drawing on her robe, she flew to the window. Her fingernails scraped a circle through the thick icy crystals. Beneath the portico below, a servant swung a lantern, the yellow halo barely reaching the circle of shadowed figures.

Nat! Her heart beat wildly as she hurried to the stairs.

When Anne reached the first landing, she heard excited voices. Her excitement about to burst, she peeked around the corner before she rushed to him.

Inside the front hallway, Jane and Bridget stood, holding a candle, flanked by the livery servants, Jake and Billy. Peggy huddled beside Bridget. Their heads were bent above the wavering candle as they listened to the cloaked figure before them.

Anne bit her lip. Jake and Billy blocked the face of the man, but an uneasy feeling snaked down her spine. Suddenly Jake shifted and Wilkens's gray eyes locked on hers.

She felt a shock run through her. His face was ghostly pale in the flickering flame. Bridget, Jane and the servants turned toward her. Their wide stares in the deathly silence told her something terrible had happened.

"It's Nat, isn't it?" Anne cried, not recognizing the high timbre of her voice. Fear pounded away at her as she ran toward them. "What's happened to Nat?"

Bridget's pale blue eyes glistened with tears. Her hand on Anne's shoulder was of no comfort. "You must be brave, dear."

Anne whirled toward Wilkens. "Tell me what's happened!"

"Nat an' Doc are in jail ready fer the gallows," he said.

Anne's breath caught. She felt as though she had been struck.

"Wilkens," Bridget said, "I'll finish explaining to Anne what happened. Jake, Billy, see that Wilkens has something to eat and a fresh bed. Not a word to the others."

The three servants scurried from the room.

Bridget tossed back her black braid and drew the green shawl about her nightgown. "Peg, bring the salts. Anne looks deathly pale. Before this night is over, we may all need them."

Jane clasped an arm around Anne while they followed the older woman to the study. After the women had seated themselves before the fire, Bridget leaned forward in the settle. "Wilkens said that the king set sail two weeks ago. News has come from a Paris newspaper that the king arrived safely in France with Lord Wilmot, praise God." She managed a shaky smile. "Minutes after the king's ship sailed..." Bridget's voice quaked and Jane reached for her mother's trembling hand. "Roundheads swarmed the wharf, and Nat, Doc and the others were arrested—"

"But how did Twining happen to be at Shoreham?" Anne interrupted, her mind wild with fear.

"Wilkens said one of the men who befriended the king recognized him, even through his disguise. Apparently he had overheard them speak of their plan to find a boat at Shoreham. He sold the information for a sack of gold."

"What happened next?" Anne asked, afraid of the answer.

"Twining arrived in Shoreham with a tavern maid from Tom's inn," Jane explained. "Moll Standish, I think Wilkens said—"

"Oh my God." Anne jumped to her feet. "Oh, my God."

Jane and Bridget turned and stared at her.

"It's all my fault." A raw and primitive grief overwhelmed Anne as her fingers clenched the hair at her temples. "I'm as guilty as if I pointed the finger at Nat, myself."

Bridget put her arm around her. "Calm yourself, dear. Sit down and—"

"No, you don't understand." Anne pulled away, refusing comfort. "You see, inside my locket is a picture of my mother. Recently, my father told me that Colonel Twining had been betrothed to her before she married my father. Twining had a copy of my mother's miniature, as well. Obviously, when Moll told him of my locket and the description of the miniature inside, that would have proved to him that Anne Lowell was the woman who had been with Nat at the inn. Since Moll could identify Nat, that's all Twining needed to prove it in court."

Bridget and Jane exchanged glances, then Bridget spoke first. "It's too late for blame, Anne, and besides, it doesn't matter now. Please, try not to upset yourself."

"Mother is right, Anne. What's done is done." Jane glanced back at her mother. "Wilkens said that the men have been taken to London. Wilkens didn't know which jail, but I'm certain Major Wellington will inform me when he hears the news. He'll be down on us like locust, questioning me about my husband's politics."

"What will you tell him?" Anne asked, suddenly aware they were all at jeopardy.

Jane's thin face tightened with worry. "We'll deny any knowledge of his politics," she said bravely, although her trembling belied her words.

Bridget's chin tilted up. "It's not uncommon to have mixed politics within a family. Look at Anne's father and his brother, George." She smiled softly. "Our family's friendship with the Wellingtons will put us in good stead if Twining should decide to come snooping."

Anne stared at these two women with disbelief. "Deny any knowledge?" Her mouth fell open and she stared at Jane. "How can you sit there and deny any knowledge of your own husband?"

Jane averted her gaze, her fingers twisting the folds of her nightgown. "Anne, that's enough! We must be strong together."

Anne clenched her jaw. She didn't want to be strong. She wanted to hear Bridget's plan to get the men out of prison. She felt a wretchedness she had never known before. "Bridget, you *must* do something. You're very powerful in Roundhead circles—"

"Anne, calm yourself." Bridget's blue eyes hardened to icy chips. "Many people are at risk now. The king is safely in France, but now our work must truly begin. To return Charles Stuart to the throne will take careful planning. Money must be secretly raised to overthrow Cromwell." Bridget reached for Anne's hand. "We must be more diligent than ever."

Anne shook off Bridget's hand and stepped back from the two women. "Nat and Doc will be put to death unless we do something! Don't you understand?"

Bridget gave her a patient look. "Aye, I understand, my dear. More than you'll ever know." Bridget's voice quaked, and Anne remembered what Nat had told her of his father's march on Bridget's ancestral home in Ireland. All of her family were slaughtered like sheep.

Guilt, frustration, fear and anger warred within her as Anne fought back the threatening tears. "I'm sorry, Bridget. I know you've suffered, but wouldn't you have tried to save the lives of your family in Ireland, if you could?"

"I couldn't have prevented it any more so than you can, now." Bridget's eyes shone a warning that she would not be disobeyed. "We have Royalist sympathizers in London who will risk their lives to help Nat and Doc. But we must be patient."

Anne slumped back in a defeated heap. It was hopeless. Bridget and Jane were of the same cloth as Nat when it came to politics. "What is so glorious about being noble if it means you lose all that you love?"

Bridget's eyes brimmed with unshed tears. "This night is one of victory," she said, with the familiar defiant jut of her chin. "Our king is safe. I'm certain the Black Fox is rejoicing in his heart, even though he's imprisoned."

A fresh stab of remorse struck Anne. *Dear Nat. He was lunging back and forth against his chains, cursing her name to the heavens for her foolish, stubborn duplicity.*

Bridget pulled a lace handkerchief from her robe's pocket. "Nat knew he was endangering his life when—"

"No!" Anne screamed, jumping to her feet. "No! No! No!" She whirled away from them. "Nat's a fighter, and he'd expect us to do something!"

Bridget slapped Anne across the face with her open hand. Stunned, Anne glared back at her, rubbing her stinging cheek.

Why was she wasting her time trying to convince Bridget and Jane? If Nat and Doc were to be saved, she'd have to think of something, herself!

"I'm sorry, Anne, but you were hysterical." Bridget placed her arm across Anne's shoulder. "Let's pray together." Before the older woman could say any more, the study door creaked open and when Bridget looked up, her features suddenly appeared as though the life had drained from her.

Anne whirled around to see her father standing in the doorway, his arm around the fair-haired servant, Mattie.

"Father!" Anne rushed to his side. "You should be in bed!"

"Peg," Bridget ordered, "have Jake summon the doctor."

Peg hurried from the room while Bridget and Jane helped Anne lead him to a chair.

"I'm sorry, mistress." Mattie's face flushed crimson to her blonde roots. "But 'e swore 'e'd come down the stairs with or without me 'elp."

Bridget shot a hasty glance toward Anne. "Aye, Mattie. It's a trait that appears to run in the family."

"I heard the commotion." Jonathan paused to catch his breath. "I was sure...Nat and Doc...had returned." He gasped for air, his face pale.

Anne knelt at his feet. She stared at him, dressed in the blue satin Royalist uniform. He looked so frail and old in the flickering candlelight. "Father, let me help you to bed."

Jonathan shook his head. "I—I wanted...to pay my tribute to them...as an officer of the king's army should." He gasped again, then flinched as though in pain.

"The king is safely in France, Colonel," Bridget said, her voice strained. "The Black Fox's mission was successful."

"God be praised." He laid his head back, closing his eyes.

"But Nat and Doc have been captured..." Bridget's fingers clutched her rosary and she folded into a chair.

Jonathan's gaze flew back to Anne. "It's a valiant deed the Black Fox has achieved."

Anne knew it had cost her father a great deal of his pride to offer the compliment. She smiled her gratitude.

He slumped back against the cushion, took several deep breaths, then dissolved into a fit of coughing. When he recovered, he appeared so exhausted she felt suddenly afraid for him. Dear God, would her world ever be right again?

Several menservants rushed into the room. Anne stepped aside to let the strongest man carry her father to his chamber, as though he were an overly tired child who had fallen asleep.

Dawn had swept across the eastern horizon, streaming faint ribbons of peach and gold through the study windows. Anne took a few minutes to change from her bedclothes before returning to her father's room.

She shuddered as she splashed ice-cold water over her face and arms, but she still felt as if she were trapped in a nightmare. When she had finished her ablutions, she dressed in a rose pink wool gown of Jane's. Returning to her father's room, she found Dr. Abbott leaving.

"I've bled him, but he doesn't seem to respond." The white-haired doctor shook his finger at Bridget, standing nearby. "It's because his room isn't cold enough," he chastised. "I told you, no fires, and keep the bedroom door closed. Fresh air brings on fevers. I've warned you before!"

"Aye, doctor." Bridget shot an accusing glance toward Anne. Obviously Anne would be the only one foolish enough to do such a thing, the scolding glare said. "What else may we do for him?"

"Cut a pigeon in half and place it at his feet. It will draw the fever. A sheep's lung will do, if you have it. And keep giving him the conserve of violets." His white hair waved above his ears as he moved. "God might take him anytime or He might grant him several weeks."

Anne's throat tightened and tears sprang into her eyes as she hurried to her father's bedside. One look at the chalky pallor of his cheeks and the pale, drawn lips and she went rigid with fear. *Please, God. Don't take him from me, too. I need him so very much. All my life, those whom I've loved have been taken from me—*

"Anne?"

She lifted her head. "I'm here, Father," she said, choking on the words as she reached for his hand.

His heavy lids fluttered. "Don't be sad." His voice rasped. A stabbing realization told her there was nothing she could do. For a fleeting moment, she stood, staggered by the truth. She tried to wash the fact away from her mind, like an ink spot upon white silk, but her efforts were just as futile, the hopelessness welled inside her until it threatened to seize her very soul.

For the remainder of the day, Anne hovered over him. The servants wove in and out, and, following the doctor's instructions, they shrouded the bed with red curtains, the beneficial color for the sick.

Her father drifted in and out of sleep. Several times he called out to Elizabeth, and although Anne knew he was dreaming, several times she felt the strange sensation that someone else was in the room.

The fire had been allowed to go out and the chamber was chilly. She moistened his parched face with trembling hands as her dread mounted. Jonathan dreamed fitfully. She called to him, but after a while, he didn't hear her. He refused food, water or his medicines.

Anne lost track of the time, only remembering that she had replaced the tapers in their holders three times. Bridget insisted someone relieve her, and Anne couldn't believe it when Bridget told her it had been eighteen hours since Jonathan had collapsed downstairs.

Anne declined all offers of help. She felt as though her presence and strong will would keep him alive.

Several hours later, he lay motionless against the pillows. "Father?" she called, her heart racing with fear.

His lids fluttered open and he managed a weak smile. "Didn't I tell you she looks exactly like you, my dear?

Anne grasped his hot, dry hand in hers. "Who, Father?"

His hazel eyes darted toward the sound of her voice. "Why, your mother, of course. Elizabeth's standing beside you." His voice was feeble and weak, but his eyes were bright and filled with an inner peace. "Your mother says she's very proud of you."

Tears welled in her eyes for the first time and she couldn't stop them as she wiped them furiously away. "Please Father, don't leave me," she begged.

"Anne, listen, my dearest."

She lifted her head, her heart twisting in sorrow.

"Your mother reminded me of something." His voice was fading and she strained to hear. "She says to tell you…each new dawn brings us closer…to our destiny. Follow your dream, Anne." He squeezed her hand with unbelievable strength. "And be brave enough to listen to your heart…."

An anguished sob shook her."I will, Father," she whispered hoarsely, flicking away her tears with her fingers.

"Your love for Nat…will give you strength…to embrace the dawn, whatever fate might bring."

Suddenly he released his grip and she felt the life force leave him.

She kissed his cheek. Although his expression held such peace and contentment, she couldn't stop the uncontrollable weeping any more than she could stop what she knew had happened.

After a few minutes, the muffled sound of sobbing and a hand at her shoulder caused her to look up at Bridget and Jane standing beside her. Bridget's lips moved silently, her rosary beads clicking in her shaking fingers.

Jane drew Anne to her and Bridget embraced them both, weeping, sharing their grief as they tried to comfort her.

After a long time, Bridget said finally, "I'm glad you were with him in the end. It was a great comfort for him to have you there," she added, her soft brogue thick and ragged.

Anne's throat constricted. Remembering the look of love and peace on her father's face, she knew that she was not the only one with her father. "My mother, Elizabeth, was with him," she whispered, fresh tears spilling down her face. "She was with us both."

Chapter Sixteen

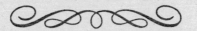

"My dear Anne, you must eat something," Bridget urged, ladling mutton broth from the silver tureen into a bowl and passing it to Anne. "You've eaten nothing since..." Her voice faded, as though saying the words, *since your father died,* would dissolve Anne into a puddle of tears.

Actually, Anne had not cried since early morning when he had died; she felt so dry and numb inside, tears were impossible. Through the ravages of her grief, her one thought was of Nat. How could she go on if she were to lose him, too?

"Did you hear me, dear?" Bridget's lace-capped head tilted in question. "I asked you if you're feeling up to talking about the arrangements?"

"Whatever you decide will be fitting," Anne murmured, while her mind wrestled with how to break the news of her decision to Bridget. She glanced at the woman beside her, her head bent over her meal, her mind in deep reflection. This dear soul, whom Anne had grown to respect and love as if she were her own mother, would move heaven and earth to stop her. Anne bit back the taste of regret. But there was no other way. Regardless of the emotional price, she had to leave for London.

"Jane, may I have a few words with you?" Anne began, after the meal was over and they had gone upstairs.

"Of course, my dear," Jane replied with compassion. "Would you like me to stay with you awhile?" Since the news of Doc's imprisonment, dark blue shadows framed Jane's gray eyes. The usual pink had left her cheeks, leaving her fragile looking.

Anne nodded, then pushed open the door. The scent of dried lavender rushed out at them as they entered the chamber. A servant had already turned back the blue-and-white coverlet upon the feather bed. Fresh candles flamed from the silver holders, and a bright cheery fire crackled noisily in the grate.

Jane seated herself by the hearth while Anne sat on the edge of the bed. She hesitated only a moment before plunging in. "I'm leaving for London in the morning," she began shakily. "I'll plead with Colonel Twining for Nat and Doc's lives."

Jane's mouth dropped, her face blanched white as her lace cap. "That's folly!" She bolted from the chair. "Surely Twining has broken your marriage contract by now. He'll have you tortured until you tell him everything about the people who have helped you. Then he'll hang you along with Doc and Nat. You must be mad if you think otherwise."

Undaunted, Anne continued. "I've already thought of that. I'll tell Twining that I came down with a lung fever and only recently recovered. I'll tell him it was the Black Fox who saved me from death and I've been trying to make my way back to London all this time."

Jane paused, her narrow shoulders rigid beneath the black silk. Then she took a deep breath. "Anne, my dear," she said as though speaking to a child. "It's admirable of you to want to help, but it's not necessary. In London, our supporters are working to gain the men's release, as we speak."

Anne rose and stood before the fireplace. "I'm leaving tomorrow, with or without your help."

"But you can't!" Jane gasped. "You'll be putting everyone, including yourself, in danger for... nothing!"

"Perhaps, if I fail... but what if I can change Twining's mind?" Anne closed her eyes and prayed for a miracle. "My father told me that Twining had been deeply in love with my mother. I'll beg Twining to consider my plea as the daughter of the only woman he ever loved."

Jane shook her head, frowning. "A foolish, romantic notion."

"But what if I *can* convince him? Isn't it worth a try?"

Jane stared into the crackling fire. After a few minutes she gazed back at Anne, deep in thought.

Anne placed her hand on Jane's shoulder. "Please, with your help, I know we can save them."

Jane's gaze lingered in the leaping flames. "The gold reserves for the king's restoration effort are stored here." Jane fixed her gray eyes back on Anne. "Wilkens offered to bring enough gold to our supporters in London to bribe the men's escape, but he's been through a great deal for one so old. Even with another week's rest, he might still be too weak to ride." Hope enlivened Jane's gray eyes. "Perhaps if you brought the gold to London, our loyalists might be able to arrange the men's release before their trial."

"I'll do it," Anne cried. "The livery servants won't disobey Bridget and saddle a horse for me, but if you ask for a horse, I can ride to the first inn and sell it for my coach passage to London. Ask to have my father's horse saddled."

"Your father's horse was killed in battle." Jane's brow wrinkled in thought. "You're right about the servants. None would disobey my mother. However, Jake and Billy are Doc's servants, and while he's away, they'll not dare disobey me."

An overwhelming rush of gratitude washed over Anne and she breathed a deep sigh of relief. "Thank God," she muttered.

Jane paced back and forth in front of the crackling logs. Pink splotches of color brightened her cheeks. "I'll ask Jake to harness the horses. He'll take you as far as the first inn, but he can't let anyone see the Rosemoor crest on the coach door. He'll let you out near the inn, then you'll go the rest of the way on foot."

"He can leave my trunk by the side of the road by the inn."

Jane nodded, circling the floor as she thought. "You'll need coin to pay for the change of horses...a lunch and flasks to drink."

"Several changes of clothing."

"Aye, I'll give you my plainer things," Jane agreed.

Anne rushed to her. "You won't be sorry, Jane."

Jane hung on to her. "If only I could go with you, but I can't leave Mother. Besides, I might hear news from the major that might prove valuable."

Anne smiled. "It's best I go alone. Besides, I feel God answered my prayers. And you know I'll do everything in my power to save the men we love." When Jane released her, tears welled in her eyes.

"I know you will, my dear." She wiped her eyes. "Now, we have work to do. I've a small trunk you can use. It's plain. No one will recognize it. And I'll be back with clothing and the special pouches of gold." Jane's eyes flashed with hope and her voice rose with excitement. "Saints, what I'll tell Mother in the morning is beyond me," she muttered as she opened the door.

"You'll think of something." Anne watched Jane roll her eyes as she closed the door behind her.

Fifteen minutes later, Jane returned carrying a small trunk. "Do you know how to use this?" she asked, opening the lid and lifting out a white silk petticoat. Perplexed, Anne watched as Jane unfolded the undergarment and pulled out a pistol from a long, hidden panel concealed in the skirts.

Anne's eyes widened. "God's bones. What a piece of handiwork to keep up your skirts!"

Jane's cheeks pinked; she grinned back at her. "You might be glad you've got it, traveling alone," she said, removing the musket ball from the cloth bag. "Have you ever shot a wheel-lock pistol?" she asked, ramming the wadding down the bore.

"Nay, but I saw Nat shoot one at the Pied Bull Inn."

After showing her how to load the firearm, Jane put the weapon in Anne's palm. "Remember to do this," she instructed, showing her the proper grip. "Hold the butt in both hands, steadily but not tightly. Then cock it like this, and gently pull back the trigger, while eyeing down the top of the barrel." Jane squinted her left eye and made believe she pulled back the hammer. "Pop! That's all there is to it."

Anne gripped the cold metal in her hands, and imitated what she had been shown. She trembled slightly at the reality that she may actually have to use it.

"Aye, that's it." Jane slipped the pistol back into the specially sewn flap of the underskirt, along with the cloth bag of musket balls and laid the ruffly garment on the bed. "Wear it while you're traveling. It's best to be prepared."

Anne swallowed but nodded in agreement. After Jane held up plain garments for her approval, she wrote the address of Twining's town house in London and the name of the vicar at London's Christ Church Vicarage and Almshouse and pressed the slip of paper into her hand. "After you deliver the gold to Vicar Trueworthy at Christ Church, I pray you'll return to Rosemoor." Jane smiled slightly. "Although I doubt I hold little persuasion to change your mind."

Anne returned the smile. "I'm confident I can persuade Twining, especially with Vicar Trueworthy's help."

Jane nodded, her mouth a firm line. "So be it." She watched her steadily. "And of course, if you can get word to him, Babson will help you."

"Babson?" Anne stopped dead still. "Babson?" she repeated, unable to believe her ears.

Jane glanced up, surprised. "I thought you knew. He was your father's manservant before Jonathan married your mother."

Anne felt confused. "Aye, but that was a long time ago. Babson was like a father to me when my mother died, but after the war, he changed. When Uncle George became my guardian, Babson asked to take leave and join the Roundhead army. He—"

"Nay, Anne. He did that to gain your uncle's trust. Babson was the spy who helped Nat at Wycliffe Manor. He helped many a priest and Royalist through to safety during the civil war." She paused and watched Anne's face. "Babson's loyalty to your father has never faltered. How did you think your father managed to visit when you were a little girl?''

Anne slumped back in the chair, her knees weak. "Babson must have thought I was such a foolish chit."

Jane gazed at her warmly. "Not now, my dear. Next to my mother, you're one of the bravest women I've ever known."

The autumn rains had begun the morning Anne left Rosemoor, turning the post roads into a muddy quagmire. With the generous gold Jane had given her for her own use, Anne rented the finest coach and six available, and a team of drivers who eagerly accepted the challenge to bring her to London posthaste.

She rode day and night, sleeping in the coach, stopping only long enough to eat and change horses at each coaching inn. Tucked inside her skirts, Anne felt the hard sacks filled with gold she guarded with her life. The small fortune would somehow save the lives of Nat and his men, providing they were alive.

Dear God, they had to be!

During the long days it had taken to reach London, nausea dogged her with each toss and sway of the coach. Clutching on for dear life, her face buried in her lap, she had ample time to realize that her symptoms weren't so unusual after all. Hadn't she watched, with childlike fascination, the very symptoms among the servant women who were with child?

A rush of reverent elation swept through her at the dawning realization that she was going to have Nat's baby. Alone, bouncing along the rutted road, the drumming rain hammering upon the leather roof as the coach clattered toward London, a larger purpose began to unfold to her. Aye, God had taken so much from her. His mercy wouldn't allow her to arrive too late.

By the time Anne arrived at the Christ Church Vicarage and Almshouse and had delivered the two long sacks of gold to Vicar Trueworthy, darkness was near. She knew she hadn't any time to lose. She gave the coachman the order to proceed to Holborn, the residential area linking the City and Westminster.

That evening, Anne looked out at a fashionable town house, an iron gate and fence circling the small front garden. Her heart hammered with sudden dread. She peered at the flickering candlelit windows as she paid the driver while the footman carried her valise to the entranceway. She stood upon wobbly knees until the crack of the whip signaled the coach lurching away. Her courage ebbed with the sound of the wheels clacking along the stones, the horses' clip-clops fading into the fog.

Her hand trembled as her cold fingers grabbed the bronze eagle-head knocker, and the hard clack echoed along the deserted street when she rapped upon the red-lacquered door. Her heart beat so loudly she thought it would hammer through her ears.

She waited for what seemed like an eternity. Then boot steps shuffled inside. Her throat tightened as the sound grew louder.

The scrape of bolts and locks rankled her senses before the door jerked open. A shadowy outline of a hunched, maroon-and-gold-liveried manservant peered down at her.

"Mistress Anne?" gasped a man's voice.

Anne peered up. The crystal chandelier's illumination from the hall obscured his face, yet the voice was familiar. He poked his white head into the doorway. She blinked up as the lantern light spilled across the snowy, craggy-faced servant she remembered from Wycliffe Manor. "B-Babson?" she cried.

"God's breath!" His hand flew to his heart.

"Babson, am I too late?" Before she could say another word, he pressed his finger to his lips and glanced over his shoulder.

"Nat an' 'is men are in Newgate prison."

A flood of relief engulfed her. Thank God she had arrived in time. But knowing that Nat had been imprisoned in England's most notorious jail shot fear through her bones. "Is Colonel Twining in?" she whispered. "I must see him."

Babson shot a nervous look behind him. Then he stepped out of the doorway into the lamplight. "For God's sake, child. Leave here at once. It's not safe—"

Anne pushed past him, refusing to be treated like a child. "I'm here to help Nat. Let me in. I know what I'm doing."

"Twining is due back anytime." Babson's voice tightened with anguish while he scuttled after her. "And keep your voice down. The house is full of spies." He pointed to a doorway off the foyer. "This way," he urged, picking up the candlestick from the hall table as he led the way through the open door.

"Why are you here instead of with my uncle?" she asked, glancing around the ornate hall.

"When Twining left Wycliffe Manor, he asked if I might join him as his manservant." Babson's mouth twitched. "Your uncle was hardly in the position to refuse him anything after you left."

Good. Twining hadn't cut off her uncle George. She would need all the leverage she could use. Anne laid her hand on Babson's frail shoulder. "Dear Babson, you must help me free Nat and Doc—" But before Anne had a chance to finish, the front door burst open and Colonel Twining entered, his immense cape sweeping around him like enormous bat wings.

For a brief moment, Twining thought his mind was playing tricks again when he looked up and saw Elizabeth. The red gold curls escaping beneath the green tucked bonnet. The black gown that played up the blue-green fire of her eyes. The same ivory skin and defiant chin as her wide eyes held his unflinchingly. It *was* his Elizabeth, standing in the foyer as she did that night, nineteen years ago—that night she told him of her decision to marry Jonathan Lowell.

He closed his eyes for a moment and steadied himself against his cane. But it couldn't be. He blinked.

She was Anne. Anne had come back to him.

Babson stood beside her, mouth agape. He rushed to take his hat, cane and gloves.

"Colonel Twining." Fabric rustled as she dipped a curtsy. "Forgive my unannounced arrival. I know it's highly untoward, but..." Anne's eyes widened and something that might have been alarm touched her face. "Colonel Twining?"

He realized he had been staring. "Mistress Anne," he managed, and with a formidable effort tried to gather his composure. But he couldn't take his eyes from her. Millions of thoughts rushed at him as he forced his hands to calmly unfasten his cloak and allow Babson to lift it from his shoulders.

She was an incredibly beautiful woman. So like her mother. No, Anne had something more—a fiery will that flamed a defiant passion—sparking a yearning in him so profound it nearly undid him. God, he had known all kinds of women, preferring his experienced French mistress of late, but compared to Josephine, this flame-haired jewel made him feel like a young bull.

"I've come to talk to you, Colonel." She gave him a despairing look, her hands folded demurely in front of her.

"Babson," he said thickly. "Take her cape, then have Mrs. Minton prepare a room. Also, send word to her uncle that she is safe with me." He dismissed the servant with a flick of a hand.

"Come, my dear. We'll talk in the withdrawing room." He took her arm, and as she swept beside him, the fragrance of violets drifted to his nostrils. For a moment, he was reminded of the rush a hawk must feel when swooping down on its prey.

When she was seated by the fire, he poured two drafts of brandy and waited for her to begin.

"I've come to offer my apology for insulting you, Colonel. I behaved like a foolish chit when I ran away from my uncle." She paused and gave him a pleading look. "I didn't appreciate...your offer of marriage." Her gaze dropped to her fingers playing nervously with the black silk gloves in her lap. "And..."

"And now you do?" he finished for her.

A flash of surprise crossed her face, but she recovered quickly. "I—I meant only to apologize for my actions, Colonel."

Resentment rose through him as he realized she had no thought to honor her contract. Then why had she come? "You're shaking," he said, hoping to hide his irritation and impatience. He handed her the brandy. "I hope you haven't taken a chill."

"I'm sure I haven't, thank you." Her eyes never left his. "I don't care for a brandy."

"But I insist." He held out the crystal goblet, the prisms sparkling with firelight. When she took it, her icy fingers brushed his as she seized the glass and took a sip of the amber liquid.

For the brief moment their fingers touched, he felt another jolt of desire. *How he wanted her.* His manhood hardened, straining against his breeches. How he wanted to take her to the floor, now, and be done with this charade. But a slow curl of control slowly returned to him as he took a seat, instead, and crossed his legs. He could take her and he would, but first, he would hear why she came to him.

"It was rumored you dressed as a boy and followed Dr. Herrick and his wife from Wycliffe Manor where you came upon the Black Fox and his band. Did the doctor or his wife help you with your intrigue?"

Her blue-green eyes rounded in surprise. "Of course not. It's true I dressed as a lad and stole a horse from my uncle's stable. I rode through the woods until I became lost." He watched the fine tendrils of fire-gold hair escape from under her bonnet and frame her lovely face with each tilt of her head while she talked. "I became ill and wandered for days, accepting charity where I could find it. Then the Black Fox found me, sick and helpless. He said he would take me back to my uncle, as soon as I was well, but something must have happened to him, because after I recovered, he never returned. I've been making my way back to my uncle all this time."

"Indeed?" Besides becoming more beautiful, she had also improved on her ability to lie. Her father, Jonathan

Lowell, had been a smooth-talking devil. Hadn't that rogue's honeyed eloquence turned Elizabeth from him? Surely his daughter had the gift of the devil's tongue, as well. He remained silent as he sipped from his glass. "It must have been a terrible ordeal for you." When she said nothing, he continued, "Then you never saw the rogue again?"

Anne's dark lashes swept to her lap. "Never. When I heard the Black Fox had been charged with my kidnapping, and had been arrested, I thought it only fair that you should know it wasn't true. He saved my life."

So that was it! One glance at her beautiful face as she spoke of Braydon and a blind man could see that she was transfixed by that damned rogue. Twining's fingers edged white as he squeezed the stem of his drink. Twirling the amber liquid in the crystal goblet, he tried to subdue his growing rage. She would risk facing the devil, himself, to save her lover. He could feel her eyes on him. "You'd plead for a rogue you hardly know?" He tried to keep the rancor out of his voice, but he saw from her slight flinch that he wasn't successful.

"It—it seemed like the Christian thing to do," she replied uneasily.

Desire and outrage grew within him like a two-headed demon. Before he was through, he'd strike that silly look of captivation for Braydon from her face. "And is it also your Christian duty that brought you to London to tell me that you're willing to proceed with our marriage contract?"

"Marriage contract?" Anne rose, all pretense drawn from her face. "Surely you can't accept me as...as a proper candidate after what's happened?" It was clear she had never thought he would ask her to fulfill the contract.

"Why not, my dear?" He relished her discomfiture. "You've told me your virtue is intact and that you were a victim of a childlike rebellion against your uncle, which, by your own admission, was foolish." He smiled to himself when he saw the disturbed surprise fill her face. "How could I, as a righteous Christian, hold a series of unfortunate incidents against you?"

"But, what would your...?"

Twining sat down beside her and took her cold hand in his. "My dear, either you're willing to marry me or you're not."

He watched the surprise mix with dread as she thought of an answer. "That's between you and my uncle," she said finally, hoping to stall for time, no doubt.

He let go of her hand, strode toward the brass wood box and tossed a log onto the hungry flames. "Tell me, do you know the identity of the Black Fox?" he asked, his back to her.

"Nay. I only saw him for a short time, as I told you. I never saw him without his mask."

Twining whirled around. "His name is Nat Braydon."

Anne's face paled. How he delighted at the anguish she failed to hide. She knew he knew she had been lying. He felt like a cat toying with a mouse. She forced an easy shrug, as though refusing him the satisfaction of her uneasiness.

"Braydon's the cousin of Tom Thackery, the owner of the Pied Bull Inn." He paused, studying her. "*Was* the owner, I should say. I had that den of immorality burned to the ground."

She dropped her lashes to hide the pain she felt at this latest strike of his cruelty. She thought of the brave people who had risked so much to smuggle Royalists through the Roundhead lines to safety, and a real pang of sadness and regret coursed through her. Damn this evil man.

"I see by your expression that you're surprised."

She raised a shoulder. "Why would I be surprised?" Her voice was a torn whisper. "I don't know the people you're talking about," she insisted.

"Even of the Pied Bull Inn?" His thin black eyebrows shot up and the firelight played off his sharp cheekbones, casting deepening shadows across his face. "The tavern where you and Braydon stayed as man and wife?"

Anne stiffened. "I don't know what you mean."

"Or should I call you Rosie?" His face brightened with a maniacal glee and suddenly Anne felt afraid.

"Rosie, the wench who wore your gold locket!" He lunged for her, grabbed the wool shawl about her shoulders and sent it flying across the room, exposing the bare neckline of her gown.

Anne cried out.

"You're not wearing your locket, my dear?" He coiled back at her like an adder, his eyes raking over her. "Moll Standish described your little trinket. In fact, she has been very helpful in bringing the Black Fox to justice."

Anne stumbled back, but he grabbed her and pulled her to him. "You look shaken, my love."

"It—it's not true . . ." She stopped to take a deep breath. She couldn't give in, after all this. She had to convince him. "You've been told an untruth, and—"

"Indeed I have, and all by you." His damp hands squeezed her arms, then he shook her. "Do you deny it?"

"Aye, I deny it." She clenched her small jaw and glared back at him. It would be her word against Moll's. She'd never admit the truth if he tortured her. She had to keep her pretense or Nat and everything he cared for would be lost. "I deny it."

"Good." Twining shoved her back onto the sofa. His eyes glittered with evil as his voice took on an inappropriate calm. "For I shall enjoy teaching you how to tell the truth, my little Anne." His voice softened to a mere whisper. "And before I'm through, you'll learn to enjoy it, as well."

"You believe the word of a barmaid over me?" Anne rubbed her arm where she could still feel his grip.

"All that matters to me is that you've returned where you belong." His mouth hardened as his eyes narrowed.

"But you can't hang this man for kidnapping me, when he saved me from the soldiers—"

"Saved you from *my* men?" Twining wheeled around at her. "*My* soldiers would have returned you to your uncle, posthaste!"

"Your men would never have believed me if—"

"Stop it!" He pounded his fist on the table. "I've listened long enough." He lunged at her, his face only inches

from hers. "Your precious highwayman will hang at Ty-
burn the day after tomorrow along with Tom Thackery and
Doc Herrick."

"No, please." Anne's head turned away, her shoulders
shook with emotion. "On my mother's grave, spare them!"

He cupped her chin and forced her to look at him. "Your
mother stood in this room and made her choice. She got
what she deserved. You, however—" He jerked her to him
and when she stopped fighting, he tightened his hold on her
arms. "I see I've managed to shed a little light of reason on
your mind."

"Don't kill him. Please," she begged, hating herself for
it. "Please, I'll do anything . . . anything to save him."

"Anything?"

Anne bowed her head and nodded. His iron grip took her
chin and lifted her head back. His gray eyes held a strange
expression. Finally he spoke.

"We will be married, immediately."

This can't be happening! Her mind whirled. *But it's my
mother you want, not me.* Anne tried to twist her head free,
but he yanked her back. His eyes shone with rage. A cry of
anguish escaped her. "Surely, you jest."

The cunning grin straightened and he glanced over her
with a look of the familiar lechery she remembered. "You'll
discover, my dear, that I never jest about what I want."

Panic and despair increased in her mind. She had done
nothing to further Nat's chance for escape; instead, she had
trapped herself, as well. "And if I won't marry you?"

"You will," he answered smugly. He strode to the side
table and picked up the goblet of brandy. "You see, I've re-
considered my decision on the highwayman."

Anne's heart leapt with hope. "You mean, you're going
to let him go if I marry you?"

He snickered. "What a child you are. Ah, you'll delight
me in my old age." He watched her, his eyes bright with
cruelty. "Braydon will not hang. You have my word, providing you give me a written letter to him, telling him of

your change of heart and your decision to marry me."
Twining's eyebrows lifted as he waited for her answer.

Anne tried to understand what drove this twisted, maniacal thinking. "You call that a bargain? To rot away in jail
instead of hanging?"

"You're still underage, and I have a signed contract by
your legal guardian."

"You won't marry me, because I'm pregnant with Nat
Braydon's child."

Now it was Anne who watched with satisfaction the
stunned look of shock wash across the colonel's face.

"You're lying."

"No, Colonel, I'm not." She placed her hands defiantly
on her hips. "Now, do you still want to marry me?"

Twining stared at her, dumbstruck. For all he had put her
through, seeing him this way returned some of her mettle.

"If it's true, I would think you'd wish as early a marriage as possible." His expression was one of testing, bait-
ing. He drained the brandy and went for another.

"I would think by now, Colonel, you would know that I
care little for convention." She watched his eyes rake over
her, his mind scheming behind those gray orbs. Finally he
strode to within a sword's length from her and glared at her.

"Aye, we have a deal." The confident tone reappeared in
his voice. "We'll be married as soon as possible, and you'll
tell everyone the child is mine."

"Never. However, I'll agree not to disclose the father—"

"You have no bargaining power with me!" He grabbed
her wrist and pulled her to her feet, his mouth twisted with
rancor. "You'll tell everyone the child is mine. Refuse, and
you'll watch Braydon hang. Then I'll lock you away and
you'll never see your bastard child. Is that what you want?"

"You're mad!"

"Not as mad as you if you refuse my offer."

Anne jerked from his grip and sat down. With her head
in her hands, she tried to think of something, but she had
failed completely. She should have listened to Jane, for she

had done nothing but risk her unborn child's life, and done nothing to help the man she loved.

"I'll marry you. I won't deny that the child is yours, and..." She lifted her head and met his eyes. "Spare Nat, Tom Thackery and Doc Herrick, and I'll be an *obedient* wife to you."

Twining's eyes flickered with understanding at the further offer she was making. Desire tightened his loins. "And you'll write the note to Braydon that I dictate?"

"Aye, but I also want your promise in writing, as well."

"Agreed." He watched her full bosom heave with short, agitated breaths at the final agreement. "I'll allow you to watch the men board a vessel for France. That should satisfy you of my good word."

She nodded, closing her eyes.

"Then for what it's worth, dear lady, you've saved your lover's life."

A wave of nausea threatened at the thought of the devil's bargain she had just made, but it had been worth it. Nat, Doc and Tom would be saved.

His gray eyes flickered with a strange emotion. "I'll ring for a servant who will see you to your quarters." He strode to the wall and yanked on the bellpull. "Sit at the desk, my dear. There's a parchment and quill in the drawer."

Anne stared at him. "Surely that can wait until tomorrow?"

"You'll be much too busy with your marriage plans for writing letters, my dear." Twining shoved the ink pot closer to her. Now, write exactly what I tell you."

Anne took the quill and dipped the nib into the ink. As he dictated the outrageous words, she cringed, ignoring the sickening feeling in the pit of her stomach. The only way she could make it through this ordeal was knowing that Nat would never believe the lies she was being forced to write. Never! He knew she loved him, and as soon as she could, she would get word to him that she was well, and they were to have a child together. At least his life and that of Tom and Doc had been spared, and they would be sent to live safely

in a neutral country, until she had a way for them to be together again.

"You may sign it any way you wish," Twining said with
a wave of his hand. He watched as she signed it simply,
Anne.

He took it, perusing it. "Yes, this will do quite nicely."

Anne rose and put the plume down. Her knees felt weak
and she needed to be alone. She felt ill, but all she would
think of was that Nat and the men were saved. Nothing else
was important.

Twining pulled the bell cord, and a servant appeared.

"Mrs. Minton. Show Mistress Lowell to the blue suite,
then send in Babson."

"Aye, Colonel."

Anne followed the woman out the door without giving
Twining a word or customary curtsy.

Twining noticed the slight but only chuckled at her spirit.
Nothing could dull his elevated mood. Nothing. He lifted
the candle closer and reread the elegant scroll. "What a
stroke of God's grace," he said aloud, clutching the parchment to his chest. He was still reading the letter addressed
to Nat when Babson tapped on the door, paused and entered the room.

"Have my coach brought 'round, and have a sentry
posted in front of the blue suite. Under no circumstances is
Mistress Anne to leave her chambers."

"Aye, sire."

"That will be all, Babson." He watched the old man bow
curtly and leave the room.

Taking a seat beside the fire, Twining removed the me-
dallion from his vest pocket and stared down into the lovely
smiling miniature. The flames roared with a sudden gust of
draft.

*Aye, Elizabeth, your daughter looks like you, but she has
the heart of that devil you married. But Providence has sent
her to me, as well as your grandchild. I promise you, now
that I've got them, I'll never let them go.*

He smiled, gazing for a long moment, then snapped the keepsake shut and put it away. With careful precision, he rolled up the document and placed it in the leather case. He hadn't felt such satisfaction in a very long time.

He watched the log sputter and sparks fly up against the fireplace screen only to burn themselves out and fall harmlessly to the fire.

Worry not, Elizabeth. I'll see to it that, like her father, Anne atones for her sins.

Chapter Seventeen

A whip cracked and a man's bloodcurdling scream ricocheted off the stone walls of Newgate prison, awakening every chained prisoner on the second floor. A jolt of compassion shot through Nat as he watched the latest example of cruelty by the turnkey called Crabbe. No sooner had Crabbe raised the whip again than the shackled prisoner—a slightly built, white-haired old man—jerked back, and a cry for mercy ripped from his throat.

A rat scurried from the shadows where Tom stretched to the full length of his chains to reach within several feet of where Nat and Doc Herrick lay. "Just like I told ye," Tom whispered. "That flea of a runt, Crabbe, likes the smell o' blood." With his free hand, he scuffed at a bug crawling along the stone wall. "'Ow I'd like to get me 'ands on 'im, just once."

So would they all, Nat mused, studying the circle of twenty or so prisoners observing the beating. In the flickering lamplight of Crabbe's lantern, Nat could see the hate and the yearning to have one last chance at Crabbe before the gallows.

Doc rolled away as far as the shackles at his ankles would allow and softly retched in the shadows, more a dry heave, Nat thought bitterly. For the past week since their imprisonment, Doc had kept little in his stomach, the result of witnessing the inhuman atrocities of the hellhole of Newgate.

"If only we could bribe Crabbe as easily as we bribed the other guards," Tom whispered again, "breakin' out of 'ere would be easy."

Nat watched Crabbe hurry from the room down the torch-lit passageway in summons to a call. So far, the little bully had kept a respectful distance from them, yet Nat had seen the sadistic longing in Crabbe's eyes. No doubt, Twining had paid the turnkey to refrain from using the whip on them, for whatever his own nefarious reasons. But Nat knew it was fear of Twining, not money, that kept Crabbe in tow.

"Somehow we've got to try to take Crabbe, ourselves," Nat whispered. "When we escape, the bribed guards will look the other way or keep their distance, but they won't help us overpower Crabbe. They know he's Twining's straw man."

The clatter of boot steps caused Nat to turn to see Crabbe scurrying back, his lantern bouncing light along the stone walls. Following the turnkey, the caped figure of a man marched behind. A feeling of foreboding shot though Nat.

"Shh. We'll talk later." Pretending sleep, Nat watched through slitted eyelids the swinging light of Crabbe's lantern spill across the sprawled bodies of the sleeping prisoners.

Clacking footsteps grew louder along the uneven granite floor. "'E's down at the end, sire," cackled Crabbe's monotone. Nat's instincts heightened when the boot steps stopped a foot in front of him. The clink of keys swinging from the chain around Crabbe's waist banged against the knife sheath at his hip. "On yer feet, Braydon," Crabbe shouted, jabbing the toe of his boot into Nat's ribs. Nat refused to flinch as he eased himself carefully to his feet, prepared to block any sudden move from the whip Crabbe always carried. Although the unaccustomed lantern's brightness nearly blinded him, Nat knew instinctively the identity of the tall, wiry man looming behind Crabbe. Colonel Twining, his lower face obscured by the overpowering perfumed white handkerchief held to his nose, stepped from the shadows and glared at him. Nat took a step toward him.

"That's close enough, Braydon," Twining said. "Or do you prefer to be called the Black Fox?"

"What do you care? Any man who would imprison men without so much as a trial—"

"Here, watch that mouth, Braydon, or—" Crabbe drew the whip, but Twining placed his hand on the turnkey's forearm.

"Don't waste your time trying to tame a fox, Crabbe," the colonel said smugly. "It will always be an animal."

Nat shrugged. "I'm afraid you've lost your beauty sleep for nothing, Twining. I still won't answer any of your questions."

"No need." The colonel waved the handkerchief. In the wavering light, Nat saw Twining's eyes flicker with dark amusement. "It is *I* who have information for you."

Alarm coursed through him, but Nat refused to show it. With theatrical motions, Twining unfolded a cream-colored parchment from the leather case while the turnkey raised the lantern. In a commanding voice, Twining read from the neat, even script.

"My dear Nat,
I will return to my rightful place in society when I become Mrs. Edward Twining, tomorrow afternoon. My marriage to the colonel will provide me the life-style I was born to.

I feel it my Christian duty to offer my encouragement to purge yourself of your sins against God and the Commonwealth by confessing your crimes posthaste.
Respectfully,
Anne"

Folding the paper away, Twining grinned broadly. "Mistress Lowell appeared at my town house, unharmed, relieved that her duress was over." His eyebrows arched imperiously. "She wished that I deliver this to you immediately. In all her excitement with the wedding details, she unselfishly wished that you should purify your soul with a confession."

Nat threw back his head and laughed. "I thought better from you, Twining. Do you really think I'd believe such dung?"

Twining's features hardened and his voice edged with the malice Nat remembered. "We'll see who has the last laugh, Braydon." He thrust the parchment in Nat's chest. "Read it yourself. That is, if you can."

Nat fixed his eyes on Twining. "Why should I read your dribble that you forced some maid to pen?" He watched Twining's glittering outrage grow. "I have only one answer for you." Nat leaned forward and spat on the colonel's ruffled shirt.

"You swine!" Twining jumped away, stabbing at his chest with the handkerchief.

Crabbe reached back and cut loose with the whip across Nat's chest. "I should cut yer tongue out—"

"Enough, Crabbe." Twining jerked Crabbe's arm back, recovering himself. "I want him conscious tomorrow when I bring my beautiful bride to see what a pitiful animal he really is." The mockery of his words didn't quite reach the hate in his gray eyes. Twining placed the handkerchief back to his nose. "Come, Crabbe. We'll let the animals be for the night." He chortled, and the sound made Nat want to shove the lacy cloth down Twining's throat.

Crabbe drew the lantern high for one last look and muttered a coarse oath as he shuffled after the colonel, the ring of keys jingling from the chain at his belt.

Ignoring the stinging pain and the wet, sticky ooze dampening his shirt, Nat swore after the footsteps receded, rage and frustration tearing at him.

"Easy, friend." Doc parted his shirt and peered at the open slash that cut across Nat's chest before the light of the turnkey faded down the hall. "Oh, God!" Doc winced.

"That gash'll get worse in this pest 'ole," Tom added, his face troubled.

"I wonder what that arrogant bastard has up his sleeve?" Nat said, staring into the darkness.

Doc looked up, brow tight with worry. "Maybe he didn't believe me when I swore that Jane and Bridget knew nothing of my political affairs," he whispered. "Maybe Twining sent soldiers to storm Rosemoor..." His voice broke with emotion. "What if he found Anne's father?"

"Nay," Nat replied. "If that were true, Twining would have thrown it in our faces." He wiped the blood that trickled down his abdomen. "It's something else." He paused, staring at the unlit passageway. "But whatever trick that pompous ass has hatched, I'd stake my life on one thing." He gazed back at Tom and Doc. "Although I've never seen Anne's handwriting, I know she didn't write that letter."

In the elegant bedroom suite of Twining's town house where she had spent the night, Anne sat in front of the fireplace and watched the clock above the mantel tick away the minutes. It was almost seven. She had been awake when the dour Mrs. Minton brought her a basin of cold water for her morning ablutions and a change of clothing, more than an hour ago. In fact, for most of the night, Anne had lain awake, stunned and mute, her mind tumbling over what she could do to make certain Twining would carry out his part of the bargain and free Nat and the others.

But it was useless. Even if Twining signed an agreement to free Nat, the colonel could rescind the order the moment she failed to please him. Even long after they married, he could change his mind and command Nat to jail...or worse. She shivered, more from her thoughts than the damp, chilly room.

In a few short hours, she would be made to prepare for a wedding to a man she despised. The memory of Twining's hot hands, digging into her shoulders as he shook her, pressed back into her thoughts. Dear God, could she really go through with what she'd promised? At Rosemoor, surrounded by the memory of her father's love, Bridget and Jane and the loving thoughts of Nat, she had believed she could surmount anything. Now, alone in Twining's house, remembering the undisguised lust in the colonel's eyes, she wasn't so sure.

Anne squeezed her eyes shut and prayed for the strength that she would need this day. *Her wedding day!* No, today would only be a mockery. She would always remember her real wedding day as that golden morning in the autumn woodland, against a wreath of golden leaves in her hair and the bouquet of cedar that Nat had gathered when she knelt beside him, before God, beneath the blue canopy of heaven and the rolling autumn countryside of their beloved England. Before the gentle woodland creatures, with the bird's song as their symphony, they exchanged their promise to love each other until death parted them.

Anne ached with the pain of despair. How could she pretend to go through with this mockery? In her heart, she was already married, before the truth of God, and she carried the proof of their love in the tiny babe within her.

An orange ember sizzled from the small fire and popped against the screen. She pressed her hand against her stomach. Merciful God, she must find the strength to do whatever she could if there was a chance to save Nat. Raising her head, she drew in a deep, sharp breath. *For her child, she must.* Squeezing her eyes shut, Anne tried to imagine the baby. The tiny face would have Nat's laughing dark eyes and deep chestnut hair. Their son would be strong, brave and honorable like his father, and she would tell him stories of the Black Fox and teach him of honor and duty like Nat would want her to. She pressed back a fresh rush of tears. Aye, as long as she carried this precious life, she wasn't alone. She would think of her baby and remember the love and goodness of the man she cherished, and that love would give her the strength she needed to do what she must. She cradled her arms about herself, rocking back and forth, the image of her baby and Nat giving her strength.

The scrape of the metal bar opening across the lock brought her head up. For an instant, she feared it might be Twining. But that was absurd. Although he wanted her, she knew he had too much conceit to ravish her. Otherwise, he would have taken her, there, last night, when she saw the desire in his eyes. All that stopped him was his vanity. She shuddered with the realization. He would make her come to him, knowing how she despised him, and he'd glory in his power over her.

Mrs. Minton pushed open the door, her stiff black skirts rustling with the smell of lye as she marched near. "The colonel is waiting for you downstairs." Her frowning expression raked over her. "He'll not be pleased with your appearance," she added, her black brows knitted with disapproval.

Anne got to her feet, shaking out her skirts. "What's wrong with my appearance? The gown you brought me fits well enough." Usually Anne would have been curious how a bachelor would have access to such an elegant gown—yellow silk with white lace at the throat and wrists—on such short notice, but she had too many other pressing things on her mind. She remembered the servants' gossip linking Twining's name with many influential women of London society. No doubt he kept some of their finery here, in the town house. The thought that he had numerous sources for his carnal desires gave her a brief feeling of relief.

"You appear haggard. Didn't you sleep well? You look ill."

"I'm fine." Anne would give the woman no reason to run to Twining with tales.

"Humph!"

Anne couldn't tell if Mrs. Minton believed her or not, but at least the old woman didn't press her with further questions as the bony fingers poked and straightened the lace at her collar. Anne felt like swatting the woman as one would a pesky fly, but instead, she gritted her teeth and allowed the servant to fluff the billowy yellow sleeves and flatten the satin ribbon about the waist, amid disdainful sniffs.

Anne glanced into the reflecting glass while Mrs. Minton tightened the yellow bow that caught her red gold hair at the back of her head. Aye, Mrs. Minton had been right. Dark shadows were etched beneath her eyes, and her cheekbones were more pronounced from the effect of the nausea. She clasped her hands over her stomach, as if to protect the tiny life inside her.

Finally Mrs. Minton cast a cursory glance from Anne's satin slippers to the bow on her head. "Follow me," she ordered, as though Anne were finally presentable. "You'll have breakfast with the colonel when you return. Best hurry. The coach is waiting.''

Anne felt much too overdressed for a weekday morning, regardless of what Twining had planned, but she decided it would be foolhardy to protest. When they left the room, the two sentries straightened sharply and fell into step behind Anne as she swept past them in the wake of the older woman. Their boot steps clanked along the wooden stairs, echoing throughout the hall until the Roundheads took their positions outside Twining's study where he sat hunched over the desk, quill in hand.

Apprehension skittered up Anne's spine after Mrs. Minton left them alone. She looked around more closely than she had last night. The low fire crackled noisily amid a thick layer of ashes in the grate. Stacks of papers littered his desk beneath the thick candle sputtering low in the holder. Anne wondered why the maids hadn't replaced the candles or cleaned the grate. A fresh fire hadn't been laid this morning. Her eyes swept to the colonel. By the look of him and the room, he hadn't been to bed.

Had he worked all night arranging their marriage appointment so soon? During the Commonwealth, weddings were replaced by marriages before the civil magistrate, and she knew Twining wielded a great deal of influence. If the colonel demanded an immediate wedding, he would get it.

Anne waited, afraid that he would tell her they were leaving for the magistrate's office, but she refused to show her discomfort. Finally, after he had kept her waiting long enough to show his power over her, Twining lifted his head. She saw his gaze sweep over her and the obvious appreciation in his face that he couldn't hide.

He stood, dropped the quill and studied her from head to foot. "Enchanting. Truly enchanting." He offered her a chair.

"I prefer to stand." Anne tilted her chin, enjoying the small act of defiance.

"As you wish," he obliged civilly, but she couldn't help but notice the flush of annoyance that colored his cheeks. "Before we leave, there's something I want you to wear."

The silky tone made her skin crawl. He opened the desk drawer and pulled out a small chest of inlaid ivory. He lifted the lid and placed several small black velvet bags upon the desk.

Silently she watched as he removed a necklace with glittering green stones and a matching ring from the second bag. "It's much too early in the day for such ornamentation," she protested, feeling uneasy. Twining had impeccable taste. He would never flaunt such ostentation unless he had a very good reason. She ran her tongue across her dry lips. "Where did you say we are going?"

"You'll find out soon enough." he answered, moving toward her. It was useless to argue. When he stood in front of her, their eyes met. She was shocked to see what looked like hatred piercing the gray depths. A cold chill coursed through her.

He placed the ring on her trembling finger. By chance, it fit perfectly. Flashing prisms of brilliant stones encircled the larger green gem. She had never seen emeralds or diamonds before, but recognized them from her reading. Their beauty was lost to her. She refused to show any emotion as his eyes scrutinized her face.

He placed the heavy necklace around her throat. "I'll help you with the clasp, my dear." His attempt at graciousness made her feel more anxious than his temper of last night.

"You're wearing the Thurston emeralds, in case you didn't know." He made a condescending, chortling sound at the back of his throat. The lavish rows of emeralds, encircled with diamonds, felt like a noose around her neck. She refused comment, repulsed by his fingers at the back of her neck. She prayed he would hurry and get whatever spectacle he had planned over with so she might retire to her chamber. Her head ached, the nausea had returned and she felt extremely fatigued.

He whirled her to face him, his eyes on the necklace at her bosom. "That emerald necklace and ring was bought by my grandfather when he made his fortune in wool. One day it will be given to my first son to give to his wife on their wedding day." The mention of their child, she knew, was a direct reference to her baby, as though to keep her in line. She ignored the comment, afraid she would be unable to control her tongue. How she would have loved to slap that arrogant look from his face.

"You haven't told me where we're going," she said instead.

His face lit up with a smile that caused her apprehension to grow. "Hurry, our coach awaits. I'll tell you en route."

The coach and six wheeled past the row of fashionable town houses that lined Newberry Lane, still shrouded in chilly, early morning mist and chimney smoke. She snuggled deeper inside the heavy red woolen cape and fur muff he had given her to wear before they left. Again, the clothing fit as though it were made for her. No doubt, his mistress and she were the same size. It had been dark when she had arrived last night, and this was the first glimpse of London she had seen. A heavy feeling of despair hung around her as Twining droned on about trivial details. Why didn't he tell her where they were going?

Ten minutes later, she pulled back the leather curtain from the window, watching the early morning vendors' carts wheeling to market, beggars arguing over a tossed coin, villagers walking or on horseback. As they drove closer to the City, the air smelled dank and reeked with the smell of garbage. She drew back the curtain in disgust.

Seated across from her, wrapped in the fur lap robe, Twining eyed her with interest. "The wind is coming off the Thames. It's usually not quite so foul. You'll get used to it." His mouth twitched in droll humor.

"Where are we going?" she snapped, her patience at an end. The swaying of the coach and the fetid smells made her stomach turn. The incessant clip-clopping of the horses' hooves upon the cobbles sounded like drums pounding in her head.

"We're going to Newgate prison, my dear. You will have the opportunity to speak to your lover, and tell him of your marriage today."

A sudden surge of excitement shot through her at the thought that she would finally see Nat, talk to him, tell him that she loved him, but almost as quickly, her excitement changed to wary skepticism. She watched his enjoyment grow at her reaction and she forced herself to gain control of her emotions. With her heart hammering, she said in an even voice, "I wrote the letter you dictated. Isn't that enough?" *But of course! Nat hadn't believed it. Now, Twining needed her to tell Nat in person.* "And what if I refuse?"

"Suit yourself." He sighed and waved his hand in that foppish manner she had come to hate. "But your lover received a rather nasty cut from the whip last night." He paused, enjoying her alarm. "Unless a doctor sees to that gash very soon, he could die from it." Twining fussed with the cuticles of his fingers. "He may not be alive by the end of the week," he said in an offhand manner.

Anne leaned forward. "You promised me that nothing would happen to him."

"How did I know he'd be so stupid as to get himself flogged?" He arched the thin brows in feigned innocence.

"If he didn't believe my note, what makes you think he'll believe my words?" The coach leaned sharply around a curve. She grabbed the hand strap, throwing her to the side.

"You'll make him believe you, if you want to see him live."

Anne stared back into his hard, chipped-granite eyes. Beneath her cape, she felt the heavy jewels circling her neck. Now she understood Twining's insistence on her ostentatious dress and jewels. He really thought that Nat would believe she could be so easily bought. Well, Nat would never believe it. He would know she was only doing it to save him. Finally she nodded. "And when I convince him, you'll give me your assurance that his wound will be properly taken care of?"

He nodded, grinning with that innocent expression. If Anne hadn't known the evil mind that worked behind that smile, she might have been taken in by his guise.

"It should be quite simple for you to convince Braydon that it's your wish to be married to me." He flicked his hand again. "Tell him you'd rather live in splendor than squalor."

Anne turned her gaze back out the window. "How will you know what I tell Nat?"

Twining grinned as though relishing her discomfort. "A turnkey will be with you. He'll provide me with a full report." Twining's eyes glinted with obvious pleasure. "And unless you put on a very convincing show—" he reached out and grabbed her wrist "—your lover's death will be on your conscience." His face was within inches of hers. She could smell the sickening perfume of his clothing. "For only you, my dear, have the power to set him free."

He released his grip and she flinched, wishing what he said wasn't true but knowing full well that it was. For the remainder of the trip, Anne tried to pull her jumbled thoughts together and think of what she would tell Nat. She sat immobile, forcing her pain beneath a facade of haughty composure, her agony tearing her up inside.

The coach veered sharply down Newgate Street and before the three-storied stone jail came into view, Anne could sense the dissolution and despair in the features of the hawkers, streetwalkers, and men and women who recognized the wealth of the coach's occupants and rushed to beg for a coin. Anne turned her face away, saddened by the want and pain in their eyes as the unwashed hands and arms banged on the polished lacquered door and scratched at the leather curtains.

Twining thumped his cane on the roof of the coach and the lash of the driver's whip and loud curses thundered over the cries of the crowd as the coach lurched forward amid the mob's screams and profanity. Anne held her stomach and forced the imagined sight of the sick and helpless thrown aside as they rode past. Nausea suddenly overwhelmed her and she hoped she wouldn't be sick. Pray God, she could get through this day.

Once inside the prison, nothing could have prepared Anne for the wretchedness of Newgate Jail. She felt as if she were stepping into hell as she followed the gatekeeper called Pike and his swinging lantern through the large cellar that comprised a central tavern for, as Pike explained, the selected prisoners who paid the turnkeys for special privileges. She

caught his glimpse at her over his shoulder, his leer raking
her from head to foot. There was no mistaking his offer to
take a bribe, if she chose to offer him money for a treat for
the prisoner she would visit. As there was only room for
them to proceed in a single file, Twining walked behind her,
and she wasn't sure if he had caught the exchange with Pike.

It was too dark to see the prisoners as she walked past toward the gigger, the hall where prisoners were allowed visitors. She could only imagine their beseeching faces. Odors
of excrement reeked around them. Something wet and furry
brushed her slipper while she followed Pike along the torch-
lit halls of damp, musty stone. Her feet skidded on something slippery; she clenched her teeth, unwilling to make a
sound, lest Twining heard and relished her agony.

From the shadows, a hand reached out and grabbed at her
skirt, calling out a name, while another moaned, the frail
voice begging for mercy. The acrid stench of unwashed
bodies, sour old vomit and the hot coppery smell of blood
brought bile to her throat. Her eyes stung from the stench
and her throat constricted in pity with each step taking them
deeper into the hell of Newgate.

Cries rang out amid the clanking of shackles and chain as
they climbed a short flight of stone steps and turned into
another roomful of prisoners. Thankful for the darkness,
Anne blinked back tears for the despair of the sobbing,
hacking, wretched souls caught up in this misery.

Anne buried her face in the fur wrap about her neck and
clutched her skirts from the grabbing hands along the narrow hall. Her yellow silk gown and satin slippers were completely ruined with filth. She knew that Twining had
planned this down to the last cunning detail. How she hated
him for his cruelty.

"Wait here, Colonel," the gatekeeper said, "while I go git
Crabbe." He motioned toward a wooden table and chair in
one corner. A few feet away, a torch burned, providing the
only heat and light.

Out of nowhere, a short, dumpy man appeared, looking
as if he belonged in this place. The sputtering lantern he
carried illuminated the ring of keys at his waist. "Bring the

Black Fox here,'' Twining ordered, and reached into his jacket pocket while the turnkey waited, his jaw slack. Pulling out his money bag, Twining tossed several gold coins upon the wooden table. "Visitors are expected to provide the prisoners with food and drink, isn't that so, Crabbe?'' Twining's face twisted in arrogant pleasure. "You might want to provide Braydon with this small diversion."

"Nat won't want your money," she said, tossing her shoulder.

"Suit yourself, my dear." In the darkness, she could hear his faint chuckle. Crabbe, the turnkey, grabbed the coins and smiled a toothless grin at her, then left to bring Nat.

"I'll be in the next room when you're through." Twining turned and she heard his footsteps recede, but her attention was drawn straight ahead, her gaze straining into the shadows for Nat. The darkness was so thick and deep she felt she could cut it with a knife.

Dear Nat, what can I say to you? The lantern barely threw enough light to reach where she sat, a few feet away. The dim torchlight above splashed eerie shadows across the wet stone block walls. She huddled, waiting, her heart beating with the excitement of finally seeing Nat and the dread of what this hellhole had done to him.

Up ahead, staggered boot steps grew louder and she leaned into the darkness for any sign of him. Suddenly the familiar wide-shouldered figure stepped into the circle of lamplight.

"Nat!" Anne moved toward him but halted, her eyes straining against the changes in this man she loved. He was stripped naked to the waist. A dark beard covered his face, the fine scar along his cheekbone white against the dark of his skin. His long chestnut hair touched his shoulders, yet he was as ruggedly handsome as ever. She cried out when she noticed the encrusted gash below his left breast. Twining had told the truth. Dried blood caked the wound, and she knew if he didn't receive the proper herbs and ointment, he might die.

She reached to brush the hard muscle of his shoulders, and with the single touch of his skin, fell against his chest, her arms circling his neck. *Nat, Nat, I love you,* she yearned to whisper in his ear, but she didn't need to. He knew. Hot, salty tears sprang unheeded down her cheeks, and when he didn't respond, she drew back. It was then she saw that his wrists were shackled behind him. Heavy chain bound each of his ankles to a short heavy weight, allowing him only short steps. "Oh, Nat..." Her throat constricted with grief and desperation.

From the flickering torchlight, she watched his dark eyes rake her up and down, coming to rest at the glittering jewels at her throat. "I didn't believe Twining when..." His voice lashed out at her, but he stopped, his jaw clenched so tightly the muscle above his temple bulged.

The grinning turnkey pulled a stool closer, then perched on it with his legs crossed beneath him like a trained monkey. At his side, coiled up like a snake, she saw a thin leather whip.

"Is it true?" Nat's stony mask couldn't hide the rage she saw in his eyes. Despair and hurt coursed through her at the accusation on his face. A wave of nausea rolled through her and she reached out to him to steady herself. She felt him flinch at her touch, and the pain from his rejection tore her apart more than the searing nausea.

"Answer me. Is it true?"

His question cut her like a knife. There was no way she could explain. The turnkey would report everything, just as Twining had said. Anne swallowed, taking a deep fortifying breath, hating what she had to do. "Aye it's true. I'm to be married this afternoon."

She could hear his unsteady breathing. Finally he said, accusingly, "Twining said you had traded my life for your father's."

My father? But my father is dead! She struggled to keep from shouting it. How devious of Twining to taunt Nat with her alleged betrayal. But if she revealed that she had found her father, Twining would have known she had knowledge of the Royalists' spies and he'd never stop until he got the information from her.

Anne met his hard gaze. Dear God, how could she ever make him understand? "Please, Nat. The reason matters not—"

"Don't you know that I would have gladly given my life for your father if you had asked me?"

His answer was an aching whisper and she thought her heart might break. Of course she knew that, but how could she make him understand the real reason? "Nat, please..." she managed, biting back the tightening in her throat.

The turnkey leaned closer, as though straining to hear her.

"Get back to the table, Crabbe," Nat growled.

The turnkey sneered, eyes menacing, but he obeyed.

She had to say something to make Nat know she hadn't betrayed him. "I've chosen to marry the colonel because he's a noble gentleman and any maid would be honored to be his wife." Surely Nat would know instantly that she didn't believe such nonsense. She searched his face for a sign of his understanding.

But his dark eyes shadowed a deeper warning. "If you've done this to save me, then that would be a deeper betrayal, for how could you believe I'd want my life bought at such a price?"

Don't you know? she thought helplessly. "Because I— I—" Tears began to choke her as she fought for the words she needed to help him understand that she carried their child and she didn't think she could live if he were to die.

"Twining is going to hang me, regardless of what he tells you," he whispered. "I'm ready to die for my beliefs. But you've thrown away the one thing that has sustained me— this beautiful thing we've had together. Don't you know that, now, my life isn't worth anything knowing you'll be with him?"

Anne couldn't fight back the torment of his words as an oppressive weight of desperation filled her. She had nothing to say in her defense. She had failed him again.

"When I first saw you standing here like something out of my dreams, I wanted to rip these chains apart and take you in my arms. But now, for the first time since I've been in this hellhole, I'm glad my hands are locked behind me."

Nat turned and struggled with short, mincing steps until he reached the shadows that swallowed him up.

Crabbe jumped to his feet. Grabbing the lantern, he shot after Nat, the light splashing wildly about the damp stone walls.

Anne stood there, listening to the fading footsteps, feeling shattered and broken inside. How could she have been so foolish as to believe Nat could understand her wanting to save him? *I love you, Nat,* her heart cried out. *I'll love you, always.*

After what seemed like only a moment, Twining appeared with a lantern, a lace handkerchief at his nose. "Congratulations, my dear. That was very nice, indeed."

Anne turned on him. No doubt he had been within earshot all along. Her voice was edged in hate. "I'll expect to see him released, and a doctor to tend his wounds, as you promised, before we exchange our vows today."

"And you will. En route to the magistrate's office, where we'll exchange our vows, we'll stop to watch your lover and his rogues board *The Blithe Spirit.*" He smiled a malevolent smile. "Thanks to you, my sweet unselfish Anne, they'll set sail tomorrow for the New England Colony to begin their new lives.

"And if you lie to me—"

"There's very little you can do about it, my dear. But no need to worry, I'm a man of my word."

At that moment, her only hope was that maybe, once Nat was free, she might get word to him of their child and that she loved him. She had to lean on that thought if she hoped to garner the strength to go through this charade.

And if Twining broke his pledge to her, she would find some way to even the score. She jerked the lantern from him, swept up her skirts and proceeded back toward the prison gate to her own private hell.

Chapter Eighteen

When Crabbe escorted Nat back to the prison room, Tom and Doc hadn't returned from their morning exercise in the press yard. Nat was glad for the few minutes he had to be alone with his raw emotions. Never had he felt such savage heartbreak as when he saw Anne, standing like a beautiful fantasy amid the squalor of Newgate. Although he heard her speak and felt her touch, a part of him still couldn't believe she had been here, telling him she would wed Twining today.

Nat tried to close his mind from the truth, but God help him, he still loved her, wanted her with the deepest of his being—even knowing she had betrayed him. Fool that he was, he had wanted to break off the shackles and hold her, kiss her until she confessed that she loved only him.

Nat peered into the murky shadows, ignoring the aching sounds around him. If he could forget his idealism, he might even understand her betrayal. But his ideals had always been a wall between them. She had never understood how he could be prepared to die for what he believed. But he had always hoped, deep in his heart, that they could be together. He slammed his fist with brutal force against the wooden stake that held his chains. Fool! Damned fool!

His thoughts were interrupted when Crabbe brought Tom and Doc back from the press yard. Although it was morning, daylight never broke through the slitted windows above. The darkness swallowed up even the faint halos of the men's

candles, and for the moment, Nat was glad no one could see
his pain.

After Crabbe had left, and Nat briefly explained to Tom
and Doc what had happened, no one spoke for a long time.
Finally Tom leaned his barrel chest upon his arm shackled
by a long chain to a stake above his head. His long, matted
hair hung along his neck, the deep brown curly beard made
him look like a wild man. "I'm sorry, Nat."

Nat shrugged, curling his legs under him in a futile attempt to keep warm. He moved slowly in order to prevent
the gash across his chest from bleeding again. Maybe the
pain of his body would push the thoughts of Anne from his
mind.

A rat's claws ticked across the stones as it scurried beside
him. Doc shuddered and tried to sit up. "I'm sorry for you,
Nat." His voice lowered. "I'm sorry for Anne, as well."

"Women!" Tom whistled. "I've never understood 'em."
He scraped his free arm against his chains. "I thought by
now that Moll would 'ave come an' visited me." His burly
shoulders drooped forward as his arm sagged above him.
His weary face looked sorrowful, lost in his own thoughts
of that dark-haired beauty.

Nat frowned at the mention of Moll Standish. Since Tom
had been arrested earlier and taken to Newgate, he hadn't
known of the details of Nat and Doc's capture. When they
met later in prison, Nat couldn't bear to tell Tom who the
eyewitness was who had permanently sealed the Black Fox's
fate.

But he would never forget the look of betrayal in Moll's
flash of dark eyes when he was brought before her, chained
like an animal. Nor would he ever forget Twining's smug
gloating afterward, as he ordered Nat and Doc to be
hanged, without so much as a trial.

Nat had asked Doc to swear never to tell Tom of Moll's
treachery. Tom had enough pain, he mused bitterly. Let him
believe the woman he loved was true.

During the coach ride back to Twining's town house,
Anne remained silent, her mind on how to undermine the

terrible cruelty that Twining had done. She couldn't bear to have Nat believe his life meant nothing due to her betrayal.

She shook back the threatened tears at the thought that after today, she might never see him again. She squeezed her eyes shut. No, she mustn't think of that. There would be time enough, after Nat sailed to freedom, that she could afford the luxury of her feelings, but not now. Now, she needed all of her strength to carry out her part of the bargain with Twining.

But first, she had to speak to Babson. He was her only hope. If she could sneak a note to Nat and tell him she was so sorry for everything that had gone wrong. If only there was some way he could find it in his heart to forgive her.

When they returned to the town house, Anne overheard Twining order the groom to keep the coach harnessed; he would be going out again. Hopefully, Twining would leave without Babson.

Twining, in excellent spirits, solicitously granted Anne's request to retire alone to her chamber, remarking that she should rest for their marriage ceremony in several hours. After he collected the necklace and ring from her, he insisted she leave the study before he locked the jewels away. More than likely so she wouldn't know where he kept them, she thought dryly.

After she had gone upstairs, Mrs. Minton helped her change into another of the mysterious gowns that Twining had instructed her to wear. The high-necked, rose-colored, expensive wool serge reflected good taste and refinement, although she would have preferred one of Jane's plain gowns in her valise.

Anne gulped the plate of food the housekeeper had brought, hoping to get rid of Mrs. Minton. When the woman finally left with the tray, Anne heard the guard slide the bolt in place. Immediately she rushed to the window and twitched back the lacy panel. It had been dark when she had arrived last night, and this morning, they had left for Newgate before the sun had lit the early winter sky. For the first time, Anne studied the stark grounds. The windows were locked from the outside. If she broke the glass, it would be

impossible to escape. The courtyard below was surrounded
by high fencing. No doubt, well thought out by the master
of the house.

But every room of the house couldn't be so well fortified. She whirled around, her hand pressed to her forehead. Babson would know. Yet she dare not send for him
without a very good reason; it would alert Mrs. Minton.

She remembered that, after her father had left for war,
Babson would fix her broken toys, dry her tears when she
skinned a knee, or hammer the broken heel on her slipper
before her maid discovered it and brought her to task for her
carelessness.

Of course! She'd call Babson to repair something! But
what? She glanced about the room. Everything about the
expensively furnished bedroom spoke of meticulous order.
She dashed to the valise and threw back the lid. The small
trunk had very few items: Jane's neatly folded clothing, a
pair of slippers, the ruffled petticoat containing the wheel-
lock pistol tucked inside its hidden pocket. Her heartbeat
quickened as she thought of an idea.

She slammed the lid down and locked it, then hid the key
beneath the clock on the mantel, her pulse pounding with
excitement. Next, she tapped lightly on the chamber door.

"What is it, mistress?" the soldier asked.

"Please summon Mrs. Minton." She held her breath
while the clack of boot steps faded down the hall. In a few
minutes, she recognized the housekeeper's heavy footfalls
approaching.

The sliding of the bolt outside the door caused her breath
to catch. When Mrs. Minton pushed the door open, Anne
was kneeling in front of the valise. "I've lost the key, and I
can't budge the lock."

"Foolish thing to do." She picked up the porcelain candlestick beside the bed and glanced around the floor.
"Where'd you have the key last?"

"I think it slipped out on the street, last night," Anne
answered, hoping to put an end to Mrs. Minton's searching.

"Careless chit," the housekeeper mumbled under her breath, but loud enough for Anne to hear.

"Ask Babson to bring a steel bar to pry the lid open. I must have an item from my trunk immediately." Anne imitated the forceful manner of Colonel Twining when addressing the woman.

"What is it you need?" the woman asked derisively, banging on the lid with her thick fists, to no avail.

Anne got to her feet and straightened her skirts. "Mrs. Minton, I'm not accustomed to being questioned by a servant. May I remind you that in a few hours, I will become Colonel Edward Twining's wife, and the mistress of this house? I demand that you treat me with the proper respect," she added, glad her full skirts hid her trembling knees. "Now, summon Babson here at once, or I shall have to tell my future husband that I was detained from my wedding because of *you.*"

The woman stepped back, eyes wide with outrage. She folded her arms, her face beet red.

Anne held her ground. "I'm waiting, Mrs. Minton."

After a long pause, the housekeeper shifted her weight, turned and trounced out the door.

Anne crumpled back onto her knees and let out a relieved sigh. God's bones, she might come to enjoy being a tyrant!

Within a few minutes, Mrs. Minton returned with Babson, who carried a short poker. "You'll never open the lock with that," the housekeeper chided, bending over him, arms akimbo. Anne wanted to dismiss the woman, but it might make her suspicious.

As if he could read her mind, Babson said, "Mrs. Minton, go back to the kitchen and see that Prudence shines the silver till it sparkles. The maid's a bit lax if left on 'er own."

Anne straightened her shoulders. "And be quick about it."

The older woman glanced from Babson to Anne. "Humph!" Her stiff, black skirts swished as she moved toward the door. She paused a moment and tossed a dour glance at Babson. "That poker's too big to do the job proper!" She slammed the door after her.

Anne threw her arms around the frail old man. "Oh, Babson, there's nothing wrong with my valise," she whispered. "I needed an excuse to speak to you." She jumped up and dashed to the mantel to fetch the key. Next, she unlocked the trunk lid and hurriedly hid the key back under the clock.

"I've news for ye, as well." His thin face flushed with excitement. "Before dawn, I snuck away to see the Vicar Trueworthy. 'E said a few o' the king's men are ready to 'elp Nat an' the others escape, an' with the gold ye brought 'em, most of the turnkeys can be bribed t' look the other way."

"Oh, Babson, that's wonderful news."

"It's not all good news. One o' the turnkeys can't be bought. Crabbe's 'is name, an' 'e's Twining's man. The vicar said Twining's made a deal fer Nat, Tom an' Doc t' sail to Prisoner's Island in the Caribbean. Sold 'em like cattle, 'e did. They're t' be boarded on *The Albatross* later today."

Her knees very nearly gave way as she remembered Nat's words. He knew Twining couldn't be trusted, but in her desperation to save Nat she hadn't wanted to believe it. But now, she couldn't ignore it, and the anger of betrayal shook her. But what had she expected from such a loathsome creature?

"Babson, we've got to get the men out before Twining has them put aboard."

"I'm afraid it's too late. Twining told me 'e'd be gone for several 'ours. I've a feeling 'e's at the docks, right now, settin' 'is evil plan in motion." His face gentled with compassion as he looked at her. "Mistress Anne, what was yer news?"

Tears choked inside her throat. "I had hoped you could take a note to the prison for me, but..." She forced herself not to cry. "I wanted him to know...I love him."

Babson nodded, sympathy and regret misting his eyes. She clung to him, her heart obviously breaking with misery. "There, there," he soothed. "There's not much we can do."

She lifted her head and wiped the tears from her face with her fingers. "But there must be something!" Her eyes fixed on his helpless expression "I have a few gold pieces left from what Jane gave me. You must try to bribe Twining's turnkey to let Nat and Doc go."

He shook his head and made a low sound in the back of his throat. "It would take more than gold to pay 'im off. Twining already pays 'im well to do 'is dirty tricks. It's against the law what the colonel's doin', but with 'is money and power, 'e gets away with it." His white brows twitched in disgust.

The memory of Pike, the gatekeeper, and the bold hint that he'd readily take a bribe came to mind. "Do you know where Twining keeps the emerald necklace that I wore this morning?"

He shook his head. "Not in the house. I'm sure 'e took it with 'im."

Anne's mind whirled with another idea. She opened the trunk and showed Babson the ruffled petticoat concealing the weapon. When she explained what was inside, and that Jane had shown her how to use it, his face turned ashen.

"Mistress Anne, that's a dangerous thing if Twining was to find it." He paused, as if someone might overhear. "Let me take it and the bag of coin. While Twining's gone, I'll try and get a message to Nat."

"Babson, could I . . . go with you?"

"Saints! Never!"

"But . . . what if I dressed up as a . . ." The milling beggars and streetwalkers outside the jail came to mind. "I know!" She jumped to her feet. "Do you think the Vicar Trueworthy would lend us a few robes?"

"Aye." Babson's hazel eyes brightened with understanding. In fact, Sarah, the laundress is a . . ." He cleared his throat. "Close friend of mine." He grinned, his pale face blushing like a young lad's. "Sarah repairs the clothing for the almshouse."

Anne smiled. "Do you think Sarah can find an outfit for me to wear? Maybe something from the servants' rooms. We'll go to Newgate, and you'll say you're to have prayers with Nat and the others. I'll go as a streetwalker—"

"Mistress Anne!" His hand shot to his mouth.

"Please, Babson, I'm going with you, and that's final. Now, hurry and leave. There's no time to lose."

He sat back on his knees, his face white with shock. "But what do you plan to do?"

"It will be easy. Listen! I'll distract the turnkey while you grab his keys. I'll keep him busy while you go through the gigger—the prisoners' visiting room. I can draw you the floor plan of the jail."

His hazel eyes grew round with excitement. "I'll ask Sarah for four of the vicars' robes. Once the men are un-shackled, they can walk out of Newgate as men of the cloth."

She hugged him with the thrill of success.

"Aye, it's worth a try." She hadn't seen him beam with pleasure like that since she was a child. Suddenly a sense of dread curled along her spine. She felt that Babson knew that hit or miss, he could never return to Twining or the life of an innocent rustic. If their plan failed, he would find himself in Newgate, condemned to death with Nat and the others, as well as herself.

It was as if Babson knew what she was thinking. He smiled and squeezed her hand. "Aye, ye 'ave yer father's spunk, lass."

She blinked back the sting of tears, deciding to tell him later of her father. Instead, she smiled back. "A Royalist's daughter never had a nicer compliment."

They both stood up. "The vicarage is a few miles away," Babson whispered. "I'll take a horse and when I return, I'll tie a white rag on the fence outside yer window."

"When I see it, I'll sneak downstairs and meet you behind the house."

"How will ye get past Mrs. Minton and the two Round-heads posted at yer door?" he asked, his expression grim.

She waved airily. "I do it all the time," she lied. She hated telling him a fib, but she didn't want to upset him. "Don't worry," she said with a wink. "I'll be there."

He narrowed his eyes and brushed himself off. "All right, but I think I've got the easier task."

Before she could reply, footsteps shuffled outside the door and the metal bolt scraped open. Mrs. Minton charged into the room. Her glance flew immediately to the trunk, and Anne couldn't help suppress a smile that the woman's black eyes widened in surprise when she saw the trunk lid ajar.

Babson's eyes twinkled as he picked up the bar of steel and strode toward the door. "The master's touch," he muttered as he swept past her.

Anne smiled sweetly at Mrs. Minton's thunderstruck expression. "You're excused, Mrs. Minton. I'll take my nap now. I'll call you if I need anything."

Anne paced back and forth in front of the window, panic increasing by each tick of the clock above the mantel. It had been almost an hour since Babson left, and she was afraid that, any minute, Mrs. Minton would barge in, telling her that the colonel had returned and it was time for her to prepare for her wedding.

She glanced at the clock. Exactly two o'clock. Pray, everything would go according to plan. Her eyes shot back to the hearth. The fire burned low, with just enough flame to cause the effect she needed, yet not enough to burn her hands when it was time to shove the wad of clothing up the chimney.

Everything looked in place. Anne moved stiffly toward the fireplace. She wore Jane's multilayered petticoat, the firearm wedged along one leg, tied in place by the custom fastenings Jane had carefully sewn. She took a nervous breath as she gathered the plain gown from her valise and tied it in knots before soaking it in the water pitcher. The wad lay waiting, ready to be crammed up the chimney hole by the fire poker as soon as she saw Babson's signal.

She smiled at her ready ingenuity, so useful to her as a defiant child in a strict Puritan household. She glanced back

to the window and her pulse quickened. Babson had just left
a small white streamer on the lower fence post. Quickly she
grabbed the soaked gown, tightened the knot around the
poker, then pushed it up the fireplace with the poker. It was
easier than she had thought. The chimney was smaller than
the ones at Wycliffe Manor. The ball of wet clothing stuck
easily, cutting off the air from the chimney opening. Immediately, thick, gray smoke billowed into the room, hiding the poker. Anne held the apron over her face while she
leaned the poker up against the back of the chimney, the rod
supporting the tight wad in place.

She tried not to cough as the dense rolls of smoke filled
the room. Waiting until the last minute, Anne pounded on
the door. "Fire! Fire!" The soldiers opened the portal, and
the clouds of smoke rolled into the hall. "Bring water!,"
Anne cried. "Get help! Fetch Mrs. Minton!"

The two soldiers bounded down the hall, swords clang-
ing against their heels. Anne rushed after them, careful to
listen for Mrs. Minton or more soldiers coming back to fight
the fire.

Smoke choked the hallway, and as she started downstairs, she heard footsteps coming around the corner.
Quickly she dodged back up the stairs and into the next
bedroom, closing the door.

Leaning against the wood, she drew a deep breath. Her
eyes opened and she gasped at the sight in front of her.
Across the room hung a life-size portrait of her mother. For
a moment, the likeness took her breath away. It was an ex-
act replica of the miniature in the gold locket!

She looked about the lavishly furnished room. Sheer,
frilly curtains, deep emerald satin ensconced the bed hang-
ings and coverlet. In the corner stood an open wardrobe,
brimming with gowns, hats, boas, capes. Her hand brushed
the elegant gown she wore. So this is where the elegant
clothing had come from that Twining had insisted she wear!
She shivered with the realization of Twining's consuming
love for her mother.

Men's voices and footsteps clambering up the stairs
brought her back to the present. She cracked the door and

watched as Mrs. Minton and the soldiers stormed into the next room. Quickly she sped down the stairs. Thank God, the hall and lower landing were empty. From the loud choking and coughing upstairs, Anne knew she had only a few minutes before they discovered she wasn't in the bedroom.

The door to Twining's study was ajar. God's bones, she hadn't thought of that! What if he had returned? Somehow, she had to sneak past the open door.

"Hurry lass, I've a 'orse saddled and waitin'."

Anne jumped with a start at the familiar voice. Babson, his white head and face obscured by a hood, stood hiding inside Twining's study. He was dressed in the brown wool vicar's robes, with a long, gray bulging cloth sack slung over his shoulder. She would never have recognized him in a crowd.

He grabbed her hand and led her through the back of the house out toward the narrow lane. A sprig-tailed mare chomped on grass along the verge.

Her heart beat a tattoo as she mounted behind the old servant. Babson kicked the horse's side, and they galloped off toward Newgate Street.

Nat studied the small, wiry turnkey while Crabbe dished out the daily plate of gruel on a tin and handed the putrid-smelling portion to him. Crabbe enjoyed the close contact with the men, allowing him to size them up, no doubt. The ring of keys hung in plain sight from the chain around Crabbe's waist, as though daring the inmates to grab for them. Nat needn't have heard the prisoner's stories about Crabbe slicing off an ear or lashing out an eye with the whip to know what sort of black soul he had.

"Back off in the corner, Fox," Crabbe shrieked, "or ye'll taste another bite of me leather." Crabbe's toothless face twisted into a sneer.

Nat conceded, although he recognized the boastful talk never quite washed away the look of fear in the small pig eyes of the bully. Nat took the tin plate and dragged the ankle weight to the corner out of the sputtering light of Crabbe's lantern and ate in silence.

Crabbe strode, dragging the whip, to where Tom stood shackled to the high-ceiling brace. When the turnkey stretched his arms in order to reach the seven-foot bar to unlock Tom's wrists, Nat saw a glint of steel from what Nat presumed was the handle of a poniard or small sword tucked inside Crabbe's trousers. So the little bully carries a hidden blade, Nat mused.

Silently Tom lowered his stocky arms, free of the shackles, if only for the brief time the prisoners were allowed to eat. He couldn't prevent the grimace of pain, however.

"Who made this slop?" Tom asked the turnkey, his cynical laughter ringing after him.

"It's not so bad," Crabbe said. "Ye don't want to hurt Cook's feelings, now do ye?" he quipped sarcastically.

"Cook, hell!" Tom answered. "More likely the stable hand made this stew."

"That's enough of yer tongue, or I'll cut it out fer ye," Crabbe snapped. Chuckles rippled along the shadows where the other prisoners sat chained, and it pleased Nat to know their spirit hadn't been completely crushed by the bully, Crabbe.

"That puny little weasel! How I'd like to pinch 'is face off," Tom muttered, his gaze following Crabbe's halting lantern light along the enormous room full of wretched souls.

"You might get a chance," Nat whispered, and hunched closer. "I noticed he uses the same key to unlock all of the shackles."

"So?" Tom frowned. "That's no 'elp to us as long as those keys are around that little crupper's middle."

From the nearby darkness, an acrid smell rose as the sound of urine splashed upon stone. Nat shuddered as Crabbe's laughter faded in the distance.

Nat forced down the last of the swill from his plate and tossed the tin to the stone floor with a clank. "I received a message from the vicar from Christ Church," Nat whisered. "The guards have been bribed and won't offer resistance if we can somehow manage an escape."

"Except Crabbe," Tom added, then spit in disgust. "We always knew the little wart was Twining's man."

"I think I know how we can handle Crabbe," Nat said. Tom and Doc stared at him with rapt attention. "Crabbe has a blade sheathed to his belt," he continued. "When he comes back to lock us up, we'll jump him."

The promise of escape hung for a long moment before Doc broke the spell. "Do you really think it's possible?"

Nat cocked a brow. "If we fail, what do you think they'll do with us? Hang us?"

Tom and Doc laughed. Both men gulped the remainder of the meal and tossed aside the metal plates with a hollow sound. Nat smiled to himself. Bloody hell, even if the escape plan were to prove fruitless, at least thinking of it might keep up the men's mettle for the short time it took them to rot in this Hades.

Before Crabbe returned with the water bucket, Doc inched closer to Nat. "Hurry, before Crabbe comes back," he whispered. "I've got something for your wound."

Surprised, Nat raised up on his elbows and turned toward Doc's profile silhouetted against the faint light across the cavernous room. "Lean closer while I pour this on your wound." Doc shuffled his feet until he faced him. "Quick, before Crabbe comes back to lock our hands again."

"What is it?" Nat strained to see Doc pull a small cloth bag from his belt and open the drawstring.

"It's salt." Doc managed a half smile. "Try not to scream, 'cause when I put it on your gash, you'll think Satan's got ye."

"Where the bloody hell did you get salt?"

"I bartered with one of the other turnkeys when we were in the press yard."

"What did you give in exchange fer the salt?" Tom asked, watching with interest.

Doc narrowed his eyes and looked nervously over his shoulder at the swinging light from Crabbe's approaching lantern. "Well, if you see one of the turnkeys sportin' my fancy black Puritan hat, don't make sport of him, eh? I told him he looked as grand as ol' Ruby Nose, himself.''

Nat felt a genuine sense of gratitude for his friend. "I'm obliged for your sacrifice, but I've got another idea for it.'' Tom and Doc both straightened. Nat leaned closer and whispered his plan to the two men, who excitedly agreed.

Tom crouched back while Doc tossed Nat the bag of salt, then shifted his legs back into the shadows.

The next few minutes of waiting were pure torment. They had one chance to succeed or they were dead men. Nat bit back the thought that he may be leading these two friends into immediate death, but he also knew that Doc and Tom would not last as long in Newgate as he. They would rather die fighting than rot away.

The decision to escape had come easily, after he had returned from seeing Anne, bedecked in jewels and finery, confirming she had betrayed his life. In fact, he welcomed a quick death rather than knowing each day of his life, she was with *him*.

Nat spit back the white-hot anger that threatened to consume him. He'd think about how he'd deal with Anne later. Now, all that mattered was escaping this hellhole and settling the score with Twining.

Crabbe swung down the lantern a few feet away, the light streaking long shadowy fingers across the stone arches and walls. "Git t' yer feet an' raise yer 'ands, Fox," Crabbe barked at him, the whip coiled and ready in his right hand.

Nat waited, fixed a darting glance to Doc and Tom, then rose slowly to his feet. Crabbe snatched up the shackles from the floor and stood ready to clamp them around Nat's wrists, his mouth a tight line. "'Urry up, Fox. I ain't got all day.''

With the salt bag hidden inside his large palm, Nat held his arms out to the turnkey. Crabbe reached over with the shackles and in one smooth move, Nat hurled the coarse salt in Crabbe's eyes.

"Acckk!" Crabbe's fists flew to his eyes. Tom thrust his burly arm around Crabbe's neck, biceps bulging in the lantern light as he flexed back against the man's throat. The turnkey, terrified and blinded with pain, folded to the ground. Nat pulled the long, narrow blade from the leather sheath at Crabbe's waist and tucked the poniard inside his boot. His fingers fumbled at the key ring at Crabbe's waist. Each moment felt like hours as he squinted in the dim lantern light, searching for the large iron key Crabbe used to unlock the foot shackles.

Crabbe writhed and moaned in protest, but Tom's balled fist shot out and landed square on Crabbe's jaw with a smack. The turnkey's body slumped, like a stuffed doll, into Tom's arms.

Nat found the key, freed himself, then Doc and Tom. He twisted around for signs of other guards, but so far, nothing had been observed out of the ordinary except by the prisoners nearby. Unsure of what had taken place, the men strained closer for a better look.

Doc removed his shirt and stuffed it into Crabbe's mouth. Tom picked up Crabbe's limp form and strode to the next line of surprised prisoners, shoving the unconscious man at them. "'Ere, lads. Bind 'is 'ands before ye 'elps yerself to is keys chained to 'is waist. Then pass 'im down to the others."

The prisoner's excited cries rose, but Tom cautioned, "Keep yer voices down." Tom blew out the lantern, knowing the prisoners' eyes were accustomed to the darkness and wouldn't need the light to escape.

He picked up Crabbe's whip and fell in step behind Nat as the trio began their way toward freedom.

Chapter Nineteen

Anne's stomach turned and she fought back nausea as she and Babson shouldered through the throngs of beggars, prostitutes and visitors massed outside the main gate of the prison. Babson had sold the horse for a few coins, knowing that the cutthroats would have stolen the animal if he had left it tethered. "We'll rent a skiff an' row along the Thames if we escape," he said.

"When, not if," she retorted, giving him a wink. It heartened her to have her childhood friend with her again.

He peered nervously over his shoulder, the hazel eyes searching the crowd. "Hurry, lass. By now, Mrs. Minton will 'ave told the soldiers you're gone, an' Twining will know right where you'd go."

A film of sweat beaded her upper lip although the late November cold froze her to the bone through the thin wool shawl. Babson wore two vicar's robes over his thin frame and the other two robes were contained in the gray cloth bag he slung over his shoulder. She clutched the nubby shawl about her shoulders, her fingers tightening the knot as she crammed into line with the other visitors. Her hands shook as she felt beneath her shawl for the hard coins tied into a knot inside her apron string. Each step she took, the heavy pistol tied by the linen strands beneath her skirts pressed reassuringly against her thigh.

She looked up and her heart hammered beneath her breast at the prostitutes, waiting for a prisoner's visitor to buy them as a favor, like a pint of beer or a candle. Al-

though the most mournful profession, Anne had heard that
many young girls preferred it to the lesser wages of supporting themselves as manure gatherers, farm weeders or
dairymaids. Anne glanced away in pity and caught the
gatekeeper's stare. As luck would have it, he was the same
keeper who had seen her with Twining. Knowing she had the
colonel's protection, he would not dare force himself on her.
His pockmarked, bulbous face grinned with recognition. He
broke away from the doxies and walked toward her, the
heavy ring of keys he carried clinking with each step.

The keys! She only had to flirt with him, divert him long
enough for Babson to steal his keys and take them to Nat.
She could distract the guard long enough, she hoped, until
Nat and the others came for her. She must do it!

"Thought you'd be back." His whiskey-colored eyes
raked over her. Babson loomed protectively and Pike
straightened when he recognized the vicar's robes. "You
here to see a prisoner?"

Anne swallowed, her arms crossing over her breasts in a
defensive gesture. She glanced from Pike to Babson, then
back again. "Aye," she managed, keeping the tremor from
her voice.

Babson pushed several coins into the gatekeeper's beefy
palm. "I'm to say prayers with the Black Fox and his men.
Colonel Twining's order," he explained.

Pike glanced down at the glittering coins in his hand.
"The colonel ain't said nothin' t' me." He drew a finger
slowly along his scraggly beard, as though stalling for another coin.

Babson pushed several more coins at him. "Consider
yourself told." His voice was strong and to the point.

Raising the lantern, Pike squinted into his hand. A shrewd
smile spread across his coarse features. Then he peered at
Anne. "It's not enough!" he stated defiantly.

"Not enough?" Babson repeated, his mouth agape.
"There's more gold in your palm than you'll see in a life-
time."

Pike glared at Babson. "The gold and 'er." He put the coins in his pocket, then motioned with his chin to Anne. "Leave 'er 'ere while you're with the Fox."

Babson looked aghast. "But . . . she's a lady, not some—"

Anne felt the shudders of revulsion ripple through her. She touched Babson's arm. "I'll be all right until you return," she whispered. "Now, hurry." Each minute ticked away at the men's chance for escape.

Pike smiled. "'Ere's yer lantern, vicar." He sneered, shoving Babson toward the dark passageway, the lantern's light swinging wildly along the stone floor.

Babson stumbled, then straightened, casting Anne a worried look. She knew Babson remembered that without her, the men wouldn't have access to the pistol she carried. "I'll be along to say prayers later," she added, hoping the servant would understand that she planned to follow him as soon as she had managed to get the keys from the gate-keeper.

Babson nodded, a helpless look upon his face. Resigned, he snatched the lantern's handle, turned and shuffled down the passageway toward the gigger, the sputtering light splashing shadows across the stone archway.

When Babson was out of sight, Anne glanced back at Pike, praying she could distract him long enough to steal his keys.

"Follow me, beauty." Pike grabbed her elbow and pushed her along the wall to the side door. Unlocking it with the smallest key, he pushed the door open, shoving her inside. A scream caught in her throat when she thought of what would come next.

The smells of a stable rushed up to her as her eyes blinked against the darkness. The room was empty except for a stool and a pile of straw in one corner. She drew back, her mind spinning.

The gatekeeper's eyes bulged as he watched her, his tongue running over his lips. "I've never 'ad a lady before," he muttered, his whiskey eyes devouring her like a starving man devouring a leg of mutton.

When the time came, Anne had hoped she would only have to mimic the flirting, teasing way that Moll used to banter with the men at the Pied Bull Inn. She knew, now, that hope was gone. She recognized the animal lust in Pike's eyes—the same as the soldier who had tried to force himself upon her at the inn. But no one would come to her rescue this time.

Pike plopped the lantern on the floor and stepped menacingly toward her. She edged toward the shadows, the pistol bumping against her left thigh. With her heart hammering, she drew her hands behind her, drawing her skirts up in back, hoping to untie the weapon from her thigh before he found it.

Pike lunged at her, his left arm pressing her against the cold stone wall while his right hand tore at the knotted shawl, finally tossing it to the ground.

Her mind fought to block out his groping as her fingers searched the fabrics of her skirts for the weapon's bindings. Her damp fingers tugged at the fastenings. Terror froze her mind to the reality that she could do nothing to stop him having his way with her.

She arched her back, allowing her fingers to find the pistol handle and pull it free. *Don't drop it!* she commanded, her blood freezing in her veins.

He fumbled with the delicate lacings at her breasts. His legs pinned her to the wall. She flinched back in horror, the cold wet stones scraping her back. *Run! Run! Run!* Panic screamed inside her mind. *Nat! I can't leave without Nat!* Not until she had the keys.

"I'll bet ye don't play lady with the Fox." His hot breath curled in her ear. "If ye want ta be alone with 'im, ye'll let me 'ave yer fancies first." His breath smelled of rotted teeth.

Bile rose to her throat. She felt his hands paw the front of her skirts. She screamed. His hot hands pressed on her thighs, his mouth pushing against hers. The room spun with revulsion. The nausea that had threatened her all day finally rose to her mouth. She doubled over with uncontrolled retching.

"Why ye bitch—" He jumped aside and wiped the vomit from his sleeve. She heard the soft clink of keys drop from the hook at his belt and fall among the straw along the floor.

"Dammit t' 'ell, ye vixen!'' Ye made me drop me keys!'' He jerked the lantern up, his back to her as he crouched over the floor, searching. With renewed hope, she straightened, wiped her mouth on her apron and steadied herself while she watched him scuff the loose yellow shafts along the floor with the toes of his boots.

Afraid he would call the other guards for help, she stepped where she thought she heard the keys fall. "I—I'm sorry..." she lied, less than a foot from him. "I—I'll help you find them."

Suddenly the ball of her slipper stepped on the hard metal objects. "I saw them drop over there," she said, pointing to the center of the room.

He hunched over, his back to her, searching the ground. For a moment her mind floundered, then she stepped forward and with both hands on the barrel, using every ounce of strength born from desperation, she brought the pistol's butt down on the back of his head with a crack. A hoarse cry escaped him as his body toppled forward to lie in a crumpled heap.

She may have killed him! She pushed away the thought, forcing her mind on the precious keys at her feet. She snatched the ring of keys with one hand, grabbed the lantern with the other and whirled toward the door. Too much time had passed. She must find Nat.

Breathless, she rushed to the entrance, but before she could touch the handle, the door burst open. Colonel Twining glared down at her. In one sweep of the room, his cold gray eyes pierced her with understanding.

The prisoners' shrieks of freedom and cries of victory clamored behind them as Nat, Tom and Doc crept along the shadows, waiting for the guards to look up in surprise and grab their swords when they realized a prison break was taking place.

"This one's mine," Tom said, flashing a scabbard in his palm at the sound of running footsteps echoing along the stone arch ahead. He leaned against the wall and waited as the man's shadow splashed ahead of him.

Nat peered at the hooded, robed figure. "Tom, wait!" but Tom had already jumped out, grabbed the man and held a knife to his throat in one smooth motion.

"It's a man of the cloth," Tom exclaimed, his face white with astonishment. He lowered the knife and released his grip on the man. The hood fell back, revealing the familiar friend.

"Babson!" Nat whispered in astonishment, quickly pulling him to the safety of the shadows. "How the—?"

"Mistress Anne," Babson cried, gasping for breath. "She's holdin' off Pike, the gatekeeper."

"Anne?" He scarcely heard him, his mind filled with the image of Anne with that vermin, Pike. "Where are they?"

"In the keeper's lodge..." he answered, "by the main gate." He took a deep breath, untying the cord at his side. "Wait. Ye can't go without these." Inside his robe, he had two vestments folded over the back of a waist cord, and one robe tied across his stomach. In the lantern light, Nat saw his thin face break into a grin. "I should 'ave brought another robe for yer beard."

Nat grinned, grabbing the robe and tossing it on, not losing a step as he ran toward the iron gate at the front of the prison. Once there, he waited, studying the crowd of visitors milling by. A few minutes later, Tom, Doc and Babson joined him.

"Most of the guards are upstairs quelling the riot," Nat said, feeling relieved. "The few remaining we can handle."

"Pike and Anne must still be inside," Babson whispered.

A murderous rage filled Nat's mind at the thought of what Pike was doing to her. "I'll go in first," he said, his voice cold as steel.

"We'll go with ye," Tom offered. "We'll rush him and take him by surprise."

Nat nodded, and at his signal, the four vicars strode purposefully through the crowd, their hoods hiding their faces. When they reached the wooden door of the gatekeeper's lodge, Nat glanced over his shoulder to be sure they hadn't been followed before he pushed open the door.

"We've been expecting you, Fox." In the corner, Twining sat on a stool, his arm holding Anne crouched down across his knee. In the subdued light, there was no mistaking the glint of the sword at Anne's throat. "Come in and shut the door. I want to see your face when I draw the life from your lover." His cold eyes gleamed with strange pleasure.

Anne remained stiff, her face white against Twining's red jacket. Her hair spilled out in thick tangles, and in the incredible danger, the thought of how remarkably beautiful she was flitted strangely before him.

"Let her go, and I'll give myself up," Nat said, taking a step toward him.

"Stay back," Twining warned, jumping to his feet, pulling Anne with him. "I'll call the guards and have you placed back in chains, but first..." He smiled and pulled Anne closer. It was then that Nat saw that Twining's hand clamped cruelly at the back of her hair.

"Drop your swords and knives in that corner," Twining commanded, his eyes motioning to where Pike, the gatekeeper, lay sprawled in the straw.

"Your lover is quite ingenious, Fox. She whacked Pike's thick skull a jolly good one. He'll be hearing bells for a few days, I'd imagine." Despite Twining's attempt at humor, Nat recognized the controlled fury in his voice.

"There's nothing to be gained from killing the lass," Nat said, his voice low. "Our escape was a mistake, and we're going back." He held his hands up in an act of submission, his eye on the sword at Anne's throat.

"True, except for one thing." Twining's mouth twitched. "We must dole out a proper punishment for you, Fox." The sharp edge of hate glittered in Twining's cold eyes. "To lock you up or hang you is not enough." His eyes traveled over him with cold calculation. "I thought it would be a just punishment to have you think she betrayed you. How any woman could prefer a rogue like you to me is beyond comprehension, but..." He pursed his lips. "But our Anne quelled that little plan with her latest trick." He pulled her head back at a cocked angle, and Nat was afraid he might snap her neck.

"But to suffer the loss of your beloved..." Twining's eyes flickered strangely for an instant, then the ruthless hardness returned as readily as before. "That will be your punishment, Fox." He yanked Anne by her hair, her bright blue-green eyes moistening with pain. "For the rest of your life, you'll know how it feels to have lost the woman you love, to have her life taken from you, as easily as—"

"Killing Anne won't solve anything." Doc took a step forward, but Nat jerked him back.

Babson leapt forward. He threw off his hood, as if proud of his duplicity.

A look of genuine surprise crossed Twining's face as he recognized his manservant. In that brief instant of shock, Nat lunged for Twining's wrist. Doc and Tom pushed toward them. In the crush of brown robes, the swish of a blade was followed by a high-pitched scream.

Anne stumbled toward the ground, but Nat reached out to her before she fell to the floor.

A whir of a blade sang through the air as Tom and Doc jumped back from the glint of Twining's sword. He stood and the lifeless body of Babson fell in front of him.

"Well, well, I must say, I'm surprised." Twining peered down at Babson's still body, a red stain spreading across the servant's chest. "I'd never thought the little sniveler had it in him."

Anne's hands flew to her mouth in horror. "Babson! No!" But Nat held firm.

"There's nothing you can do for him, now," Nat whispered in her hair. She buried her face in his shoulder.

"What's goin' on?" ordered a guard outside the door. When the door creaked open, Tom and Doc quickly rushed the two guards who burst into the room. In one powerful punch, Tom brought the first man to his knees, then grabbed the second man and pulled him into the chamber.

The guard drew his sword, but Tom threw a right fist to his jaw, and the large man fell like deadwood.

"Doc, take Anne outside and meet me where we had planned," Nat ordered, his eyes on Twining. "The colonel and I have some unfinished business."

"I've relished this moment, Fox," Twining said.

Nat pulled the poniard from his boot.

"Nat, no!" Anne cried, but Doc grabbed her and stepped back a safe distance into the corner. "Please, I must stay..."

"Doc, get her out of here!" Nat commanded.

Twining jumped up, all pretense of amusement gone, his face a serious mask. "I've never carved a fox with a sword before!"

"Nor have I poked out the heart of a swine with a dagger before," Nat retorted, enjoying Twining's dark flush of anger in reaction to his taunt. He was at a disadvantage by the short weapon, but if he could keep stoking Twining's anger, the diversion might work long enough for the others to escape.

"No," Anne screamed, falling to her knees. "I won't go without you."

Doc pulled Anne to her feet, forcing her to leave. Tom leaned his ear to the door before opening it, then rushed outside. Anne struggled for a look back. "Look out!" she screamed, her eyes wide, just as Twining lunged forward, but not before Nat sensed it and leapt back out of his reach.

When Anne and the others had left the room, a tremendous feeling of relief washed through Nat.

"How I've dreamed of this," Twining snarled, twirling his sword in the air. *"En garde!"* He thrust forward. In the small room, Nat parried, but Babson's body lay sprawled in the middle of the room, and to avoid stepping on him, Nat broke his concentration for an instant, allowing the tip of Twining's sword to nick his shoulder.

Nat jumped back, stalling for as long as he could, praying Tom would think to steal a horse until they could get to the river and steal a boat. The longer he could stall Twining, the better...

"The fox is looking for his hole?" Twining taunted with a slight swagger. "No place to run, eh?" With a whir of steel, Twining sliced the air, the blade arcing the air within inches of Nat's chest.

Twining lunged into another assault, his form artistic and precise, his face wild with glee. "Too bad I can only kill you once, you scoundrel!"

Nat kept on the defensive, watching, waiting. Twining's confidence could be a foil, he thought, studying his enemy's perfect footwork. Twining's reputation as a superior swordsman was well earned, and although his exactness made him doubly dangerous, it was also his weak point.

At the next thrust, Nat jumped back just in time to hear the whisk of the blade below his ear. Twining screeched like a falcon barely missing its prey.

Nat measured the distance from Twining, then he paced several steps around the room, to stand within two feet of Babson's lifeless body. Nat waited, but only for an instant. Twining thrust with renewed force, but this time, his right foot caught on the edge of Babson's robe, momentarily throwing off his attention. Nat took advantage of the opening. In one quick move, he plunged the blade deep into Twining's chest. Only luck could have guided Nat's thrust to hit the fatal mark.

Twining gasped, blood rushing from his mouth, his eyes round with surprise as Nat pulled the knife from the colonel's chest. He staggered, his knees giving way finally as he crumpled to the floor. Immediately, the pale glassy eyes rolled backward, and Nat knew Twining was dead. Somehow, Nat couldn't help feeling pity for the wretched creature.

After wiping the blood from the blade, Nat returned it to his boot, straightened his robe and pulled the hood over his head while he made his way out the door. Although it was daylight, the torches had been removed from the stone archways, by the handful of guards or the prisoners fleeing the jail.

Nat strode through the crowded jail, his head down, until he reached the gates. He moved between an old woman and man. His arm crossed the couple in a gesture of comfort, as he moved with them past the new gatekeeper, who must have just come on duty. The old couple looked up. "Go with God, my children," Nat whispered, his step quickening.

He crossed Newgate Street, his eyes blinking against the daylight. After all the days in the murky prison, he was nearly blinded by the sun.

"Vicar!" A familiar man's voice called and Nat turned to see a stately lacquered coach and six waiting nearby. In the driver's seat sat a frightened man dressed in a uniform, wedged between two vicars. Anne's face peeked out from the leather curtain inside the coach. A sudden surge of gratitude coursed through him as he ran to the coach, the hem of his robes flying about his boots.

"Head north to the boat stations along the River Fleet," he ordered, holding on to the side of the coach by the luggage rack.

Tom yelled to the horses. The whip sang through the crisp winter air. The coach lurched forward, wheels clacking as the horses' hooves thundered along the cobbles of the narrow lane.

Chapter Twenty

The coach pressed hard down Newgate street, swerved past Pye Corner to Holborn, then veered north along the River Fleet.

"There's a post ahead to rent boats," Nat yelled to Tom, seated on the far end of the driver's bench. The white-faced coachman sat in the middle and Doc crouched on the end. "Pull over there," he ordered, pointing to a copse of scrub evergreens.

"Watch him, Doc, while I have a word with Tom." Nat jumped down from the coach and walked with Tom until they were out of earshot from the coach. "All of London will be searching for this coach when news of what happened spreads," Nat whispered. "Unhitch the horses. We'll leave the coach here. Tie up the driver and blindfold him, then put him inside the coach. Let him overhear that you've let the horses loose, and that we're planning to steal a boat and head upriver."

Tom nodded, understanding immediately. "That'll give the ol' boy a nice tale to tell the soldiers when 'e's found. But what will we really do?" he asked, scratching his beard.

"We'll each take a horse and split up. Free the other horses. Then you and Doc will ride west through the fields until you come to the village of Chelsea. It should take you a little more than an hour. Meet me by the stand of oak at the old Chelsea church. It's near the embankment on the Thames."

284 Embrace the Dawn

Tom nodded, then hurried to follow his orders while Nat strode to speak to Anne, who watched from the waiting carriage.

She observed the familiar, purposeful stride, feeling overwhelmed with gratitude that he was safe. She had died a thousand deaths, waiting, wondering, bargaining with God for Him to spare Nat's life and let him escape unharmed.

Anne pulled back the leather curtain and waited, squeezing her hands together in further thanks to God for answering her prayer for his safety. If only He would grant that Nat find it in his heart to forgive her and... But with all Nat's virtues, forgiveness was not one of them. He had never forgiven his father, and that hate had nearly destroyed him.

The soft rap on the carriage door interrupted her thoughts. "May I have a few words with you?"

Her fingers shook as she pulled back the stiff leather and gazed with longing at the ruggedly handsome face framed by the coach window. He still wore the nubby brown robe, the hood carelessly thrown back over his tousled shoulder-length hair.

"Twining is dead." He said it matter-of-factly, his dark eyes shaded by the slant of his black lashes as he waited for her reaction. When she gave none, he continued. "We have only a short time before the soldiers find Twining's coach and driver, but it will be long enough for us to escape London." His gaze swept her face. "Are you feeling up to riding bareback?"

"Of course." She glanced toward Doc unhitching the horses and to the low copse of pine where Tom was tying up the driver's hands. "Where are we going?"

"Away from London as quickly as possible. The others will split up, but you should ride with me. We'll join the others later."

Without hesitation, Nat helped her from the coach.

When she stood next to him she noticed the bloodstained rip in his robe at the shoulder. "You've been hurt!" She reached out to touch him, but he flinched from her touch.

"It's nothing," he said curtly. "Hurry, we must leave."

She felt a pang of remorse as she remembered his words: *I don't think I could bear to touch you.* She bent her head, forcing herself not to cry as she blinked against the crisp, wintry breeze that tore at her skirts while she strode toward the pawing horse Doc Herrick held for her.

Within minutes, she followed Nat's lead, riding hard upon roads rigid with frost. They galloped past small cottages and houses, smoke curling out the chimneys with the steel gray River Thames on their left. A dismal sleet had begun to fall, turning the December countryside a misty gray. Before long, the cottages spread farther apart, the land rolling gently ahead of them.

An hour later, they trotted to the grove of stately oak trees where two riders waited upon the ridge.

When they approached, Doc Herrick spoke first. "Let's all go to Rosemoor, Nat." The cold wind roughened round pink circles upon his freckled cheeks.

Tom squinted, wiping ice crystals from his beard with his hand. "Aye, Mistress Bridget knows contacts who'll arrange passage to Bristol."

"From Bristol, we can go anywhere." Doc added, as though he had already decided his plans.

"Rosemoor is a wise choice, Doc." Nat's mouth twisted in thought. "It's well fortified with secret rooms. You'll be safe until you and Jane leave England."

Tom pulled up the hood around his head. "Jane will be so glad to see that ugly face of Doc's, she'll do anythin' 'e says."

Tom and Doc chuckled, but Nat's expression remained serious. "Bridget will never leave, but you and Jane must. Bridget will be believed when she says she knew nothing of our activities. She has loyal friends—contacts—who will see you safely out of the country."

A look of relief spread over Doc's face. "Aye, I'll convince her."

Nat glanced toward Tom. "And what are your plans, Cousin?"

Tom scowled, scuffing his feet on the frozen ground. "I've some unfinished business..." He gazed out at the dark swirling river coursing toward London, his brows knotted into the familiar frown. Anne thought his mind was on Moll and what might have happened to her. "I'll go see what's left of the Pied Bull. I'll ask the neighbors and try to find out where me mum is."

"I know where Emma is," Nat said.

Tom's face brightened with surprise.

"Aye. She's at our childhood cottage by the river. Emma had often said that if anything were to happen, it would be where she would want to remain with her memories."

"Aye, she would," Tom agreed. "I'll go there directly, an' once I tell 'er we're all safe, I'll work till I get me a piece o' land." His face split into a grin. "Build another inn an' tavern, I think. For 'ow can the Black Fox ride without an inn to come 'ome to?"

At the mention of the Black Fox, Anne shot a cursory glance toward Nat, but his attention was on Tom. "When you reach the cottage, you'll find my horse. Ride Shadow to Rosemoor. Before my uncle Alex died, he saw to it that I was left property from my father's inheritance. I've never wanted it until now, Tom." He paused, and Anne could see the admiration and respect for Tom shine from Nat's dark eyes. "Tell Bridget that I want you to have it." Nat smiled at the grateful expression on Tom's face. "The money will more than enough build a new coaching inn."

Tom shifted uncomfortably beneath the bulky robe, but his face expressed more than words what Nat's generosity meant.

"Tom, when you see your mother, tell her I wish her well," Anne added, her throat constricting. Loving memories of the spirited old woman would remain in her heart forever.

The three men turned toward her, as though waiting to hear her plans. For the first time, she realized she had no place to go. She had always presumed she and Nat—but Nat would never forgive her—besides, even if he might, how could she bring a child into a world where his father might be arrested any day? Unless Nat would leave England. She looked away.

Doc said, "Anne, you're coming with us to Rosemoor, aren't ye? Your father will want to hear all about your adventures—"

"My father died in mid-November," she answered sharply, surprising herself. An icy gust fluttered a long wisp of hair and she pulled it from her face. She felt Nat's stare of surprise upon her. "The night before he died, Wilkens brought the news that the king had safely arrived in France." She forced back the sting of tears at the bittersweet memory. "It was as though my father held on for that moment. He said he was very grateful to the Black Fox and his men." She turned to Nat, but his expression was unreadable. *Nat, now you know that I couldn't have bargained your life for my father's.*

"If ye don't go to Rosemoor, lass, where will ye go?" Tom asked.

"I still have the money that Jane gave me," she said with determination, her fingers feeling the knot in her apron. "It's more than enough to take me where I want to go."

Nat hesitated, then he pulled the hood up around his face. "Before I return to Rosemoor, I've some things I want to talk to Anne about," he said to the others. His face straightened and she felt a sudden chill go through her.

She stiffened, knowing what was in his heart. She knew Nat's glorified honor would never permit her to leave without his attempt to explain why he could never forgive her. But she already understood. And she couldn't bear to hear him say he couldn't forgive her for bartering herself to Twining. She knew he was noble and that the Black Fox could never take such an unprincipled maid as a wife. He needed a woman cut from the cloth of a firebrand like his Aunt Bridget or his cousin Jane. He'd never understand a wife who would move mountains for such a trivial thing as love.

Anne bit back the bitter truth. He'd never forgive her, even though he'd try. Even now, the only thing that kept him from leaving her here at the Chelsea churchyard was his lofty sense of nobility.

Very well. If he didn't love her, then better she know now, before she would be foolish enough to tell him she was to have their child. God's bones, with his burden of nobility, he'd insist she marry him and he'd be miserable. Well, she was through trying to make people do things they couldn't find in their hearts to do for themselves. She hung her head.

Nat exchanged clumsy hugs with the men. Doc and Tom kissed Anne on the cheek. "Good luck," they cried in unison.

Anne waved, her eyes brimming with tears. "Give my love to Jane and Bridget," she added as she watched them mount their horses and ride off.

After they had gone, Nat rode his horse beside her. "Until you decide what to do, I thought you might like to stay with Emma." His voice was low. "She'd like that, I know."

She glanced up at him and felt unsettled by his nearness. "Aye. I could catch a ferry at the river and go to Bristol," she said, feeling less nervous with a plan, albeit a spontaneous one. "I could be on a ship and out of England before the authorities found me and questioned me about the colonel's death." Nat was whisper close and she felt herself shiver in response.

The nubby wool hood cloaked his face in shadow, the coarse robe stretched taut across his wide shoulders. Her knees felt like jelly, her heart beat with a wild fervor.

The bloodstain from his fight with Twining hadn't become larger, she noted, and she decided not to ask about it. She avoided his eyes; she couldn't stand for him to see the heartbreak she knew was in her face.

Through fields fallen silent by winter's cold, they galloped, following the hedgerows, skirting the forests until they came to a ridge overlooking a valley.

"The hamlet of Bloomsley lies a few miles to the north," Nat said, frost forming puffs of mist as he spoke. "There's an inn where we can spend the night. We'll be safe. They won't have heard of the news of the prison escape for a few days, and no one's looking for a vicar and a young woman."

Cold, bone weary, hungry and thirsty, she would have gladly slept on the frozen ground. With all the strength she had left, she nodded, then urged the horse to follow Nat's lead.

The Yellow Rose Coaching Inn stood alongside the deep-rutted road toward Bloomsley. Her gaze swept across the two-story stone structure, its gabled roof, touched by the dormant rambling rose canes that covered an arbor which obviously lent itself to its name. Smoke curled invitingly from several chimneys; candlelight winked from the downstairs windows.

An hour later, Anne was warming herself by the hearth in the only room left that had a fireplace. Nat had offered to sleep on a thin pallet in the unheated common room shared by the male travelers down the hall, and if that's what he wanted, she wouldn't try to stop him.

A light tapping on the door invaded her thoughts. She rose, her heart pounding with dread, knowing that Nat had come to finally speak to her. When she pulled the door open, he stood, freshly bathed, clean shaven. He had changed into a blue woolen shirt and a leather pair of breeches he must have bartered with the innkeeper for in exchange for chores. The worn leather molded itself to his hips and the long length of his muscled thighs. The periwinkle shirt was cut too small for him, the wool stretched taut with each breath he took across the broad, muscled chest, tapering tightly to the lean waist. His hard, muscular biceps bulged with the weight of the covered tray he carried.

She gazed up into his serious face and braced herself, forced a polite smile and bid him enter. Without a word, he placed the tray beside the fireplace table, and the welcoming aroma of mutton stew, hot bread and ale wafted through the room.

Motioning him to a fireside chair, she moved the candlestick closer and sat across from him. Nat sat, crossing his long legs. She watched the firelight soften away the lines of fatigue from his face. "I've been wanting to talk to you ever since we've left London," he began. "I know this isn't the time, but . . ."

She stiffened, the urgency in his voice brought her senses to high alert. "While I was in Newgate, I had a lot of time to think..." His dark eyes fixed on his hands in his lap.

She didn't want to hear it. Instead, she wanted to reach out and touch the strong jaw, run her finger along the fine scar beneath his cheek. Tonight, she wanted to be with him, to remember how the scent of his skin reminded her of the shadows among the cedars. To watch the special look in his dark brown eyes when she whispered his name. She ached to touch his hair, rich chestnut brown, wild and thick about his shoulders.

He met her stare. She blinked, feeling the warming color rise to her cheeks. "I—I'm so tired," she said, her hand brushing across her brow. "I'm afraid I'll fall asleep before you finish," she exclaimed, the weak excuse the only thing she could think of to hurry the agony of his words.

"I'm sorry to hear of your father."

Anne bit back the ache. "Aye," she managed, her voice tight. For one helpless moment she yearned for him to take her in his arms, tell her that he would never want anyone but her.

"You've lost so much."

She closed her eyes and bit her lip. *Not as much as losing you, my darling.* She felt the rough touch of his fingers on her cheek and her eyes fluttered open. Dear God! If he didn't want her, then he shouldn't touch her. She arched away from his reach. Fighting to control her shattered pride, she murmured, "We've all lost a great deal." He was so close she could feel the heat of him. "Tom lost the Pied Bull Inn, Bridget will lose Jane and Doc when they leave for France, and Moll lost Tom. But the important thing is that the king is safely waiting to regain the throne, wouldn't you say?" The words were sharper than she would have liked.

He didn't answer, but asked a question instead. "Would you risk it again, Anne, knowing the cost?"

She watched the firelight play among the planes and angles of his face. His words formed a question, but his eyes spoke the answer. Surely he would have, and she guessed the others would have, as well. But would she?

"Aye, I would," she admitted frankly, knowing if she hadn't, she would never have met him. She averted her eyes to the fire. *Dear Nat, don't you see? That's the difference between us. I don't care if I live under Cromwell or Stuart as long as you're with me.*

"So, where do you plan to go with your pouch of gold?" His manner was as offhand as if he were asking her the time of day.

"I—I'm not sure. I remember the stories of the New World I read to my father. I remember thinking of the freedom, the chance, the adventure in the colonies. I think I might go there." Regret of things lost settled over her as she remembered her dream of moving to the Delaware or Maryland colony with Nat. "Royalists fled there during the war to avoid prosecution."

"Aye, I've several close friends who relocated to the Maryland colony." He eyed her with curiosity.

"I could be a governess, or anything I put my mind to," she said with a confidence she didn't feel. She would have him remember her with dignity and pride, if the pretense killed her.

He looked so handsome in the firelight, if he didn't leave immediately, she didn't know how she could keep from throwing her arms around him. "Is there anything else?" she asked instead. "I'm extremely tired and wish to go to bed."

"I couldn't leave without thanking you and telling you what a brave thing it was for you to go to London and face Twining."

She looked up at him, waiting for what she knew was coming. *Brave but foolish.* She took a deep breath. "I never told Twining that my father had died, for fear that he might learn I had met Royalist sympathizers. He'd never rest until he forced names and places from me."

She saw other questions in his eyes. "Bridget was against it, but Jane helped me."

His eyes widened with surprise. Although she didn't tell him, she knew Jane would have done anything if there was a chance of saving Doc. She smiled wistfully. "I wish I could be a fly on the wall and see Jane's face when her husband rides into the courtyard to her welcoming arms.''

Nat's brown eyes deepened to dark velvet. ''If it were not for you, she might not have known that joy.''

For a moment she thought he may believe that love was worth fighting for. ''Do you believe my sacrifice was worth it?'' she asked, unable to help herself.

''I think Jane and Doc will, when he takes her in his arms.''

But what about you? Obviously he hadn't changed his mind. ''Do you have anything else to tell me?'' she asked, hoping her voice didn't betray her heartbreak. ''I'm so very tired.''

''Anne, I can't have you leaving, believing you're to blame for my arrest.'' His mouth thinned into a firm line. ''Moll gave Twining some farfetched story she made up in order to save Tom. She would have said anything for him.''

''Wilkens told us what happened. I knew when Moll saw my locket, something terrible might happen because of it. I'll never forgive myself—''

He reached to cover her lips with his fingertips. ''Don't, Anne.'' Tenderness crept into his voice. ''It was only a matter of time before I was caught.'' He saw her wince and he knew she remembered the many times he had told her that very thing.

''I didn't understand until this morning when Twining brought you to see me at Newgate.'' He saw the pain flash across her beautiful face at the memory. ''When I stormed back to my cell after you confessed you were marrying Twining, Doc and Tom told me that they had received news that instead of hanging, Twining was sending us to the slave colony in the Caribbean. That's when I knew you had sacrificed yourself to save our lives.''

''Twining said he'd let you go free in the New World....'' She felt like a fool for believing his treachery, but at the time it was the only hope she had to save him.

She looked into his face. ''And does Tom forgive Moll?''

"I never told Tom about Moll's involvement. Besides, what does it matter? Tomorrow, when he arrives at the cottage and finds Moll with Emma—"

"Moll? How do you know she's with Emma?"

The dimple in his cheek deepened and his eyes twinkled mischievously. "I'm becoming an expert on women and what they'll do for love." He cocked a brow as he reached for her. This time she didn't move away. "Moll would want to be close to the man she loves," he said in a low voice. "And until then, she'd want to remain with his mother so they can comfort each other."

"Oh, Nat." Her throat tightened. "So that's why you told Tom to go to the cottage." A deeper feeling engulfed her. "Then . . . you've forgiven Moll for betraying you?"

He smiled and pulled her closer. "Moll thought she was saving Tom's life. She did the only thing she knew. I can understand and forgive her sacrifice because of you." Pain, longing and want raged within him. "After all, she did it for the greatest thing in the world."

Anne held her breath, searching his face.

"Love."

Through the veil of tears, Anne saw the tenderness and love shining through his magnificent eyes. "Love?" she repeated, afraid she had misunderstood him.

"I love you, my Anne. Even when I saw you with Twining, I knew I'd never stop loving you. I was wild with jealousy, and I struck out at myself for being so foolish and losing you."

"But . . . you couldn't help—"

"Maybe not, but I can now." He yanked her into his arms. "If you want to leave, I can't keep you from going, but I only ask that you give me another chance to make you fall in love with me again."

"Again?" Startled, she couldn't believe what he was saying. "Nat, I've never stopped loving you. I've—"

"But you said you were leaving for the Maryland colony."

"I thought you didn't want me. You were remaining in England to help Charles Stuart return to the throne—"

"Aye, and the Black Fox will carry on, as always, but Tom has agreed to take up the fight. When I realized what you had sacrificed for me, there was no way I could live without finding you and winning you back. I'd have risked anything to break out of Newgate and to find you."

She pressed her wet cheek against his shirt, her arms clinging to his neck. "If you've known how long I've waited for you to say that."

He lifted her chin. "If you want to go to France, I'll go. I'll go to the New World, anywhere with you. But are you willing to leave everything familiar, everything you love?"

She smiled in that familiar way that lit her eyes. "Aye, it would mean taking it with me."

He thought his heart would break with happiness.

She tightened her arms around his neck, her lips finding his. She slid her hand along his face, the innocent gesture arousing him, filling him with need. Everything about her affected him that way. God, he would never get his fill of her.

After a long kiss, he whispered brokenly, "Then you'll marry me?"

"Marry?" Her eyelashes fluttered open, her eyes meeting his in a look of love.

"Aye, my beautiful vixen..." He pulled her close and tangled his fingers into her thick red gold hair. "And I'll never leave you again, I promise." He sealed his words with a kiss.

Rapture filled her heart until she ached with it. "My love." Her voice could barely be heard. "Of course I'll marry you."

"It'll be a fresh start, just the two of us."

She blinked back the tears of happiness. "Well...not quite." She smiled through her tears. "There's something else I must tell you," she whispered, her small hands cradling his face. A swell of tenderness and passion rose inside her breast. "I'm going to have our baby," she managed brokenly.

"Our baby?" Nat pushed her back and stared at her. Then, unable to restrain himself, Nat picked her up and

virled her around. "Our baby?" he repeated, his heart
eating with joy. Suddenly he stopped, his face shaken. "I—
—didn't mean to be so rough..." He carried her gently to
ae side of the canopied bed. She couldn't stop the tears of
by as she clung to him. He laid her carefully in the feather
ed and propped pillows around her, as though she were a
orcelain doll.

"I won't break," she laughed, pulling him down beside
er. She sat against the pillows, her fingers unlacing his
airt. "Oh, Nat, your wound!" She could feel the bandage
rapped around his chest.

"That's not where it hurts," he said, grinning. He began
o speak again, but her lips stifled any chance for speech.
This isn't a time to talk, my husband-to-be." She smiled
nd a teasing light came into her eyes. Her fingers removed
is shirt and he felt a surge of passion course through him.

"You'll never get any sleep if you do that, wench." His
es darkened with desire as he began undressing her.

In trembling need, her fingers shook as she ran her hands
ver the bunched muscles of his shoulders while he loos-
aed the ribbons at her breasts and parted the fabric with his
isses.

Anne arched back against the pillows, and in her most
racticed tavern wench dialect answered, "Aye, an' it's not
eep I 'ad in mind, m'lord."

Epilogue

Marseilles, France
September 1652

Anne tightened the woolen bunting around the precious infant in her arms and took a deep breath of the crisp, salt-filled air. Along the pier reaching from the fish markets to the shore along the harbor, gulls squawked over leftover morsels of fish while waves splashed upon the glistening rocks in well-timed rhythm. A strong breeze from the west caused whitecaps to lift and bob upon the blue-green Mediterranean Ocean. The clear dawn held promise of fair sailing weather, she knew. Besides, the crew of the *La Marseillaise* had said as much last night at the *Maison Vert*, the inn where she and Nat and their daughter had spent the night.

Nat strode up and put his arms around her. "It's time we leave for the west pier," he reminded her gently. "The tide's changing and we're the last to board."

Anne pulled back the bunting from their baby's tiny face. "I was just telling Elizabeth that we'll be sailing from a port the Greeks first colonized centuries ago," she said with enthusiasm.

"And what did the babe reply?" Nat asked, enjoying the delightfully amusing way his wife carried on conversations with their daughter.

"Elizabeth said she would rather hear the tale of the Black Fox rescuing her mother from the soldiers at the Pied Bull Inn," she answered playfully, smiling up at him.

"Aye, our daughter has her mother's thirst for adventure," he said. He kissed the top of Anne's shiny hair.

The baby mewed a tiny cooing sound and grabbed his finger, tugging gently. The brush of red gold hair atop her perfectly formed pink face caused his heart to quicken. Never had he known such joy as when he held Anne and their baby in his embrace.

Anne looked up at him, her blue-green eyes full of love and trust. "Come, my darling. If we don't hurry, they'll leave without us, then what will Bridget say after she went to all the trouble to have the ten trunks of furniture and belongings shipped here?" She laughed. "I don't want to be the one to tell her," she added merrily.

"Nor will I be the one to tell Tom and Moll after they spent two weeks helping her pack them." His rich laughter joined hers.

"Then it's best we hurry so we don't get left," Anne said, giving him a playful poke.

Nat cradled his tiny daughter in one arm, his wife in the other. The wind whipped the hems of their capes about them as they strode across the grassy knoll toward the pier.

A half hour later, *La Marseillaise,* the three-masted ship bound for the New World, sailed in the distance. White and pristine, she bobbed up and down against the pink-ribboned sky.

"Your hands are cold," Nat whispered, gently squeezing her small hand in his warm palm. "Are you frightened at the thought of leaving France?"

"Of course not, my darling. I'm excited, that's all." She smiled wistfully, watching the coast fade from sight. "I keep remembering something my father said," she whispered, her gaze on the pink and golden sunrise. She blinked back the tears of happiness as she glanced at her handsome husband and their precious infant. "He said that each dawn marks a step toward one's destiny. Embrace each new challenge with courage, for love will find the way to overcome whatever fate has in store.''

Nat held his wife and daughter in his arms as he considered her words for a moment, then he pulled her around to face him, setting his mouth to hers. "I can face anything with you at my side, my Anne," he said between kisses.

"And I'll always be there," she answered, her heart brimming with happiness.

* * * * *

Harlequin® Historical

MORE ROMANCE, MORE PASSION,
MORE ADVENTURE...MORE PAGES!

Bigger books from Harlequin Historicals. Pick one up today and see the difference a Harlequin Historical can make.

White Gold by Curtiss Ann Matlock—January 1995—A young widow partners up with a sheep rancher in this exciting Western.

Sweet Surrender by Julie Tetel—February 1995—An unlikely couple discover hidden treasure in the next *Northpoint* book.

All That Matters by Elizabeth Mayne—March 1995—A medieval about the magic between a young woman and her Highland rescuer.

The Heart's Wager by Gayle Wilson—April 1995—An ex-soldier and a member of the demi-monde unite to rescue an abducted duke.

Longer stories by some of your favorite authors. Watch for them in 1995 wherever Harlequin Historicals are sold.

HARLEQUIN®

PRESENTS
RELUCTANT BRIDEGROOMS

Two beautiful brides, two unforgettable romances…
two men running for their lives….

My Lady Love, by Paula Marshall, introduces
Charles, Viscount Halstead, who lost his memory
and found himself employed as a stableboy by the
untouchable Nell Tallboys, Countess Malplaquet.
But Nell didn't consider Charles untouchable—
not at all!

Darling Amazon, by Sylvia Andrew, is the story of
a spurious engagement between Julia Marchant
and Hugo, marquess of Rostherne—an engagement
that gets out of hand and just may lead Hugo to
the altar after all!

Enjoy two madcap Regency weddings this May,
wherever Harlequin books are sold.

REG5

From author Susan Paul

This spring, don't miss the first book in this exciting new series from
a newcomer to Harlequin Historicals—**Susan Paul**

THE BRIDE'S PORTION
April 1995

The unforgettable story of an honorable knight forced to wed
the daughter of his enemy in order to free himself from
her father's tyranny.

Be sure to keep an eye out for this upcoming series
filled with the splendor and pageantry of Medieval times
wherever Harlequin Historicals are sold!

Harlequin® Historical

Gayle Wilson

**The talented new author from
Harlequin Historicals brings you
the next title in her series set amid the
sophistication and intrigue
of Regency London**

THE HEART'S WAGER
April 1995
The compelling story of an ex-soldier and a casino dealer who must
face great dangers to rescue his best friend from certain death!

Don't miss this delightful tale!

And you can still order THE HEART'S DESIRE
from the address below.

To order your copy of THE HEART'S DESIRE (HH #211), please send your name,
address, zip or postal code along with a check or money order (please do not
send cash) for $3.99 for each book ordered ($4.50 in Canada), plus 75¢ postage and
handling ($1.00 in Canada), payable to Harlequin Books, to:

In the U.S.	In Canada
3010 Walden Avenue	P. O. Box 609
P. O. Box 1369	Fort Erie, Ontario
Buffalo, NY 14269-1369	L2A 5X3

Please specify book title(s) with your order.
Canadian residents add applicable federal and provincial taxes.

HHT-2

Harlequin® Historical

Claire Delacroix's UNICORN TRILOGY

The series began with UNICORN BRIDE,
a story that *Romantic Times* described as
"...a fascinating blend of fantasy and romance."

Now you can follow the Pereille family's ongoing quest
in the author's April 1995 release:

PEARL BEYOND PRICE

And if you missed UNICORN BRIDE, it's not too late
to order the book from the address below.

HARLEQUIN®

Don't miss these Harlequin favorites by some of our most distinguished authors!
And now, you can receive a discount by ordering two or more titles!

HT#25577	WILD LIKE THE WIND by Janice Kaiser	$2.99	☐
HT#25589	THE RETURN OF CAINE O'HALLORAN by JoAnn Ross	$2.99	☐
HP#11626	THE SEDUCTION STAKES by Lindsay Armstrong	$2.99	☐
HP#11647	GIVE A MAN A BAD NAME by Roberta Leigh	$2.99	☐
HR#03293	THE MAN WHO CAME FOR CHRISTMAS by Bethany Campbell	$2.89	☐
HR#03308	RELATIVE VALUES by Jessica Steele	$2.89	☐
SR#70589	CANDY KISSES by Muriel Jensen	$3.50	☐
SR#70598	WEDDING INVITATION by Marisa Carroll	$3.50 U.S. ☐ $3.99 CAN. ☐	
HI#22230	CACHE POOR by Margaret St. George	$2.99	☐
HAR#16515	NO ROOM AT THE INN by Linda Randall Wisdom	$3.50	☐
HAR#16520	THE ADVENTURESS by M.J. Rodgers	$3.50	☐
HS#28795	PIECES OF SKY by Marianne Willman	$3.99	☐
HS#28824	A WARRIOR'S WAY by Margaret Moore	$3.99 U.S. ☐ $4.50 CAN. ☐	

(limited quantities available on certain titles)

	AMOUNT	$	
DEDUCT:	**10% DISCOUNT FOR 2+ BOOKS**	$	
ADD:	**POSTAGE & HANDLING**	$	
	($1.00 for one book, 50¢ for each additional)		
	APPLICABLE TAXES*	$_____	
	TOTAL PAYABLE	$_____	
	(check or money order—please do not send cash)		

To order, complete this form and send it, along with a check or money order for the total above, payable to Harlequin Books, to: **In the U.S.:** 3010 Walden Avenue, P.O. Box 9047, Buffalo, NY 14269-9047; **In Canada:** P.O. Box 613, Fort Erie, Ontario, L2A 5X3.

Name: _____

Address: _____ City: _____

State/Prov.: _____ Zip/Postal Code: _____

*New York residents remit applicable sales taxes.
Canadian residents remit applicable GST and provincial taxes.

HBACK-JM2